'A
o

'High-octane act...
imagined alien civilizatio.. ...
belter from one of our best exponent..
adventure'   *Daily Mail*

'This is page-turning SF with a distinctive identity and brutal, stylish action sequences, all of which adds up to a compulsive read . . . A sharp, distinctive piece of sci-fi, and Gibson has certainly proved himself a name to watch out for'   *SFX*

'Handles a big plot with some aplomb'   *BBC Focus*

'The inventiveness and sense of wonder are raised a notch and the novel is a page turner you do not want to put down . . . In the top class of the field alongside Peter F. Hamilton or Iain M. Banks'   *FantasyBookCritic* blog

'A fast, exciting read with a dramatic twist towards the end'   *SFFWorld.com*

Gary Gibson has worked as a graphic designer and magazine editor, and began writing at the age of fourteen. He's originally from Glasgow, but currently lives in Taiwan. His previous novels include his Shoal trilogy plus the standalone books *Angel Stations*, *Against Gravity*, *Final Days* and *The Thousand Emperors*. He's also written *Marauder*, a book connected to the Shoal universe. His latest novel is *Extinction Game*. You can find out more about Gary and his work at garygibson.net.

By Gary Gibson

Angel Stations
Against Gravity

The Shoal Trilogy

Stealing Light
Nova War
Empire of Light

Final Days
The Thousand Emperors
Marauder

Extinction Game

Gary Gibson

EMPIRE OF LIGHT

Third Book of the
Shoal Trilogy

TOR

First published 2010 by Tor

This edition published 2013 by Tor
an imprint of Pan Macmillan, a division of Macmillan Publishers Limited
Pan Macmillan, 20 New Wharf Road, London N1 9RR
Basingstoke and Oxford
Associated companies throughout the world
www.panmacmillan.com

ISBN 978-1-4472-2411-2

5 7 9 8 6 4

A CIP catalogue record for this book is available from
the British Library.

Phototypeset by Intype Libra Ltd, London SW19 4HE
Printed and bound by CPI Group (UK) Ltd, Croydon CR0 4YY

Visit www.panmacmillan.com to read more about all our books
and to buy them. You will also find features, author interviews and
news of any author events, and you can sign up for e-newsletters
so that you're always first to hear about our new releases.

For Emma

Previously, in _Stealing Light_ and _Nova War_

When humanity finally reaches the stars, it is only possible with the help of the Shoal, rulers of a vast empire of interstellar trade routes over which they maintain absolute control through their monopoly on faster-than-light technology.

A human expedition to the Nova Arctis system subsequently uncovers the first of the Magi fleet, derelict but highly advanced starships originating in the Greater Magellanic Cloud. Dakota discovers she is uniquely adapted to bond with these thanks to her machine-head implants. When the Shoal-member 'Trader in Faecal Matter of Animals' destroys the entire system rather than allow them to escape with the secret of superluminal travel, Dakota, in the company of Lucas Corso, is able to use a Magi ship to jump to safety.

Captured by a Bandati colony many light-years distant, Dakota and Lucas become pawns in a deadly game being played between the Bandati and the Emissaries, a hitherto unknown starfaring species with whom the Shoal have been engaged in a frontier war for millennia.

Trader, believing that a nova war is inevitable should the Emissaries discover that the superluminal drive can also be used to destroy whole star systems, attempts a pre-emptive strike. The plan backfires, and the war spins out of control, threatening to eradicate life throughout the galaxy as system after system is wiped out.

Dakota knows that if any way exists to bring the war to an end, it lies with the Maker, a mysterious entity responsible for seeding the faster-than-light technology in caches scattered across the face of the universe . . .

ONE

Consortium Standard Year 2544

Seventeen thousand light-years from home, drifting through an unmapped star cluster on the edge of the Core, Dakota Merrick finally stumbled across the first faint signals that betrayed the Maker's whereabouts.

The signals utilized compression techniques of dazzling sophistication in order to cram the maximum amount of information into the smallest possible packet burst. A less sophisticated vessel than her Magi starship might never have been able to distinguish the signals from random noise.

She followed the transmissions back to their point of origin, passing through a dense cloud of cosmic dust filled with stars so young that their planets had barely formed. When her ship finally emerged from the cluster, she came across dozens of shattered Atn clade-worlds orbiting far out on the edges of much more ancient systems.

More stray transmissions drew her towards a halo cluster a thousand light-years above the galaxy's ecliptic plane. She drove her starship forward until the Milky Way slowly revealed its shape astern, the Core now a brilliant bar of light wreathed in black smoke.

As time passed, she picked up the signals of ancient emergency beacons, still active after more than a hundred and fifty thousand years. Before very long it became clear she'd stumbled across the remnants of Trader's own expedition from long ago. She found coreships that had been reduced to airless hulks, their hailing systems still firing out fading requests for help long after their crews had turned to dust.

The transmissions grew more dense, and Dakota found her attention drawn more and more to the vicinity of a red giant on the edge of a star cluster. Long-range sensors finally revealed the nature of the Maker: rather than being a single entity, it proved instead to be a vast swarm of objects interlinked via instantaneous, faster-than-light tach-net transmissions. There were trillions of them, scattered across an area of several light-years, with the red giant at its centre.

The swarm filled the superluminal ether with short-range bursts of data, a cacophony of unintelligible voices all shouting to each other across enormous distances.

While the ship closed in, Dakota spent her time drifting through the infinite virtual worlds held in the Magi ship's memory stacks, subjective days and months passing in what were only seconds in the universe beyond the hull. She became a flock of birdlike creatures that flew through the dense air of a high-gravity world, diving into the waters for prey. She experienced life as a twist of self-aware magnetic vortices in the photosphere of a star, then searched through the ruins of a drowned city in the body of an eel-like creature whose remote ancestors had built it, then forgotten their past. Her own body felt like a distant memory, and in truth it had long since been subsumed into the body of the ship, freeing her mind to roam at will.

There was a part of her that wanted to stay locked away in these worlds for ever, while another part still remembered what it meant to be human.

Dakota had become aware she was being haunted.

At first the ghosts remained out of sight, vague presences of whom she caught only fleeting glimpses, but over time they grew more solid, more real. They carried the voices and faces of people she'd known and loved, and who had died because of her. She found herself wondering if it meant she was losing her mind.

'Do you see?' one of them cried, following her through a maze of data. It had Josef's face. 'The swarm isn't just a cloud of interconnected objects – they're a single entity. When we listen to its transmissions, we're listening to its *thoughts*.'

'Go away!' she screamed, fearful of the memories he aroused. But even as his ghost faded, she realized what he'd said was true. Each member of the swarm – each *component* – was a single neuron in an enormously distributed brain. The Maker was alien in a way she had never encountered before; it had taken the principles of instantaneous communication by tach-net signal and used it to create a new kind of machine life. But then she remembered what she had become, and wondered whether she was really so different.

A few days later – as measured in the external universe, at any rate – Dakota had the ship rendezvous with one of the swarm-components. She proceeded cautiously, wary of how it might react to her ship's presence, or her gentle probing of its internal systems. When it appeared that no resistance would be offered, she had the starship draw the component inside it.

For the first time in over a year, Dakota reconstituted her physical body, creating a space within the starship both for herself and for the newly captured component. Her dark hair flopped across her eyes, the deep browns of her pupils again topped by the thick black commas of her eyebrows.

The swarm-component was perhaps ten metres in length, delicate sensors and neural conduits hidden beneath a series of tough plates streaked and pitted from centuries of microscopic impacts. That it was a Von Neumann machine, capable of endlessly replicating itself, was clear; isotopic measurements and analysis of its hull showed that the raw materials used to construct it had been drawn from asteroids and drifting interstellar bodies.

Since her arrival in the red giant's vicinity, Dakota had discerned a variety of different types of component. Some appeared to act primarily as relays for transmissions within the body of the swarm, while others did nothing but carry out repairs on other components, either by manufacturing parts or breaking down older machines in order to construct new ones. Still more appeared to be scouts ranging far from the main body, perhaps in order to locate resources. The particular component Dakota had chosen to study was, she suspected, close to the end of its useful life.

She flexed her fingers, feeling the half-forgotten play of muscles, and realized that she wasn't alone. She felt her skin freeze when the ghost stepped out from behind the component's pitted bulk to regard her with calm grey eyes.

He wasn't a true ghost, of course, merely a doppel-gänger of her dead lover, Josef Marados, now made flesh from her own memories. A way, perhaps, for her increas-ingly rebellious subconscious to combat the growing loneliness of being so very far from home.

At least, that was the rational explanation.

'This thing's alive,' he commented casually, as if pick-ing up the thread of a conversation. 'You know that, right? But it doesn't seem to know we're here.'

Dakota had a sudden vivid recollection of Josef's

bloodied corpse lying crumpled on the floor of his office on Mesa Verde. She hadn't been to blame for his death, not really; at the time she'd been under the murderous control of Trader in Faecal Matter of Animals, an agent of the Shoal. He had exploited fatal weaknesses in her machine-head implants and turned her into his unwitting puppet. She knew this, and yet the guilt remained.

If I act like the ghost is real, then that means I really am crazy.

But she did, anyway. She couldn't help herself.

'I . . . I think, with some time and effort, I could use it to try and communicate with the rest of the swarm.'

The ghost laughed, eyeing her with a half-smile that suggested he saw through to the deep well of uncertainty at the core of her soul. 'Time,' he replied, 'is the one thing you might not have.'

He meant the red giant, of course. It was now weeks, perhaps only days from death. A new and entirely natural nova would result, as it expelled most of its mass in one single cataclysmic blast. Despite the obvious danger, untold billions of the swarm-components remained within close proximity to the star, like fireflies dancing at the edge of a forest fire.

'Don't.'

Dakota stared at the ghost with a puzzled expression. 'Don't what?'

'You were about to apologize. Don't start saying you're sorry for killing me.'

'I wasn't—'

'You made me, spun me out of your memories, and that means I know every thought in your head even before it appears. Now,' he said, leaning down with hands on knees to peer at the component's hull, '*this* is interesting . . .'

Part of her wanted to touch the back of his neck, in case his skin was still warm and soft and carried the same scent as the man she'd known. Instead, she had her ship feed her highly magnified images of the component's exterior. It was studded with millions of extremely miniaturized tach-net transceivers, each one packed with dense molecular circuitry.

This particular component appeared to have a relatively simple function, storing and analysing data from all across the electromagnetic spectrum as well as more exotic phenomena such as gravitic fluctuations and superluminal tachyon drift. If the swarm did have an overarching intelligence, as she suspected, it was almost certainly an emergent property resulting from its sheer complexity.

Dakota lightly touched the fingers of one hand to the component's hull and closed her eyes, tense despite herself. She could hear the whisper of its transceivers, and realized it was still in communication with its brethren.

Perhaps she could tap into that flow, talk directly to the swarm . . .

She hesitated, drawing her hand back.

'Go ahead,' the ghost prompted. 'It's the opportunity

to talk to something that's been alive for billions of years.'

'It's also responsible for creating the caches. The same ones that destroyed the Magi and could still destroy us. What if I . . . made it angry?'

'Life, Dakota, is a series of opportunities preceded by risks. We have the chance to finally find out what the swarm's ultimate purpose is. So go ahead and try.'

She nodded, and put her fingers once again on the component's hull, listening to the swarm's chatter. What had been unintelligible noise suddenly became clear, and what she learned was so shocking she pulled her hand back with a gasp.

'It's trying to . . .'

'Re-engineer the universe,' the ghost finished for her. 'A project it doesn't expect to finish until billions of years from now.'

'That's incredible,' she said, 'but how does it help us?'

'Look here,' said the ghost, directing her attention to one particular strand of data. 'There – a way to stop the nova war.'

Once again, she placed her hand against the component's hull. More data came pouring through, almost swamping her conscious mind.

The ghost grinned in jubilation. 'Did you see?'

She nodded. 'I saw it. We've really found something.'

A name, fished out of the depths of the Maker's collective intelligence, and a little more besides.

*

'*Mos Hadroch.*' Severn rolled the phrase around his tongue.

They were walking side-by-side through a simulation of the streets of Erkinning, on Dakota's home world of Bellhaven. The winter winds felt so entirely real that she had bunched her hands into fists, pushing them deep inside down-lined pockets, a padded collar pulled up close around her neck and chin. The scent of food and the sound of voices drifted to them from the direction of the city walls, where Grover refugees taking advantage of the daily amnesty had set up a market.

Dakota had murdered Chris Severn while he'd been recovering in an Ascension clinic, cutting out his heart and watching his life-support read-outs flat-line. Another figment of her mind made real, whether she liked it or not – dressed up in the skin of someone who'd died because he'd made the mistake of loving her.

'Whatever it is, it means a lot to the swarm,' Dakota replied. 'It meant something to the Magi as well, but what that meaning is still isn't clear.'

'The Mos Hadroch is a legend,' Severn told her, stopping off at a stall to buy hot tea for them both. 'Or as good as, anyway. There are no surviving records to prove it really existed. It's a weapon, supposedly, built by a predecessor civilization in the Greater Magellanic Cloud.'

Dakota drank the bitter black tea and felt its heat diffuse down her throat. 'It can't be that much of a myth if the swarm wants to find it. We need to try and find out what else it knows.'

Severn frowned. 'You might want to exercise some caution. Trader found out, the hard way, that the swarm can be lethal.'

'There's not enough time to be cautious,' she muttered irritably. 'We need to find out everything we can.'

'Knowledge won't be much use to you if it only gets you killed. The swarm acts like we're beneath its notice, but how can we really be sure?'

More days passed, and the starship learned how to decipher more of the data streaming through the captured component's transceivers. For the first time, an accurate picture of the swarm's origins began to form, where before she'd had only disparate fragments of knowledge loosely knitted together with conjecture.

Once the starship learned how to tap into the swarm's senses, Dakota was able to look out on the universe through trillions of eyes.

She eventually discovered that the swarm was very, very old – and not alone. There were others scattered through distant galaxies, having seeded themselves across the face of the universe over vast epochs of time. The origins of this particular swarm dated back to a time when the Earth's sun had barely coalesced from interstellar dust.

It was clear that these swarms maintained contact with each other, despite the vast distances that separated them, by some means Dakota did not yet understand. Although tach-net communications were instantaneous, the amount of energy required to boost a signal so enormously far staggered the imagination. How the swarm obtained the requisite energy was a question that, at least for the moment, might have to remain unanswered.

Mos Hadroch. The term turned up again and again, and it soon became clear that, whatever it might be, the swarm regarded it as a major threat to its primary mission, even while its precise nature remained frustratingly elusive.

'We're getting nowhere in trying to work out what the Mos Hadroch is,' said Dakota. 'I'm going to get in contact with the other navigators back home, see if they can help.'

She was standing with Josef's ghost on the roof of a kilometres-high structure on an otherwise deserted world drawn from the ship's memory. A real-time image of the red giant hung above them, great loops of fiery plasma torn from its surface outlining the flux of its magnetic fields.

He looked at her with a doubtful expression. 'What could they possibly do? For all we know, the Mos Hadroch might be somewhere back in the Greater

Magellanic Cloud – or might not even exist anymore. Maybe we should be trying to think of something new.'

'No, you don't understand. The Shoal abandoned a coreship before they left our part of the galaxy. What if there's some clue buried in its data stacks? Or in the wreck of the godkiller back in Ocean's Deep? There are navigators back home who've been flying their own Magi starships for a couple of years now. If I send them everything we know, they might find a correlation within minutes.'

I'm talking to myself, Dakota thought, as she studied the ghost. *That's all he is: another part of me that thinks it's someone else.* More evidence, if it were needed, that her mind was now unravelling.

'The risk of making contact with home is enormous, Dakota. It's suicidally risky.'

'How do you mean?'

The ghost turned towards her. 'Think about the energy cost of transmitting a signal across seventeen thousand light-years, all the way back to Ocean's Deep. Without enough power, it'll de-cohere into random noise before it even gets there. You're going to have to drain the drive's energy reserves to make sure they receive the message.'

'So?'

'It'll take the ship days to claw that energy back out of the vacuum, and until then she won't be able to carry out any superluminal jumps. We'll be at the swarm's mercy, if it decides to turn on us.'

'We're at a dead end here, anyway,' Dakota insisted.
'We have to act now.'

'It's a mistake,' the ghost warned her.

'No. It's a risk, but one we're still going to have to take.'

TWO

Nathan Driscoll looked up and noted that one of the suns had gone out.

He stepped back, his hands greasy with gore and his nostrils full of the scent of burned flesh, and watched as an evac team carried away the injured soldier he had been tending, and then loaded him into a waiting air-ambulance. The medbox units that had once been an integral part of the ambulance's interior had long since been stripped out, so the soldier's stretcher was instead slotted into one of several brackets, the rest of them already occupied by other injured men and women.

Nathan studied the pattern of dim red balls that clung to the coreship's curving ceiling, a dozen kilometres above the city of Ascension, his breath frosting the air. He couldn't work out precisely which of the thousands of fusion globes had just failed, but he had sensed the sudden, marginal drop in ambient light; the world had just become a little bit darker than it already was. He pulled his scarf tighter around his neck in a futile attempt to counter the biting cold.

He brought his gaze back down, and in that moment saw her.

A group of refugees – perhaps a dozen men, women and children in all – was making its way past the ruined façade of a mall about half a block away. Probably they'd been forced to abandon their homes as the fighting between the Consortium and Peralta's *terroristas* spread along the banks of First Canal. Despite the half-light, Nathan had spotted a woman with long brown hair gathered up in a band, her terrified features smeared with dirt.

It was only the briefest of glimpses, but his heart leapt nonetheless.

Ilsa.

Almost as soon as he'd spotted her, a cadence of ground-rattling thumps heralded the return of a four-legged rover-unit from the battle, troopers clinging to its sides while the most seriously injured were lifted on to pallets mounted on top of the rover itself. Nathan rushed forward with the other two volunteer medics, and helped to load the wounded into another air-ambulance that had dropped to the fractured tarmac almost as soon as the previous one had lifted off.

Nathan began to doubt himself, even as he worked. It had been the merest, most fleeting glimpse: only part of her face had been visible. She had been wrapped up in layers of clothing, a rag pulled tight around her neck to ward off the plummeting temperatures; because, ever since the Shoal had abandoned them, the temperature had dropped even as the light failed. It didn't take a genius to realize the coreship was dying.

Nathan pulled himself up inside the second air-ambulance, along with Kellogg and the other new volunteer whose name he'd already forgotten. The ambulance's jets began to whine, preparing for take-off, but his mind was on other things.

He was almost certainly mistaken, of course, as he imagined he saw Ilsa everywhere he looked: in the faces of the troopers and volunteer aid workers, or among the refugees who vastly outnumbered them all; or the corpses that had come to fill the streets and canals as the fighting intensified.

But then again, this *might* have been her. It might have been Ilsa. If he could find her . . . if she was still alive . . .

Nathan hopped back down from the open rear of the ambulance. He could see no sign of the refugees, but he guessed they were heading for the shores of the canal. His fluorescent plastic waistcoat – meant to identify him clearly as a non-combatant – flapped around his waist in the backwash from the jets.

'Nathan!' Kellogg bellowed down at him. 'What the fuck do you think you're doing?'

Nathan looked up, shook his head. 'I saw someone I know,' he yelled over the noise.

More than likely the refugees intended to wade across the canal under cover of darkness, since the bridges were frequently targeted. If they could get to the other side, they had a chance at escaping the worst of the fighting.

'Nathan, get the fuck back in!' Kellogg yelled again. 'Once this thing goes, it goes!'

'I'll find my own way back,' Nathan replied, and started to jog away, heading towards the canal. Kellogg yelled something else, but the words were lost as the ambulance's VTOL jets lifted it high above the ground It tipped its nose in the direction of Third Canal and northwest, and began to accelerate.

The streetlights had been down ever since Peralta had targeted the city's primary fusion reactor systems. Nathan stripped off his waistcoat and shoved it deep inside a pile of rubble.

He jogged on past the ruined mall and kept going, squinting into the deep shadows as he went. He alternated between running and walking until he finally arrived exhausted at the banks of First Canal several minutes later. His bones ached, and more than ever he felt the slow onslaught of late middle age.

Nathan crossed the street and peered down the embankment at the black waters. The dark shapes of bodies drifted by, carried along by the artificial tide. Ice had formed on either side of the canal, and he squinted up and down its length until he sighted a huddle of dark shapes moving along the path at the foot of the slope, maybe fifty metres away.

Nathan slipped and skidded down the steep stone facing of the embankment until he reached the path they were on. Some of the refugees were already braving the ice and the freezing cold to wade across the slow-moving waters.

'Hey!' he yelled, waving as he came towards them.

Several turned and shouted out in fear, assuming, in the dim light, that he must be one of Peralta's soldiers. A few more threw themselves further into the water and started swimming frantically.

Nathan slowed down and raised his hands. Their faces, even in the faint light, were clouded with terror and suspicion. 'I'm not with Peralta or anyone else,' he yelled. 'I'm just looking for somebody. I thought she might be . . .'

Then he moved a step closer and saw her: an angular woman with brown hair, her eyes dulled by fatigue. It wasn't Ilsa, though. Now he could see her more clearly, he could only wonder how he might have made such a mistake.

'What the hell are you doing, running straight at us like that?' one of them demanded, his face looking bruised and ugly in the dim light, fists bunched in readiness at his sides. Like the rest, he wore several layers of extra clothing to try and keep the cold out, the topmost layers already ragged and worn.

'I'm sorry, I—'

Bright light suddenly flared down on them. Nathan crouched instinctively, and squinted up the embankment towards several figures that had suddenly appeared there, silhouetted by arc lights mounted on top of a rover. He heard one of the refugees mutter the word *terrorista*, but Nathan knew these new arrivals were Consortium troopers.

Some of the troopers quickly made their way down a series of steps leading to the waterside path, their weapons held up in readiness against their shoulders. The rover came closer to the rim of the embankment, its blunt, instrument shrouded head swinging slowly from side to side, scanning the environment constantly for threats. Its brilliant light shone down on the filthy waters, illuminating the bloated shapes of the dead.

One of the troopers came up close, pushing her visor up to reveal a small round face, a lick of dirty blonde hair pushing out from under her heavy black helmet. *Karen*, he realized with a shock. Sergeant Karen Salk, his sometime lover.

She grabbed his arm and pulled him away from the rest of the refugees, who had finally realized they weren't in immediate danger. The rest of the squad kept their weapons raised regardless; *terroristas* had a habit of hiding amongst those fleeing from the fighting.

A military transport of similar design to the air-ambulances dropped down towards the road that ran parallel to the top of the embankment.

'Kellogg said you'd run off in the middle of a fucking combat zone!' Karen shouted at him. 'I mean, what the *fuck* was going through your head?'

Nathan found he couldn't frame an answer, so he

remained mute as she tugged him towards the steps, and the beckoning lights of the transport waiting above.

Several minutes and a dozen kilometres later, the same transport dropped down towards a camp that spilled out along the streets lining both sides of Third Canal. Smoke rose from clusters of tents and prefabs where a sea of refugees warded off the freezing cold by burning furniture and anything else combustible. These were the lucky ones, awaiting immediate evacuation; in the surrounding city, there were tens of thousands dying more slowly of starvation or freezing inside their homes.

The transport's lights picked out the landing pad on the roof of the clinic and began to drop towards it. Nathan glanced out of a window and saw in the distance the great flickering wall of energy that delineated the nearest perimeter of the coreship's human-habitable zone. Closer to hand loomed the black shape of one of the sky-pillars, a great, carved rock limb that was only one of hundreds supporting the coreship's outer crust.

'Hey. Nathan, you stupid bastard. Wake up. It's me. Karen.'

Within minutes of disembarking from the ambulance, he'd crawled on top of a spare trolley in the clinic, and passed out. He groaned and sat up, blinking in the harsh lights and rubbing at a sore spot on his arm.

Karen regarded him with a mixture of scorn and pity. She'd taken off her helmet and matte-black body armour and let her hair fall down to her shoulders. One of the doctors stood next to her, a dark-skinned woman in disposable paper clothing.

The clinic, unlike almost anywhere else currently in Ascension, was warm. The doctor leaned in towards Nathan and pulled one of his eyelids up, shining a bright light directly into his pupil.

'Seems okay,' she remarked, her voice brisk. She then took out a hypo and aimed it towards Nathan's arm, almost before he realized what she was doing.

'Hey!' he shouted, sliding off the trolley and out of her immediate reach.

The two women stared at him with almost identical expressions of exasperation.

'For God's sake, Nathan,' said Karen. 'Doctor Nirav is trying to *help* you.'

'Thanks, but I don't need any shots.'

'What, you fucking *phobic* or something?' she replied in a voice full of scorn.

'Command think Peralta's got his hands on some kind of nerve agent,' explained Nirav. 'That means everyone gets a shot, and we also take a blood and DNA sample at the same time. Everyone has to do it, no exceptions.'

Nathan glanced warily towards the doctor. 'Forget it. No samples of any kind, either.'

'Why the fuck not?' asked Karen.

'Sorry,' said the doctor, patting a pocket. 'Got that already while you were out cold. So how about you stop whining and take the shot now, so I don't have to get some of the guys from security to come here and hold you down while I give it to you anyway?'

He hesitated, and even thought about making a run for it and taking his chances outside before they could identify him from his DNA sample. But where could he go? His work as a medic had given him a sobering overview of just how bad things were in the city; outside lay only a cold and hungry death.

Instead he nodded, and Nirav pressed something cold against his neck. There was a hiss and a sudden jolt of pressure against his skin, and then it was over.

A block of ice immediately settled into the pit of his stomach. It had only ever really been a matter of time before they worked out who he was, and there was literally nowhere he could run.

As Nirav departed, Karen folded her arms and studied him with a mixture of motherly concern and mild contempt. 'To be honest, Nathan, after the way you ran off back there, I was worried maybe you'd caught a whiff of that nerve gas and gone crazy. *Who* was it you said you saw?'

Nathan shook his head. 'I made a mistake.'

She sighed and reached out to tug him closer to her. 'How awake are you?'

'Not very.'

She shook her head. 'Not the right answer,' she said,

pushing a hand through his hair. 'It's been a long day, Nathan. Let's go back to my place.'

What Karen called 'her place' was a room in a commandeered administrative block on the other side of the main refugee camp. She had cleared it of most of its remaining furniture, whatever hadn't already been burned or looted, and had installed a spare cot from the clinic. Technically this was against the rules, but nobody seemed to care enough to enforce them. The illicit arrangement did have the advantage of giving her and Nathan some privacy.

A small portable heater glowed in the dark nearby, illuminating Karen's warm lithe body from behind her. Nathan slid his hands around her waist, then moved them up to cup her small breasts. Her tongue felt wet and salty as it licked against his lips. He felt himself stiffen, a wave of sudden, needful ardour washing over him.

She grinned and slithered expertly on top of him, quickly sliding him inside her. She was already wet. Her hands pressed down hard on his chest, the sensation almost painful, then she began to move, her hips grinding slowly.

Even the building's basement generators, augmented by their tiny heater unit, could not together quite keep the cold out, and soon he shivered, his skin prickling in the frigid air. He thought of the bodies he'd seen floating along the canal, picked out by the rover's unforgiving searchlights, and felt his ardour begin to fade.

'I'm not sure I can,' he muttered, and felt a sudden wave of fatigue wash over him. It had been, as she had said, a long day. 'Maybe we should try and get some sleep.'

'Shut up,' she said, her voice ragged, hands pressing ever more forcefully against his chest. 'Don't disobey the orders of a superior officer.'

I'm not in your fucking army, he thought. But he dutifully held on to her plump thighs and banished those images of death and decay from his mind, concentrating instead on the tumble of her hair across her shoulders and the moistness of her lips when she leaned down to kiss him. To his surprise it worked, and he listened to the increasing hoarseness of her breath just before she climaxed and came to a gasping halt. Her head tipped back, before she finally collapsed against his chest.

'Oh fuck, I needed that,' she moaned.

'You're welcome,' Nathan muttered. He glanced towards the window, where he could see the underside of a sky glowing a dull red.

Karen slid back down beside him and lay there for a few moments, her head resting on his shoulder. He sensed something else was on her mind and, after a few minutes of silence, she pushed herself up on one elbow and stared down at him.

'So who was she?' she asked, regarding him with a serious intensity.

Nathan gazed at her blankly until he realized she meant Ilsa. 'What makes you think I was looking for a she?'

'Intuition.' Karen's expression softened a little and she smiled. 'I'm not saying you have to *answer*. I'm just curious.'

'Does it matter?'

'You know, Nathan, it doesn't take a genius to guess you're hiding something.' She rolled on to her back beside him and sighed. 'I guess there's never going to be a good time to tell you this.'

'Tell me what?'

'I'm being reassigned. They're sending several new expeditions into the rest of the coreship, and I've been asked to join one. We might even try to penetrate the command core this time round. It'll be a joint operation, undertaken with the surviving Skelites and Bandati in the other zones.'

'What are you hoping to find? The coreship is dead.' He'd seen external shots of the starship taken by the Legislate ships that arrived a few weeks after the Shoal had abandoned it. Almost all its drive-spines had been burned away as it escaped Night's End. Early hopes of finding a way to pilot it back to Consortium territory had been quickly dashed, but contact had now been made with races in the other environments, including one or two previously unknown to mankind.

Karen frowned. 'You understand what I'm saying, don't you?'

Nathan smiled and stroked her hair for what he guessed would likely be the last time. 'That we won't be seeing each other any more, is that it?'

'I wasn't sure how you'd react.'

'I think we both always knew a day like this was coming.' He looked inside himself and realized he wasn't lying. Life had been grim, desperately so for too long now, and their time together had helped keep him sane. 'No more chasing after General Peralta, then,' he added.

'You must be relieved.'

She scowled. 'Peralta's a dead man. He's never leaving Ascension alive. He must know it too, but he just keeps fighting.'

Nathan found himself wondering what she might think if she were to find out he had been in Peralta's employ until a few months before. The warlord, faced with a stark choice between arrest and execution on the one hand and a slow, lingering death on the other, had demanded safe transportation off the coreship for himself and his inner circle, almost as soon as the first relief operations had arrived. The Consortium had other ideas, however, and Peralta had then made good on his threat to carry out attacks on refugees until he got exactly what he wanted.

Ilsa had been amongst the first to slip away from Peralta's compound under cover of night, and ever since he had made his own escape a few months later, he had been searching for her so they could find a way out of Ascension together. He had hoped his volunteer work on the ambulances would improve their chances of being lifted out of the coreship, once he'd found her.

'Unless he can find a way to mix in with the rest of the refugees and slip past you,' Nathan suggested. He was careful to keep his voice casual.

'They scan everyone who goes through,' she replied, and yawned, pulling herself in closer to him. 'With DNA profiling, biometrics, the works. Don't you worry, there's no way in hell anyone gets on to a ship without us knowing exactly who they are.'

'That's good to know,' he muttered, staring up at the ceiling, and wondering if Nirav had yet checked his DNA profile against the Legislate's security databases.

'Hey. Wake up.'

Nathan grumbled and shook his head, opening bleary eyes. He could tell it was dawn because the light outside the window was now marginally brighter than during the night. Karen was already sitting up, the thick grey blanket pulled up around her naked breasts.

Two men stood by the open door to the office, dressed the same as any other troopers except for the grey shoulder markings that identified them as internal security. They were armed with pulse-rifles.

'Ma'am,' one of them said to Karen, throwing her a salute but unable to hide the smirk on his face. 'Sorry to wake you, but we've got orders.'

'What goddamn orders?' she snapped.

Nathan glanced down towards Karen's pistol, still in its holster and half-hidden under her tangled clothes, and decided his chances of surviving a shoot-out were minimal in the extreme.

'We're here to take Mr Whitecloud into custody,' said the trooper who'd spoken. 'The orders came from Representative Munn. You'll see they're marked highest priority.' He passed the credentials to her.

She scanned the papers for a moment before looking back up. 'Ty Whitecloud?' she asked, looking utterly confused. 'Who the hell is Ty Whitecloud?'

'He is, ma'am,' the trooper replied, nodding towards the man who had been calling himself Nathan Driscoll.

Karen turned to stare at him like she'd never set eyes on him before.

THREE

PRIORITY MESSAGE Code ALPHA security rating 15
Compiled by OFFICE OF SECURITY @ OCEAN'S
DEEP/DATE:2544:6:6 via Hubert Tach-Net Array.
Authorized by WILLIS, OLIVARRI, OUSPENSKY.

REPORT SUMMARY FROM:
Navigators GILLIES, SATIE, YUSEF, MAZZINI,
YOSHI
Direct observations of artificially induced
novae to date: 15
Sightings of Emissary fleets: 13
Estimated Threat Level at time of report: 7
(0–10)
Notes: Navigators GILLIES and YUSEF report
contact with Emissaries at 0.91+0.78
kiloparsecs 2544:6:2+2544:5:29
Location of Navigator SATIE unknown following
last report: filed under MISSING.
SUMMARY ANALYSIS: Dispersal of Emissary fleets
in region designated 'Long War' suggest likely
contact with colonies in maximum 1.577×10^7
seconds

RECOMMENDATIONS: 1:CITATION for Navigator
SATIE. 2:Raise Threat Level to 8(0—10).
PRIORITY MESSAGE ENDS

OFFICE OF SECURITY

The blow was unexpected, a hard jab that caught Lucas Corso on the side of his ribcage and half-spun him around. He staggered slightly before regaining his balance and quickly dropped into the correct defensive posture, ready for the next assault.

'You're dead already,' Breisch snapped, flexing the fingers of his free hand. The other held a short sword, its blade slightly curved and razor-sharp. 'Attack, not defence.'

Corso scented his own blood, mixed with sweat, where Breisch had slashed him across the chest. He kept his breathing under control and snapped out with his feet and arms in a series of coordinated lunges, pushing his opponent back across the training suite.

Corso yelled with each lunge, barking his anger as Breisch dodged and dipped and spun out of reach. He sucked in air, legs slightly bent at the knees, almost a dancer's posture.

Breisch was right: if this had been the real thing, he'd be dead by now. He was slipping badly, and the reasons were all too obvious.

A priority alert then appeared in the form of a softly

glowing lozenge of light projected from a ceiling-mounted mechanism. Breisch saw it and immediately relaxed into a non-combat posture, legs straight, hands clasped behind his back. His skin was slick with sweat, so at least Corso knew he hadn't made it too easy for his teacher.

'That was a bad slip you made,' Breisch told him calmly 'We're going to have to work on your response times. It's a weakness that any half-decent fighter could exploit, Senator.'

'I appreciate that, Mr Breisch,' Corso replied, picking up his shirt and using it to wipe the sweat from his neck and face. Breisch was one of the best deadly-combat trainers in the Freehold, and it had taken a lot of money to persuade him to leave Redstone and become his personal trainer.

'The gravity here on Eugenia may also be an issue,' Breisch added. 'We may have to work on more strategies for coping with different strengths of gravity, particularly if you keep moving around as much as you have been.'

'Noted,' Corso replied. 'We'll pick up from here tomorrow morning.'

Breisch nodded and left the room. Corso stepped through to a shower room and washed the blood and sweat away, then used some coagulant to stop the bleeding before applying a strip of bandage to the wound.

'Report,' he said to the air, once the water had shut off.

There was a soft chime in his right ear, and a female

voice with rounded tones began to speak. 'Nisha here, Senator Corso. There's been another sabotage attempt. A robot cargo transport deviated and made straight for Eugenia. The good news is that we caught it long before it got anywhere near us.'

'You're certain it was sabotage? Not just a systems failure?'

'The platform's brain had been very expertly hacked, Senator. There's no doubt it was deliberate.'

Corso groaned silently, and started to towel himself dry. Another crisis to deal with. 'Anything else?'

'An urgent request from Ted Lamoureaux, who wants a meeting with you straight away. Something for your ears only, he said.'

'First things first.' Anger flowed like heat through his thoughts; there had to be some way to make people understand he wouldn't tolerate these constant acts of terrorism. 'We need to be seen to be reacting to this strongly and positively. Do we have any idea at all who's responsible for the sabotage?'

'Nothing clear as yet, but we've got analysts taking the transport's brain apart right now.'

Sometimes he wondered just whose bright idea it had been to give him this much responsibility, and then he reminded himself, for the millionth time, that he had volunteered for the job. Previous investigations of attempts to either kill him or hurt the colony in Ocean's Deep had a nasty habit of running into dead ends. Would-be executioners and saboteurs either proved to be mercenaries with no knowledge of who'd hired them, or simply turned up dead by the time the Consortium's own intelligence services tracked them down.

'Who's our most likely suspect?' he asked. 'I'm talking governments here, Nisha. Who would you say wants rid of me the most of all this week?'

'I would guess . . . the Midgarth security services are near the top. There are rumours they've been soliciting secret talks with both Morgan's World and Bohr. In addition, they've been openly vetoing our request to take part in the next round of crisis talks. Also, some of their more recent candidates for navigator training turned out to have connections deep within their respective intelligence communities. We rejected them, naturally.'

'We've been sitting around while other people take potshots at us for far too long. Where's Willis right now?' Corso asked, referring to his security head back at Ocean's Deep.

'Probably asleep, Senator. I reckon Leo Olivarri would be on active watch-duty about now.' Olivarri was Willis's deputy.

Corso grunted and checked the bandage in a mirror, to make sure it wasn't going to slip. His arms and chest were marked with a fine criss-crossing of scars, like memories of pain and death carved into his flesh.

He started to get dressed, pulling on an anti-ballistic vest made from compacted layers of genetically enhanced spider-silk, then a formal dress shirt on top. A carefully concealed holstered pistol was next, followed by a slim blade tucked down the back of one boot. He kept himself armed at all times these days, and had recently spent a lot of time in the company of men like Breisch, learning how to properly use the various weapons he carried. In the two years since Dakota had left, his chest had broadened and any excess fat had drained from his face, lending him a much more angular appearance. His fingers had grown calloused from months of weapons and hand-to-hand combat training. There was a long, dark burn mark on the inside of his left arm, invisible beneath his shirt – testament to a challenge he had taken part in less than a year before.

'All right, Nisha, this is what we're going to do,' he said, pulling on his jacket. 'Tell Leo to wake Willis up. I want them to locate and round up every Midgarth representative to the Fleet he can find at Ocean's Deep, and have them hauled in. They can call it protective custody, but make sure that, one way or another, at least some of them are formally arrested and charged on suspicion of espionage.'

'I'm not aware that we have sufficient leads to warrant any such arrests, Senator.'

'It doesn't matter. Do it anyway. If they don't like it, they can catch the next ship going home.' He thought for a moment. 'And if we can't find any leads, keep them locked up, anyway. Let's see if *we* can stir up some shit for a change.'

'They won't be happy, sir.'

Understatement of the century, thought Corso, but

said, 'Fuck them. I also want all of their representatives' assets, financial and otherwise, frozen pending an immediate investigation. Have the office put together a general press release after the fact, nothing too specific. But I want it worded in such a way that it's clear we intend to take a stand. Even if Midgarth isn't involved, maybe some of the others will think twice if they think their heads might wind up on the block as well.'

'Yes, Senator.'

The chime sounded again, indicating that the link had been broken.

Corso took a deep breath, and pulled a small vial out of his jacket pocket. He shook a couple of pills out of it and swallowed them dry. How many hours a night of sleep was he getting these days? Four, maybe five?

The medication helped, but he knew he was overdoing it.

Corso exited the gym and met the half-dozen heavily armed men and women that comprised his personal security detail in the building's lobby. From there it was a short walk across an open plaza to the domed building that housed Eugenia's government offices. His guards surrounded him, their weapons discreetly tucked into pockets or within easy reach inside jackets. Tiny security devices whirred in the air around them like mechanical insects, scanning for anything that might be missed by ordinary human eyes.

Eugenia had started life as an asteroid and, like so many of the larger bodies scattered throughout the Sol system following first contact with the Shoal, had been transformed by using the Shoal's own technology. A gravity engine had been buried at the asteroid's core, while shaped fields completely surrounding it retained a pressurized atmosphere and protected it from radiation. Fusion torches – suspended from poles that pushed through the shaped fields like pins through soap bubbles – shone heat and light down on the tiny world.

It was the first boosted world Corso had ever found himself on, and he couldn't say for sure if he was enjoying the experience. His stomach lurched every time he caught sight of the impossibly close horizon.

For all that, Eugenia was one of the largest of the Main Belt boosted worlds, and a little over two hundred kilometres in diameter. It had started out larger, but its original rough, potato-like shape had been less than ideal, so it had been blasted and sculpted into something more approximating a sphere. It had even been allowed to retain Petit-Prince, one of its two small moons. An iron sculpture of Saint-Exupéry's Little Prince stood near the centre of the plaza, gazing up at a point where his namesake would pass overhead every five days.

But before very long, the asteroid and its moons were going to become eternally separated. The Little Prince was going to have to make his own way through space.

Yugo Stankovic, one of Corso's aides, was waiting for him in the foyer of the government building.

'All right, Yugo, Nisha already gave me an outline of what's happened. Is there anything else I should know?' Corso asked, as Stankovic matched pace with him. The security detail made their way elsewhere while Corso and his aide headed for a bank of elevators.

'What she told you, she got from me. We managed to disable the cargo platform remotely without any further incident, but it was pretty close.'

'How bad could it have been?'

'It could have wiped us out. The Consortium's own intelligence services are working hard at stopping any word of this getting out to the media, and Eugenia's prime minister took the chair of an emergency session about five minutes ago.' Stankovic smiled and shrugged. 'We're not invited, of course.'

An elevator arrived and they stepped inside. 'Who's in charge of figuring out who's responsible?'

'Lieutenant Nazarro of our own Authority security is working on it with the local security heads in a separate meeting,' Stankovic replied. 'I should have an initial report from him within the hour.'

Corso flexed his hands, and found himself wishing for a more tangible enemy. All the careful manoeuvring of the last few years was coming to nothing. Whoever was responsible for these acts of sabotage was doing a good job of remaining eternally elusive, leaving him with the near-certainty that the only ones capable of covering their tracks so thoroughly were precisely those govern-ments that coveted the Peacekeeper Authority's power the most. As far as most of them were concerned, he was the one thing standing between them and the stars.

The elevator doors hissed open and they stepped into a suite of offices. Ted Lamoureaux was already there, sprawled on a couch.

'Ted,' said Corso, stepping forward and shaking Lamoureaux's hand, after the other man stood up to greet him. 'Good to see you. We'll talk through here.'

The starship navigator was a slight, pale-featured man in his thirties, with a perpetually worried look. He was also – in common with Dakota Merrick and every other Magi-enabled navigator within the Consortium – a machine-head, his skull filled with consciousness-altering technology that made him uniquely suited to interfacing with the starships that Dakota had summoned to Ocean's Deep.

Lamoureaux followed them into an office with a wide picture window. Hundreds of newly installed drive-spines – spaced equidistant from each other all around Eugenia's surface – were visible beyond the window. They were a recent addition, an essential part of the asteroid's slow transformation into a full-fledged starship. Each spine was hundreds of metres tall and gracefully curving, giving Eugenia the appearance from a distance of some enormous space-going bacterium coated in metallic cilia.

Corso dropped on to a couch. 'Whatever it is you

wanted to talk to me about is going to have to wait a few minutes. I need to know why Eugenia's new FTL drive still hasn't arrived.'

'It's all in my report.'

'Yeah, I know. Just humour me, Ted.'

Lamoureaux shrugged and slipped a ring from the finger of one hand, then dropped it on to the active plate of an image unit set up near the window. He touched the machine's controls, and an image of an airless dwarf planet appeared above the plate, slowly rotating. A Maker cache had been found there little more than a year before, at Iota Horologii – the Tierra system, as it was more commonly known. Other images appeared, cut-away schematics showing the cache's layout, a kilo-metres-deep shaft drilled deep into the planet's crust, with thousands of needle-like passageways extending out from the shaft.

One of these passageways, Corso knew, contained a machine called a drive-forge, a template-driven fabricator that could manufacture new superluminal engines for faster-than-light travel.

The Tierra system had briefly been home to a Uchidan colony before the Shoal Hegemony had reclaimed it without explanation. The uprooted colonists had been evacuated to a new home on Redstone, an ill-fated decision that left the Uchidans in a state of near-permanent war with the Freehold colony already long established there.

Much more recently, it had been discovered that the

Shoal had been actively suppressing knowledge of the existence of these caches for a very, very long time. When they'd discovered this particular cache orbiting out in the very farthest reaches of the Tierra system, the Shoal had reneged on their existing contracts with the Uchidans.

But now the Shoal themselves were gone, and the cache had been quickly rediscovered, and subsequently placed under the control of the Peacekeeper Authority. Corso had been locked in a political battle with the Consortium Legislate ever since, desperate for the resources and personnel needed to exploit the cache, but forced to make more and more concessions in order to get them.

'All the latest research is right here on this data ring,' Lamoureaux explained. 'It can take up to a couple of weeks to produce a single superluminal drive, and as soon as one is finished half a dozen different colonial governments, with their own agendas, start threatening embargoes and worse if we don't give it to them. At the moment most of the drives are meant to go into ships intended for relief operations throughout the Consortium, but we've got no guarantees that's what they'll get used for. That and about a hundred other reasons are why there are so many delays, and why Eugenia doesn't have its drive yet. And that's before we even get to considering the increasing rate of neural burnout in our machine-head pilots. We've had to retire nearly a third of our longest-serving navigators in the past six months.'

'"Neural burnout"? Is that what they're calling it now?'

'That and the bends, but the neurologists prefer not to call it that. It's primarily affecting the ones who've been piloting Magi ships the longest.'

'Like yourself.'

'So far I've been fine, but it might only be a matter of time.'

'And we still don't know what's causing this?'

'Nope.'

Corso leaned back and stared up at the ceiling, suddenly feeling wearier despite the pills. 'In other words, we're even more fucked than we already were.'

Lamoureaux spread his hands. 'Look . . . I don't want to be the one to have to say this, but if things keep on the way they are, we're going to wind up losing navigators faster than we can replace them. We might then be forced to give the Legislate at least some of what it wants.'

'Specifically?'

'Relaxing the rules governing the recruitment of new navigators. Allow the Legislate, and the governments it represents, to share the responsibility for finding and training them.'

'Which would leave the Peacekeeper Authority without any purpose. Or authority.'

Lamoureaux's expression was carefully non-committal.

'Yugo,' Corso asked, 'your thoughts?'

'If I can speak candidly?'

Corso nodded.

'I think Ted's right. If we don't make major concessions now, the Legislate might claim we're being unreasonable and merely blocking them. That might be just enough of an excuse for them to try and make a grab for the Tierra cache. The Allocation Treaty means a certain proportion of finished drives go to them, so if they then decided to carry out a military action against us, they'd have the means and resources to do it.'

'Not to mention,' Lamoureaux added, 'a lot of ships are being retro-fitted to make it harder for them to be remotely grabbed by machine-heads. That means we might not be able to stop them, even with the help of the Magi ships. Unless we threaten to blow up their suns.'

'Not even remotely funny,' Corso muttered. Clearly he was going to have to intervene directly over the business of Eugenia's drive. 'Whatever else it is you came here to tell me, I really hope it's good news.'

'We received a transmission from Dakota Merrick.'

Corso tried not to look too startled. 'It's been, what, more than a year? I was beginning to . . .' *To wonder if she was even still alive*, he almost said.

'She's rendezvoused with the Maker,' Lamoureaux continued. 'We received a targeted burst from her several hours ago. According to what she sent us, the Maker is really a swarm of space-going machines, quite vast in number. The evidence points to a single, unified intelligence, even though its individual components are apparently spread out across a number of light-years.'

Lamoureaux reached out to the imager once more, and the Tierra cache was replaced by something that looked more like a metal sculpture created by a psychotic than it suggested a space-going vessel.

There's something evil-looking about it, Corso thought, even though he knew it was pointless to attribute human qualities to something so very clearly alien.

'The swarm possessed data relating to something called the "Mos Hadroch", which it apparently regards as a serious threat,' Lamoureaux explained. 'According to the Magi's own records, it's some kind of weapon of phenomenal power, but – until now – there was never any evidence that it even existed.'

Corso stared at the image of the swarm-component. 'And this means it does?'

'Dakota came up against a blank wall, and asked us to see if we could find any correlation with anything known to us. Imagine our surprise when we did. Now, look at this.'

The swarm-component was replaced by an image of a lumpy-looking asteroid. 'This is an Atn clade-world,' Lamoureaux explained. 'You can find them out on the edge of many systems in the Consortium.'

'I know something about them,' observed Corso. 'I studied some of their machine-languages. They travel everywhere at sublight speeds.'

'And they usually stick to the very remotest part of a system. If Dakota's findings are anything to go by, the depths of interstellar space are even more densely infested with them than we thought.'

An image of an Atn now appeared next to the hollowed-out asteroid. A large, rectangular metal body, covered in a curious alien calligraphy, sat on top of four stumpy legs. At the end of each leg, thick, splayed metal claws gripped the ground, while a mass of mechanical manipulators extended from a slot just below the brick-shaped head.

'Since they can visit parts of the galaxy we ourselves couldn't until recently, there was always the chance we might learn something from them,' Lamoureaux continued. 'Which is why we've been studying them carefully ever since we came into contact with them.'

Corso nodded. 'And?'

'Imagine our surprise when we stumbled across references to a "Mos Hadroch" in some research papers written just a couple of decades ago by a specialist who's still around. The term crops up in relation to one specific Atn clade called "Eclipse-over-Moon".'

'So what do we know about them?'

'Practically nothing, and the term shows up only once, and in an oblique reference at that. But the man who actually wrote the papers knows more about this particular clade-family than anyone else alive.'

Corso nodded. 'Then we need to track him down.'

There was a look on Lamoureaux's face as if he was trying to make up his mind whether or not to tell Corso something. 'Already on it, and . . . I'd like your permission to get him to Ocean's Deep as soon as possible.'

'Granted. Who is he?'

'His name is Ty Whitecloud, Senator.'

Corso sat stock-still for a moment, then stood up carefully. 'No,' he said, very simply, and turned towards the door.

'Senator, there isn't anyone else who knows as much about the Atn as he does.'

'Perhaps you didn't hear me the first time, Ted. I said no. There are other people who could—'

'With the greatest respect, Senator, but there aren't,' said Stankovic. 'It's a pretty rarefied field.'

'I know a little about Atn machine-languages, Yugo. I've even read one or two of Whitecloud's papers. But there are others we could try.' He thought for a moment. 'Anton Laroque and Sophie Sprau, for a start. They're leaders in the field.'

Lamoureaux shook his head. 'We checked them out already. Laroque was in Night's End when it was destroyed, and Sprau's extremely elderly and on life-support back on Earth. She isn't expected to survive more than another couple of weeks. That leaves only Whitecloud.'

'He's a war criminal,' Corso barked.

'Sir?' asked Stankovic, looking puzzled.

Stankovic was from Derinkuyu, Corso remembered then, a long way from Redstone. 'Whitecloud is a Uchidan,' Corso explained. 'Or at least he worked for them.

One of the bright lights of their scientific community at one time. Do you remember the Port Gabriel incident?'

Stankovic's eyes slid to one side as he strove to recall buried memories of media reports from years before. 'In the general details only.'

'The Uchidans found a way to control the minds of machine-heads sent to Redstone as part of a Consortium peacekeeping force. Uchidan skull implants aren't, after all, that fundamentally different from those of machine-heads. They identified a flaw in the machine-head architecture and exploited it. The result was a massacre that killed a huge number of non-combatants.'

'And Whitecloud was implicated?'

'He was,' said Lamoureaux, cutting in, 'but he was a minor figure in the research project, not at all involved in the actual implementation. It's important to make that distinction.'

'That doesn't make him any less respon—' Corso snapped his fingers. 'I remember now. Whitecloud escaped from custody, years ago. And now you know where he is?'

Lamoureaux nodded. 'Legislate agents tracked him down in Ascension a couple of weeks back and he's being held in a barracks prison there. Turns out he'd been hiding under an assumed identity for years. It's possible we could spring him, but we'd have to move fast.'

Corso regarded him with a pained expression. 'Ted . . . if it came out that we were employing *war criminals*, we'd be kissing any chance of concord with the Legislate goodbye for ever.'

'Well, that gives us a serious problem, Senator,' Lamoureaux replied, 'because if Dakota's on to something, we're going to need Whitecloud very, very badly.'

Corso glanced at the door and fantasized for a moment about just walking out of there and having nothing to do with what Lamoureaux was suggesting. And yet, at the same time, he sensed – not for the first time – the inevitability of having to compromise what he had once considered the immutable beliefs and values he had long held dear. After the last couple of years, he was almost getting used to it.

He sighed and sat back down. 'You're a machine-head yourself, Ted. How can you even contemplate this?'

'Because sometimes you just have to live with the cards life deals you, Senator. I have good friends who would never talk to me again if they had any idea what I'm suggesting here. If there was another way, believe me, I'd take it. But Whitecloud was far from the worst of them.'

'And that's in your best professional judgement?'

'It is, but we need to move fast on this. Most of the Emissary forces are still kiloparsecs away, but advance scouts have been observed engaging with Shoal fleets a lot closer to home. I'd like to go to Ascension and take charge of this myself, with your permission.'

'Alright, fine, if that's what it takes,' Corso replied, a void seeming to form deep inside his chest. 'Tell Willis he's to rendezvous with you there as well. Olivarri can take 'care of things at Ocean's Deep for now. You understand,' he added, 'that if any word of this gets out . . .'

'It won't.'

Lamoureaux left a few moments later, and Corso noticed the fusion globes outside were beginning to dim in preparation for evening, the ghostly band of the Milky Way gradually becoming visible.

Somewhere out there, entire star systems were being destroyed all along the frontiers of the Long War, a vast region encompassing the outer rim of the Orion Arm. There were reports of fleets so vast they were almost beyond comprehension, and these made the idea that Dakota or anyone could possibly affect them seem hopelessly deluded. But they had to try.

'If this doesn't work,' Corso said, so quietly that Stankovic had to strain to hear him, 'then the only thing left to do is save what we can.'

'Senator?'

Corso stared out beyond the fading fusion globes, picturing the light spreading out from distant novae like a fiery cancer. 'If we don't find a way out of this mess, we're going to have to dispatch ships, as far away as we can, and found new colonies in some other part of the galaxy where the war can't reach them. At least that way we might save some.'

He stood and moved towards the door. 'Arrange for a priority message back to Dakota. Let Ted know about it, too. Tell her what we've found out and make sure she's kept up to date whenever something new comes up.'

Stankovic hesitated. 'What about Whitecloud? Do we mention him?'

'Dakota was at Port Gabriel during the massacres. I think we'd better not mention him at all, don't you?'

FOUR

Next time, the interrogators were different.

The first one to enter Ty's cell was balding and middle-aged, with loose wisps of hair curling around his ears. A younger man closed the door behind him, his own head carefully shaved. The older one had the look of a civil servant, and wore a sombre-looking suit with a high collar. His younger companion was dressed more casually.

'My name is Rex Kosac,' the older man explained, as Ty lifted himself up from the narrow plastic shelf that served as his bed, 'and my colleague here is Horace Bleys.'

Ty gazed at them warily, trying to adjust the thin paper uniform he'd been given to wear. 'You're not part of the staff here, are you?'

Bleys glanced around the tiny cell and wrinkled his nose, perhaps becoming aware of the perpetual scent of detergent and urine that clung to every surface. His flattened nose, thick, muscled hands and general air of barely suppressed violence suggested he was Kosac's bodyguard.

'On the contrary, Mr Whitecloud, I administrate this facility,' Kosac replied.

Ty sat up straighter. 'When they brought me here, they said I would be formally arraigned within a couple of days.'

Kosac shook his head sadly. 'That's not why I'm here, Mr Whitecloud. I just wanted the chance to meet you before . . .' he glanced at Bleys with a smile, as if he'd caught himself on the verge of saying something he shouldn't. 'Well, you're our most famous resident, as a matter of fact.'

A helicopter passed over the prison, the sound of its blades dopplering as it descended towards a nearby landing pad. The muffled sounds of men shouting and trucks pulling up outside continued unabated day and night.

'Would you like to know how we found you so quickly?' asked Kosac, his grin increasingly feral.

Ty cleared his throat, his mouth suddenly dry and his tongue feeling heavy. 'I assumed it was the blood sample.'

Kosac frowned. 'Blood sample?'

'A doctor took it from me at a clinic. I assumed you were running automatic gene-profiling and matched it to a sample that was taken from me before I was due to be handed over by the Uchidans.'

Enlightenment crossed Kosac's face. 'Ah! I see. No, on the contrary, we picked up a friend of yours a couple of months back. Ilsa Padel – you know her?'

Ty nodded, a terrible feeling of inevitability beginning to overcome him.

'She tried to exit the coreship along with a group of refugees. She almost got past us before we figured out who she was. She was *extremely* helpful when it came to identifying key members of General Peralta's senior staff in return for certain concessions. Even if we didn't have the blood sample, Mr Whitecloud, it was still only a matter of time. And hiding right there in the clinic! Well,' – Kosac shook his head as if sorrowful, 'that was always going to make it easy for us, wasn't it?'

Ty slumped back against the wall. 'I see.'

Ilsa. Few others could have had the opportunity to betray him so thoroughly. Apart from her, only Peralta had been aware of his true identity. Ty felt a tide of bitter melancholy well up as he remembered all the times he had searched for her, unaware she had already bartered him for a more comfortable cell or a shorter sentence.

His first sight of the barracks had been at dawn. The block-shaped prison building was tucked into one corner of a large fenced compound belonging to the permanent Consortium military presence stationed in the coreship. Rover-units with heavy armaments mounted on their backs surrounded it, while supply trucks and transports constantly arrived or departed. The corridors within teemed with black-suited troopers, their faces more often than not hidden behind visors.

His first night in this cell had convinced him that he would not survive to see the morning. The single window above the toilet bowl looked out over a courtyard surrounded by a high concrete wall. An automated guntower equipped with IR and motion sensors stood on a skeletal tripod in one corner of the courtyard, while most of the rest of it was stacked with pallets containing emergency supplies, the spaces in between forming narrow corridors.

Ty had watched as guards dragged three men in rags past this maze of pallets and towards the courtyard's rear wall. One of the troopers raised a pistol to the back of the head of each in quick succession, dispatching them with quick and brutal efficiency. The pistol emitted a muted bass thump with each shot that Ty felt more than he heard.

He had soon collapsed on to the plastic shelf and spent the rest of the night waiting for his own turn to come. He could imagine the cold biting wind on his face, the chafing of the plastic ties around his wrists, and his last sight of those cracked grey concrete walls before a single shot took out the back of his skull. Instead he woke to another day, and then another after that. But every night the same drama was repeated: one or more figures would be marched out to the rear of the courtyard and executed. Yet nobody ever came for him.

Not until now.

*

Kosac stepped over to the window and peered out. 'Tell me,' he asked, 'how did you wind up with the Uchidans? I believe you grew up in the Freehold.'

'I grew up on a farm, Mr Kosac. My father was murdered on the orders of a corrupt senator, and I had to stand and watch as an entire agricultural facility and several thousand acres of land that should have been my inheritance were stolen from my family.' He shrugged. 'After that, switching sides was easy.'

'I see.' Kosac stepped away from the window. 'You trained originally in biotechnology, but switched careers. Why?'

'After I arrived in the Uchidan Territories, I developed an interest in the Atn. They're a form of extreme bio-tech, after all, engineered rather than evolved, so it wasn't really that much of a career change. I obtained a Consortium-funded research grant and made a name for myself studying them. My work took me all across human-occupied space, and I spent several years far from home. But when the war with the Freehold became intractable, I found myself conscripted into Territorial Research and Defence when I finally returned.'

'And so you did your duty, because of your faith in God?'

Ty regarded him with a weary look. 'Uchidanism has nothing to do with faith, Mr Kosac. It has much more to do with logical certainties and inescapable mathematical truths.'

'Really,' said Kosac, clearly unimpressed. 'Perhaps you could elaborate for me.'

'I'd rather not.'

Kosac nodded briefly at his companion. Bleys stepped forward and grabbed Ty's hair, then slammed the back of his head against the wall behind the shelf he sat on. Ty groaned and slithered on to the floor, tasting blood where he'd bitten his tongue.

'Humour me,' said Kosac.

The two men waited while Ty pulled himself back up on to the shelf. He dribbled blood and Bleys handed him a handkerchief. Ty took it, pressing it to his mouth until he was ready to continue.

'Uchidanism is . . . is based on objective observation and statistical probability.'

'What probabilities?'

'That life, by its very nature, always seeks to preserve itself within a universe that has a finite span, and that the ultimate endpoint of technological development is the direct manipulation of the most fundamental laws that govern nature.'

Ty swallowed again. The words came easily, memorized long ago but still clear in his mind. 'There are good reasons to believe we live not in the original universe but in a simulation, possibly one of many. Reality, at its most base level, is little more than an expression of various mathematical formulae; therefore, once you acknowledge these simple truths, the idea that our world could be anything other than *created* becomes ridiculous.'

'I'm disappointed, Mr Whitecloud.' Ty looked up at Kosac. 'I don't know much about Uchidanism, but I know something about personal faith. I believe we pay for what happens in this world in the next.'

Bleys had turned away slightly, reaching up to touch the side of his head. Ty noticed for the first time the man wore a comms bead in one earlobe.

Ty looked back at Kosac. 'Why are you asking me these questions?'

'Because I'm probably the last person you'll ever speak to, and I wanted to know what kind of man does the things you've done.'

Ice gripped Ty's heart. 'I'm to be arraigned. Taken off the coreship to be tried.'

Kosac smiled sadly. 'In a less imperfect world, perhaps.'

'Sir?' said Bleys, and Kosac turned to him. 'We got a report that the Authority's people are on their way here. I think we should hurry.'

The ice spread long frozen fingers deep into Ty's bowels. 'I'm too valuable for you to just shoot,' he croaked.

'No, Mr Whitecloud, you're not going to have a chance to escape a second time.'

Ty stared backwards and forwards between the two men. 'Escape?'

A moment later two armed and visored guards appeared at the cell door, and Ty knew the worst was yet to come.

*

The two guards entered the cell and dragged Ty out into the corridor, where one slammed a shock-stick into the back of one knee. He collapsed on to all fours. A second blow sent him sprawling on his belly.

A moment later his arms were twisted painfully behind his back, and he felt the plastic ties being clipped into place around his wrists. He was pulled upright a moment later and pushed towards a service elevator at the far end of the corridor. His legs gave way under him, but the guards dragged him along between them, regardless.

They pushed him inside the elevator and forced him to his knees, then hauled him back out, once they had arrived at the ground floor. Ty managed to find his feet, and was shoved towards a steel door at the far end of the corridor, a thin but freezing trickle of cold air seeping past its frame and carrying with it the scent of oiled metal and decay. One of the guards stepped forward and unlocked the door, revealing stacked pallets as it swung open.

Ty clenched his teeth at the blast of frozen air and tried to hunch up, his paper uniform providing him with so little protection that he might as well have been naked.

He realized he was weeping as they dragged and shoved him out into the courtyard. Everything seemed to get a little farther away, as if he were experiencing the world at one remove, reduced to being a passenger within his own skull.

They pulled him towards the wall at the rear of the courtyard. He was close enough now that he could make out the dark stains where the wall met the ground. For the first time, he saw a door set into the wall over to his right, where it had been hidden from his view in the cell by a pile of crates. It stood open, a military transport parked on the street outside. A guard stood by the door, his visor pushed up, arguing with two men who looked too healthy and well fed to come from Ascension.

One had a thick woollen hat pulled down over his stubbled skull, but Ty still saw the irregular grooves and bumps disfiguring his cranium, which marked him out as a machine-head. He was tall and gangly, with a worried expression, whereas his companion was small but wiry and muscular-looking. The second one's gaze locked on to Ty the instant he came into view.

'That's him,' Ty heard him say, over the unending hubbub of activity. The machine-head glanced first at his companion, then at Ty. Then they both pushed past the guard they'd been talking to and headed straight for him.

'Hey!' the guard shouted, dropping his rifle from his shoulder and following them. 'You can't—'

'The fuck?' said the machine-head's companion, stopping for a moment to glare back at the guard. 'What was it about our authorization you *didn't* understand?'

Ty's own guards had halted at the commotion, but then they seemed to come to some mutual, unspoken decision and resumed pushing him towards the wall.

'Hey, stop right there!' shouted the small, muscled man. 'Don't take another single fucking step. Do you understand?'

'We have orders,' one of Ty's guards grated. 'If you've got a problem with it, take it up with Director Kosac.'

'Oh, we will,' said the other man, coming closer. 'You,' he said, turning back to the guard who'd tried to stop them. 'Tell them who I am.'

'Commander Willis, sir,' the guard replied with clear reluctance. 'Head of Ocean's Deep security.'

'That makes me one of the people responsible for the entire relief operation out here. And that,' he continued, coming up closer to one of Ty's would-be executioners, 'means you do *exactly* what I say. So here's the deal,' he continued, his voice softening now into an agreeable we're-all-friends-here tone of conciliation. 'We want this man for questioning.' He glanced briefly at Ty. 'Your name is Ty Whitecloud, isn't it?'

Ty managed to nod.

'Those aren't our orders, sir,' one of Ty's guards said. 'Our instruction is immediate execution.'

'Who told you that? Director Kosac?'

Ty glanced to one side, just in time to see the guard nod.

'Well, Director Kosac is about to get a spiked boot up his ass that's going to bounce him all the way out of Ascension and into a job someplace that's going to make his time here look like a fucking holiday.' Willis smiled broadly. 'And if you don't do exactly what I tell you, and

I mean *to the fucking letter*, I'll make sure you're there to keep him company. Now,' he added, gesturing to Ty, 'since you've already seen our credentials, how about you do precisely what we tell you to, before you make things worse than they already are?'

Ty felt the grip on his shoulders tighten for a few seconds, then relax.

'Sir,' said one of his guards, before letting go of him altogether.

'This way,' said Willis, taking Ty's elbow and leading him towards the waiting vehicle.

Ty followed in a daze, as the machine-head moved up on his other side.

'Mr Whitecloud,' said the machine-head, leaning down a little to speak to him, 'my name is Ted Lamoureaux and you are a very, very lucky man. I hope you'll be grateful enough to be as cooperative as we're going to need you to be.'

Lamoureaux touched a panel on the side of the transport and a door slid open, warm air wafting out from within. Ty drew in the smell of oiled leather and cheap plastic, and felt tears prickling the corners of his eyes.

Lamoureaux gestured inside.

'My hands,' said Ty. 'Please.'

'Shit,' he heard Willis mutter behind him, and a moment later he felt the plastic ties fall away from his wrists. He brought his arms back around, wincing at the pain in his shoulders, and climbed inside the vehicle.

The interior was cramped, and the air felt hot and

close to him, after being out in the freezing cold. There were two rows of seats facing each other, and Lamoureaux and Willis sat down opposite Ty. The transport started to move a moment later.

'Where are you taking me?' Ty asked.

'Well, that depends on exactly how cooperative you're feeling,' Lamoureaux replied.

'Kosac told me someone was coming for me, but he wasn't going to let me escape.'

He watched the two men exchange glances.

'Well, that's it,' Willis muttered. 'I'm going to get a kick out of burying that little shit up to his neck in trouble.'

'Mr Whitecloud,' said Lamoureaux, his tone dry, 'can you tell me if the term "Mos Hadroch" means anything to you?'

Ty nodded slowly. 'It's an Atn term: a transliteration based on an analysis of ancient Atn sound recordings. It means a machine for passing judgement.'

'And you've been living under the "Nathan Driscoll" identity for some years now, isn't that correct?' Lamoureaux prompted.

Ty nodded slowly, unsure what to admit to just yet.

'We'll stick with the Driscoll identity for now,' said Willis. 'Seems you've had quite the varied career, haven't you, Ty?'

Ty shrugged uneasily and still said nothing.

Lamoureaux's eyes became momentarily unfocused. *He's accessing data from somewhere*, Ty realized.

Lamoureaux blinked and looked at Ty. 'You have an implant,' he remarked.

'You can tell?' Ty asked.

Lamoureaux shook his head. 'No, not that it stopped me trying to detect one. But it's noted in your records. Is it still active?'

'No,' Ty replied. 'The Uchidan authorities disabled its higher-level functions before I was to be handed over to the Legislate. You should know that Uchidan implants aren't programmed like the machine-head variety. Spontaneous networking isn't what they're designed for.'

'I'm aware of that, Mr Whitecloud.'

'Why are you asking me questions about the Atn? Nobody cares about them except a few underfunded university departments.'

Lamoureaux responded by pulling a case out from under the seat beside him. He opened it and extracted a bundle of printouts and handed them to Ty.

'Can you identify these?' he asked.

Ty studied the documents for a good minute or two before looking up again. 'These are the spiral forms of the wall-glyphs found inside almost every Atn clade-world,' he said. One set of glyphs – a crescent placed next to a full circle, both of them at the centre of a tight spiral of lines and squiggles – was immediately familiar. 'If all you wanted to do was identify the Atn clade-family concerned, I could have told you as soon as you said the words "Mos Hadroch".' He tapped the crescent and circle. 'This is the identifier for Crescent-over-Moon. They're the only clade with which that term is associated.'

Willis leaned forward. 'What exactly is a "clade"?'

'The Atn have clans, or clades, distinguishable by small differences in their written languages. They appear to be quite distinct from each other, and rarely intermingling.'

Lamoureaux fixed him with an intense stare. 'What we want to know, Ty, is whether the Mos Hadroch is a tangible artefact. Can you tell us that?'

A tide of fatigue threatened to swamp Ty. Living in a state of perpetual terror, he had found, required a great deal of constant energy. 'Look, Mr . . .'

'Lamoureaux.'

'Mr Lamoureaux, I can't tell you how grateful I am for what you did back there, but what happens if I answer your questions? Are you going to take me back to be executed, once you've got what you need?'

'No,' Willis replied. 'You're under our jurisdiction now, but we're going to have to get you out of Ascension before Kosac or someone like him figures out a way to change that. But in return we expect your full and unhesitating cooperation. If we think you're holding out on us, or being less than honest for one second, then, yes, you go straight back where we found you.'

'Why,' asked Ty, 'is it so important that you know about the Mos Hadroch?'

'Tell us exactly what you think it might be, for a start.'

The transport took a series of fast turns, slinging the three men from side to side. Whoever was in the driver's seat – assuming the vehicle wasn't automated – was in a hurry to get to their destination.

'I said it referred to a machine for passing judgement, but the modifier "Mos" could mean "weapon" equally as much as it does "machine". The Atn are a notoriously uncommunicative species, and that fact unfortunately means that sometimes all we have to go on is educated guesswork.'

'There are academic papers that seem to suggest the Mos Hadroch is some kind of god,' said Lamoureaux.

Ty made a dismissive noise. 'Laroque's idea. The man's an idiot. There's nothing to suggest the Atn share our concept of deities. I'm not sure they're even really sentient, at least not in any way we ourselves can understand. Where I do agree with Laroque is that they're an artificial species of some kind, but if there was ever a purpose behind their creation, it's either been lost to time or they just don't want to tell us. All the evidence suggests they haven't evolved or changed in any significant way in millions of years. They're more akin to intelligent space-going termites than anything else.'

The transport came to a sudden stop, and Ty nearly slid out of his seat. The hatch clanged open and Lamoureaux climbed out first, while Willis gestured for Ty to follow the machine-head into the bustling noise beyond.

He saw they were at an airfield, where the cold hit him like a wall. Helicopters were parked in ranks, and guarded by rover-units whose electronic eyes constantly scanned the nearest rooftops. A world-pillar rose in the near distance, dwarfing the buildings clustered around its base. Near the helicopters were several heavy air-transports, from whose open bellies packages and crates were being lowered to waiting trucks. There were even a few dropships nearby, the concrete beneath them blackened and cracked.

The driver turned out to be a guard wearing a Legislate trooper's uniform. He exited the front cabin and took hold of Ty's right arm.

Willis led the way, and it was soon clear they were heading for one of the dropships.

Lamoureaux kept pace with Ty and his guard. 'Remember, as far as anyone's concerned, your name is still Nathan Driscoll.'

'I'll need a change of clothes,' said Ty. He could hardly speak for his teeth chattering.

Lamoureaux and Willis exchanged a glance. 'Should have thought of that,' Willis muttered, as if it were the machine-head's own fault.

'Okay,' said Lamoureaux, looking annoyed. 'There's probably spare engineering jumpsuits on board the dropship. If I can find one, you can use it.'

Ty nodded in a daze, half-convinced some unbelievably cruel trick was being played on him.

Either that, or he really was about to finally leave Ascension behind for ever.

FIVE

The dropship lifted from the concrete not long after they boarded, accelerating hard until it passed through an open portal in the coreship's ceiling, more than a dozen kilometres overhead. A screen mapped the dropship's progress for the benefit of the three men, now strapped into couches in a space not much larger than the rear of the transport that had brought them from the compound. Half an hour later the dropship rendezvoused with a cargo ship that had been commandeered by the Consortium for the relief effort.

Four men were waiting for them as they disembarked. They were all dressed in plain clothes, but their muscular physiques, air of watchful attentiveness, and the zippered jackets that failed to conceal the bulge of holstered weapons, all strongly implied a career in security. Ty himself had been given a jumpsuit three sizes too big for him.

'You're on your own for the next couple of days,' Lamoureaux told him. 'But there's some material I want you to look over in the meantime. You'll find it waiting for you in your berth.'

'Where *are* we going?'

'Ocean's Deep.'

Ty was then quickly escorted through the vessel's narrow, claustrophobic passageways. It had been some years since he'd last experienced zero gravity, and at first he sprawled about clumsily. By the time his body started to remember how to manoeuvre, he found himself deposited in his berth for the nearest journeys. A single private berth containing only a heavily padded acceleration seat and a voice-controlled comms unit.

The berth was cramped and utilitarian by most standards, but after the deprivations of life in Ascension it felt almost decadent in its comfort. Ty wedged himself inside the awkwardly tiny toilet and pulled off his jumpsuit, quickly sponging the grime and urine from his skin.

The water was warm and, as he washed himself, he felt some of the tension and horror of the past few years – the slow dying by cold and starvation – begin to drop away like a second skin he could finally slough off.

He then pulled the oversized jumpsuit back on, and tested the door into the berth. He was far from surprised to find it had been locked from the outside.

After a few minutes' experimentation with the comms unit, he discovered that it was linked into both local as well as interstellar public tach-net relays. Before very long, he'd managed to navigate his way to a live feed that showed the coreship's surface.

He gazed down on a forest of shattered and twisted drive-spines. Other ships were visible closer at hand, scattered through the surrounding void, and most were clearly of human construction, but mixed in with them were a few quite unlike anything Ty had seen before.

These latter were equipped with drive-spines that curved out and then forward from a bulbous central hull. Ty realized, after a moment, that these must be the alien Magi ships, news of which had arrived with the first rescue and relief missions.

A heavy cargo lifter drifted in front of the nearest Magi vessel, giving Ty the perspective he needed to see how truly immense the alien craft were. A thrill of awe burned its way up his spine and into his brain. There was a sinuous, organic quality to them that made them look less like something manufactured and more like something that might have evolved in some limitless ocean.

After a while, he managed to drag his eyes away from this spectacle long enough to pull up whatever details he could find concerning the destruction of Night's End, and everything that had happened since. He absorbed the details with the ferocity of a man starved for knowledge, learning of the Fleet Authority based at Ocean's Deep, along with what little was known of the Magi starships – and the rumour and conjecture surrounding those directly or peripherally involved with their discovery. Lamoureaux and Willis's names turned up frequently, though not nearly so often as those of a Dakota Merrick and a Senator Lucas Corso.

He checked the external view to see if anything had changed, and realized the nearest of the Magi ships was drawing closer. By the time it was almost abreast of the cargo ship, the stars were obscured by an energy field.

And then, in something less than the blink of an eye, the coreship was gone, along with its attendant fleet of human and Magi vessels. Instead there was only the broad sweep of the Milky Way, and the diamond sprinkle of stars both near and far away.

A data file appeared on the display, with a confirmation request. Ty activated it and found himself looking at an up-to-date library of research into the Atn, including not only all of his own published work, but also a set of documents marked 'classified'.

He speed-read through the summaries of several of the classified files, with a fascination that slowly gave way to anger mingled with envy. Clearly some of his fellow exo-anthropologists had been engaged in classified research for the Legislate: work he'd had no inkling of during his long years of exile.

He read the papers in more detail, soon becoming lost in their minutiae, his struggle for survival on the streets of Ascension now slowly fading into a memory.

Three days later, the same four security personnel escorted Ty into an orbital station within the Ocean's Deep system. A central hub many kilometres long was surrounded by a series of pressurized rings that spun constantly to provide gravity, all of them connected to the hub by spokes that also served as part of the station's transport system.

He stared around, goggle-eyed, as he was taken down one of the spokes and into the interior of a ring, which proved to be dominated by ancient, crumbling towers of Bandati design. The air smelled sour and damp, and slightly foul.

Enormous windows set into the ring's inner rim faced in towards the hub, the gas-giant around which the station orbited intermittently visible as the ring turned on its axis. Ty watched for a few moments as the planet slowly slid past.

A shadow passed overhead, and he caught sight of a Bandati soaring from one tower-platform to another, with wings spread wide.

He found Lamoureaux and Willis waiting for him in a prefab admin building located in the shadow of one tower.

'First things first,' said Lamoureaux, once Ty's escorts had departed. 'You read the files I sent you?'

'Yes, yes I did.' Ty gave a little half-laugh. 'I had no idea Laroque was doing any kind of secret research, or that the Atn were involved in the smuggling of restricted technology. Why would they do that?'

'They needed things from us. Access to manufacturing facilities, certain processing technologies they could make use of. Sometimes it's easier for them to barter for what they need than build it from scratch way out there between the stars.'

'And in return?' asked Ty.

'In return,' Lamoureaux replied, 'they'd either give us information about whatever was out there in the greater galaxy that the Shoal didn't want us to know about, or they'd supply us with banned technologies.'

'All right, but Crescent-over-Moon never dealt directly with humanity. We only know they even existed because I found one of their clade-worlds, and that turned out to have been abandoned for tens of millennia. The reference to Mos Hadroch is *incredibly* obscure. I still don't understand why you care about it so much.'

Willis spoke up. 'First things first, Mr Driscoll. Was there anything at all in the data we gave you that can help us figure out where the Mos Hadroch is, or what it can do?'

'Yes, there was. Particularly the set of stellar coordinates.'

'Coordinates?' Lamoureaux asked, his eyes taking on a faraway look as he accessed remote information being relayed to him.

'Laroque found them on one of the secret expeditions, and dismissed them. He believed Crescent-over-Moon were a dead end. If he'd even bothered just once to try and correlate his findings with my own, he might have been on to something. But he was too short-sighted.'

He paused for breath, aware of the way the two men

were staring at him. He'd have to learn to control his outbursts.

'You're saying you might actually know where it is?' asked Lamoureaux.

'May I?' Ty asked, nodding towards a comms unit in one corner of the room. 'If you have a copy here of the same files you sent me, that is.'

Lamoureaux nodded to Willis, who shrugged and palmed the unit awake. Ty stepped past the two men and brought up a series of images of Atn glyphs arranged in tight spirals. Large pieces of these spirals were missing.

'You know the strangest thing about the Crescent-over-Moon?' Ty asked. 'You can sometimes tell you're on one of their clade-worlds just from the sheer destruction that's been visited on them. At first I thought they might be targets of some kind of pogrom from other clades, since that might also explain their relative isolation.'

Lamoureaux got that faraway look again for a moment. 'There's no reference to that in any of your work,' he pointed out a moment later.

'That's because it's unsupported speculation, not fact. It's possible some of their asteroids had merely suffered impacts with other stellar bodies long after they'd been abandoned.'

'But you don't believe that?'

Ty thought for a moment. 'Let's say that the over-whelming consistency with which their clade-worlds appeared to have been targeted suggested other explanations.' Ty manipulated the images until some of the damaged text-spirals were aligned next to each other. 'Some of these partial glyphs were taken from Crescent asteroids found after I went on the run. Bring them together with fragments taken from other Crescent asteroids, and there's a clear match.' Ty caused the fragmentary spirals to slide on top of each other until they clearly matched.

'I'm still not sure what we're looking at,' said Willis.

'These glyphs, when put together, refer *specifically* to the Mos Hadroch. They're essentially a set of galactic coordinates referring to a region of stars a little over a thousand light-years away,' Ty explained, his finger pointing to different parts of each spiral.

'What about stellar drift?' asked Lamoureaux.

'The Atn coordinate system was designed to take that into account, and as a result it's extremely reliable. The coordinates don't so much refer to a single point in space as a projected path for a star or group of stars. I've identified a white dwarf system in the catalogues that matches the numbers very closely.'

'That still leaves the question of what the Mos Hadroch *is*,' Willis remarked.

'We need to get this back to Dakota fast,' Lamoureaux muttered to Willis. 'To Senator Corso as well.'

Ty looked between the two men, his throat suddenly tight. 'You're going out there, right?'

'Where?' asked Lamoureaux.

'You've got material proof the Mos Hadroch is

something tangible, with a defined location a thousand light-years from here. Until very recently a discovery like that was always going to be of purely academic interest, since the Shoal were never going to let us go that deep into the galaxy. But that's all changed now, hasn't it?'

'That's far from decided,' Willis replied.

'You lifted me out of Ascension, practically kidnapped me out of the hands of the security services. The Legislate is probably at your throats for that, am I right?'

Willis's face was carefully blank, but the look on Lamoureaux's face made Ty sure he was on the right track. 'Get someone else to check the data if you like,' Ty added, 'but there's no one better qualified. If you're going out there, you're going to need to take me with you.'

SIX

When the attack came, it was swift, brutal and very nearly deadly.

With time, Dakota came to realize she had failed to pay proper attention to subtle changes taking place within the captured swarm-component. That it was a Trojan Horse became evident only with hindsight, its outwardly simple structure belying a technology far more sophisticated than she had even suspected.

The component had responded to Dakota's careful probing of its memory banks by sending its own, undetectable feelers deep into the data cores of her Magi starship, entwining itself in the ship's neural networks like a hand taking a firm grip on a living heart. At the same moment the swarm turned on her, the captured component launched its own, primarily informational attack from within.

Dakota spun through the starship's limitless virtual depths, appalled by the wholesale vandalism the component had unleashed on her ship's femtotech arrays, until she found Josef's ghost waiting for her on the balcony of a library complex long since turned to dust and ruin.

'Look,' he said, gesturing at the sky.

Dakota gripped the balustrade and followed the direction of his hand, to see a black cloud of viral agents blotting out the sky.

She felt her insides grow cold and liquid. 'There wasn't any indication that the component was remotely capable of launching an attack like this! We analysed it inside and out. It just doesn't make sense!'

She shifted into another virtual environment, and sensed Josef keeping pace with her. The next time she looked at him, she was appalled to see his features grow suddenly blurred before snapping back into focus.

'We know now that the swarm can reassign each of its components to a new purpose at any time,' he reminded her. 'The component we captured was adapting itself to a new purpose from the moment we brought it inside the ship. We should never have let it remain in communication with the rest of the swarm.'

'But why did it wait so long?' she demanded. 'Why not just attack us when we first got here?'

'The only logical answer is that the swarm deliberately fed us the data about the Mos Hadroch. Notice, it didn't attack until Corso sent back confirmation that he'd found something.'

'The swarm used us to help it find the Mos Hadroch,' Dakota realized. 'It wants it just as much as we do.'

'Exactly. And now it'll tear this ship apart until it finds those coordinates.'

Josef's face began to melt and Dakota spun away in

horror. She found herself in an environment she had never visited before, and watched with sick horror as viral agents tore it to shreds, leaving her tumbling into a chaotic void where once there had been land and sky.

She shifted to another, more stable environment, where Josef's partly reconstituted form joined her after a little while.

'I don't know how much longer I can hold myself together,' he warned her, little more now than a voice attached to a blur of static. The blur then shifted and almost resolved into other faces from her past: Corso, Severn, even her mother, all drawn from her dreams and memories. 'The data cores are starting to purge themselves, shutting themselves down as a last-ditch measure. The swarm's almost penetrated the ship's command levels. You have to . . .'

Dakota watched as Josef dissolved into a cloud of random noise – dead a second time. She burrowed her way deeper into the starship's networks, hiding in realms as yet unaffected by the ravages of the viral agents.

A silent battle raged for the next several days. Huge swathes of the ship's neural structure were destroyed, but eventually the balance tipped, and another forty-eight hours saw the last few surviving viral agents isolated and finally destroyed.

As soon as Dakota had regained full control over her

ship, she sent the swarm-component spinning back out into space.

It was a pyrrhic victory at best. The swarm had learned far more from her than the reverse. In the meantime her ship drifted, silent and crippled, its self-repair mechanisms struggling to mend the worst of the damage.

Dakota watched helplessly as the swarm all around now entered a period of renewed activity. Thousands of its components were being refashioned into weapons, and it wasn't long before the first of these came vectoring in towards her with deadly intent.

A dozen hunter-killer components made contact with the hull of her ship and began burning and drilling their way into its interior. She reached out with her mind and shut them down before they could penetrate too deeply, but there were legions more to take their place. Another dozen separated from the main body of the swarm and closed in for the kill.

Her only recourse was to jump as far away from the vicinity of the swarm as possible, but the battle for control of the ship had drained the energy reserves it needed to make a jump of even a few light-years. Then she recalled that the swarm had been observed to maintain a certain minimum distance from the near vicinity of the red giant.

She might not have enough power for a long-range jump, but a very short-range jump was another matter.

Before the next wave of hunter-killers could reach it, the Magi starship summoned up just enough power to jump a few AUs closer to the dying star. The star field beyond the hull remained unchanged, but the red giant grew huge and corpulent.

A storm of transmissions flickered back and forth through the vacuum around the ship. Dakota knew she hadn't escaped the swarm, but she *had* managed to buy herself a few hours of breathing space.

Her ship once again began the process of clawing energy out of the vacuum in preparation for its next jump. In the meantime yet more hunter-killer components vectored inwards, and Dakota tracked their progress with sick despair.

The ship managed to repel them, but not before serious damage had been inflicted on its drive-spines. It managed to carry out a second jump regardless, less than an hour after the previous one.

This time the red giant blotted out half the universe, and the swarm had become distinctly less numerous.

The ship's sensors picked up a cluster of several hundred swarm-components undergoing heavy modification, at a distance of a few million kilometres. Closer observation showed that drive-spines were being fixed to the hulls of these components.

Another attack. Dakota jumped her ship so close to the red giant that it was effectively *inside* the star, orbiting at the very outermost limits of its atmosphere: an attenuated red mist heated to a few thousand degrees Kelvin. There were limits to how long the ship could survive in such an intense environment, but Dakota was running out of options.

More importantly, it was too hot for the swarm, and for the moment the attacks ceased.

Hours and then days passed in the external universe, and Dakota watched as the swarm's newly constructed superluminal fleet jumped en masse out of the vicinity of the red giant.

She had little doubt they were making straight for the coordinates pinpointing the location of the Mos Hadroch. She had got what she wanted from the swarm, but it was a victory laced with a particularly bitter aftertaste.

Dakota drifted on through the remnants of dead worlds, her mind filled with the confused whispers of terminally damaged Magi minds, their voices like ghosts in the ether, half-heard gabbles lost in hissing static.

There was a slim chance she could still make a long-range jump to safety before the star blew but, given that her starship had been almost terminally crippled by the swarm's concentrated attacks, there were no guarantees it would survive the attempt. Instead a plan slowly formulated in her mind: to use the remaining energy reserves to transmit a warning back to Ocean's Deep.

It was one of the hardest choices Dakota had ever had to make, but she came to a decision quickly. She fired off a single high-energy burst of coherent data towards Ocean's Deep, across the immensity of the galaxy, an act that left her starship nearly powerless and adrift.

And then something strange began to happen, over the following hours and days. In the face of its inevitable destruction, Dakota became aware the starship had spontaneously abandoned all efforts to repair itself. For reasons she could not yet understand, it instead began working at reintegrating whatever scattered fragments of her mind hadn't been compromised or destroyed by the swarm's vandalism.

The star itself entered a period of increased activity during this time, sending great fiery gouts of plasma sailing out across the void. Meanwhile her ship picked up major disruptions in the heat-flow at the star's core. There were, perhaps, only a few hours before the star went into terminal collapse and shrank, before ejecting its outer layers. There was enough energy to make a short-range jump, but she already knew she could never outrun the impending nova.

In the last few moments before the end came, Dakota found herself in a room full of objects that might have been mirrors – mirrors capable of capturing the light from several more spatial dimensions than her mind was capable of perceiving.

She saw reflections of herself, of other lives she might have lived if she had only made the choices that led to them. They were hazy reflections at best, might-have-beens and never-weres, glimpses into worlds that never quite became solid enough to be real.

Dakota found her attention drawn to one particular such vision, clearer than all the rest. She saw herself as she had been before the swarm attacked, when most of her memories had still been intact.

She never had a chance to find out why the ship had shown her this. The red giant's core chose that moment to collapse, releasing all its energy in a titanic blast that would, with time, become visible throughout the entire galaxy.

In her last moments of awareness, before the wave-front tore the ship apart, Dakota saw the billions of swarm-components nearest the expanding wave-front suddenly focus and direct the explosive energy of the nova in a way she couldn't even begin to understand.

A few seconds later, there was nothing left of Dakota or the starship itself but a whirl of superheated plasma, carried onwards and outwards.

SEVEN

He had sheltered within a dozen systems scattered across the great starry whirlpool of the galaxy, some of them inhabited, most long abandoned but still filled with billion-year-old ruins; and yet no matter how far Trader in Faecal Matter of Animals fled, the creature that called itself Hugh Moss always found a way to track him down.

He had almost been caught in the ruins of a vast dome rising from a plain of ashes, all that was left of a vast repository of knowledge left behind by a civilization that would have dwarfed the Shoal Hegemony, had it not immolated itself a hundred million years before. Trader had sought shelter in the cold iron ruins of a star caught for eternity in a temporal loop, now home to insane AIs imprisoned for crimes long forgotten; and yet Moss tracked him down even there.

He had been sheltered for a while by the Ascended War-Minds that ruled a dozen systems hard by the great black hole at the galaxy's heart. Moss had fallen upon him once again, and Trader again fled for his life with mocking laughter ringing in his ears.

Centuries before, Hugh Moss had begun life as a

Shoal-member called Swimmer-in-Turbulent-Currents. He had been made an example of by Trader as punishment for his attempt to broker peace with the Emissaries by having his body radically altered, cell by cell, until he was transformed into something neither human nor Shoal.

The process had driven Swimmer insane, and towards the end of the battle for control of Ocean's Deep, Dakota had given Hugh the means to find Trader, regardless of how far he fled across the face of the galaxy, so that he could exact a terrible revenge upon his tormentor.

But now, at last, Trader would be free of the monster.

Trader had parked his yacht in orbit around the moon of a gas giant, in an unoccupied system no more than a few hundred light-years from the Hegemony's borders. Within a few hours, a Shoal coreship had appeared within range of his yacht's scanning instruments, a planet-sized craft with heavy weaponry dotting its armoured crust. The coreship had quickly manoeuvred itself into one of the moon's Lagrange points, precisely balanced between the gravitational attraction of the moon and the gas giant it orbited.

When the arranged hour of the meeting arrived, Trader departed his yacht and dropped towards the moon's dense atmosphere, protected from the hard vacuum of space by a shaped-field bubble that surrounded him and contained the liquid environment he required for breathing. A cloud of machines the size of dust-motes followed him down, spread out around him for kilometres.

Trader directed his descent with gentle pulses of energy applied to different points around the spherical field's surface. Before long he was dropping down through a near-impenetrable layer of cloud until, at last, the darkened oceans beneath were revealed to him, and the great towers that rose from their liquid depths.

Trader guided his field-bubble below the surface of the waters. He had been one of the Shoal Hegemony's most adept agents for more than a hundred millennia, tasked with suppressing any knowledge of the existence of the Magi ships, a duty he had pursued with aggressive diligence. That he had been granted this private audience with Commander-of-Shoals only proved how desperately the Hegemony needed his unique skills once more.

Trader made his way towards a cathedral-like building, its apex long ago drowned beneath the waters, and made his way inside. He soon found himself within a high-vaulted space and set about deploying the microscopic defensive units he had brought along in preparation for this meeting.

Through the lenses of more devices seeded through the ocean surrounding the tower, Trader watched the descent of Commander-of-Shoals's own private vessel. Its belly cast a deep shadow across the ocean, before plunging deep beneath its surface. It came to a halt on a sub-aquatic plain a few kilometres distant before disgorging its sole occupant.

After that, it was just a matter of waiting.

'Trader in Faecal Matter of Animals,' said the Commander once he arrived within the cathedral chamber, 'I can't say it's a pleasure. Why did you pick this . . . place for our meeting?'

'It used to be a Meridian outpost, Commander,' he explained. 'They disappeared off the galactic stage a long time ago, a fact that tends to curb occasional bouts of hubris on my own part.'

'I see,' the other Shoal-member replied, clearly unimpressed. 'I presume you heard about General Desire?'

Desire-for-Violent-Rendering had been Trader's superior commanding officer. 'Executed for crimes against the Hegemony,' Trader replied, noting how the Commander's manipulators were tipped with razorsharp steel. 'Or so I heard.'

'Oh, it's quite true. And the same would happen to me if anyone got even an inkling I was here with you. Now why don't you say whatever it is you have to say, so I can get out of this hell-hole?'

All around the chamber, a thousand tiny but lethal devices armed themselves. 'I take that to mean you've considered my terms?'

Commander-of-Shoals twisted his manipulators in anger. 'Have you *no* conception of what's happened in the last few days? The home world is destroyed, and the Hegemony is on the verge of being torn apart. Do you really think I have any interest in playing these ridiculous games of yours?'

Trader fanned the waters around him with his fins. 'I don't understand.'

'It was hit by asteroids converted for short-range superluminal jumps and accelerated to relativistic speeds. Totally wiped out, Trader.'

'I . . . I never heard of this,' Trader stammered. It had been some time since he'd last had an opportunity to check on the progress of the war. 'The Emissaries?'

'On the contrary, recidivists who blamed the Deep Dreamers for the war, and didn't have too much of a moral problem with wiping out a few hundred million of our fellow Shoal-members while they were about it. You can imagine the chaos.'

Trader suddenly remembered General Desire-for-Violent-Rendering telling him the Dreamers had predicted their own demise. 'I can, yes. I am . . . sorry to hear of this.'

'Sorry!' Commander-of-Shoals barked. 'A plague of fire spreading across the face of the galaxy because you gambled on the Emissaries having no nova-class weaponry, and you're *sorry*. I wonder how sorry you'll feel once the Hegemony's interrogators get hold of you?'

'I understand that Desire was a sacrifice to public opinion, but I must remind you that *you* were the one who gave Desire his orders, as he gave me mine. I could easily have implicated you.' Not to mention dozens of key members of the Hegemony's highest ruling councils.

The Commander's manipulators rippled in grudging

agreement. 'Yes, yes, Trader. I know this. And I'm grateful that you didn't. But concerning these terms of yours . . . the Mos Hadroch is an old fish's tale, a daydream, nothing more.'

'It was enough to bring the Magi across the void to our galaxy. I headed an expedition to the Maker swarm which found evidence to suggest it was much more than a story.'

Commander-of-Shoals's steel-tipped manipulators clicked as their razor edges clashed with each other. 'An expedition, I recall, that ended in ignominy and failure. There's a limit to how much you can demand of me in return for your silence, Trader. I came here only because your record of past service earns you a final audience. The Emissaries are making tremendous gains, while we are pushed back and back. But if all you have for me are pipe dreams of yore, then I suggest you leave now in peace for ever and make yourself a new life somewhere very, very far away.'

'This may interest you, then,' Trader replied, making a gesture.

A tiny sparkling glyph representing a data package appeared, hovering in the water between them. Commander-of-Shoals regarded it warily, then accepted the package with visible ill grace.

Trader waited while his superior scanned the package's contents. 'This is the first I've heard of this!' Commander-of-Shoals exclaimed after some moments. 'There was a *second* expedition?'

'One I myself led a few centuries after my encounter with the Maker. Except this time I travelled to the Greater Magellanic Cloud itself.'

'Why was I never made aware of this?'

Trader twisted his manipulators in the Shoal equivalent of a laugh. 'With all respect, Commander, you are a soldier, good for taking and giving orders. There was no need for you to know. We spent the better part of fourteen centuries roaming what had once been the most densely populated regions of the Cloud.'

'Do not keep me waiting, Trader. What did you find?'

'I found the proof that the Mos Hadroch exists, or did once exist, but found no trace or clue to its whereabouts – that is, until recently. The Maker is still searching for it.'

He declined to mention that this new knowledge originated in intercepted transmissions originating from Ocean's Deep.

'Then it *is* in our galaxy? And it's real?' Commander-of-Shoals swam closer. 'What exactly *can* it do?'

'You will find the details in the data package I just gave you.'

Commander of Shoals tapped two steel-tipped manipulators together and a small ball of light appeared between them. Shoal glyphs flickered rapidly before finally freezing in place. The Commander read what was there, before dismissing the projection after several moments.

'Remarkable,' said Commander-of-Shoals, the twist

of his manipulators indicating he was impressed. 'A solution of quite stunning elegance.'

'Based on my own findings, the Mos Hadroch takes advantage of certain flaws in the design of the caches seeded by the Maker swarm. If anything, the existence of such flaws tells us that whatever beings created the swarm were rather less godlike than the Magi believed them to be.'

'This is a tremendous achievement, Trader. Yet I can't help feeling that recent events have failed to bring you the humility you claim to value.'

'I'm not interested in your petty character judgements,' Trader snapped. 'Do you accept my terms? I will find the Mos Hadroch, rid us of the Emissaries, and bring this war to an end.'

'Have you considered that it might be easier for me to simply hand you over to my interrogators and have them extract the information from you?'

'I have considered it, Commander, and you do indeed have that option, if you wish to see the finer details of your own illegal subterfuge become immediate public knowledge throughout the length and breadth of the Hegemony. If I were not to have taken such precautions, I would not deserve the reputation I have.'

'Then on behalf of the Hegemony, I see that I have no choice but to accept your terms.'

'And . . . ?'

Commander-of-Shoals's manipulators signalled defeat. 'And if you succeed, we will reinstate you to your former position within the Hegemony, with full resumption of special rights and privileges. But let me be clear that there are many within the upper ranks of the Hegemony who would be more than happy to see you die in this attempt.'

'Then I shall take added pleasure in my triumphant return. Now, there were certain other matters contained within my terms . . .'

'Ah, yes, a fleet of your own, and the capture of the monster you created out of Swimmer in Turbulent Currents. Neither, I fear, will be possible.'

'These are fundamental requirements,' Trader responded angrily. 'That . . . *creature* has chased me across the entire face of this galaxy. Wherever I flee, he manages to find me. And without a fleet of my own, my chances of success are severely reduced. Surely you can—?'

'No, Trader, I cannot,' Commander-of-Shoals replied coolly. 'I will, however, supply you with his current location. That may give you some small advantage, whether you choose to confront or escape him. He calls himself by a human name these days, doesn't he? Hugh Moss?'

Beyond the vaulting walls of the tower chamber, thousands of lenses showed to Trader the waters around the Commander's vessel beginning to boil. 'We have no fleets to spare, certainly not on the scale you've requested. If I were to provide them to you, it would lead to certain questions being asked – questions I would not care to answer. And if such a scandal were to be exposed at a time such as this, it would shatter the Hegemony so thoroughly that no weapon, no matter how legendary or powerful, could possibly save us.'

'If you refuse to help me, you condemn us all to death!'

The Commander paused in the act of turning to leave. 'I am offering you the slim chance of returning a victorious hero, rather than as a fugitive. Which is more than some might think you deserve. Find your own fleet, if you can, Trader. Then return triumphant, or do not return at all.'

EIGHT

A holographic simulation of the Milky Way filled the shallow dome of the debriefing room as Corso entered, angled so that the wispy trail of a spiral arm hovered just a few metres above the floor. The air inside the room felt pleasantly chilly, the atmosphere in the rest of the Bandati orbital station being too warm and humid for his comfort. He had only just arrived back at Ocean's Deep aboard a transport called the *Kilminster*, along with more than a hundred newly recruited technical specialists who would continue on to the research base at Tierra.

Lamoureaux stepped towards him from out of the gloom. 'Senator.'

Corso nodded and dropped into one of twenty chairs arranged around the circumference of the room and facing towards its centre. 'I literally just came down the spoke. I got your report about Whitecloud. Where is he now?'

'Still up at the hub, on board a ship. Ray and Leo both felt it was safer keeping him there.'

Corso nodded tiredly and glanced towards the

glistening star-simulation. 'Fair enough. How about we get started?'

Lamoureaux nodded and stepped back towards the centre of the room. 'This is where we are,' he said, turning slightly to regard the simulation.

A minuscule ball of light representing the Consortium blinked into life deep inside the Orion spiral arm. It was easy to miss amongst the surrounding starscape.

'I can never get over how tiny it looks,' Corso muttered.

'It *is* tiny,' Lamoureaux agreed, 'on the galactic scale of things. Now, remember some of what I'll be showing you consists of best guesses and conjecture.'

'That's fine.'

Half a dozen yellow pinpricks, their brightness oscillating rapidly to make them stand out from the surrounding starscape, appeared at various points scattered through the Orion Arm and beyond. Lines representing trajectories connected each pinprick to the ball of light representing the Consortium.

'The yellow dots represent the furthest points reached by our experimental probes,' Lamoureaux explained.

'I thought we sent out more than this,' said Corso with a frown.

'We did. We lost contact with some, particularly the ones we sent in the direction of the Emissaries. They might have been captured or destroyed, but they managed to return useful data before they disappeared.'

Corso grunted. 'What about the Magi ships we sent out to reconnoitre?'

'We suffered some losses, but there are others out there trying to trace the progress of the war. The probes are a lot more disposable, and even with just this many we've managed to identify the location of quite a few of the Shoal's tach-net transceiver relays. The relays boost transmissions around the Shoal's territory, and their signal strength is uniform. As a result we were able to work out the rough shape and size of the territory covered by the relays.'

As Corso watched, a roughly ovoid section of the Milky Way, encompassing a large chunk of the Orion Arm and reaching in towards the core, changed in colour to a uniform magenta.

'And that's the Hegemony?' he asked, not quite able to keep his voice under control. *An empire made of light*, he thought to himself.

'So we think.' Lamoureaux glanced over at Corso and smiled on seeing his expression. 'There's some guesswork involved, like I said, but we're still looking at a region several thousand light-years across at its widest point.'

'It's incredible, but it's still not quite the galaxy-spanning empire they sold themselves as.'

Lamoureaux nodded. 'Not quite, no. But huge enough.'

'And the Emissaries?'

Lamoureaux nodded. 'Coming up next.'

Another region of space, immediately adjacent to that representing the Hegemony, now changed colour. It reached towards the rim of the galaxy, and encompassed an area roughly half that of the Hegemony itself.

'You can see the galaxy's outer rim puts a clear boundary on their expansion,' said Lamoureaux. 'So, unless they want to stick to the halo stars, they have to pass through Shoal territory in order to access the rest of the Milky Way.'

A translucent blue panel appeared in the simulation, placed between the two empires and brushing against the outer rim of the Orion Arm. Corso recognized it as the region of the Long War.

'We think their conflict with the Shoal has forced the Emissaries to expand sideways, up and down the outer arms,' Lamoureaux continued. 'But with the escalation to using nova-class weapons, they're clearly pushing the Shoal's fleets back towards us and deeper into the Orion Arm.'

'And how long before the fighting actually reaches us?'

'Based on the latest analyses, not long. We may have less than six months before they arrive here in force. Most of the strategic analysts I've spoken to think the Shoal are preparing for a major retreat in order to bolster older, better-defended systems closer to the heart of their territory. That way they sacrifice us as well as a lot of their other client species, but stand a much better chance of either surviving the war with their culture intact, or more likely – judging by how it's playing out so far – reaching some kind of détente.'

Corso shook his head and quietly swore under his breath. A tightness in his scalp heralded an oncoming migraine. 'So exactly where was Dakota last time we heard from her?' Her garbled warning had been forwarded to him on board the *Kilminster* less than twenty-four hours before.

'Over here,' came the answer. Another brightly coloured pinprick appeared far around the curve of the galaxy, between three and three and a half kiloparsecs distant – a little more than seventeen thousand light-years from Ocean's Deep. The simulation of the galaxy rotated rapidly until the icon representing her last-known location was directly overhead, while the Consortium now hovered just underneath the ceiling.

'As you can see,' said Lamoureaux, 'she's gone a long, long way.'

'Show me the coordinates Whitecloud dug up. Draw a line from here to there.'

Lamoureaux nodded, and a single pale line reached out from the Consortium towards a sparse stellar region not much more than a thousand light-years away.

Corso let out a sigh and stood, before walking around under the simulation and peering up. 'All right,' he said, reaching up with both hands and wiping them across his face as if he could scrub the fatigue away. 'What do we have that's ready to travel to Whitecloud's coordinates and see what's actually there?'

'There are five Magi starships here in Ocean's Deep, but the only currently available navigators were all supplied by the Legislate. That means I can't guarantee any of them aren't supplying information back to the Legislate security services.'

'That's all?' Corso snapped, sounding scandalized. 'What the hell about our own people?'

'They're all either out on relief missions or they've been hit by neural burnout. The way things are going, we're going to need more of our own ships to be equipped with superluminal drives than we thought. But in terms of our present situation . . .' Lamoureaux hesitated.

'What?'

'Even if a Magi ship was available, it's going to have to tow a ship with enough room for an expeditionary crew. There aren't any big enough, apart from the *Mjollnir*, and she already has her own superluminal drive. But, as you know, she's being prepped for a relief expedition to Ascension.'

'Really?' Corso thought hard for a moment. 'Put her up there, Ted.'

Lamoureaux complied, the galaxy fading to be replaced by an image of the *Mjollnir*, a colony-class frigate belonging to the Freehold. She was similar in appearance and construction to her sister-ships *Agartha* and *Hyperion*, both long since destroyed within the Nova Arctis system. She was also one of the few vessels in existence with the capacity to carry a significant proportion of Ascension's trapped population to safety, a task for which she was currently being readied at Ocean's Deep. Her maiden faster-than-light voyage had brought her here from Redstone to be refitted just for that purpose.

'The *Mjollnir* could do it, then?' said Corso, staring up at the floating image. 'How long before she's ready?'

'She's ready now,' Lamoureaux replied. 'Senator . . . at the very least, you'd need to get the authority of the Consortium's Central Trade Council as well as the Freehold Senate. And the fact is, they're not going to give it to us. If you think things are looking shaky for us now, I don't even want to think about what's going to happen if we commandeered the *Mjollnir*.'

'Screw the CTC,' Corso replied. 'And the Senate. I don't need to ask anyone's permission to commandeer her.'

Lamoureaux looked doubtful. 'How does that come about?'

'There are specific clauses relating to overriding emergencies. Just look them up. I think that beating Dakota's swarm to the Mos Hadroch, assuming that's really where it's headed, fits anyone's definition of an emergency.'

'It's going to break the Fleet Authority's back, if you do this,' Lamoureaux warned.

'Let me worry about that. How soon could we reach those coordinates with the *Mjollnir*?'

Lamoureaux made a resigned sound. 'Two weeks

there, more or less. And the same again to get back home.'

Corso stared back at him, thunderstruck. 'That fast? It's taken Dakota, what, two years to get seventeen thousand light-years?'

Lamoureaux shrugged. 'She didn't go in a straight line, Senator, because she had to hunt far and wide to find the Maker's trail. We've been sourcing data from the Magi ships that's helped us greatly increase the efficiency and reach of the drives coming out of the Tierra cache.'

'Then there's no other recourse. Who's in charge of the *Mjollnir*?'

'Eduard Martinez.'

Corso nodded, recognizing the name. 'I've met him,' he replied. 'Good, that might make things easier.' Martinez was very much a progressive in Freehold politics, which meant Corso might not have to replace him in command.

'But the Ascension relief operation?' Lamoureaux reminded him. 'The *Mjollnir*'s scheduled to be going there in the next couple of days. How are you going to square that with the Legislate?'

'It's a short-term loss for a long-term gain,' Corso replied.

Lamoureaux gave him a strange look, and Corso realized just how cold-hearted he'd sounded. 'If we save some people at Ascension instead of heading straight out to those coordinates, we might lose something that could save *us all* from the Emissaries,' he explained. 'If the Legislate doesn't want to think ahead, then I'm going to have to do it for them. Get hold of Martinez for me, and set up a secure, one-on-one tach-net link to Akiyama at the Office of Representatives while you're at it, and route it to my quarters. Flag it urgent and top-priority.'

'Senator, with the very greatest of respect, do you really think we can pull this off?'

Corso glanced back at Lamoureaux, as he headed for the door. 'You'd better hope we can, Ted. Because if we can't, we're screwed.'

NINE

The sun was low on the horizon. Cool wind teased her dark hair, while saltwater foamed and splashed over her bare toes where she sat at the water's edge, her baggy cotton trousers rolled up above her ankles. She knew, without looking, that further up the beach behind her stood a single-storey cabin on stilts, with tatami mats scattered welcomingly on its floor and a futon rolled up in one corner.

None of it was real, of course, but she didn't know who she was, so it hardly mattered. She knew something had been threatening her because, when she tried to remember where she'd been before the beach, all that came to her was a sense of unease and foreboding.

In the meantime, she knew she could happily wait here on the beach for ever.

Sometimes she glanced down at her arms and legs and didn't recognize them. The knowledge that something was missing – that some essential part of her had been lost for ever – slowly formed in the back of her mind, but somehow she didn't seem to feel anything about it: no anger, remorse or bitterness. Only the awareness that something that should have been there, now wasn't.

After a long while she remembered a star, angry and red, reaching out to swallow her. She remembered there had been machines like dark metal locusts filling the universe like a plague.

A little while later, she remembered dying.

What might have been hours or days or years later, her name came back to her: *Dakota*. She formed the sound with her lips, working her jaws around it in ways that felt unfamiliar, as if trying the vowels out for size.

She turned, seeing that a bamboo table laden with fresh fruit stood near the cabin, and in that instant it was as if a switch was thrown inside her. Sudden hunger overwhelmed her, and she stood and walked over. Once she'd eaten her fill, she crawled inside the cabin, unrolled the futon and went to sleep.

She dreamed she was a little girl again. The cabin's open doorway and the strip of beach it framed became a tall window looking out on cobbled streets lined with buildings made of brick and steel. She lay with her head in her mother's lap, listening to the gentle rhythms of her parent's voice, while flakes of snow drifted down from out of a sky so pale it was almost white.

*

The next time Dakota opened her eyes, she was somewhere else.

She knelt naked on a rocky shore entirely unlike the one she had found herself on before. Faces and places that should have been familiar to her spun through her mind like pieces of a shredded book flung into the heart of a whirlwind. She was incomplete, an unfinished puzzle with missing pieces.

The air had a strange, coppery taste to it, and when she turned to look behind her, instead of a beach hut and table she saw only forbidding-looking cliffs topped with tangled blue-green flora. The roofs of buildings like gold-plated tombstones rose above the jungle, while the distant peaks of mountains were visible further inland.

She looked out to sea, and saw massive towers like minarets rising out of the ocean, several kilometres out from the shore. Something about them made her sure they were very, very old.

A Magi ship rested on the shore, looking as if it had been beached there. It dwarfed the nearby cliffs and towered far above her, its bulbous body angled upwards as it rested on its drive spines. Waves lapped against the curve of its partially submerged hull.

That was when Dakota realized the Magi ships were never going to let her die.

She stood and stared up and down the beach, cold prickling her bare skin, and tried to remember what her mother's face had looked like. Nothing came to her except the memory of gazing out on to a snow-laden street. It seemed much of her life on Bellhaven had been reduced to that one sliver of memory; the rest was gone for ever.

Somehow, whatever essence – whatever fundamental core of self-identity – she had carried within her had been transported across the light-years and used to rebuild her. Her memories of a beach and a hut had been part of the process of integration, as they had started to put her fragmented memory back together. It shouldn't have worked, of course: she should have become a stumbling Frankenstein mess, a lopsided thing only half-alive, and yet here she was.

She heard whispering voices all around her, as if the beach or the waves or the sand itself had suddenly become conscious. It took her a moment to realize they were coming through her implants.

We had to make do with what we found, they announced.

The minds of the Magi ship, she realized. Not the same one that had carried her to the Maker; that was gone, turned to superheated dust and scattered across the cosmos, along with the original Dakota.

'But you didn't do it to help me,' she moaned. 'You brought me back because you wanted me to lead you to the Mos Hadroch.'

It had to be done, they replied. *We want to help you, Dakota. You don't ever have to die if you don't want to, not really. Not any more. We made you whole again – or as whole as we could make you.*

She wanted to wade out into the water, to let herself sink as soon as she could no longer feel anything solid beneath her feet, but soon realized she didn't have the strength or the will to do it. And even if she could, she knew the ship would just resurrect her again.

A bundle of what at first appeared to be rags lay close by but, when she stepped over, Dakota found they were clothes, identical to the ones she'd worn when she'd left Ocean's Deep a few years before. She picked them up, thinking that at least she wouldn't freeze to death if the nights here were as cold as the day was warm.

As she dressed, she glanced up at the curved under-belly of the Magi ship, and imagined it giving birth to her here on the shore, spitting the clothes out after her and watching over her until she blinked her eyes open for the first time.

She pulled the jacket around her shoulders. 'Why am I here?' she asked the air.

There was a message, the voices whispered in reply. *It used Shoal protocols, and was directed to Ocean's Deep. Indecipherable to all but you.*

They fed the message to her: a stream of data encoded using encryption techniques developed jointly by the Shoal and Magi – before one had committed genocide against the other.

The message was from Trader in Faecal Matter of Animals, and it concerned the Mos Hadroch. It detailed a rendezvous here on this world's shore, where dull grey waters lapped against broken shale.

What am I made of? Dakota wondered, panicked by the thought. She reached down and pinched the flesh of her forearm between thumb and forefinger. It felt like ordinary flesh and blood but, if she'd been remade, how could she be sure her knowledge of what flesh should feel like hadn't also been changed? After all, she wasn't even real, just a dead woman's memories prodded into life and given the illusion of independence.

Not true. You are *alive,* said the voices from within the starship.

'Shut up!' she yelled, her hands curling into fists by her sides. 'I didn't ask for this.'

She stepped closer to the waves and bent down, scooping some of the water up in the palms of her hands. Feeling experimental, she called on her filmsuit, and to her amazement it coated her flesh at once.

They had rebuilt more than just her body: she still had her filmsuit, even her implants.

Your ship calculated the precise phase state and non-arbitrary superpositions for every particle within your body, as well as gathering together the remaining fragments of your mind that were distributed throughout its neural stacks, said the voices. *That way when it transmitted—*

'I said *shut up!*'

The voices fell silent.

There was a disturbance in the ocean, and a moment

later a submersible of some kind emerged, halting a few metres from the shore. Dakota saw its hull was covered with tiny waving strips like flagella, which presumably propelled it. A hatch opened on its upper surface.

He's waiting for you, Dakota heard the voices say.

She stared up at the starship one last time, with a mixture of unease and disgust, then waded out to the submersible.

The cilia began to thrash against the water as soon as she had climbed inside. She stared out through the submersible's tinted, transparent walls as the hatch closed above her. The craft soon began to sink beneath the ocean's surface.

Something else had changed, she realized. For all that she could still hear the voices of the virtual entities that occupied the Magi ship, that deep, near-instinctive grasp, the near-total symbiosis she'd felt with them, had somehow faded away to nothing.

The original navigators were born to their task, the starship's voices told her. *They were created, their genetics manipulated so they could fuse their minds with their ships almost from the moment they came into life. Other Magi ships remade the physical structure of your cortex, but it was only a temporary measure, a stopgap whose consequences could never be precisely modelled. We . . .*

Dakota ignored them, squeezing her eyes tight until the voices finally retreated once more.

When she opened her eyes again, bright beams of pale yellow light had flickered into life, radiating out from a dozen points around the submersible's hull and picking out ruins on the seabed.

The submersible diverted around a vast, weed-strewn hulk that must have been kilometres long. At first she thought it was a collapsed tower, but as the lights picked out the dark shapes of nacelles and heat-dispersal fins, she realized it was a spacecraft that must have plummeted into the ocean long ago.

The ocean floor gradually slipped out of sight, and the submersible began to thread its way between vast columns that Dakota guessed must be the towers she'd seen earlier from the shore. Eventually the submersible headed straight towards one, before passing through an oval opening in its side, which led into a shaft at least a hundred metres across. The submersible began to rise through that shaft, ascending before long into an air-filled cavity.

The hatch opened with a hiss. Dakota pushed her head out and saw that the submersible was now floating in a wide moat between the tower's outer wall and an enormous circular platform surrounding a column rising at the tower's centre. Windows made from some crystalline material provided a view of the ocean waves from a few metres beneath the surface.

The platform itself was quite wide enough to support a Shoal superluminal yacht, floating on a bed of shaped fields. Waiting next to it, as Dakota had known he would be, was Trader in Faecal Matter of Animals, safely contained within a field-suspended sphere of water.

Dakota pulled herself out of the hatch and jumped down on to the platform, which looked and felt like black glass as she reached down to touch it. Trader drifted closer, and she watched how his manipulators clutched and wriggled beneath the wide curve of his body.

When he spoke, the familiar tones of his synthesized voice seemed to fill that dank underwater space.

'Once again, mellifluous greetings,' he said. 'Did you enjoy your trip to the Maker? And don't say I didn't warn you.'

'F . . .' She cleared her throat with some difficulty, and dug her fingernails into her palms, then tried again. 'Fuck you, too, Trader,' she finally managed to say, and touched her throat with nervous fingers.

'I congratulate you on having survived your encounter, Dakota. Few ever do.'

She stared back at the alien and felt a familiar seething anger well up inside her. It was easier to give in to the feelings of the old Dakota – the *real* Dakota, as some treacherous part of her mind insisted on thinking of her.

'Yes, Trader. I survived, and I got your message. Now tell me how you know so much about what I found out there.'

'The Consortium is an open book to those with the means to decrypt its most secure transmissions.'

'Not good enough. I was only ever in contact with other machine-head navigators.'

'The Shoal could not have brought about the deaths

of the original Magi navigators without having the means to intercept their communications traffic, a skill that remains with us. You can be assured, however, that the coordinates you recovered from the Maker stay a secret with me. Even the Shoal Hegemony remains unaware of the expedition.'

'What expedition?'

'The expedition your friend Lucas Corso recently sent out towards the coordinates associated with the Mos Hadroch, of course, Dakota.'

She nodded mutely, and realized she had no idea just how much time had passed since the red giant had turned nova. It might have been days, or weeks, or much more.

'I don't know what it is you want, Trader, but there are a thousand reasons why I shouldn't listen to anything you have to say.'

'And yet here you are.'

I didn't ask to come here, damn you. 'The last time I saw you was on Morgan's World. You already knew about the Mos Hadroch, didn't you?'

'In this I must confess my guilt,' Trader replied smoothly.

'You could have just told me, and then I never would have needed to go out there.'

'But I had little more than a name at that time, Dakota. You found out more than I ever did when I myself visited the swarm long ago. You even managed to find a possible location.'

Dakota felt her hands twitch with barely suppressed anger. 'If I could, I'd kill you, Trader. I'd . . .'

Her heart was hammering, and she felt on the verge of a panic attack. Too much was happening too soon.

She slumped down on the slick black glass extending underfoot, and listened to the wet slap of water against the platform's edge. 'Why here?' she asked, looking briefly around. 'I mean, what is this place?'

'This world?' Trader turned slowly within his sphere of water, glancing from side to side. 'Its occupants have long since passed on, as you may have guessed. There was a time when the civilization that built these towers strode amid the stars. They had an empire of a kind that stretched across thousands of light-years. Their name for themselves might be loosely translated as "Meridians".'

'So what happened to them?'

Trader's manipulators wriggled under his body. 'They never discovered a Maker cache until it was much too late and their culture had become terminally fragmented. Before that, they learned the secret of exceptionally long life and journeyed aboard ships that crawled between the stars at sublight speeds. One branch of the species became aquatic, while the rest remained air-breathers; the reasons why remain unknown. These towers are emblematic of happier times, when the two sides coexisted relatively peacefully, but eventually they tore themselves apart. They could not destroy stars as effectively as you or I might, but they certainly had the means to shatter worlds. If they had survived to face the Shoal

Hegemony, they would have presented us with a formidable challenge.'

'So does that have anything to do with why you chose this place?'

'They left behind weapons of the most remarkable power. Weapons that we will need, Miss Merrick, when we begin our journey.'

Dakota stared up at the alien. '"Journey"?'

'First, my dear Dakota, let me recount to you the full tale of the origin of the Mos Hadroch, as far as it is known. It is said to have been created by a species who were forerunners to the Magi, and who saw several of their own worlds destroyed in the early centuries of the nova war that set the Greater Magellanic Cloud ablaze. This vanished race developed the Mos Hadroch as a means to counter the dangers inherent within the Maker caches, but were themselves destroyed before it could be implemented. The Mos Hadroch itself vanished for ever and, for lack of evidence that it ever existed, it became little more than a phantasm, a fable that gained credence through the simple accumulation of age.'

Beyond Trader, Dakota saw dark shapes with wide ragged fins passing slowly by the tower, bioluminescent algae making their skin glow with sinuous patterns of green and yellow.

'But you thought it was real enough to go after the Maker swarm yourself,' she said.

'Before you departed, I told you of my own journey to the Maker. Although ultimately disastrous, it was not entirely a failure. I came away with the knowledge that the Mos Hadroch was of paramount importance to the swarm. After the Maker turned on my fleets, I remained locked in time-stopped stasis for decades until rescuers found me cast adrift in a cloud of wreckage. All I retained for my efforts was that single sliver of knowledge, that somewhere out there existed a weapon that might be used to prevent the nova wars the swarms are programmed to provoke with their caches. But its location has remained elusive – until now.'

'There must be a reason why we're here talking, and you haven't just gone to get it for yourself.'

'Precisely, Miss Merrick! And in that simple statement lies the proof of your intellect.' The alien drifted a little closer. 'You see, it is one thing to have a weapon, but another to know how to pull the trigger.'

Dakota cocked her head. 'I don't understand.'

'Precisely how would you suggest the Mos Hadroch is activated and implemented?'

Dakota stared at him, mystified. 'I couldn't begin to guess until we actually find the damn thing, whatever it is.'

'Indeed,' Trader was saying. 'Beyond a name, you do not even know what it is we are looking for. You know that it has a location, and your own people have discovered that some connection exists between the race that created it and an isolated Atn clade. But you do not know its dimensions, its size, or whether it even has a material shape.'

'But if all you yourself managed to find out is its name, then you're no better off than we are.'

Trader's manipulators wriggled suddenly with what Dakota suspected might be delight. 'On the contrary, the means of operating the Mos Hadroch has been available to me for a very long time. I acquired that knowledge long ago, on a journey to the Magellanic Clouds. A most sorrowful place it is, too: a graveyard of stars, one might say. There is life there, though sparse, living amongst the ruins of dead empires whose descendants can barely perceive the heights to which they once aspired. How ironic that the weapon I travelled so far to find should turn out to be so close to our own territory.'

'You mentioned something about a "journey". But a journey to where?'

'Why, to the heart of the Emissary empire, of course. In order to implement the Mos Hadroch in the way for which it was designed, we must penetrate the Maker cache from which they have derived the majority of their power.'

This has to be one of his tricks, she decided. 'You're fucking kidding me.'

'An amusing conceit, is it not? You must excuse my lack of transparency concerning the method of its activation, but we find ourselves in a situation where each of us may gain from the other. You must believe me, Dakota, when I tell you the Mos Hadroch must be taken to a particular cache before it can be deployed. It then exploits what one might call certain weaknesses in the design of the caches in order to achieve its full effect.'

Beyond the tower, the sun was sinking towards the horizon. Dakota's buttocks felt numb and sore from squatting on the platform. 'This just sounds like more bullshit, Trader,' she told the alien bluntly.

'You are free to doubt my words, as you are free to fly off and never encounter me again.'

Trader's yacht pinged her with a request to pass on data. She accepted it, but not without aggressively filtering it first to make sure she wouldn't encounter any nasty surprises before accessing it.

She stared at him after she had finished studying the data contained. 'You're serious? That's what it can do?'

'Impressive, yes?'

'If it's true. Look, it's what you're *not* telling me that worries me. Let's say, for the sake of argument, we get hold of this . . . this thing and fly it into Emissary territory. I've seen one of their godkillers in action, and I don't have any problem believing they'd wipe us out long before we got anywhere near one of their caches, even if we had a fleet of ships.'

'I've already mentioned the necessity of arming ourselves. The Meridians were most skilled in the art of war, and any one of their weapons would be a match for an entire fleet of human craft.'

Dakota stood up again. 'You haven't exactly made it clear what you're getting out of this yourself.'

'Why, an end to the nova war that threatens us all, of course.'

'A war you started, Trader. A war the Shoal is losing, last I heard.'

'The Hegemony desires a return to the peace we maintained for many tens of thousands of years, and I intend to facilitate it.'

'Why me, Trader? If you've got access to all this amazing firepower, why not just take it for yourself?'

'Because your Magi-mediated implants are ideal for their operation,' he replied. 'And you have proven yourself admiringly adaptable and even, dare I say it, strikingly callous in the heat of battle. It provokes a sense of admiration on my part that I would not normally experience in regard to a member of such a thoroughly retrograde and self-destructive species as your own. With an adequately equipped expedition, we could drive to the heart of the Emissary empire and still it for ever.'

Dakota shook her head. 'Here's what we're going to do, Trader. You'll give me access to whatever weapons the Meridians left here. Then I'm going back home to help out there in any way I can. Then, if I can't think of any other solution, I'll come back to you. Maybe. But I can tell you right now, nobody's going to take part in some kind of long-range expedition if they think you're involved.'

'And yet, without my knowledge of how to operate the Mos Hadroch, it's of no use to you. I fear this places you in an impasse.'

'I guess we'll have to see about that,' Dakota replied coldly.

Trader was silent for a moment, his manipulators twisting themselves into knots. 'There is one more matter which we have not yet discussed,' he said finally.

'Go on.'

'You set Hugh Moss on my trail. He dogs me even now. I have recourse to no other superluminal craft, and his urge to destroy me has not faded. He is a hindrance to our aims. And if he were to kill me, the path to peace would be eradicated for ever.'

'Not if you told me *everything* you know,' she said with a smile. 'If you really wanted peace rather than just to save your own skin, you'd do it immediately.'

'How well you know me, Miss Merrick,' he replied, his manipulators angrily thrashing the water under his belly. 'But it changes nothing. You will need my help, and we will need to journey together a long, long way. But as long as Hugh Moss is alive, he will seek to kill me.'

'So what the hell does that matter to me?'

'I have intelligence that currently puts him on Derinkuyu, a Skelite world close to the Consortium's borders.'

'No.' She turned away and walked back towards the submersible. 'I won't help you, Trader. Not after everything you've done. I'll find some other way.'

'Miss Merrick,' Trader called after her, 'you may believe you have a choice in the matter, but you do not.

There is a reason, after all, that your ship chose to deliver you to me here. Or will you lie to me and tell me you came here under your own volition?'

She hesitated. *How does he know that?*

She stopped and turned. 'I have a choice, Trader. And I choose not to trust you.'

'Listen to the minds on board your ship. Listen to what they have to say to you. They understand the situation better than you do.'

'What?'

'The Magi ships have a primary purpose, Dakota, which is to track down the Maker and destroy it. And if it can't be destroyed, then they must neutralize it or render its caches ineffective, a task for which the Mos Hadroch is explicitly designed. If you move against that central directive, the ship you use will refuse to obey your orders.'

She took a step back towards him. 'I don't believe you. You're lying.'

'Ask them yourself, then. See what they say.'

Dakota licked suddenly dry lips. 'Bullshit.'

But a moment later she knew it was true. She reeled with shock as the Magi voices confirmed what Trader was telling her.

'I don't understand,' she stammered. 'How the hell could you know what they're thinking?'

'You were, I understand, incapacitated when I first tried to contact you. Your ship, however, responded and I offered it terms. I demonstrated that the knowledge I carry is too valuable to risk losing as a result of Moss's murderous actions. Therefore, Miss Merrick, you must protect me.'

She again balled her fists at her side, trying to comprehend what was happening. 'I take my ship where the hell I like, damn you!' she yelled.

'Yes, Dakota, you do,' Trader agreed. 'Except when that interferes with its core directives. By the time you return to your own ship, you will have full control of the Meridian weapons systems, as a gesture of good intentions on my part. I think, in time, you'll come to see that your ship's course of action has been by far the wisest.'

Dakota felt the sense of betrayal as a knotted cord in her belly, twisting and untwisting. 'You can't do this,' she seethed.

'On the contrary, I have done nothing, Miss Merrick, except help you towards your goal. We will meet again, and soon.'

'I won't let you do this to me!' she screamed, but Trader had turned away already. She lurched forward, clawing at the shaped field surrounding the Shoal-member. But the shock of contact repelled her, and she collapsed on the platform, staring after the alien as his bubble rose towards an opening in his yacht.

She continued to scream her rage and beat the surface of the platform with her open palms, weeping and angry. She reached out with her mind and tried to take control of the Magi ship, still waiting on its rocky shore, but all she got for her efforts was a wash of pain that made her double up.

Once the pain had passed, she climbed back inside the submersible and let it take her back to the shore. She stared out at the ocean depths, without really seeing them, then slid down on to the submersible deck, hunched forward, knees up against her face, and hands pressed against her eyes.

Her instinct told her that everything the Shoal-member had said was probably true. But Trader was also a master of manipulation; what had been left unsaid could easily prove to be just as important.

The submersible broke through the waves a couple of hundred metres from the shore. A low rumbling sound caused her to look back towards the towers, in time to see Trader's yacht lift out of the water and accelerate upwards. A moment later she felt the command structure for the Meridian weapons systems suddenly land in her implants. It felt like she'd instantly gained a couple of hundred extra limbs.

The submarine's hatch snapped open once it reached the shore, and she pulled herself out, moving carefully while her brain assimilated what felt like a staggering amount of data. She waded through shallow surf until she once again stood in the shadows of the Magi star-ship.

Dakota collapsed on to the rough shale and closed her eyes, playing around with the command structure. Almost immediately something rumbled in the dense jungle beyond the cliffs, and Dakota opened her eyes again just in time to see a dozen silver spheres suddenly shoot up into the air above the cliffs, pieces of rock and dirt and shattered foliage sliding off their featureless carapaces. More rose from further inland, ascending to hover hundreds of metres above the ground, scattering more debris.

She turned towards the sea and saw a considerably greater number of identical spheres climbing out of the deep waters.

She sat there for a few minutes while the Magi ship's minds analysed the complex subroutines and hard AI neural structures of the command structure. Then she played around for a while, making the weapons swoop and soar like balls thrown by a sky-high invisible juggler. One tore overhead at several times the speed of sound, the roar of its passing sending small winged creatures, too weird-looking to be called birds, scattering from their perches in great flocks.

If it was up to me I'd just fly away for ever and never come back, Dakota thought to herself. Her sense of resentment had grown rather than diminished and, despite the staggering levels of destructive power hidden beneath the smooth, featureless shells of the Meridian drones, she felt powerless.

The blank exteriors of the drones proved to be a form of shaped-field technology masking a convoluted nightmare of warped space and exotic matter. She caused a dozen of them to accelerate to hypersonic speeds in the blink of an eye, and a series of powerful thunderclaps rolled over the shore in response. She looked up, seeing bright flickers of light from low orbit, as the drones unleashed primal energies in an impressive display of focused power.

Trader must have feared she would turn the weapons on him. Not wanting to disappoint, Dakota directed the drones to lay siege to the tower from which she had recently returned, according to a pre-programmed plan of attack. Wave after wave of plasma energy smashed into the tower, turning it white-hot and shattering it. She watched as a great cloud of superheated steam and debris shot upwards, a grumbling tremor spreading through the bedrock underlying the shore.

But Trader was long gone, as the ship's minds soon informed her. The violent action made her feel better regardless.

She stayed there for a while, watching as the sun dropped towards the towers, then she turned back to the waiting Magi ship.

It was time to go home. But, whether she liked it or not, she was going to have to pay Hugh Moss a visit first.

TEN

Ty was in a passageway just off of Shaft B when Cesar called in the warning.

The passageway terminated abruptly at a flat expanse of stone that differed substantially from the floor, ceiling and walls leading up to it. It featured none of the carved glyphs that covered almost every square centimetre of every other passageway throughout the abandoned clade-world. There was an unfinished quality to it, as if the Atn that had once made their home here had been interrupted in its construction.

Deep in thought, he crouched next to the unblemished wall of stone, a hand-held sodium lamp casting a sharp-edged pool of light around him. The comms indicator in one corner of his helmet visor had been blinking on and off for the past minute or so, but he had chosen to ignore it, suddenly certain that the last piece in a highly complex puzzle was about to slide into place.

Ever since the *Mjollnir* had brought them here, all the way from Ocean's Deep, Ty had wandered throughout the desolate shafts and passageways of the clade-world, convinced the Atn had left behind a message for those who knew how to read it – if not for him, then certainly for others of their own kind. There were hints, if you knew how to look, and careful study of them had drawn him to this particular passageway among all the rest.

The comms link continued to flash obstinately, and Ty finally activated it. In one corner of his visor an image popped up, of three interconnected white domes nestling together in a shallow crater. Digging equipment and spare parts for the spider-mechs were stacked out in the open. He noticed with a shock that at least one of the domes had been partly deflated.

'Nathan, you need to get back to the surface,' he was informed. Like the rest of the *Mjollnir*'s crew, Cesar Androvitch had no idea of Ty's true identity. 'Nancy's come over to help us get packed. We're going back over to the frigate.'

'But why? There's still too much to—'

'Nathan,' another voice cut in; this time it was Nancy Schiller, the *Mjollnir*'s chief of security. 'I'll explain everything when you get up here. Don't bring anything with you. Leave it all for the spiders. Just get here as fast as you can.'

She cut the connection, so that Ty hadn't even had a chance to tell her what he had found.

He pulled himself back along the passageway until he reached Shaft A, a borehole nearly thirty metres wide that cut straight through the heart of the asteroid, at which central point it intersected with a second shaft – Shaft B – running at a right angle to it. The asteroid itself was a little over thirty-five kilometres across; thousands of passageways, all identical in width but varying in depth, radiated outwards from each of the shafts.

He tapped at a panel on the arm of his spacesuit and, in response, one of a dozen spider-mechs that had been floating motionless near the centre of the shaft now moved towards him, propelled by tiny puffs of gas. The approaching device consisted primarily of a series of grappling arms that extended from a central hub a metre in diameter.

Once it had reached Ty, the spider rotated, presenting two handholds to him. Ty grabbed on to them, taking care not to look down the length of the shaft towards the asteroid's core as the machine carried him back towards the surface. Despite the minimal gravity, one such glance was sometimes all it took to send his suit's biomonitors into high alert.

Instead he looked up towards a slowly widening circle of stars no more than a few hundred metres away – the white dwarf around which the clade-world had been orbiting for the last few billion years standing out clearly amongst the rest.

A second dome had been deflated by the time Ty got back to the surface camp, which had been set up in a shallow crater a short distance from the mouth of the shaft itself. He let go of the spider-mech and allowed himself to drift slowly downwards, his boots kicking up a tiny puff of ice and dust. Then he made his way over to where Nancy and Cesar were working hard at packing the first dome back into its crate, under the harsh glare of an arc light. The *Mjollnir* was visible far overhead in the starry blackness, like a black and grey stick thrown high into the air, and which had never come down.

The frigate had taken a beating on the trip out, and it had not taken long for Ty to realize there was a very good reason why almost all the Shoal's superluminal craft comprised hollowed-out moons and adapted asteroids, since contact with the superluminal void put enormous stresses on the hull of any craft equipped with a faster-than-light drive.

The Magi starships were self-healing, but the *Mjollnir* wasn't built from the same pseudo-organic material. Along with the relatively few other human-built craft that had so far been converted to superluminal travel, the frigate was instead forced to undergo lengthy and difficult repair stops at the end of each and every jump it undertook. Outer hulls became corroded and damaged. Drive-spines required such constant repair and maintenance that onboard fabrication engines had to work around the clock to keep up with demand. While Ty and Nancy had been exploring the clade-world's passageways and caverns, Martinez and his crew had been striving to get the *Mjollnir* in full working order for the trip home.

One of the two helmeted figures now glanced up, and

Ty's suit automatically projected an icon floating beside that figure, identifying it as Nancy.

'Merrick's swarm is on its way here,' she told him without preamble. '*Mjollnir*'s on full alert, and Martinez wants us out of here within the hour.' Ty was close enough now to see the worried expression through her visor. 'I'm sorry, Nathan. We did our best.'

'How do you know it's on its way?' he asked.

'The reconnaissance probes we sent out,' explained Cesar. 'One of them picked up a lot of drive-signatures no more than thirty light-years from here.'

'Drive-signatures?'

'Sure,' said Nancy. 'Remember the briefing?'

Ty made an exasperated noise. 'There were endless briefings. Care to remind me?'

'Superluminal ships produce gravitational anomalies every time they enter or depart normal space,' Cesar continued. 'The probe's got tach-net monitors that can pick up short-range fluctuations propagating through superluminal space. So we know *something* just turned up.'

No more than thirty light-years from here, Ty reflected. How easily the words tripped off Cesar's tongue. They'd travelled a thousand light-years without any help from the Shoal, putting them on a par with the greatest explorers the human race had ever known.

'How could they get here so soon?' he demanded. 'I thought the best estimates gave us at least another month before they arrived here.'

'Nathan . . . Cesar . . . for Christ's sake, shut up and get packing, will you?'

Ty turned his attention to Nancy. 'Look, we can't possibly leave here with nothing to show, not after coming all this way. Tell me exactly how much time you think we have left, to the precise minute if it's at all possible.'

He could just make out her terse expression through the visor. 'Nathan—'

'Just humour me, okay?'

Nancy hesitated, and Cesar jumped in. 'I'd say anything from ten to twenty-four hours before they're right on our doorstep, Nathan. But I don't rate our chances of survival very high if we aren't ready to jump out of here before then.'

Ty thought hard for a moment. 'Okay, but once the swarm *does* reach this system, exactly how long do you think we have before they pinpoint our exact location?'

'Nathan,' Nancy spoke as if she were talking to a slightly dim child, 'if there was ever anything here, it's long gone now. Give it up.'

'Is that Martinez's opinion too?' he countered.

'Of course it is, otherwise we wouldn't be packing up, would we? Unless you've got any last-minute bright ideas.'

'Maybe I do. Look, we spent a week just trying to find this rock after we arrived in this system, right?'

'What's your point?' asked Cesar.

'The swarm needs to find us first, or more specifically this one asteroid out of the huge volume of them surrounding the white dwarf. Now, clade-worlds are always found within specific distances from their stars, which is one reason we managed to find this one as quickly as we did. The swarm's going to know that, but it still means we're going to have at least *some* time to finish our work before they trace us.'

'We really don't have time to debate this,' Nancy snapped, her voice getting louder. 'You've worked harder than anyone else, Nathan, and there's no reason we couldn't come back here some other time and try looking again, after the swarm is gone.'

'Think about what's at stake,' Ty insisted. 'What's going to happen if we return empty-handed?'

'Jesus and Buddha, Nathan!' Nancy finally exploded. 'Don't you *understand?* All that happens if we stay on now is we get killed, and it's all over either way! Not unless you finally think you found the damn . . .' She stuttered to a halt, and he realized she could see the grin almost splitting his face in half.

Cesar looked back and forth between them. 'What – you found something?'

'There's an anomaly,' Ty explained. 'It was right there in front of me the whole time.'

'So why the hell didn't you mention it before?' Nancy demanded, angry again.

Ty shrugged, then remembered the gesture probably wouldn't be visible to the others, regardless of how light and flexible their suits were. 'You didn't really give me a chance. I came up here when you called, and—'

'Okay,' Nancy said, cutting him off. 'Okay, *what* anomaly?'

'I'll need to show you,' he replied.

Nancy conferred quickly with Martinez and got permission for them to go back inside the asteroid. Cesar remained on the surface to supervise the spiders as they busily manoeuvred the packed tents and supplies on board an unmanned cargo transport that had just arrived from the frigate.

'I hope you know I'm risking my life for you,' Nancy muttered over a private channel, her voice tense.

'I promise I won't read too much into it,' Ty replied. The shaft walls slid past as they dropped down into darkness, each of them carried by a spider-mech. 'God forbid you might ever admit to actually liking me.'

'It's not that I don't like you; it's just that . . . I don't know.'

'"I'm just not your usual type." That's what you always say, isn't it?' he asked.

Sudden, intense sexual relationships were to be expected, while so far from home for months at a time; and such had been part and parcel of Ty's experiences while exploring other clade-worlds in years long gone by. But he never let himself forget that Nancy Schiller was a Freeholder. She was not unlike Karen, in that she was used to a life of discipline, and her body was a landscape of smooth, well-trained muscles; whenever they shared a bed, Ty would find himself wondering whether life under an assumed identity had left him with a perverse attraction to the threat of discovery.

He heard her sigh, over the channel. 'Forget I said anything,' she muttered. 'How long before we get to this chamber?'

'Not long. Does it matter?'

'No,' she grumbled. 'It's just . . .'

'What?'

She made an irritated sound. 'I just can't stand to think of those . . . *machines* hunting us through all this darkness.'

'It's not far,' he replied, knowing she was referring to the images of swarm-components they'd occasionally watched since departing Ocean's Deep.

The mouth of the shaft had shrunk to almost nothing, and now the only light came from the spider-mechs' lamps, which cast sharp-edged pools of illumination against the walls of the shaft as they rushed by. Their conversation lapsed into silence, and Ty guessed Nancy was just as intimidated by the scale of the clade-world as most people were the first time they found themselves inside one.

Before long they reached the crossroads at the asteroid's heart. Someone had directed a spider to nail up a handwritten sign indicating basic directions. Ty braked, and waited for Nancy to do the same.

'We're going into Chamber Two,' he explained, nodding in the direction of Shaft B West. 'It's pressurized, okay? That means we can—'

'Nathan, I know you're dedicated to your work, but get your head out of your ass. Remember I'm the one who writes the daily progress reports. What makes you think I don't already know it's pressurized?'

'Sorry. I was just thinking out loud. Another hundred metres, then down the hatch.'

The Atn usually left a basic assortment of data and tools behind whenever they abandoned a clade-world, but in this case there seemed to be a surfeit of artefacts both physical and virtual. The data was recorded on storage devices built around a core of self-repairing molecular circuitry, the resulting stacks resembling rows of bronzed shields embedded in the walls of dedicated chambers. Most, but not all of the data stored there still remained incomprehensible to human researchers.

The stack chamber was accessed through a pressure seal installed by spider-mechs shortly after their arrival. They passed through the airlock quickly, Ty pulling off his helmet once they were inside the chamber. He watched as Nancy did the same, shaking sweat from frizzy blond hair cut into a bob.

The chamber was rectangular, its walls crowded with the ubiquitous spiral-form glyphs. A heap of what might appear to the casual observer as nothing more than blackened junk lay jumbled in one corner. The remains of eight Atn stack-discs were embedded in the wall directly opposite the pressure seal. Each had been carefully and deliberately vandalized; fragments and chunks of the discs lay scattered all around.

Nancy knelt by the pile of junk and poked at it with one gloved finger. 'I don't know, Nathan, we've already been over every inch of this place, and I'll be seriously surprised if we've missed anything.'

Ty pulled off a glove and ran one hand over the ruined edge of a stack-disc. 'We missed one thing.' He nodded towards the pile of junk in the corner. 'That's the remains of an Atn, for a start.'

'Oh.' She stood up and took a step back. 'Are you sure?'

He glanced past her at the twisted remains, which were hardly recognizable as having ever been anything living. 'I ran a tomographic analysis on some trace organic remnants. It's definitely the remains of an Atn, and it's been subjected to extremely intense levels of heat, like something turned the interior of this chamber into a furnace. You remember what Cesar found out about those craters?'

'A lot of them were formed relatively recently, and in the same short period of time, right?'

'Exactly. It's like something turned up here, killed everything living it found, then disappeared again.'

'All right,' she said, eyeing him with wary respect. 'But if that does turn out to be the case, doesn't it lend itself rather strongly to the notion that if the Mos Hadroch was ever here, it's gone now? And you told me yourself the Atn clades used to go to war with each other. Maybe the ones in this asteroid just happened to lose a fight.'

Ty shook his head violently. 'No, the *assumption* used to be that the Atn must have fought amongst themselves, but the data we got from Merrick makes a strong case for the swarm being responsible for all the damage to clade-worlds we've found in the past.' He stared thoughtfully at the stack-discs for several seconds.

'But? I can tell there's a but.'

'There are clade-worlds in even worse condition than this one, back home, but I've never come across stack-discs that looked like they'd been as carefully and deliberately smashed as these.'

She glanced at the melted remains of the Atn, and then back at Ty. 'You think this one smashed them himself, before he got killed?'

'I think it's a fair conjecture. There was something in those discs he didn't want found. Maybe even the exact location of the Mos Hadroch.'

She stared at him like he was an imbecile. 'But if the stack-discs have been destroyed, how the hell are you going to find out?'

'By looking at things differently. For a start, we've mapped out every inch of this asteroid, but there's one passageway off Shaft A that's a hundred metres too short.'

She looked at him blankly, and he explained further. 'Look, every single Atn clade in existence follows the exact same internal architecture. It's like they have a blueprint they never deviate from. They only go for bodies of a certain size, between seventy and one hundred kilometres across. Then there are always two central shafts, and exactly the same number of branching passageways and chambers, all in the same place and according to a ratio relative to a particular asteroid's dimensions.'

He grabbed her by the shoulders and grinned. 'When Cesar called in, I'd already gone to check out that passageway – and I'd bet my life it's capped with a false wall.'

'You think there's something hidden behind it?'

'Why not? There's gear back on the frigate that can tell us if I'm right.'

Nancy carefully extracted herself from his grasp. 'Well, that's great. We can have Martinez send over some explosives so we can blow it open.'

'First we need to know how thick the false wall is. Too thick and we'll need a lot of explosives, except that could collapse the passageway on top of us and maybe destroy whatever they hid beyond. No,' he shook his head, 'first we image the passageway to get some idea what's back there. We can even drill a hole through if necessary. But we need to get started on this now, Nancy. Right *now*.'

She stared at him for another moment, then set her mouth in a firm line and opened a comms link to the *Mjollnir*'s bridge.

Ty felt a weight lift off his shoulders; it seemed they were finally getting somewhere.

*

Less than an hour later, Curtis Randall and Anton Swedberg – technical specialists – were manoeuvring new equipment down the shaft and into the suspect passageway, with the help of nearly a dozen spider-mechs. A large drill mechanism, mounted on a tripod and assembled from a kit, had been set up next to the false wall, its three legs firmly secured to the floor. The drill bit itself was hidden from view behind a flat plastic shield.

'Got word from Perez,' Ty heard Randall say over their shared comms. 'Martinez is coming online in a couple of seconds. Something's up.'

Ty glanced behind himself and saw two spider-mechs delicately directing a package down the passageway towards the false wall, casting deep shifting shadows as they passed under a string of lights positioned along the ceiling. 'What is it?'

'Anton says he spoke to Tibbs on the bridge, and *Mjollnir*'s picking up a local increase in background tach-net noise as well as gravity flux waves in the tach-net continuum. Looks like the swarm just arrived.'

Ty felt a sudden panic flood him. They were running out of time.

Get a grip, he thought angrily. He glanced over at Nancy, unpacking gear beside him, and caught the look of alarm on her face, even through her visor.

'If we're lucky, it's only a few advance scouts,' Randall added, as the two spiders came to a halt. Ty turned to them and began unstrapping the packages they carried. 'I'm sorry to be, you know, the bearer of bad news.'

Ty nodded, feeling numb. 'Then we have to—'

'Forgive me for eavesdropping, Mr Driscoll,' said Martinez, 'but I couldn't help overhearing.' Ty glanced down and noticed that the small, gold-coloured bar representing the *Mjollnir*'s commander had manifested in one corner of his visor. 'The situation's starting to look pretty desperate from where I'm standing.'

Ty could hear murmured conversations and background noises on the bridge. 'How far away are they?' Ty asked immediately. 'A star system's a big place, Commander, so we might have as much as a couple of days before they figure out exactly where the asteroid is.'

'Mr Driscoll, if the swarm gets here before we leave, it isn't going to matter a damn whether you find anything behind that wall or not.'

'I know that, sir,' Ty replied carefully. 'But all I really need is a couple of hours. You know how important this is.'

The background hiss faded for a moment, and Ty guessed Martinez was consulting with Dan Perez, one of his senior officers.

'Okay, here's what I propose,' said Martinez when he came back online. 'The instant the swarm appears, the *Mjollnir* jumps straight out of this system regardless of whether you're still on that rock or not. The same goes for everyone else who stays there, and the choice is strictly voluntary. I have to think of the crew.'

'Nobody's under any obligation to stay here and help me if they don't want to,' Ty replied, glancing over at Nancy and Curtis, 'but I know I can do it a hell of a lot quicker if I have some help.'

'What about the spiders?' asked Martinez. 'Have you considered whether you could run the entire operation from the bridge?'

'No,' Ty said straight away. 'Look, the spiders help a lot, but they're no good for fast, delicate work. They're far too slow and clumsy for what we need to do here, and it'll end up taking much longer than it should, if we have to do the entire thing by tele-operation.'

'Nathan's right,' Ty heard Nancy say. 'The spiders are fine for this kind of work only if there's no time constraint.'

'Yeah, I agree,' said Curtis. 'The more of us down here who know what we're doing, the faster we get everything done and get back out. The last of the detectors is now in place, so we should be able to pick up a video feed straight away.'

'That's fine, Curtis,' Martinez replied. 'But every analysis says we don't need more than two people down there, so I want you and Anton back here on the frigate. Nancy and Nathan, I spoke to Cesar. He's going to remain on the surface with a fast launcher. Just don't take one second longer than you have to.'

'No problem.'

Martinez cut the connection.

'Detectors?' asked Nancy.

'Muon detectors,' Curtis explained. 'We stuck them around the surface of the asteroid. They pick up traces of decaying cosmic-ray particles, so we can build up a picture of whatever's inside there.'

Ty nodded. 'Did you bring the screens?'

Curtis passed a rolled-up video monitor over to Ty, who opened and smoothed it against one wall, holding it flat there while Curtis retrieved a hammer from a spider's toolbox and nailed the monitor to the stone at all four corners.

Ty stepped back and studied the chiaroscuro of greys that appeared on the monitor a few moments later, quickly resolving into a map of the asteroid's tunnels and chambers.

'There,' Ty said excitedly, pointing one gloved finger at a shape like a fat grey worm. 'That's our passageway, right there.'

Nancy stepped up beside him and peered at the shifting image. 'There really is something behind that wall, isn't there?' she murmured, clearly fascinated.

Curtis leaned in beside them and touched the screen with one gloved finger. 'There are some dark shapes on the other side. Can you see them?'

Ty felt a burst of elation and fought to stay calm. 'I see them, yes, and I don't think this is going to be as difficult as I thought.' Glancing at Curtis, he said, 'Martinez is expecting you and Anton back at the *Mjollnir*. You'd better get going.'

Curtis nodded, and Ty could see the other's desire to

remain there warring with his fear of the approaching alien threat. Assuming they got out of this alive, they'd all of them have stories to tell for the rest of their lives.

Curtis nodded with resignation and stepped back. 'Nathan, Nancy – good luck to both of you. I'll see you back on the ship.'

Ty nodded and watched for a moment as Curtis retreated back down the passageway, before turning his attention to the drill rig. He touched a button, and the drill's bit began to cut into the wall in total silence. All he really had to do now was set the parameters, step back, and let the machine perform.

It did not take long before the passageway around them began to fill with clouds of grey-black dust as the device did its work. Ty watched the drill's readout, indicating how deep it was penetrating; it had cut through nearly fifty centimetres of rock before it signalled that it was no longer encountering resistance. Nancy watched as he pulled the drill free, and together they stepped up to the narrow opening left behind.

Nancy withdrew a long, narrow silver tube from a suit pocket and carefully slid it inside the freshly drilled hole. After a couple of seconds she pulled it back again.

The tube had contained a mobile security device modelled on a terrestrial insect, complete with a minuscule propulsion system optimized for zero-gee. After she'd repocketed the now empty tube, Nancy pushed a couple of high-intensity glow-sticks through the hole until they slid through into the other side, falling slowly under the asteroid's minimal gravity.

'Okay,' Nancy said breezily, stepping over to the screen. 'Let's see what we'll see.'

She now reset the screen to show whatever the insect-machine's lenses were picking up on the other side of the wall. After a few moments they saw a huddled shape about fifteen metres from the false partition. Other than that, the other side looked deserted.

'That's it?' murmured Nancy, unable to mask her dismay.

'Doesn't matter,' said Ty, fighting back his own growing doubt. 'There's still something back there valuable enough that someone wanted to seal it up for a very long time.'

Nancy peered at the screen. 'I can't be sure, but it looks like it might be the body of another Atn.'

A warning light blinked up inside both their visors and a priority transmission came through from Martinez. 'Nathan, Nancy; the gravity flux readings just about went off the chart during the past couple of minutes.'

'What does that mean?' asked Ty, baffled.

'It means there are even more swarm-components than we thought. Hundreds of the damn things. You should seriously reconsider returning to the ship *now*.'

'No way. There's definitely something here, but it's going to take time to get to it. You need to hold on until then.'

'I thought you might say that. I already talked to

Cesar, and he's going to stay topside for at least the next hour. Any longer than that, and every risk analysis the ship can come up with says our chances of getting out of here alive drop off dramatically. Good luck.'

Martinez signed off and Ty let out a slow, steady breath. 'You're okay with that?'

Nancy shrugged, and a faint smile tugged the corners of her mouth upwards. 'I guess I'll have to be.'

Under normal circumstances, Ty might have spent days meticulously scanning the sealed-off corridor before carefully and laboriously dismantling the false intervening wall. The present circumstances required a more direct approach, for which purpose shaped charges had already been spidered over from the *Mjollnir*.

They first drilled several more holes at different points on the rock wall. Meanwhile a computer feed from the *Mjollnir*'s bridge hovered in one corner of Ty's visor, showing a schematic of the system, along with a constantly updated animation based on the estimated location of the swarm.

Every time one of the alien machines jumped through superluminal space, it sent a faint ripple rushing through the superluminal continuum like an undulation moving across the still surface of a pond. The *Mjollnir*'s defensive systems mapped these ripples as they occurred in real time, and it was immediately clear that the swarm was spreading out to cover the whole system. Ty thought of the sheer volume of space they were trying to encompass, and wondered if the swarm really had a chance of finding them any time soon.

Once the drilling was finished, Ty carefully slid the charges into place, one to each hole, then followed Nancy back towards the relative safety of the main shaft. The spiders moved ahead of them, spreading out into the shaft beyond.

Ty and Nancy then moved to either side of the passageway's mouth. He tried to ignore the trickle of sweat he could feel rolling down one cheek, and glanced over at her spacesuited figure.

'Ready?' she asked, one finger hovering above an arm-mounted control.

Ty nodded.

'Okay. Three, two, one, *boom*.'

There was no sound, of course, but Ty's imagination filled it in all the same. Seismic taps on the surface immediately fed details of the resulting tremor back to him through his suit's readout. Barely a moment later, a thick column of grey smoke and grit came billowing out of the mouth of the passageway, spreading into the main shaft.

Nancy was now barely visible through the dust and swirling grit. 'Can't see anything on the visuals,' he heard her say.

'Too much debris for that,' he replied. 'Let's go see if it worked.'

They sent a couple of spiders in first, in case there were any really big chunks of debris still bouncing around inside the passageway, then both followed it in, moving carefully.

The explosives had worked better than Ty might have hoped, and yet the passageway immediately beyond what remained of the false wall differed little from the section that preceded it. The threat of disappointment lurked like a leaden weight in the pit of his stomach. But they finally got a good look at what they'd previously glimpsed only as an indistinct grey shadow.

It was indeed the body of a single Atn – but nothing else.

'Are you getting this?' Nancy asked. Ty looked round to see her turning her head slowly from side to side as she moved through the opened-up section of the passageway. He assumed she was transmitting live video to the *Mjollnir*'s bridge.

Ty kneeled by the Atn's bulky corpse and brought his suit's light up close to it, studying the intricate, stylized whorls and sigils engraved into its carapace. As far as he could see, there was nothing whatsoever unusual about it.

'Well, I guess that's it,' he heard Nancy announce over the general comms link. 'This is all there is.'

'Just hold on a minute,' Ty snapped irritably. 'We've barely had a chance to look around yet.'

'Come on, Nathan, there's nothing here. Let's face it, we tried and we failed.'

Ty struggled to control the quiver in his voice. 'Nothing here except for an Atn that the rest of its clade went to such enormous time and trouble to hide. Does that make sense to you?'

'I don't know. Maybe it's simply a burial chamber, and this was one of their leaders. That would explain the story of the Mos Hadroch, wouldn't it? Maybe that thing's what the Atn regarded as a king or hive-queen?'

'You're talking nonsense,' Ty snapped, running one gloved hand along the creature's carapace. 'And also you're overanthropomorphizing them. Besides, the Atn are entirely non-hierarchical. And if this place is nothing more than a burial chamber, then explain to me why a swarm of alien machines just turned up searching for this asteroid.'

'I'm just telling you what I see here,' Nancy insisted, and he could tell he'd sounded too harsh. 'A dead Atn, that's it.'

Ty stood up and looked around. All he could see were smooth, unblemished rock walls, entirely devoid of glyphs, amid swirling dust. 'All the evidence points right here,' Ty reaffirmed, thinking out loud.

'All right, and maybe it's a deliberate red herring set up to misdirect anyone coming looking for the Mos Hadroch, and we fell for it.'

The same thought had already occurred to Ty, but he didn't care to admit to it.

Commander Martinez's icon blinked back into life at the bottom of Ty's visor. 'We just picked up a mass of gravity-traces located no more than three or four AUs from here,' he informed them. 'Whatever you think you have, grab it and get out, or you risk being left behind.'

Ty could feel the blood pounding in his head, and he felt suddenly sick with anxiety. He leaned forward, again shining sharp-edged light on the dead alien's carapace markings, while he studied it for long seconds.

Think, he told himself. All they had so far was a name . . . they had no idea what the Mos Hadroch might look like, how big it was, or how small . . .

A sudden sense of excitement gripped him and he pinged Nancy with a request for a secure one-on-one link, at the same moment he severed his comms link with the *Mjollnir*'s bridge.

Nancy accepted the link, and her voice came through a moment later. 'What the hell, Ty?' she asked. 'Why did you just cut off the ship? Martinez'll throw a fit.'

'We can't go back yet.'

Her shoulders slumped, her expression more puzzled than angry.

'Look around you,' he demanded. 'What do you see?'

'An empty passageway – and a dead alien.'

The Atn were a cyborg species, and only part organic, of course; that much was well known. Not that anyone had ever managed to prove it, but the general consensus was that their long-term memories and any other data stored in their brains could be passed from one individual to the next. That way you got creatures whose individual identities constantly shifted and changed, as they each accumulated the experiences of their brethren.

What if, he wondered, *the Mos Hadroch was nothing more than some form of information, carefully hidden inside some dormant circuitry located somewhere inside what passed for this creature's brain?*

Ty shook his head, thinking hard and fast. No, that couldn't be it. If that had been the case, they'd have done as well to hide the actual stack-discs here, too, rather than destroy them in their storage chamber.

He let out a snarl of exasperation and squatted on his haunches. 'X marks the spot,' he muttered.

'What?'

'Everything points to *here*,' he said, unable to contain his exasperation. 'The records I found way back when, the spiral texts we discovered here, and even this Atn.'

Nancy said nothing, simply stood there waiting, while he stared at the Atn's metal carapace. They were hardly elegant creatures: slow and ponderous, the size of a small car. There was, he suddenly thought, a lot of room in there.

He bent down again to read more closely at the creature. There was something, he was sure, wrong with its head. He put both hands under it and tried to lift it. It moved with surprising ease, as if it were nothing more than an empty casing.

He stood up again. 'It's in there,' he declared, flushed with sudden and overwhelming certainty.

'Excuse me?'

'The smashed discs, the walled-off passageway . . .

none of it makes sense unless there's something *inside* the body.'

He stared at Nancy, his eyes bright, while she gazed back at him in mystified, thin-lipped silence. 'How can you be sure?'

'Frankly, I can't. There's just nowhere else it could be. Nobody's been in here since that false wall was put up, so it has to be *inside* that thing.'

'We don't have time to break it open,' Nancy replied decisively. 'We'd need cutting tools for that, which means we're going to have to get it back to the *Mjollnir*.'

Ty nodded. 'Tell Martinez we're coming out.'

The Atn lay with its head pointing in the direction of the main shaft, the bulk of its massive body pushed up against the wall on one side. Deciding to move it was one thing, but managing it was another. Ty got in touch with Cesar and told him what he was planning, while Nancy reopened the link with the *Mjollnir* and fielded Martinez's angry demands.

Ty glanced down at the image of the swarm's movements projected on the interior of his visor, and saw that some of its members were converging on the *Mjollnir*'s location a lot sooner than he had expected.

Nancy signed off and just stood there, looking tense and angry. 'How long did Martinez give us?' he asked her.

'Thirty minutes, that's it. And then they jump without us.'

'I just talked to Cesar,' Ty explained, 'and he's got an idea he wants to try.'

'Fine. In the meantime, let's get this thing hooked up to the spiders, then haul it the hell out of here.'

Some of the spiders were equipped with additional bits of equipment, among them a powerful oxyacetylene torch and several winches that spooled out super-strong cable. While he talked with Cesar over the comms, Ty unwound the cable from one of the spiders and fixed the carabiner lock attached to it around the dead alien's neck like a noose. Nancy did the same with another, and after a few minutes' work they'd secured the body to three separate cables.

'We're going to have to set them all to maximum burn,' Nancy muttered, surveying their work. 'But at that rate they've only got fuel for thirty seconds.'

'Is that going to be enough?'

She thought for a moment. 'Maybe. I think we should set them up for two separate burns, of fifteen seconds each.'

'Why?'

'In case we don't get it moving the first time, or if something goes wrong, we'll still have a second chance. And if this works the first time, that leaves us with extra fuel.' She gave him a steady look. 'But that only gets it out into the shaft, not up to the surface, or into the launcher.'

'Cesar's moved the launcher over the shaft mouth. He's also taken a winch off one of the other spiders, and by the time we've got our friend here out into the shaft itself, he'll have lowered that cable from the launcher, and we can just winch the damn thing up to the surface.'

'Sounds like a plan,' she admitted, but her tone gave away her doubt. 'But we might be cutting this far too close, Nathan.'

'We can do this,' he insisted.

'Yeah, well, I just hope you're right.'

The spiders were soon in place, all facing towards the shaft entrance almost a hundred metres away, their cables now knotted tightly around the alien's body. As Ty got into position behind the body along with Nancy, he glanced at her and saw her lips set in a thin, hard line behind her visor, her gaze fixed on the far end of the passageway.

'Fifteen seconds, with an initial three-second delay,' he reminded her. 'Ready?'

'Ready as I'll ever be,' she muttered.

Ty braced himself, knees bent, the soles of his boots pressed hard against the scuffed stone floor, and then he initiated the first burn.

Moments later, the thrusters of all three spiders flared in unison, and Ty's visor quickly darkened in response. Seeing the winch-lines draw taut, he put his shoulder against the Atn's inert form and pushed with all his strength. His feet almost slipped out from under him and he quickly sought fresh purchase, wondering if he'd been a fool to think something like this might actually work.

Just as time seemed to run out, the Atn started to slide forward, slowly at first, and then with increasing speed. It scraped against the stone floor and then collided with the facing wall. They stumbled after it, using their hands to try and steer it away from either side.

As the spiders finished their programmed burn, the Atn kept moving forward under its own momentum, dead limbs flailing as it drifted up from the floor and towards the ceiling, turning slowly as it went.

'Don't let it get turned around too far!' Nancy yelled. 'If it gets wrapped up in the cables, it'll pull the spiders in towards it.'

The Atn smashed into the ceiling and lost some of its momentum. At least, Ty thought, they had it moving in the right direction. It scraped grit and dust from one wall as it drifted onwards.

'Okay,' said Ty. 'Second burn, now.'

He tapped at his arm console and triggered the second blast of energy. The spiders shot towards the mouth of the shaft, drawing the cables taut once more, and dragging the Atn's lifeless form after them.

The second burn seemed to last for ever.

The spiders finally ran out of fuel, and the cables grew slack once more as the Atn drifted forward, colliding with the three spiders and grinding one of them to pieces against a hard surface. Smashed components and delicate robot arms were sent flying, but it was heading in the right direction. A few seconds later the alien's body finally sailed out into the main shaft, spinning slowly and followed by a hail of fresh debris and machine parts.

Several spiders had been hovering nearby, and their programmed sense of self-preservation made them scatter like fish disturbed by a shark as the Atn went crashing into the main shaft's opposite wall. It then rebounded at a fraction of its original velocity, tangled in cables, from the spiders still tethered to it.

Ty looked up along the shaft towards the external entrance and saw a ring of stars surrounding the bulky silhouette of the fast launcher. A cable extended down from it, its tip swaying just a few metres above them.

He grinned: Cesar had clearly been hard at work. Ty pushed himself towards the cable and grabbed hold of it.

The Atn kept rotating slowly, more or less hanging in the centre of the shaft. Ty managed to cling to one of its legs long enough to secure the cable to it. He pulled himself on top of the Atn, then opened a link to Cesar.

'Nathan,' came the response. 'How's it going down there? Are we ready to move?'

'Yeah,' Ty replied. 'Start pulling it in right *now*.'

'Sure thing.' The cable drew taut, causing the Atn's body to twist around a little faster, swinging from side to side like a huge ungainly pendulum. Ty kicked himself away from its bulk, and landed against the shaft wall just a moment later.

He felt a powerful tremor rumble through his gloved

fingertips the moment they came into contact with the shaft wall. More dust began to slowly billow out from the passageway entrance, as well as from the other passageways both above and below. He noticed a moment later that Cesar's icon had blinked out. He tried to hail him, but didn't get an answer.

'That had to be something big hitting the asteroid,' said Nancy, sounding panicky. 'Get to the surface, Nathan, *now*.'

Ty didn't bother answering. He summoned a spider and grabbed its handholds. The passageway began to drop out of sight as the machine carried him back to the surface.

Looking upwards, he realized that the launcher's attitudinal systems were having to fight to keep it in place over the mouth of the shaft. Whatever had slammed into the asteroid might have done so hard enough to increase its otherwise barely perceptible rotation, and the Atn's inert form swinging about inside the shaft wasn't helping either. It was then he noticed one of the launcher's fuel nozzles was firing only sporadically.

'Cesar? Cesar, can you hear me?' Ty yelled into his comms, but the other man's life-support icon stayed dark. Next he tried pinging the *Mjollnir*, and felt a chill sweat spring up between his shoulder blades when there was no response. He started to wonder just what they were going to find waiting for them up on the asteroid's surface.

It was possible, of course, that the frigate's crew were

under attack and too busy to reply. It was just as possible that they had already jumped out of the system, and abandoned the outside team. Worse, the frigate might have been destroyed by whatever had hit the asteroid.

He glanced down at Nancy, who was also being carried upwards by a spider, and tried to think of something he could say that might make both of them feel better. He drew a blank.

'Nancy, if something's happened to Cesar, I don't know how to fly the launcher.'

'Let me worry about that.'

Ty glanced at his visor's life-support indicators. They each had about half an hour's oxygen supply left.

The Atn was finally drawn inside the rear cargo hatch of the launcher, the craft veering to one side as the Atn crashed into its interior bay. Its boosters cut out a moment later.

'Don't worry,' Nancy said quickly. 'I just took control of the launcher.'

Ty released the spider's handholds, letting his own momentum carry him towards a set of rungs fixed to the launcher's exterior.

'Get up front and strap yourself in,' Nancy shouted, already pulling herself up the other side of the launcher. 'Move it, Nathan.'

The launcher was entirely open to vacuum, and was little more than a computer-controlled rocket platform with two pairs of seats mounted on its nose. At the rear, four primary nozzles angled outwards from the cargo bay that comprised most of the craft's volume. As Ty got into his seat, he glanced up and felt relief wash over him like a tide. The *Mjollnir* was still right where it should be.

A dense cloud of dust was rising from some point just around the curve of the asteroid's narrow horizon. A fog of ice and grit now covered its surface. Whatever had struck it must have been big.

'What about Cesar?' he asked.

Nancy was already strapped in and stabbing at the launcher's control console. 'Your guess is as good as mine.'

'He should have been here at the controls.'

'We abandoned some equipment at the camp, remember. All I can think is he must have left the launcher running on automatic, and tried to salvage some of that.' Nancy peered at the panel. 'Shit, one of the thrusters is out of action. I'm going to have to shut it off and hope I can compensate with the rest. But I'm getting close-to-fail readings on the others, so cross your fingers and hope they don't turn us into a fireball before we get back to the ship.'

'Thanks for that thought,' Ty replied.

'Just strap in and get ready. This is going to be a rough ride.'

Ty then caught sight of a suited figure drifting close to the asteroid's surface, partially obscured by the clouds of grit and ice. It took a few moments before he realized with a shock that the lower half of Cesar's body was missing. He pointed this out to Nancy and she cursed. 'He should have stayed with the damn launcher.'

'I guess he must have been hit by debris. We're lucky the launcher wasn't wiped out the same way.'

'Right now, I just want to get the hell out of here before we wind up like him.'

Something flashed out of the sky and the asteroid was struck a second time. A fresh plume of grey dust and ice shot up from its surface.

'I'm going to perform a fast burn,' announced Nancy, her voice taking on a hysterical edge. Ty twisted around to look at her, but all he could see was the side of her helmet. Suddenly it seemed important to be able to see her face. 'Then I'm going to decelerate for thirty seconds,' she added. 'Got it?'

'Got it.'

If I were the swarm, he thought, *I'd collect chunks of rock from somewhere and accelerate them close to the speed of light.* All it would take was a simple railgun technology; the rocks didn't even need to be very big to cause a lot of damage once they had reached relativistic speeds.

'Three, two, one,' Nancy counted aloud, and a second later Ty felt his heart and lungs press up against his spine while a seemingly enormous force flattened his head back against his seat. The asteroid's surface disappeared out of his peripheral view as the launcher blasted away from it.

Thirty seconds. Nancy hit a second button and cut off

the burn. The intense pressure lifted from Ty's body and they were weightless once more. He twisted around and saw how the asteroid had already shrunk into the distance. Even as he watched, something slammed into it for a third time, cleaving it like a lump of dried clay smashed with a hammer.

'Jesus and Buddha,' Nancy swore, sounding like she was on the verge of crying with relief. 'They can hear us again! I've got a channel open to the *Mjollnir*, Nathan. I think we're going to make it.'

'Are they ready to jump out of the system?' asked Ty.

'I seriously fucking hope so. They're under attack, but no direct hits so far. Deceleration burn in ten, so get ready.'

Ty grabbed hold of his armrests as the launcher swivelled round in a slow, graceful arc until it was facing back the way they had come. *No direct hits.* He stared at the expanding cloud of debris that was now all that remained of the asteroid. If the *Mjollnir* had been hit by anything like that, there would be nothing left of it.

'Here we go,' said Nancy. 'In three . . . two . . . *one.*'

The launcher had not been built with comfort in mind. When the rockets cut out half a minute later, Ty twisted around to see the dirty-grey and black exterior of the Freehold starship fast expanding towards them. He could also make out a faint blue shimmer around the frigate's drive-spines. More split-second bursts decelerated the launcher yet further, and soon the yawning mouth of a forward bay swallowed them up.

The bay doors slid shut over their heads and grappling arms reached out from the deck, locking on to the launcher and drawing it down into a cradle. Ty started to unstrap himself.

A deep thrumming sound rapidly resolved itself into a rush of air, but Ty waited until his suit gave him the signal before he pulled his helmet off, tasting welded metal and sweat as he sucked in a breath. He wanted nothing more in that moment than to get out of his suit. As he kicked away from the launcher and grabbed a handhold on the wall of the bay, he glanced across at Nancy, also with her helmet off, her face drenched in sweat.

'I'm sorry about Cesar,' was all he could say to her.

She shrugged, staring away across the bay. 'If it wasn't for him, we'd never have got that thing into the launcher.' She met his eyes. 'But if that thing's body isn't as valuable as you seem to think it is, he might have died for nothing. Can you live with that thought?'

He returned her gaze. 'Whatever it is the swarm's after, it's inside that Atn,' he replied. 'I promise you.'

ELEVEN

Several days after Dakota's encounter with Trader, the Magi ship that had resurrected her delivered her to the world known to humans as Derinkuyu, a major Skelite colony twenty-three light-years beyond the Consortium's borders.

The Skelites carved entire cities out of the deep bedrock of their worlds, creating warrens that extended far below the surface. Before the departure of the Shoal, the complex in which Dakota now found herself had been home to a small population of a few thousand human beings plus a smattering of Bandati and even, to her surprise, one or two Rafters drifting in their pressurized tanks. With the arrival of coreship refugees, the population had quadrupled overnight, spreading out to take up every last available inch of spare room in what Dakota suspected would be a claustrophobe's worst nightmare.

She wandered through a long, echoing concourse, its high arched ceiling supported by fluted stone pillars also carved directly out of the rock. Somewhere in the maze of shanty dwellings here was the Magi navigator who had agreed to act as her liaison.

Most of the dwellings she passed were constructed from scraps of plastic and metal, and even rough slabs of precariously balanced stone that looked like all they needed was a good hard push to send them tumbling onto their occupants with deadly results. Light came from a combination of glow globes and what she suspected was a bioluminescent fungus spread in dense patches across the ceiling and upper parts of the towering pillars. Her nose was tickled by the varied smells from the dozens of cooking fires that splashed pale flickering light across the lower reaches of the pillars, carrying the scent of spices and blackened meat. She wondered if any of the people sleeping and talking and eating all around her really believed that the rescue they were almost certainly hoping for would ever come.

'Miss Merrick?'

She turned to see a figure looming out of the darkness, and knew immediately this was the man she was looking for. The figure resolved into an impossibly tall black man in his late twenties, with the ubiquitous shaved skull of a machine-head.

'Miss Merrick,' he repeated, now taking her hand with a smile. 'Leroy Rivers. It's wonderful to meet you at last.'

'I should be thanking *you*,' she replied. 'I wasn't sure I'd be able to find my way around this place without help.'

'Nobody else knows you're here?' There was a precision in the way he spoke, each word and syllable meticulously phrased.

She shook her head. 'You're the only one I've told.'

Rivers bent down towards her a little, and dropped his voice. 'We should not delay. It's not safe to stay around here one second longer than we need to. I have transport nearby, and I managed to acquire one of the items you asked for at very short notice.'

She nodded, and he led her towards a small open car with tractor wheels, parked close to a pillar. 'You're part of the relief operation?' she asked.

He laughed. 'That is the idea, but it's like using a teaspoon to bail out a sinking ship. All we've managed to bring here so far are a few emergency fabricators, and yet there are people dying of diseases that are supposed to be extinct.'

'I see.'

'There is not enough room for all the refugees,' he continued, climbing into the driver's seat. 'We really need to expand into newer tunnels, but that means further negotiations with the Skelites, which is proving difficult, I'm afraid. There's been a lot of clashes between the original settlers and the refugees, but the Skelites refuse to open up more space.'

'Why not?'

'They want star-drives seeded from the Tierra cache,' he explained. 'That's their basic condition before they'll enter into any kind of negotiation.'

Dakota nodded. 'Right. I understand. They lost the coreship network along with us and the Bandati, so of course they don't want to have to rely on the Fleet or anyone else.'

She climbed into the passenger's seat, beside Rivers. He turned to look at her with an earnest expression. 'I will be straight with you, Miss Merrick. When you told me you wanted to come here, helping you find someone I've never heard of was not my first priority. But your influence at Ocean's Deep is enormous, and if the Skelites here were to think they might get their star drive, it could take a lot of the pressure off. At present it doesn't take much to start a riot here, and before you know it there's another dozen dead bodies. People generally need to know things are going to get better.'

It took an effort of will for Dakota to meet Rivers's hopeful gaze. Things, she wanted to tell him, were just as bad everywhere. There were a thousand Leroy Rivers scattered over an area of space so vast it was difficult even to contemplate, all of them desperate to ward off a coming catastrophe.

She smiled in what she hoped was a convincing manner. 'I can't make any promises, Mr Rivers, because things are bad all over. But I'll see what I can do when I get back to Ocean's Deep.'

Rivers nodded and exhaled noisily, like a man who had just been unburdened of a heavy load. He turned to her again and smiled gently. 'Thank you for telling me that.' He reached down and activated a switch, and the car's treads ground noisily.

She studied him. 'You didn't believe a word of what I just said, did you?'

'No,' he said, with a broad grin. 'Not a word. But I still had to ask.'

Dakota looked away, biting her lip in shame.

'Something for you,' he said, pulling a plastic bag, filled with something that clanked noisily, out from under the dashboard.

He passed it over one-handed. Inside she found two short metallic tubes and something that looked like the grip of a gun.

'The weapon is modular,' Rivers explained. 'All you need to do is snap the components together. The locals call these things "rat-catchers". A small, high-capacity fusion battery housed in the grip powers the plasma bolts. Like I said, it's the best I could get hold of at short notice. But you're going to have to be careful about how you use it. They have a nasty habit of going wrong if they get overheated.'

She gave him a doubtful look. 'Wrong, how?'

'The battery is a fabricator hack job that bypasses the programmed safety limits. If it gets too hot, it blows up.'

She stared at him. 'And this is seriously the best you could get?'

'Weapons of *any* kind are in very short supply here. The second-stage Skelites themselves aren't exactly lacking in armaments, but they're less than keen on supplying them to us intruders.'

'So they're all home-made efforts like this?' she asked, emptying the bag's contents on the seat between her knees.

'Yes. I think that particular one came from a fabricator originally designed for making customized kitchen components.'

Rivers put the car into reverse, and the tractor treads crunched across the stone floor as he guided it carefully between the close-packed hovels and sleeping bodies, veering close enough to outstretched limbs at times to send Dakota's heart leaping towards her mouth. She studied the weapon's components and then carefully slotted them together, the grip sliding in last. When she held it in her upturned palm it felt light, insubstantial, more like a toy than a real weapon. Hugh Moss would have access to far greater firepower than this.

'I don't mean to pry,' said Rivers, 'but you said at one point you thought you might have trouble finding your way around on your own . . . ?'

'I can't manipulate data the way I used to, Mr Rivers. I'm not much more than a passenger on the Magi ships these days.'

Rivers nodded, looking embarrassed. 'I'm sorry for asking. It seems so many of us are suffering from the bends.'

She frowned. 'The what?'

'That's what some of the other navigators are calling

it now,' Rivers explained. 'The bends, or neural burnout
– a sickness from diving too deep into the world of data
contained inside every Magi ship.'

'Really.'

'I've not been affected myself,' Rivers continued. 'But
I suspect it may only be a matter of time.'

'How long have you been a Magi-class navigator?'

'Six months,' he replied. 'Most navigators start suffering the ill effects after seven or eight months.' His smile
faded a little. 'We should be going now. I found you a
place to stay on a lower level.'

Before long they were trundling through a series of
endlessly winding passageways. Steps were carved into
the stone on either side, every thirty metres or so, leading up to open galleries cut into the side of the passageways, just below the ceiling. Terran flora was everywhere,
although much of it had clearly been engineered
specially for an underground existence. Vines dropped
down from the ceiling to brush against their heads as
they drove on, while dwarf trees – oak, ash and a few
unidentifiable hybrids – lined every district they passed
through. These trees barely came up to shoulder height,
and made Dakota feel like she and Rivers were a pair of
giants going out for a Sunday drive.

Business districts merged into residential areas, the
ceiling sometimes dipping so low that Dakota would
have had to stoop if she disembarked, while at other

times it soared to cathedral proportions, with tiers of recessed homes and businesses rising up and up, all interconnected by carved stone staircases. They moved through a cornucopia of odours, those of food cooked on open griddles in busy market places, the fragrance of pale-leaved flowers and the rankness of thousands of human bodies living for years at a time in this deep subterranean darkness. And as they moved from one district via a downwards-spiralling ramp to a lower district, the air became ever hotter, denser and damper.

'Tell me everything you know about Moss,' Dakota asked at one point.

'He turned up here slightly less than five weeks ago and established himself extremely rapidly. It's my understanding that he trains what are intended to be either bodyguards or assassins, depending on your source of information. Killers, certainly,' Rivers added, as they hurtled on.

'Assassins? But to assassinate who?'

'Well, at first the rumours were that Moss was training soldiers to act as protection for black marketeers in Derinkuyu. Then it turned out he was killing off all the black marketeers instead, and taking over in their place. Keep in mind,' he added, 'that much of this remains mere rumour and conjecture. He also supposedly has some arrangement with a tribe of second-stage Skelites living in burrows at a much lower level than this one. It's believed he's aiding them in their war with a neighbouring tribe.'

'What do you mean by "second-stage" Skelites?'

'Skelites go through three distinct stages of development during their lives. The first stage is born in pools of volcanically heated water on the surface. Those who survive go on to stage two, which is large, aggressive, extremely territorial and technologically innovative, though their existence is spent mostly in subterranean burrows like these. Those who survive their constant wars then enter a third stage, where they return to the surface and spend the rest of their existence reproducing and engaging in what I guess you might call intellectual pursuits.' He glanced briefly at Dakota. 'The second-stage Skelites are the only ones who have any contact with other species. And, of course, they're the ones who are demanding their own starships, since—'

Rivers never got to finish his sentence.

Dakota was not immediately aware that there had been an explosion – or that the car they were riding in had been pushed up from the floor of a tunnel with sufficient force to catapult it several metres into the air. Instead she now found herself some distance away from the car's burning wreckage, with no clear memory of how she had got from *there* to *here*. There were distant screams and shouts, and small fires blazed dimly through a spreading cloud of black smoke.

She sat up, looking down to see that the black liquid of her filmsuit had spilled out to protect her. Her clothes were torn and ragged, but she herself wasn't even scratched.

She jumped up and ran back to the wrecked vehicle.

Rivers must have died instantly: his head was twisted at an impossible angle, while his eyes stared sightlessly up from out of the wreckage. Dakota looked all around and observed that the tunnel was tall and narrow, with an arching roof high overhead. Galleries ran along the side walls, set back just below the ceiling. Two stone bridges crossed overhead and connected these galleries – like so much in Derinkuyu, carved directly from the living rock. Thick black oily smoke pooled under the ceiling itself, just above the level of the twin bridges.

She dropped to her knees and scrabbled around with her hands beneath the wreckage of the car, then ducked lower until her chin almost touched the ground. Peering past Rivers's corpse, she finally spotted the home-made pulse-rifle. She flattened herself to the ground and slid beneath the shattered vehicle until she could grab hold of it.

A low *whoosh* came from somewhere close by, and through the thick smoke she could see the glow of flames billowing from somewhere further along the tunnel. But the smoke was beginning to clear a little as it dispersed in both directions along the passageway, and she now saw a figure emerge, moving with deliberate purpose towards her.

Dakota pulled herself around the other side of the wreck until it was between her and the approaching figure, and there hurriedly reassembled the rifle. She kept it close to her chest and raised herself to a low crouch, wondering which was the best way to run, just as the figure came close enough for her to make it out.

The man bearing down on her had four arms: the extra pair were situated slightly below and behind what she presumed to be his original limbs. Each one of his four hands gripped some kind of weapon; she saw a wicked-looking blade, a sub-machine gun and two force-pistols. A broad belt slung from shoulder to hip was laden with cartridges, throwing knives and more pistols. She watched his face twist into a mask of fury at the same time as he raised the sub-machine gun and pulled the trigger.

Frozen until this moment, she ran off to one side, heading for a staircase that led up to one of the galleries. She was followed by a dull clinking noise, and it took her a moment to identify this as the sound of bullets striking her filmsuit before dropping to the ground, rendered harmless as their kinetic force was absorbed.

She took the steps three at a time. Bystanders who had come out on to the side galleries to see what was going on rapidly scattered as she got higher.

Four-arms stayed next to the wrecked car, but kept firing as she climbed. The bullets tinkled to the ground in a steady stream, which merely caused her would-be assassin to scream with rage.

Once she'd reached the gallery itself, she ducked out of sight. It was deserted now, but the entire passageway rang with the wail of frightened voices.

Dakota stole a glance over the side of the waist-high

wooden balustrade alongside the gallery, and saw that the assassin was standing directly under one of the two stone bridges. He fired off a few more shots and she ducked down again.

Leaning on one knee, she balanced the plastic rifle on the rim of the balustrade and aimed it directly at the underside of the bridge immediately above the assassin. She pulled the trigger, half expecting the weapon to fail completely.

Her vision turned black for a moment, before her filmsuit compensated for the overwhelming flash. When her sight returned, she had a bird's-eye view of the bridge tumbling downwards in ruin.

Four-arms wasn't nearly fast enough to get out of the way in time, and so disappeared under a mound of boulders and gravel, along with the car and Rivers's corpse.

Dakota glanced down at where her rifle should be, and found all that was left was the handgrip containing the battery, along with several centimetres of shattered plastic barrel.

So much for home-made weapons, she reflected, pulling herself upright. At least the battery hadn't blown as well.

She looked around, and could still hear the voices of people talking and yelling somewhere out of sight. Already a siren was sounding in the distance. She had no idea if four-arms had come alone, but in case he had any allies she needed to find something else to defend herself with. The filmsuit, however effective, could not protect her indefinitely.

Clearly, Dakota realized belatedly, Hugh Moss had found her first.

She made for the surviving bridge and ran across it, still holding on to the shattered rifle. It might be useless now, but someone at a distance might not be able to tell straight away. Another long tunnel stretched ahead, lit by glow-globes.

Another figure came running towards her, flames licking around his clenched fists. His head was smooth and shaved, and a satchel was slung across his bare chest. Even from a distance it was obvious there was something strange about his skin texture; it looked rather like the armoured hide of some ancient predator. He came to a stop and tipped his head back, his chest rising as if he were drawing in one enormous breath. When he lowered his head again, an enormous whoosh of flame was released from between his lips. At the same instant he drew one flaming hand back to throw something at her.

Dakota spun round and began to run back in the other direction just as a terrific explosion of light erupted behind her. She threw herself over one side of the bridge and dropped to the passageway below, just as a rush of intense heat enveloped her. She didn't even feel the impact as she landed.

She then headed downwards, following the gradually descending slope of the narrow street for lack of any better idea. She kept her arms and legs pumping furiously, ignoring the faces that sometimes loomed out of the dim light of successive tunnels and passageways, at first looking curious, then terrified as they glanced behind her. She didn't need a backward glance to know the burning man was still on her trail. Although the detonation hadn't physically harmed her, her clothes – unprotected by her filmsuit – were smoking and burning.

The street veered sharply to the right, and she threw herself around the corner, then ducked into one of the first doorways she saw. Maybe she could lose herself.

She found herself at the top of a steep and narrow stairwell, and followed it down to yet another vaulted passageway with bridges arching overhead. Taking several side entrances led her further downwards, as she ran on in her search for a suitable place to hide.

Something now rumbled from deep within the rock, growing louder the deeper she went. She soon found herself in a confined space whose roof was so low she had to almost bend double to make her way across it. Dakota realized she was now truly lost, and had to fight back her panic. She tried to connect with Derinkuyu's open access networks through her implants, but they responded with error messages that were not evident when she had met with Rivers earlier.

It had to be because of Moss. Somehow he had known she was here in the system, so he had engineered a crash in the networks servicing the local population.

Passing through a door on the other side of the

cramped space, she suddenly found herself entering a vast, cavernlike area almost as extensive as the one she had first encountered Rivers in. But this one seemed empty of residents, and the air was filled with a heavy, thundering roar that suggested a subterranean cataract.

High up above her extended a curving ceiling painted in rich dark colours, adorned with a swirl of stars and shapes that gradually revealed themselves as a depiction of coreships and planets: a giant tableau that appeared to depict the earliest years of Derinkuyu's human settlement.

Across the huge chamber, a waterfall gushed out of one stony wall, spilling a dozen metres into a subterranean lake stirred up by a whirlpool several metres across. A dozen metal walkways, at different heights and interconnected by ladders, were suspended by cables from the ceiling. They crossed from one side of the cavern to the other and, even from where she stood, Dakota could see they gave access to yet more passageways all around.

The entrance to one such walkway was right in front of her, and in the centre of it stood Hugh Moss, with an insane grin spread across his calloused features.

Dakota turned and saw the fire-breather enter the giant cavern behind her. He stopped for a moment, as if to catch his breath, then, grinning at her widely, began digging deep inside his satchel. Shortly he withdrew a wrinkled black lump that looked like a large seed of some kind.

Flames suddenly began to lick around his hands and

forearms, whereupon the seed popped and hissed, and then began to glow.

Pulling his hand back, he pitched the burning seed directly towards her. Dakota watched mesmerized for a second, as the object arced through the air towards her. She turned, throwing herself on to the nearby walkway, its metal surface clanging noisily with her every slamming footstep.

The explosion lifted her off her feet and sent her sprawling. Dakota shrieked, and twisted around on to her back just in time to see the fire-breather stepping on to the same walkway. Moss hadn't moved from where he stood.

Without really considering what she was doing, she hurled the broken remains of the pulse-rifle at the fire-breather.

The ensuing detonation ripped away the platform section where he had been standing. Dakota grabbed hold of the handrail while the entire walkway buckled under her, swaying wildly as some of its supporting cables snapped. By the time the flimsy bridge had stopped swinging and bouncing, she caught a last glimpse of the fire-breather's broken corpse being sucked into the watery depths below.

She looked back to the ledge beyond, but it was too far to jump. And no way in hell was she taking her chances with the whirlpool.

'Dakota Merrick!' Moss screeched. 'Do you remember our last conversation?'

'You'll have to remind me, Hugh,' she yelled back, her voice almost lost amid the roar of the surging water.

'I promised you that if you ever stood between me and Trader in Faecal Matter of Animals, I would do terrible things to you – things that would make you wish I had only killed you. I said, I believe, that I would make a symphony of your pain.'

'Well, we need to talk about that, Hugh.'

'What is there to talk about?'

'I need you to back off. I need Trader because he can help me stop the war between the Shoal and the Emissaries. If you don't, there's a good chance we're *all* going to die.'

She heard him laugh, and watched as he took a few steps closer to her. 'Are you appealing to my sense of decency? I'm disappointed, Miss Merrick. I thought you knew me better.'

'I'll kill you if I have to, Hugh.'

'You do realize that Trader is manipulating you, surely?' Moss moved closer. 'He's never honoured an agreement in his life. You know, I rather thought he would find a way to send you after me eventually. In fact I almost hoped this day would come.'

Fuck it, Dakota thought to herself, then hurtled towards him with a yell.

Almost at once she felt a powerful shock spasming through her body, an electric jolt that set her nerve endings on fire. Something crackled faintly just in front of her, staining the air itself a barely perceptible shade of blue.

The pain receded and she found she was caught in a shaped-field bubble. She had unwittingly run straight over a set of field-generators fixed to the floor of the walkway.

Dakota tried to stand up, but the ensuing jolt of pain was so enormous, that it forced her back on to her knees.

She waited, with a heavy, cold feeling in her gut, as Moss knelt down beside her. The shaped fields then snapped off at almost the same moment she felt her film-suit finally drain itself back inside her body. Moss reached out and touched her shoulder. She jerked away as she felt a stinging sensation there.

'Get it over with,' Dakota seethed. 'If you're going to kill me, then kill me. Just don't stand around gloating.'

'Kill you?' Moss affected confusion. 'Always that desire for death. Why would I kill you?' He gave her a lopsided grin. 'Tell me, was I right? Did Trader send you here specially to keep me from chasing him?'

'What makes you think that?'

'I can't think of any other reason you would have bothered to come here. The last time we met, I gave you my word that I wouldn't destroy Ocean's Deep, and in return you gave me Trader. That should have been the last time we ever saw each other – and yet here you are.'

'I already told you why, Hugh. I'm not going to repeat myself.'

Moss rocked back on his heels, a thoughtful

expression crossing his face. Dakota now had a good view of the long knife he gripped casually in one hand, poised close enough to slash across her exposed throat.

'Would you say I'm a man of my word, Miss Merrick?'

'I don't know what you mean.'

'Let me explain, then. I once gave you my word over Ocean's Deep. Did I honour our deal?'

'Yes,' Dakota admitted, forcing the word out.

'Then please allow me another question. Do you think Trader's the type to honour his promises?'

Dakota ground her teeth. If she made any move, he could cut her throat in an instant. 'No . . . no, I don't.'

'Then let me suggest a deal of my own, one we can both walk away from alive and feeling satisfied.'

She stared at him with an expression like a trapped animal and said nothing.

'Whatever Trader has told you,' he continued regardless, 'he *will* betray you. That's his nature. So when that time comes, you should really try and have some kind of advantage over him. Now, you gave me the resources I needed to track his ship anywhere within our galaxy.'

She licked her lips. 'Go on.'

'Allow me, Dakota, to give you in turn the means to control his ship at will. Observe.'

Dakota felt that familiar tingle in the back of her head that told her a large piece of data had just been dumped into her implants, whereupon she remembered Moss was himself a machine-head now. She discovered a moment later that she had come into possession of a complete command structure for a Shoal yacht, entirely configurable to her own needs.

She looked at him with an incredulous expression. 'Why, Hugh? Why are you giving this to me?'

'Because in exchange you will promise never to return, and to always, *always* leave me in peace. I believe you will now give me your word, and I will believe you when you give it, regardless of this particular transgression.'

'No,' she shook her head, 'it's not that simple. There's something else you're not telling me.'

He stood up now and looked down at her. 'Very well, let me put it this way. Trader's great skill is in surviving by treachery and lies. I've come close to catching up with him in the past, but he always finds a way to escape me. When he betrays you – and he will – you will have the advantage. Use it to destroy him, Dakota. Save the galaxy the trouble of letting him live.'

'And if he doesn't?'

Moss laughed. 'Will you promise me something, Dakota? When he turns on you, will you put an end to him so he can never turn on you again?'

'And you'd let me go?'

'But of course,' Moss replied, sounding almost magnanimous. He stepped away from her, and sheathed his knife.

She staggered slowly upright, breathing hard.

'So.' He smiled again, in a leathery splitting of his face

like the wide yawn of a hungry snake. 'Do we have an agreement?'

She thought over her options. Would Trader even be able to tell if she was lying?

'You're serious about this?' she asked, licking her lips.

'Quite, quite serious.'

'Then I'll do it,' she replied, and realized with a shock that she meant it.

TWELVE

Corso glanced up at the sound of helicopter blades cutting through the howl of the wind. He looked at Breisch, directly in front of him, then back up through the transparent window in the roof of their tent in time to see a shape pass across the face of one of Redstone's moons.

'Concentrate on your breathing,' instructed Breisch, without opening his eyes.

They knelt facing each other, on the antique rug spread out beneath them. The tent itself was constructed from multiple layers of highly resilient but extremely light nano-carbon, and was big enough to house up to half a dozen men with plenty of room to spare. Yet, once packed away, it was light and small enough to carry on one man's back.

Corso closed his eyes and focused on the thump of his own heartbeat, like a wet meat clock hammering out the seconds remaining before the fight. The sea hissed against the shore a few metres away. He recalled the words Breisch had repeated endlessly, until it became a kind of mantra: *Death is inevitable.* The key to survival lay only in giving up the fear of dying. Conversely, the key to victory lay in exploiting an opponent's own fear of death.

Corso opened his eyes again, unable to concentrate. Instead he studied the man opposite. Breisch was hard and wiry, with gaunt features, a veteran of a hundred challenges, which made him either one of the deadliest or luckiest fighters alive on Redstone, depending on whom you asked.

It had been a considerable surprise to him when Breisch had calmly admitted, shortly after the beginning of their professional relationship, that he fully expected to die while taking part in a challenge.

'It's better than dying old and infirm,' he had stated, in the same calm, clear tone he always spoke in. 'And, frankly, I consider it vastly preferable.'

'But you don't have to take part in challenges any more, if you don't want to,' Corso had argued. Despite his long tally of violent victories, Breisch had never requested a seat in the Senate, claiming to have no interest in politics. 'It's hardly like anyone would blame you, after so much time. You could still honourably refuse.'

'Because I'm old?' Breisch smiled more easily than anyone Corso knew. 'Even now, people still issue me challenges, because they want to be the one who finally takes me down. And one day, when I'm old enough, they'll get their wish. I can't imagine anything worse than retiring to some quiet life of public service. Better to go out fighting, don't you think?'

Corso had long since got over the irony that Breisch had once trained both of the Mansell brothers, who had been part of the fateful expedition to Nova Arctis. He had since worked hard to put his resentment and anger aside, and to accept that Breisch was not responsible for the actions of either Kieran Mansell or his psychopathic brother Udo – only for the quality of their combat skills.

A little while later, they began practising some basic moves on the broken shore outside the tent, the stars clear and sharp in the evening sky.

The old man lunged at Corso with a wicked-looking blade, constantly feinting in different directions and throwing kicks and punches when they were least expected. They were both dressed lightly despite the freezing weather, so that nothing restricted their movements.

Despite his exertions, Corso could feel the cold seeping deep into his bones, and the sound of his breathing was like a death rattle as it emerged from the breather mask strapped over his lower face. He knew his fighting skills had improved vastly over the last few months, but he didn't allow himself to forget that perpetual expression of disgust Breisch had worn throughout the first weeks of their training.

Breisch feinted again and Corso anticipated his next

move, darting to one side and turning at the same time to slash towards the old man's neck with a dull-edged blade. Before he got the chance, Breisch had responded with a backwards kick that sent Corso sprawling on to the frozen gravel.

Corso grunted as he pulled himself up. The old man was driving him even harder than usual.

Breisch looked down at him with a satisfied grin. 'I thought maybe you were getting too distracted, but you still did better than I thought you would.' He reached down with one hand and helped his pupil stand.

After a while they went back inside, Breisch warming a couple of high-protein meals on a hotplate, then retiring to his sleeping mat to rest before the coming challenge. Corso felt too wired-up to do the same.

This would be his tenth challenge since Dakota had departed, and Breisch's training was the only reason he had survived them. So far he had not been obliged to fight anyone else who also had the benefit of Breisch's intensive training, and with any luck he would never need to.

When it was almost time for the fight to start, Corso heard the sound of engines coming closer. He pulled on some thermal gear that would keep out the worst of the cold, and snapped a fresh breather mask over his face before stepping outside.

He could see half a dozen helicopters parked on a flat

area about a half kilometre inland, under the shade of a canopy tree whose massive trunk reared up for almost two hundred metres. This was a popular destination for Freeholders intent on slaughtering each other in order to gain wealth, power, women, or any combination thereof.

He watched as a balloon-wheeled truck came rolling up towards him, disgorging two passengers similarly swaddled in cold weather gear. One he recognized as Marcus Kenley, the Senate's Speaker, a round-faced man with thin grey whiskers visible around the sides of his breather mask. The other was Lucius Hilgendorf, the head of State Security under the post-coup administration, and by far one of the most dangerous men Corso had ever encountered. Above his mask, his eyes glowered like a snake whose tail had just been trodden on.

'Lucas,' said Kenley, stepping forward and shaking his hand warmly.

Like Corso, Kenley was a moderate in the Senate. Hilgendorf, who was anything but moderate, merely nodded. Kenley's job here was to act as Corso's representative both inside and outside of the ring of combat, which essentially boiled down to making sure the other side did not cheat. Hilgendorf was there to play a similar role for Corso's opponent.

'Senator Jarret has asked me to make an offer,' said Hilgendorf, stepping up to Corso. 'He wants to know if you're willing to negotiate a non-lethal outcome.'

'What you mean is, you're willing to let me live *if* I agree to surrender without a fight and automatically relinquish my Senate seat and my vote.' Corso smiled grimly and shook his head. 'Please tell Senator Jarret that if he'd wanted a "non-lethal solution", he shouldn't have issued his challenge in the first place.'

Hilgendorf was anything but a patient man. 'Senator Jarret's a war veteran and a recognized Hero of the State. Maybe you should take some time to reconsider before making any snap decisions, Senator. You're standing on pretty thin ice these days.'

'Unless you've got a serious offer to make,' intervened Kenley, 'you should remain silent, Mr Hilgendorf.'

Corso raised one hand. 'It's okay, Marcus, it's only protocol. Mr Hilgendorf's just here on a formality, isn't that right?' he said, looking Hilgendorf directly in the eye.

'We're offering you an opportunity to step down before you get hurt,' Hilgendorf insisted. 'After all, none of your previous opponents possessed the . . . *unique* skills you and Senator Jarret both share.'

Corso frowned, momentarily thrown off-balance.

'Then I'll extend the same courtesy to Mr Jarret,' he replied, unsure exactly what Hilgendorf had meant. 'If he throws in his glove, I'll let him leave here alive. Otherwise, you can tell him I look forward to meeting him in combat.'

Behind his mask, Hilgendorf's expression seemed to freeze in place. 'Very well, then. I'll pass your decision back to him.'

'You can take the truck, Mr Hilgendorf,' said Kenley. 'We'll walk to the meeting ground.' Kenley cast a questioning look at Corso, who nodded his assent.

Hilgendorf turned away without another word, and climbed back into the truck. A moment later the vehicle's caterpillar treads gripped the shattered stone beneath it, and headed back the way it had come.

'Fun ride on the way here?' asked Corso.

'How could you tell?' Kenley grumbled. 'Look . . . in all seriousness, Jarret isn't like anyone else you've been up against. He's got a hell of a reputation in the combat ring. You must know that, right?'

'And I don't, is that it?'

Kenley started to say something, then seemed to change his mind. He nodded along the frozen shore. 'Care to take a stroll?'

Corso glanced back at the tent, where Breisch was still resting. 'It'd be warmer inside.'

'Please,' Kenley insisted. 'Indulge an old man's intense paranoia.'

Corso shrugged, and they began to walk parallel to the waves beating against the shoreline. In the distance, a lighting rig was being set up at the combat ring, and soon sent beams of blazing brilliance slicing through the freezing mist that clung to the terrain further inland. The voices of the work teams racing to get everything ready in time carried to them across the still air.

Kenley stopped after a minute and turned to face

Corso. 'There are rumours that Legislate forces are planning something at the Tierra cache.'

'I guess bad news gets about fast,' Corso replied, feeling weary. 'Okay, they're not just rumours. We found smuggled shipments of armaments being taken to the research base there. There's a new batch of technical and research staff just arrived there too, and I'm not sure I can even bring myself to tell you just how many of them I think are Legislate agents.'

'But surely there must be something you can do,' Kenley protested. 'You're in charge of the Peacekeeper Authority.'

'Yeah, but nobody elected me. And I was only accepted at first because everyone I dealt with was shit-scared of so much as sneezing in Dakota Merrick's direction. Everything went downhill once she left. And now we've managed to speed up the production of new superluminal drives, it's just a matter of time before someone decides to make a grab for the cache.'

'You make it sound like there's going to be a war.'

There already is a war, Corso thought. Yet most people seemed unable to grasp the notion that a conflict happening thousands of light-years away could possibly impinge upon them. Far fewer seemed to appreciate the enormous danger they were all facing.

'The way things are looking, it's going to be a pretty one-sided war.' He lowered his voice, even though there was no one nearby who could possibly hear them over the crashing of the surf. 'Did you find out who ordered the arrest of Martinez and his senior officers?'

Kenley nodded. 'It was Jarret, after he arranged a quorum of senators through a series of back-room deals. I don't have any hard evidence, but I'm very, *very* sure he's got his hands deep in the Legislate's pockets. More than that, he has someone working for him on board the *Mjollnir*.'

Corso stopped and stared at him. 'Who?'

'His name's Simenon. Martinez's second in command.'

Corso's mask made a harsh metallic sound as he sucked in his breath. 'Damn.'

They started walking again. 'We have people on the frigate, too,' Kenley continued, 'so we have some idea what happened. The quorum sent Simenon a directive that put him in charge and gave him the authority to throw Martinez, and any of his senior officers who didn't comply, in the brig, as well as putting the remains your man Driscoll discovered under lock and key until the *Mjollnir* got back to Redstone.'

'And you think the Legislate is secretly backing Jarret?'

'I picked up a rumour that the *Mjollnir*'s next stop after here is Sol. A military R&D base on Earth's moon went silent a week back, and there's good reason to believe that's where they're going to take the remains of the Atn. They're stopping here first so they can replace the crew with more of their own people.'

'Under Simenon's command, I presume.'

Kenley nodded.

'Idiots, fucking *idiots*. All this time wasted, and we could have cracked that damn Atn open to see what's inside.'

'The thing I don't understand is why Jarret would get into bed with the Legislate like this,' said Kenley. 'He despises them and everything they stand for. It just doesn't make sense.'

'Look, we're still losing territory to the Uchidans. The whole reason for the expedition to Nova Arctis was because of pressure to found a new Freehold colony. With the whole galaxy potentially open to us, there's now an even bigger pressure to try again somewhere a lot farther away. My commandeering the *Mjollnir* gave Jarret the perfect excuse to call me out, and, if he wins, jurisdiction over the frigate then passes across to his side of the Senate House. That means control over the terms of settlement, once a new system is located, stays on their side.'

Kenley nodded, understanding. 'And then we'd be out in the cold, wouldn't we? But that still doesn't explain his connection with the Legislate.'

'The Legislate wants the remains Driscoll found, right? With me out of the way, Jarret's going to be within his rights to hand them over. And founding a colony is a very expensive business, remember. Lots of motivation there to climb right into bed with the Legislate and get busy.'

This was assuming Whitecloud had really found something significant, and not just a pile of million-year-old junk. But Corso tried not to think about that possibility too much.

'And you really think the other side of the House is going to just roll over and play dead if you win tonight?'

Corso breathed hard. 'I don't know. Maybe not. But at least, with Jarret out of the way, they're going to have to figure out some other strategy that doesn't make it so damn obvious they're in cahoots with the Legislate.'

'I think you'd better be prepared for the worst, Lucas. Things could get very ugly, even with Jarret dead.'

Corso studied Kenley's face. 'You have something in mind?'

'I think at the very least we should set up safe-houses around Unity. As somewhere we can retreat to if necessary.'

'You really think it'll come to that?'

'Worse things have happened.'

Corso nodded. 'You're talking about another coup?'

Kenley's expression was grim. 'Just tell me one thing. Are you absolutely certain whatever Driscoll found out there wouldn't actually be safer in the Legislate's hands?'

Corso laughed. 'You weren't there in Ocean's Deep, Marcus. It was a total travesty. I don't think the Legislate could have botched it more if they'd tried.'

Kenley reached out and put a hand on Corso's arm, halting him. 'Lucas . . . were you aware Jarret was trained by Breisch?'

Corso stared at him and remembered what Hilgendorf had said. 'You're certain about this?'

'Very.'

'But Breisch never . . .' he paused. *Breisch never told me.* Corso's hands curled into fists at his sides.

'Jarret is the kind of man who prefers not to pick on people his own size, if you follow me, Senator,' Kenley explained. 'He has a reputation for treachery.'

'I know that. But Breisch . . .'

'The old man has a strong sense of personal ethics, and he was deeply offended by the way Jarret misused the skills he'd learned. He finds people with influence in the Senate and first arranges for the murder of someone very close to them,' Kenley continued. 'Then he leaves just enough clues to show he was responsible, so the target winds up calling him out for a fight. Sound familiar?'

Corso heard a whine like the jaws of a trap shutting tight around him. Bull Northcutt had murdered Corso's fiancée years before, for the exact same reason.

'But why didn't Breisch warn me?'

'Maybe,' Kenley suggested, 'he's hoping you'll kill Jarret for him.'

Harsh, pumping music floated through the air towards them from the direction of the combat ring, and Corso recognized the call. He stared back towards the tent, standing further around the curve of the bay, and decided now was not the time to confront Breisch. Anyway, by now he would be waiting at the combat ring with the rest.

He turned back to Kenley. 'Come on, Marcus. Let's get this over with.'

They turned from the shore and headed inland, finding their way along a narrow path trodden through hardy grasses and spiny plants by decades of fighters and their audiences. Corso mentally reviewed his training as they walked. There were certain tricks Breisch had taught him; now he would have to watch out for Jarret using those same ploys against him.

They ascended a steep incline and were dazzled by an eruption of light and music as they reached the crest. A casual observer, with no knowledge of Freehold customs or laws, might have concluded there was a party taking place here; in a sense there was, albeit with a deadly conclusion.

Wagers would be made, small fortunes won and lost. None of it was strictly legal, of course, but old habits died hard, and everyone knew what refusing a challenge entailed.

Huge portable heating units, scattered here and there, pumped out heat, while a speaker system filled the air with crunching martial pop; tales of the Freehold's legendary warriors and their excesses bellowed over a monotonous beat.

The audience for this challenge was sixty to seventy strong. The few women present were either wives and mistresses, or more likely whores flown in for the pleasure of the senators, military officers and hard-faced bureaucrats standing around in anticipation swilling hot beer.

The combat ring itself was a circle of open ground marked by a perimeter of hissing flares pushed deep into the soil. It extended a little over eight metres in diameter, more than enough room for two men to try their damnedest to kill each other.

A muffled cheer went up from dozens of breather-equipped throats when they saw Corso and Kenley approaching. Jarret's entourage considerably out-numbered his own, which comprised a dozen or so of his advisers and various Senate staff gathered together over to one side, a few looking distinctly uneasy. They knew what they would face if Corso died today and there was no one left to protect them in the Senate.

Corso scanned the rest of the crowd until he saw Jarret himself, standing with the bearing of a king returned from a victorious campaign, his arrogance barely masked by the tan-and-silver breather he wore over his lower face.

Corso's own senior Senate staff approached him and he was glad to see Nastazi, Velardo and Griffith all present. These three were the men Corso trusted. The rest were good enough at their jobs, but one or two of them were probably spies.

'McDade's your marshal for the challenge,' declared Nastazi. 'There's even a rumour he pulled strings in order to get the job.'

Corso nodded. 'Well, the man hates my guts, so that's hardly surprising. Anything else I should know before I murder his nephew?'

'There was a move within the Senate to block us from flying out here to witness the fight,' said Griffith, behind whom the flares hissed and spat sparks into the night. 'They cited security measures: a report that the Uchidans had got wind of the fight, and might try a strike against the Aaron peninsula while it's taking place. Be warned, they mean to fight dirty, Senator.'

Corso paused, staring out into the darkness. He was thinking of Dakota, but why had she popped into his head just now? She had already disappeared, swallowed up by the mystery of the Maker, leaving him alone and defenceless as head of the Peacekeeper Authority.

The music peaked, and he listened carefully as the address system was handed over to McDade, who began to list both parties' grievances as a precursor to the challenge itself. The next step would be to offer both himself and Jarret one last chance to back out of the contest.

'Is there any truth to that report?' Corso replied quietly to Griffith. 'Is it likely the Uchidans would use a high-profile challenge like this as an opportunity to carry out a tactical strike while everyone's looking the other way?'

'There are a dozen reports of suspected offensives every day, Senator. I imagine they just picked one of them and blew it up out of proportion. They're trying to make it look like you're disrupting the normal process of Senate business, by making a nuisance of yourself.'

'I *am* making a nuisance of myself,' Corso replied. 'That's the whole point.'

Breisch approached, moving with the kind of casual, easy grace that came from years of intensive physical training. Corso drew in a breath, forcing himself to keep calm.

'I gather Mr Kenley's spoken to you about my connection with Jarret,' said Breisch. 'I'm sorry I didn't tell you before.'

Corso couldn't keep the mixture of confusion and anger out of his voice. 'So why didn't you?'

'I made you work harder than you ever have before, Lucas. There's a part of you that always stands back, that refuses to wholly engage with the fight. You've learned, over the past few days, to put that part of yourself to one side and fight without distraction. I cannot emphasize how important a step forward that is. If I'd told you about Jarret, you would have likely fallen into a false belief system, and concluded that Jarret might be more than an even match for you.'

Breisch shook his head. 'Besides, I only trained him for a short while, and he's never picked fights he can't win. But this time is different. He's undoubtedly more skilled than most of those you've faced, but you're more than capable of defeating him.'

Corso took a moment before replying. 'I think I might have done the same in your position, but I need to know I can trust the people around me implicitly.' He reached out and took Breisch's hand and shook it. 'I want to thank you for everything you've taught me, but I won't be requiring your services any more.'

Breisch didn't seem surprised, merely nodded his head fractionally. 'I wish you well, Lucas. You exceeded my expectations.' Then he turned and walked back to join the crowds waiting for the contest to start.

McDade, now finished with his preliminary announcements, jumped down from the marshal's platform and headed over to Corso.

'Senator,' he acknowledged with a nod.

'Mr McDade, I hear you worked quite hard for the chance to be marshal tonight.'

McDade met Corso's gaze easily. 'We may not agree on many things, Senator, but you still deserve the same chance to fight for what you believe in as do any of the rest of us. I can't say I'll be sorry if you lose, but any man prepared to walk into a combat ring deserves respect, whether or not he walks back out of it.'

'Jarret's a known killer. He's murdered people who didn't have a chance of beating him. Are you sure he deserves that level of respect?'

Corso watched as McDade fought to control his temper. 'The Senate floor's the place for debate, Mr Corso,' he replied tautly, his manner suddenly much more formal. 'I'm here in my official capacity as judge and marshal of this challenge, to offer you your final opportunity to back down.'

Corso listened as McDade continued with the familiar litany: 'You may stand down from this challenge, with honour, while waiving your rights to your Senate seat and your family's inheritance. If you decline to do so, the challenge will not end until either yourself or Senator Jarret is formally pronounced deceased. Do you agree to such terms of challenge?'

'I agree to the stated terms, Mr McDade. I am both willing and of sound mind, and wish to challenge Senator Jarret to a duel to the death.'

McDade looked over at Kenley. 'Will you attest that you have heard and witnessed Senator Corso's decision?'

'I attest to the Senator's decision, and uphold his right to participate,' Kenley responded.

McDade nodded. 'Good luck, Senator,' he said finally to Corso, then glanced briefly over at Jarret, with a small smile curling up the corners of his mouth. 'Because you're going to need it this time.'

Corso stared back at him calmly, watching as McDade turned on his heel and went over to read the same terms to Jarret.

'How did it ever happen?' he asked Kenley, over the din of music and voices. 'How did they turn me into one of them?'

Kenley shrugged. 'You said yourself, the only way to beat them was at their own game. Besides, the way you're going, most of the opposition is going to wind up dead before long.'

Corso grinned at this. The copters and trucks formed

dark silhouettes against the evening sky as he looked west, towards the great swell of the ocean beyond the shore, and spotted the figure of a woman standing well apart from the rest, too far outside the pools of illumination cast by the lights for him to make her out clearly.

Somebody shouted for quiet, and people began shushing each other. The music was replaced by an angry buzzing sound as it was turned off.

McDade strode to the centre of the combat circle, and began. 'This Challenge takes place regardless of the legal restrictions placed on us by the Consortium trade treaties, and is therefore not officially recognized by our Senate.' His amplified voice rolled out across the hills beyond the canopy tree. 'However, we here, every last one of us, will attest to the God-given rights of the victor as derived from the ancient precepts of our society. We came here to escape the bloodless atheism of the Consortium and the moral corruption of our fellow human beings. We came here to build a society of warriors willing to fight for their right to participate in our democracy, and who do not constantly live in fear of death. It is my firm belief' – McDade was clearly happy for this opportunity to lecture Corso and his entourage – 'that justice and might will win out this evening, and that we will overcome our oppressors and those who stand against us, for together we are strong, and they are weak.'

A huge cheer went up from the crowd gathered around Senator Jarret.

'This challenge,' McDade continued, 'takes place because Senator Corso chose to commandeer our proud flagship the *Mjollnir* for reasons that have never been properly explained nor justified to the Senate's satisfaction. Since Senator Corso has refused to relinquish his Senate seat, and until these questions have been answered to the satisfaction of all, Senator Jarret has asked that the two of them should meet in a challenge of deadly combat. Is there anyone here with reason to believe this contest should not take place?'

There was, of course, no answer.

'All right, then,' McDade finished up. 'This is a senatorial contest, and the winner can, in turn, be challenged at any time by any citizen or non-citizen who chooses to do so.'

Corso returned his attention to Jarret and his memory flashed back to the time he had similarly faced Bull Northcutt on the shores of Fire Lake. Both men were of a piece: hair shaved close to the skull, active subdermal tattoos that recorded previous kills in graphic detail, and thickly overdeveloped muscles that hinted at steroid abuse. Jarret had stripped down to a pair of loose camouflage-style trousers and a light shirt that clung to his augmented musculature. His exposed skin glistened with thick grease that would be good for keeping the cold out for a few extra seconds. Clearly the man was gambling on an early win.

At that point, McDade stepped out of the ring and removed an antique pistol from within his own bulky winter gear. Following their cues, Jarret and Corso both stepped just inside the ring's perimeter. Two long, curved knives lay, crossed over each other, at the ring's precise centre.

McDade raised the pistol high over his head, its barrel pointing upwards. 'On my mark,' his voice boomed over the sound system.

Corso pulled off his heavy coat and threw it outside the circle. His skin wasn't greased, but he wore a tight, long-sleeved tunic made from layers of fibre that efficiently contained his body heat. Already the cold bit savagely at the exposed skin of his neck and face where it wasn't covered by the breather mask.

McDade fired a single shot high into the air, then retreated quickly back into the crowd.

Corso sprang forward, as if someone had sent an electric jolt through his body. Jarret simultaneously threw himself towards the knives and grabbed one.

It was the obvious first move for both of them to make, and Corso had been gambling on this. Instead of reaching for a knife, he aimed one booted foot at Jarret's head, connecting with a dull smack. But Jarret saw it coming at the last second, and responded by slashing out low with his newly acquired weapon, aiming for Corso's thigh and the delicate femoral arteries.

Corso jumped back out of reach, the blade missing him by millimetres. Jarret came up fast and they faced each other warily, both now oblivious to the baying of the audience.

Jarret was undoubtedly daring and vicious. For all his accustomed bluster and swagger on the Senate floor, he was now thinking strategically, his movements considered and economical, despite the intense violence of the moment.

Breisch had taught Corso that it was not always necessary to go straight for a weapon; the overwhelming desire of one's opponent to get hold of one was another weakness to be exploited. From personal experience, Corso knew that it was a move that could end challenges in seconds rather than minutes. However, instead of disabling his opponent, Corso's opening ploy had left him on the defensive, and lacking a weapon of his own.

Jarret came towards him fast, moving his knife in swift patterns through the air to make it harder to block. Corso feinted to one side, then managed to grab Jarret's knife-hand before flopping on to his back.

Jarret was pulled along with him, and as Corso hit the ground he shoved both feet into his opponent's stomach, so that the momentum of the fall carried Jarret over the top of his head. Corso meanwhile kept a tight grip on Jarret's hand and wrist, twisting hard.

Sharp grit dug into Corso's back even as he caught sight of Jarret's pained, tight-clenched expression as he rolled past him. The man's knife-hand was seriously injured now, placing him at a serious disadvantage.

A soft murmur arose from the watching crowd, and Corso estimated they were already almost a minute into the challenge.

He got himself back upright, surreptitiously scooping a small handful of dust and grit into his left hand. He found he was now close to the centre of the combat arena, the remaining knife within easy reach. He took it, and found Jarret ready facing him once more, his own blade now grasped in his weaker left hand. By now the cold would be seeping in past the dense grease coating his skin, sapping his strength. Corso could feel it now an icy numbness spreading through his arms, while slowly and inexorably weakening him.

Corso caught sight once more of that same lone figure standing well back from the howling mob of onlookers. It seemed impossible, but in that moment he felt certain it was Dakota.

He went on the attack, moving in fast, and gratified to see Jarret take a defensive step backwards in response. Corso swung his knife towards his opponent's head, but Jarret ducked easily, and attempted to parry left-handed. Corso dodged the blade and threw the handful of grit straight into Jarret's eyes.

As Jarret backed off, something slithered across his eyes. Corso realized that he had artificial nictitating membranes – secondary eyelids. He had hoped to blind his opponent, but the ploy had not worked.

Corso covered his brief disappointment by going on the attack once more. Jarret stood his ground, blocking Corso's stabbing thrust and taking the opportunity to punch him hard in the throat. Corso jerked back, ignoring the pain, and moved in close to his rival once again.

When he had the chance, he grabbed hold of Jarret's injured hand once again, and twisted it as hard as possible.

Jarret's teeth clenched in agony, then Corso felt something slice through the flesh over his ribcage. He twisted away, but did not dare spare a glance down in case Jarret took advantage of his distraction.

At least two minutes had passed, and the fight became more desperate, Jarret feinting towards Corso, then kicking out hard once he was close enough. Corso neatly avoided the kick and threw himself forward, trying for a chance at Jarret's jugular. Instead Jarret managed a successful slash at Corso's back, scoring a deep flesh wound.

They hit the ground together, Corso on top. Jarret lost his grip on his knife once again and it spun out of reach. Corso tried to get in close with his own blade, but Jarret fought furiously, pressing the heel of one hand against Corso's face while maintaining a grip on his knife-hand with the other.

A deep thrumming began to fill Corso's ears at the same moment he realized most of the blood staining the ground immediately around them was his own. He had to finish it right now, or he was going to die.

He let go of his knife and used his feet to propel himself in an arc over the top of Jarret's head that landed him on his back, head to head with his opponent on the frozen soil. Then he quickly reached up and wrapped both arms around Jarret's neck before the other had a chance to twist out of the way. Corso sat up quickly, digging the heels of his boots into the hard soil and pulling Jarret after him, twisting his neck backwards.

Jarret struggled and let out a gargling scream, then there was a terrible, sickening crunch as his neck snapped. He twitched spasmodically for a few moments and then fell still. Corso released him and struggled back to his feet, before retrieving one of the knives and stabbing it into the ground to signal the end of the challenge.

Kenley and some of Corso's staff darted forward, grabbing hold of him before he crumpled to his knees. His entire body now felt like it was on fire. As if from a great distance, he heard McDade call out the duration of the fight: three minutes and twelve seconds, Corso's longest-lasting challenge yet.

The air was filled with shouting and booing from Jarret's angry supporters – as well as from those who had bet on the wrong man.

'Close,' Corso mumbled, half aware of Kenley's face near to his own. 'Too close.'

'You'll be fine. The doctor's ready to stitch you up now.'

As they carried him out of the combat ring, he looked around again to see if he could spot Dakota – but she had vanished, if she had ever been there at all.

Corso was gently heaved on to a stretcher, and realized Breisch was holding one end of it. He was then lifted into the back of an aid-copter originally used for ferrying injured soldiers out of the battlefield.

'Put him down now. The rest of you, outside,' he heard Breisch order. 'Everyone but the doctors.'

Someone pushed a needle into his arm and Corso tasted peppermint on his tongue. Two faces hovered within view, as he saw scissors cutting away his shirt, revealing a wound in his side which was much deeper than he had realized.

For a little while, everything seemed to get increasingly far away.

'Second wound's on his other side,' he heard a doctor say. 'We'll have to turn him. Ready . . . *now.*'

Everything got dark.

THIRTEEN

When Corso next opened his eyes, he found himself in a private room inside a hospital. The curtains were open, and the only light in the room came from the twinkling skyline of Unity beyond. The Senate building was visible towards the centre of town, a dome wreathed in artfully tangled girders and lit from beneath by floodlights.

An ambient video loop of a shoreline under a vault of grey clouds cycled across an expanse of wall next to the door. He mumbled a series of commands until he found one that caused the loop to switch off, then let his head fall back against the pillow, enjoying the sudden silence.

'You're back, I see.'

Corso lurched up in surprise. Breisch had been sitting the whole time in a chair to one side of the bed, nearly invisible in the shadows.

'How long?' Corso managed to ask, before letting his head sink back. His throat and mouth felt raw and ragged.

Breisch lifted himself out of the chair and stepped over to stand beside the bed. 'You've been out cold for two days. The med boys patched you up good, though. That was a hell of a fight.'

'I thought I was a dead man.'

'You very nearly were. You kept your head, though, when Jarret didn't. He thought he had you figured out.'

It was coming back now, yet it all felt like it had happened a million years ago. 'I remember now. Listen, I'm sorry I—'

'It's all right,' Breisch cut him off. 'I think we'd gone about as far as we could with your training anyway. I just wanted to be here when you woke up. There's somebody else here who's been waiting to see you since they choppered you in.'

Corso watched as Breisch stepped towards the door, pulling it open.

'Wait . . ' began Corso.

'Good luck, son,' said Breisch. 'I've enjoyed working with you.' He stepped through and was gone.

Corso stared at the closed door, then tried to lever himself into an upright position. The right side of his chest still felt like it was on fire, so he moved with extreme care. Something shifted against his ribcage under the bed sheet, but before he had a chance to investigate, the door opened again and Dakota walked in.

'I don't think they'll like it if you move around too much,' she declared, looking him up and down.

Corso froze where he was, then slid back down with

infinite care. 'Until I saw you back there, I was sure you were dead,' he grunted.

Dakota headed past his bed and perched on the edge of the windowsill. The lights of the city now illuminated her from behind, colouring her skin a pale bronze.

'In a funny kind of way, I was,' she replied. 'And I can't make up my mind whether I still am.'

He tugged the bed sheet down with his left hand and saw, to his horror, that something not unlike an enormous caterpillar with semi-translucent flesh lay across the gash in his chest. He could see blood – *his* blood – pulsing through its body, while its dozen legs impaled his severed flesh, holding it in place.

'The wonders of modern biotechnology,' Dakota said. 'But don't worry. One of the doctors said it'd die and fall off in a couple of days once you've healed up.'

Corso let the sheet fall back into place, thoroughly disturbed by the sight.

'You simply disappeared,' he said. 'We got your final warning about the swarm heading our way . . . then nothing. What the hell happened to you, Dakota?'

'The swarm turned on me the instant I let my guard down.' She shrugged. 'I thought I was studying it, while the whole time it was siphoning off the same data you sent to me. When it attacked, I was trapped. I had to use the last of my ship's energy reserves to send that final communication.'

'But you got away. You escaped, and now you're here.'

'It's not as simple as that.'

Corso groaned and tried to sit up again. His head was pounding. 'I need to get up.'

She hopped down from the windowsill and stepped over to the bed, gently pushing him back down. 'There's nothing needs taking care of so badly that you have to go anywhere right this instant.'

'Tell me exactly what happened. What did you mean, *It's not as simple as that?*'

She forced a faltering smile. 'You'll recall how the swarm had gathered close by a red giant. Well, it blew – turned nova. At first I thought it was just the natural end of the star's life, but I can't help wondering if the swarm helped it along.'

'But you jumped to safety before the star turned nova?'

She shook her head. 'No.'

'Then . . . I don't understand.'

'The next thing I knew, I was most of my way back home. The ship had reduced me to information just before it was destroyed, and used the very last of its power reserves to transmit all of that to another Magi ship, located not much more than a few days out from here.' She gave him a ghost of a smile. 'They'd rebuilt me, except it seems something was lost during the transmission.'

Corso stared at her in mute shock, as she continued. 'I can *feel* there's a lot missing. Sometimes I try to remember something, and there's only a little fragment, a picture or a face or something I can't even make out properly, and that's all.' Her expression became hopeless. 'It's like there's now this yawning hole where a lot of my life used to be.'

Corso struggled to find an adequate response. 'But you're here, you're alive, aren't you? At least—'

'No,' she cut him off abruptly. 'I remember *dying*, Lucas. I'm not sure how I'm supposed to feel about that.'

'Dakota, if one of those Magi ships did what you say it did, then that's . . . that's *incredible*. That makes you just about one of the luckiest people alive.'

She shook her head. 'But I'm not *me*. The *real* me died.'

'You know, some people would say that's just semantics.'

She looked at him sharply. 'So if someone made an exact copy of you and it tried to murder you, that would be okay because it's got all your thoughts and emotions and memories, even your sense of self-identity? Would you – the *real* you, that is – be any less dead?'

Corso opened his mouth, then hesitated. 'No,' he said, a little reluctantly. 'No, I guess I wouldn't be. But if I knew I was going to die, I think I'd feel a lot better knowing I'd still be carrying on in some way.'

Dakota's voice took on a harder edge. 'But you'd still be dead, either way. And the copy would still only be a copy . . . I've been thinking about this a lot.'

I can tell, thought Corso, but kept silent.

'There's a part of me,' Dakota continued, 'that thought it meant I was free of my former responsibilities. That I could just fly away and not give a damn about the Long War or the Emissaries or anything like that. *This* version of me wasn't in Nova Arctis or Night's End, no matter what my memories may say. So I don't *have* to care about any of this.'

'All right,' he replied. 'So why even bother coming here?'

'I wasn't given a choice.'

He took a moment to process this statement. 'I don't understand.'

'The Magi ships are all hardwired to stop the Maker. Even if I wanted to disappear, the one that brought me back from the dead would never let me.'

'But you're its navigator, of course you can—'

'No, I can't,' she interrupted. 'Not any more.'

'Why?'

She sighed. 'Let's just say there's been a fundamental change in my relationship with the Magi ships, since I was brought back. I'd tell you more, but this really isn't the right time.'

'Why not?'

She had slipped her jacket off as he spoke, revealing bare shoulders poking above an armless vest. 'Because I don't want to think about that right now,' she answered.

Corso fell silent, watching as she pulled the vest up over her head before dropping it to the floor. His mouth became instantly dry as he studied her smooth belly and small firm breasts.

'I ought to warn you I'm not in the best of shape right now,' he said.

'Just tell me if it hurts,' she answered, quickly unzipping her boots and throwing them to one side. Her trousers and underwear followed a moment later.

Corso stared at her in the dark, feeling his body respond instinctively despite his injuries and the medication, and he was suddenly reluctant to recall just how long it was since he'd last been with a woman. There'd been no time for anything but work over the past few years.

She pulled the blanket to one side and slid on top of him, straddling his hips. Without thinking, Corso slid his hands up the taut surface of her belly. She quickly manoeuvred him inside her, and then reached down with both hands to grip his sides, taking care to avoid touching him where the caterpillar-like creature knitted his flesh together. Before long she was rocking her hips back and forth in a steady rolling motion that shot spikes of pleasure up his spine.

He started to thrust, raising his hips from the mattress, but she shook her head. 'No. Stay still.'

He watched her for the next several minutes, with no small pleasure, as her breath started to emerge in short sharp gasps, her head tipping back as she came closer and closer to climax. He reached up, sliding his hands further up and gently cupping her small breasts again. Her flesh felt so supple and smooth, and entirely human, that he found it impossible to believe her story. She still felt completely real.

The look of intense concentration on her face made him remember other times, first on board *Hyperion* and later in a Bandati tower on a distant world long since wiped out. He wondered again about her story: if she really had been recreated somehow, reborn from the flesh of one of those alien starships . . .

That killed it for him.

He felt his ardour rapidly drain away, but a few seconds later Dakota gripped him painfully hard, before letting her forehead drop against his chest.

After a minute she looked up and gave him a questioning look.

'I think it's the meds,' he muttered, embarrassed.

She gave him a look of careful appraisal, as if she wasn't sure whether to believe him or not, then wordlessly lifted herself up and off him, before dropping down beside him, and pressing up close. The heat of her skin felt like a furnace against his own.

'If you had that performance planned, I hope you warned the staff to give us some privacy,' he muttered.

'I don't think we're likely to be disturbed.' She reached up to stroke a finger along his jaw line. 'That man Breisch, who is he?'

'He taught me how to fight.'

She raised herself on one elbow and gazed down at him. 'What happened to you, Lucas? I saw the whole thing, and you killed that guy in cold blood. It was . . . brutal. I thought you stood against that kind of thing.'

Corso shrugged. 'Seems it's the only way to get anyone here to listen to me. A lot of people want me dead, and the rest won't take me seriously unless I play them at their own game.'

'But that doesn't mean you had to—'

'It does,' he retorted 'Things got a lot harder once you were gone, Dakota. The Fleet's lost most of its power, we're a spent force – and the Freehold isn't the only one desperate to undermine us at every opportunity.'

'But you had it in your power to place sanctions against uncooperative worlds.'

'Yes, but not the moral authority, and their governments knew it. The only people who were getting hurt by the sanctions were refugees dumped on worlds without the resources to deal with them. Too many people were dying, Dakota. We had to give in, especially once some of the navigators broke ranks.'

She bristled. 'But we were only taking on navigators if we were sure we could trust them.'

'There's only so many old-school machine-heads available, so of course we had to take in navigator candidates whose backgrounds we couldn't always check and loyalties we could never be sure of. Most of the first batch of navigators, like Lamoureaux, were on our side, but two thirds have burned out for some reason we don't understand. As it is, we're barely maintaining the lines of physical communication that hold the Consortium together.'

'It's that bad?'

'After you left, I split my time between Ocean's Deep and Redstone, trying to stop things falling apart here after the coup. At first I got treated like a returning hero, but it wasn't long before I realized I'd made a lot of enemies without really trying. They were practically lining up to call me out with challenges. I learned to fight because I couldn't see any way out of that, not if I was to have any hope of retaining some influence. I wanted to show them I could meet them on their own terms and still beat them. But instead things just went from bad to worse.'

'But now we know the Mos Hadroch is real.' She again traced the curve of his jaw with a fingertip. 'You found it and you brought it back? Now you know what it is, am I right?' There was an intensity in her expression, a touch of avarice to the gleam of her eyes.

'No, it's still locked away on board the ship that carried it back here. That's the reason the contest took place – Jarret wanted control of that ship and whatever it brought back with it.'

He saw shock alternating with anger in her expression, as she replied. 'Things haven't really changed so much while I've been away, have they?'

'I'm afraid not, no.'

'All right, so what *do* we know about the Mos Hadroch?'

'Nothing, really. It's not even certain we *did* find it. What we found was the body of an Atn sealed up inside a hidden passageway on an abandoned clade-world. And . . .'

He had been on the verge of saying Whitecloud's real name. The sedatives were making it hard to think straight.

'It's possible what we're looking for is locked away inside the Atn's body,' he continued quickly. 'Except, as soon as it was brought on board the *Mjollnir*, it was locked away under Senate orders. The Legislate's arranged a secret deal to have the thing's remains shipped to Sol as soon as some essential repairs are finished.'

Dakota was staring at him open-mouthed. 'I . . . I didn't know any of this,' she said finally. 'We can't just leave it in the hands of people who don't know what they've got. Not if you've really found the Mos Hadroch.'

He glanced past her towards the window. Dawn's first light was reddening the horizon. 'Jarret's death means I can't be challenged over the *Mjollnir* any more, but there are people in the Senate who'll do almost anything, I reckon, to stop us getting hold of what Driscoll found.'

Dakota pushed herself up on one elbow and gazed down at him with a determined expression. 'Then obviously we need to get on board before that happens,' she said. 'We have to take the Mos Hadroch somewhere else.'

'Where?'

'Deep into the heart of Emissary territory,' she told him. 'A long, long way away.'

'Take it *into* Emissary territory.' Corso stared at her, slack-jawed. 'You have to be kidding me.'

'We need to head for a cache located deep inside their territory, which has certain unique vulnerabilities the Mos Hadroch is designed to exploit. We'll have backup, though: alien weapons, hundreds of them. If it comes down to a confrontation – and it almost certainly will – we should have a good chance of surviving.'

'And I suppose if I asked where you found these "weapons", you'd tell me?'

She smiled faintly. 'Not just yet.'

He groaned and started to haul himself out of the bed.

'Are you sure you should be doing that?' Dakota asked.

'Fuck it, it's been, what – two days now?' He winced as he lowered his feet to the floor. 'I don't know what the hell might have been happening in the meantime.'

He padded naked over to a locker, grunting in satisfaction when he found his clothes neatly pressed and waiting for him.

Corso started to get dressed, moving slowly and carefully, and clearly still in a great deal of pain. 'Here's the way I see it, Dakota. I sent a frigate, which also happens to be one of the Freehold's few assets of any value, out to a remote location on your say-so. That challenge I just barely survived the other day is one consequence of that decision. Now you're talking about flying into the heart of a deeply inimical, wildly hostile and considerably more advanced civilization, and attacking what I'd guess to be one of their primary resources. To be frank, it sounds like suicide.'

'I know how it sounds, but it's the only way to get the Mos Hadroch to function the way it's intended to.'

'And just what is that?' he asked, stepping closer. 'You mentioned something about a "vulnerability".'

In that moment Dakota herself looked as small, frail and vulnerable as he'd ever seen her. 'It's difficult to explain.'

'I just killed a man, and risked the crew of our flagship on an expedition halfway across the galaxy to track this thing down, and that's the best you can say?'

'Let me remind you of the facts,' she replied, her tone defiant. 'The Emissaries are already on their way. The swarm is still out there somewhere, looking for the Mos Hadroch. You're just going to have to take me on trust for now, because I'm pretty much working out things as I go along.'

'Assuming we really have found the Mos Hadroch,' he pointed out, 'and not just an alien corpse.'

She was silent as he finished buttoning his shirt up. He closed his eyes for a few seconds, thinking hard, before turning to her again.

'Who else knows you're here on Redstone?'

'Nobody apart from you and Ted Lamoureaux.'

'Good, let's keep it that way.'

'Why keep it a secret?'

'Because the more I think about it, the more I think things are going to get very nasty. If my enemies even suspected you were here, they might consider it de facto proof that I was planning an attack on the frigate.'

She slid off the bed and came towards him. 'And are you?'

'Let's say I've already been thinking of contingency plans in case things didn't work out the way I wanted them to.'

'So when were you thinking of putting them into action?'

Corso stared out at the helical twist of girders that framed the Senate building, before answering, 'As soon as possible.'

FOURTEEN

Lamoureaux was already there a few days later, when Corso arrived at the spaceport a few kilometres outside Unity. Its turbos humming loudly, his automated taxi blew up a storm of grit as it dropped down on to the blackened concrete plain a short distance from the vehicle that had brought Lamoureaux.

Lamoureaux wore a fur-lined parka, a cheap breather mask strapped over his mouth and nose. The sun was bright, but still low on the horizon, burning away the freezing mist that clung to the ground.

'Ted,' Corso greeted him, climbing out of the taxi and stepping towards the other man. 'Thanks for coming here.'

Lamoureaux nodded uncertainly. 'I don't know if you heard the news this morning.'

'I'm afraid I did, yes.'

The Consortium had finally made their move, taking over the research station servicing the cache within the Tierra system. Legislate-registered military cruisers equipped with newly minted superluminal drive-cores had moved in, while Fleet representatives throughout the system had been placed under arrest.

Lamoureaux nodded. 'Now maybe you can tell me why I had to come to Redstone under an assumed identity, *without* my Magi ship.'

'I'm sorry about all the subterfuge, but it was necessary, believe me. I needed to be sure nobody knew you were here at all.'

'I watched some of the local news broadcasts. They really don't like people with implants here, do they?'

'Not generally, no.'

Lamoureaux reached up to fiddle with his mask. Corso saw he hadn't put it on right, and stepped forward to adjust the straps for him.

'I don't know how the hell you manage to go around with these things on,' Lamoureaux muttered. 'I've only been out in the open for twenty minutes, and already it's driving me crazy.'

'I grew up having to wear these things any time I went outdoors,' Corso replied, stepping away again. 'And it gets to be second nature. Might as well complain about having to hold your breath if you go diving. How does that feel?'

'Better,' Lamoureaux admitted, tentatively touching the device where it pressed against his face, 'though I'd still rather not be wearing it at all. Now, do you mind telling me why all the subterfuge?'

'Because there's an extraordinary motion due to go through the Senate this morning to have me removed from my seat and placed under arrest on charges of sedition against the state,' Corso explained.

'Then we have to get you out of here promptly. We need to get you back to Ocean's Deep.'

'No.' Corso shook his head. 'By the time we got back there, it'd be just as dangerous. Think about it: the strike against the cache, the dispute over the *Mjollnir* – it's all tied together. Now there are rumours the *Mjollnir*'s going to be leaving orbit again in a few days' time.'

'But it only just got here,' Lamoureaux protested.

'Nonetheless, I've got good intelligence it's headed for the Sol system. We can't allow that to happen.'

'So what do you plan on doing?'

'We need to get on board and take control before it can leave.'

Lamoureaux searched his face. 'You're serious, aren't you? What was the point of fighting Jarret, then?'

'I made the mistake of thinking the people behind him would stick to their own rules. But they were just gambling I'd be the one to wind up dead, and thus solve all their problems.'

Lamoureaux shivered. 'You haven't told me exactly where we'd take the *Mjollnir*.'

'Did you know Dakota's still alive?'

Lamoureaux nodded warily. 'Now that you mention it, yes. I didn't know until she got in touch with me a few days ago, asking me not to tell anyone. I didn't even know if she'd told anyone else.'

'She came to me a few nights ago and said me she

wants to take the Mos Hadroch into Emissary territory, to one of their own caches. She claims that's the only way it can work.'

'Fly the *Mjollnir* into Emissary territory? That's crazy.'

Corso smiled grimly under his mask. 'If you've got any better ideas, I can't wait to hear them. Because I've been doing nothing but trying to think of alternatives and, assuming Dakota isn't insane or making up stories, I can't think of any.'

'Things might be a lot simpler if she *was* crazy.'

'She claimed she died out there when she tracked the Maker down,' Corso told him. 'That it destroyed her and her ship, but that it somehow preserved her mind and transmitted it to another ship closer to home. I want to know if you think that's remotely possible.'

'Shit.' Lamoureaux stamped his feet a few times on the frozen concrete, and shoved his gloved hands deeper into the recesses of his silvered parka. He stared off into the distance for several moments, towards a couple of rapid-orbit cargo ships idling on the concrete a few kilometres away, steam trickling out from their main nacelles.

'All right,' he said at last, 'you're worried she's been hit by whatever's taken down a lot of other machine-heads. What I would say is that she isn't any crazier than any of the rest of them, and none of them has shown the least sign of being delusional. And also there are . . . depths to the Magi ships I can't even begin to explain to someone who hasn't experienced them. The Magi were verging on godlike when they disappeared, Senator, so I suspect it's probably the least of the tricks they could pull off.'

He stared past Corso, chewing the inside of a cheek.

'You've got something else on your mind?'

Lamoureaux met his eyes. 'I've got to tell you, Senator, that interstellar piracy was pretty high on my list of career options when I was twelve years old, but I'm balking at it now.'

Corso grinned. 'Did I even say you were coming along?'

Lamoureaux laughed, the sound strangely muffled by his breather mask. 'I'm not sure what else you expect me to do. My Magi ship is still back at Ocean's Deep, otherwise maybe I'd be able to grab control of the *Mjollnir*.' He shrugged. 'Dakota could do the same.'

'No, she couldn't – and neither could you. The *Mjollnir*'s had manual circuit breakers installed in case of exactly that eventuality.'

'Huh?' Lamoureaux shook his head. 'But surely that's crazy. Don't the Freehold have their own machine-heads now?'

'Yes, out of necessity, but they don't really trust them either.'

Ships all throughout the Consortium had been hastily modified to prevent them from being taken over by hostile machine-heads linked to Magi ships. A lot of damage could be effected in the brief seconds it took an unaugmented human pilot to react to a hostile takeover, but once he had thrown the switch, the attack could be stopped immediately.

'Well, that makes it a little more complicated, doesn't it? If Dakota's also going on this expedition of yours, you won't need me, will you?'

'On the contrary,' Corso replied. 'I'd need you along to help me keep an eye on her, and because I need people with me I can trust. So what do you say?'

Lamoureaux scuffed one booted foot against the concrete before letting his shoulders sag as if in defeat. 'What else am I going to do, Senator? Sit around along with everyone else and wait for the Emissaries to arrive? It's not much of a choice.'

Corso grinned and put a hand on the machine-head's shoulder. 'I don't even know if it's going to come to an armed assault, but it might.'

'You have the resources to do that?'

Corso nodded. 'The *Mjollnir*'s going to have only a skeleton crew when we board, so it's extremely unlikely we'll face any serious opposition. Not that you'd be expected to carry a gun or anything like that; you'd be following us in only once we feel sure it's safe.'

'So who else is going?'

'Hopefully the *Mjollnir*'s usual commander, a man named Martinez, and one or two of his senior staff. I'm not sure the expedition would even have happened if not for him. He's currently under house arrest, but I'm working on tracking him and the others down.

226

Whitecloud's been spirited away, but assuming we find him too, he's coming with us. Leo Olivarri and Ray Willis should get here any day. Once I've had a chance to explain what I've got in mind, I'm hoping they'll agree to come along also.'

Lamoureaux shook his head and grinned visibly beneath his mask. 'You realize how insane all this sounds.'

The way he said it, it almost seemed like a compliment.

'Our plan is to board the frigate in less than a week, when it's scheduled for final maintenance and diagnostic checks. Security will be low, and we won't get a better chance.'

'And if it all goes wrong? If I don't hear from you, or they arrest you or kill you meanwhile, what then?'

'Then I'd advise you to find some way off Redstone and out of this system as fast as possible. Until then, we've got a lot of work to do.'

FIFTEEN

The return journey aboard the *Mjollnir* had proved a difficult time for Ty. As soon as he and Nancy had reached the safety of the frigate, the ship had jumped to a point a few hundred light-years distant, while the Atn's remains were placed under guard in the ship's laboratory complex. Ty had been turned back when he tried to enter the labs, and told in no uncertain terms he was not to be allowed access to the Atn's body for the remainder of the journey.

It had soon become clear there were political machinations taking place far beyond the frigate, which Ty could only guess at. Martinez vanished from the bridge, and if not for Nancy he might never have known the Commander had been confined to his quarters while his second in command, Simenon, assumed control. Other members of Martinez's senior staff had also quickly vanished from the ship's centrifuge, replaced by hastily promoted members of their crew. An angry confrontation with Simenon over access to the Atn's remains had ended with Ty barred completely from the bridge. He had risked his life to retrieve the thing, yet his every request was dismissed out of hand.

On arriving back at Redstone, teams of armed soldiers had boarded the freighter, rapidly separating Ty from the rest of the crew without explanation. Before long he was ferried down to a spaceport and transferred to the windowless rear of a robot truck that drove away immediately.

He still had no idea where he was being taken, or whether or not he was under arrest.

The vehicle drove for over an hour before finally coming to a stop and unlocking its doors. Ty stepped out into what appeared to be an underground garage, where a man with impossibly wide shoulders and a face like granite was waiting for him.

Ty did not fail to notice the way the man's pale grey eyes widened the moment he saw him. Yes, Ty thought, with a growing sense of doom. The man was clearly trying to remember where he had seen him before.

'Mr . . . Driscoll,' the Freeholder rumbled. 'Welcome to Redstone.'

Ty nodded, and fought back the tight knot of panic gathering in his stomach. He started at a sudden noise, then realized it was only the truck reversing back up the ramp that led into an industrial-sized airlock.

'My name is Rufus Weil,' the Freeholder continued. 'You'll be staying here for a day or two.' Weil paused, and again those pale grey eyes roved around Ty's face, as if trying to place him. 'If there's anything you need while you're here, just let me know.'

'All right,' said Ty, still watching as the airlock's inner door closed on the truck. 'Where exactly am I? And why am I even here? Nobody would tell me anything.'

'You're in Unity, the Freehold's capital. And you're here because of a matter of security. There are questions over exactly who has jurisdiction over the *Mjollnir*, and the Senate requests that you stay here until they're sorted out.'

'How long is that going to take?' Ty demanded, feeling scandalized. 'And what about the . . . remains I recovered?'

'Those are high-level security questions, Mr Driscoll, and I'm not allowed to discuss them. All I can do is ensure you're comfortable while you're here, and apologize for any inconvenience.' He waved towards a nearby bank of elevators. 'This way, please.'

Ty stood his ground, unwilling to share the small, confined space inside the elevator with this Freeholder. He did not want to have to stare into those quietly accusing grey eyes any more than he had to. 'What exactly is this place? Am I a prisoner here?'

'No, sir, you're a guest. This is a residency for officials from other settlements when they're visiting the Senate. You'll have an entire suite allocated for your personal use.' Weil once more indicated the waiting elevator. 'Please, now. You'll be here no more than a few days.'

Ty considered his options and decided he had none.

He swallowed nervously and stepped towards the row of gleaming silver doors.

As the elevator carried the two of them upwards, in silence, Ty could feel beads of sweat forming on his brow. The interior of the elevator was mirrored, so that there was no way he could avoid Weil's persistent, accusatory gaze. Any doubts Ty had that his paranoia was getting the better of him vanished under that fixed stare.

Several minutes later Ty was relieved to find himself alone in what indeed appeared to be a luxury-sized suite, whose picture windows looked out across the city. He listened to Weil's footsteps padding away down the corridor and leaned his head against the door, taking several long, deep breaths until he felt his nerves start to settle back into equilibrium.

No doubt about it; Weil knew who he was – or certainly had strong suspicions. The Freeholder, Ty estimated, was in his mid-to late thirties – just about the right age to have taken part in the abortive, Consortium-backed assault against the Uchidan Territories more than a decade before. Also just the sort of person to wonder if he had seen Ty's face on some long-ago news bulletin.

But even his sudden fear of being uncovered could not entirely distract from the frustration at being prevented from studying the body he had risked his life to recover. He felt sure that within its dusty shell lay the summation of all his life's work: a suitable antidote to the rank failures of the past.

An armchair faced the window. He fell into it, suddenly exhausted, and stared out through the glass. A warning sticker detailed the fatal consequences of either opening or breaking the window without having a breather mask handy. As a native of Redstone, he knew full well how deadly the planet's naked atmosphere was. So if things got bad enough he could . . .

No. He slammed the arm of the chair and leaned forward, chewing on a knuckle. Suicide was not an option. He had thought it was finished when the Territories decided to hand him over to the Consortium, and even then he had escaped. No matter how bad things looked, there was always a way.

Ty brooded for a while longer, then stood up and stepped over to the door. He was pleased to find it was not locked, but a man of a distinctly similar build and demeanour to Marcus Weil sat in an easy chair down the far end of the corridor, next to the elevator.

'Sir,' said the man, rising, 'can I help you?'

Ty shook his head and forced a smile. 'No, thank you.'

He ducked back inside, closing the door and listening to it click as it swung to. He might not be locked in, and it might be a comfortable suite, but it was definitely also a prison.

He returned to the armchair, and watched the sun track its way across the sky, just thinking.

Ty woke, much later, to find himself in darkness.

He shook his head, rubbed tired hands through his hair and staggered into the suite's bathroom. When he emerged from the shower, wrapped in a bathrobe, the first trickling light of dawn was showing itself beyond the glass of the window.

He lay down on top of the bed and soon fell asleep again.

Later in the morning, the same man who had been set to guard him the night before entered the suite with a breakfast tray. He placed it on a table by the armchair, along with a shrink-wrapped bundle.

'Who are you?' Ty demanded, still groggy with sleep.

'Hibbert, Mr Driscoll.' He nodded to the shrink-wrapped package. 'We ran a fresh change of clothes out for you earlier this morning. If they're not right, let me know.'

'What happened to Weil?'

The Freeholder regarded Ty with a carefully blank expression. 'Mr Weil works on a different shift, Mr Driscoll. Enjoy your breakfast.'

Despite his misgivings, Ty ate ravenously, delighted to have the opportunity to consume real food after the limited fare of shipboard meals. When he had finished, he stood by the window and watched people passing through the city streets far below.

There were certain parallels here with the Uchidan settlements, of course; underground tunnels similarly linked most of the buildings in Unity so that, in order to go about their lives, the citizens barely needed to step outdoors for months at a time. Most of those out in the open were maintenance workers or those there by necessity. He could almost have forgotten about the intrinsic barbarism that lay just under the surface here.

When he felt ready, Ty activated the suite's comms system, but soon found it had been crippled: getting a message of any kind out was impossible. He tried to access local news services, but all were blocked except for one dedicated to the ongoing war with the Uchidan Territories.

He got dressed and again went out into the corridor, finding Hibbert back in his seat by the elevator.

'My comms unit doesn't work,' Ty explained. 'I can't send any messages. How the hell am I supposed to call anyone while I'm stuck in here?'

'It's a security issue, sir, and it might take a couple of weeks to clear up. I'm afraid you're going to have to—'

'A couple of *weeks?*' Ty yelled, stepping up close to the other man. 'Weil said a couple of *days.*'

Hibbert stood, towering over him. 'Please, Mr Driscoll. You're going to have to return to your r—'

Ty stepped past Hibbert and towards the elevator. Hibbert swiftly pressed something against his side, and the next thing Ty knew he was lying curled up on the floor, spasms of pain racking his entire body. He was distantly aware of Hibbert grabbing him by both feet and dragging him back into the suite.

Weil delivered Ty's breakfast the next morning, and also his lunch and dinner. No word was said about the previous day's incident, and Ty was far from inclined to risk being zapped a second time, or even to engage Weil in conversation. Instead he endured the silent tension until Weil stalked back out each time, closing the door behind him.

The next day passed in much the same way, and the day after also. Ty found that, if he leaned against the window and peered straight down, he could see part of the ramp leading into the basement garage, almost directly beneath. He watched as unmanned supply vehicles entered and departed through the airlock. But most of his time he sat in his armchair, brooding and staring out across the city.

It took a few seconds before Ty realized that the comms unit really was registering an incoming message.

Slouching in the armchair, he had been drinking his morning coffee, the window half-opaqued. It was his fifth day in captivity, and the remains of his breakfast lay on the table, waiting to be picked up by Hibbert.

He stared unbelievingly at the comms unit. *A message?* Did Lamoureaux and Willis know he was here? Were they trying to get him out?

The door opened suddenly and he jumped up, suddenly full of nervous energy. Hibbert gave him a wary look before approaching the table. He had clearly not noticed the glowing message icon floating above the comms unit's imaging plate.

Ty moved quickly to one side, so that Hibbert's view of the comms unit would remain blocked as he reached down to pick up the tray.

Hibbert instantly froze and stared at Ty with eyes full of the threat of incipient violence.

'Nice morning,' Ty blurted.

Hibbert's gaze turned contemptuous. 'Sir,' he merely replied, then picked up the tray and left the room.

Ty sagged slightly as Hibbert closed the door behind him, then he turned to the comms unit and opened the message.

It was, he found, a list of instructions encoded in simple text. The message itself read like something out of some hoary old spy 'viro.

```
This message will delete itself within
300 seconds of being opened. When you are
ready to leave the Senate residency,
stand at the window of your suite, facing
outwards, and wave your left hand.

The response will come within no more
```

    than a half hour of your performing this
    action. Please be prepared to move
    quickly.

Ty stared back out over the city, aware he was standing
in plain view of an entire metropolis. Anyone could be
watching from any one of thousands of windows. He
thought about waving his hand immediately, but something made him hesitate.

Surely, he thought, if Lamoureaux or Willis were
behind the message, they would have identified themselves in some way? How could he be sure the message
wasn't some kind of trap – that if he did stand there and
wave his hand, some assassin armed with a rifle, and in
league with Weil, would not endeavour to take him out
with a long-range shot?

He felt trapped by his own indecision.

When he finally turned back to the message, hovering
like a mirage within the dark shallow bowl of the unit's
viewing area, it was just in time to see it vanish of its own
accord.

Later that night, Ty opened his eyes to find the keen
edge of a blade held close to his throat. A moment later
a hand clamped over his mouth.

'Not a fucking sound,' said Weil, leaning over him.
'Do you hear me? So much as a squeak, and I'll skin you
alive before I cut your throat.'

Ty nodded, dizzyingly aware of the blade pressed against his flesh. He hadn't even been sleeping, just resting with his eyes closed on the bed. Weil had entered the room and pushed the knife against his throat without making a sound.

'I know who you are,' Weil hissed. 'I knew the second I set eyes on you. I was part of the detail sent to receive you from the Territories, but you got away before we could pick you up.'

Ty panted, his breath whistling sporadically through his nostrils. His bladder felt on the verge of unleashing a tide of urine.

'I lost a brother because of what you did, you and the rest of those Uchidan god-fuckers. He wasn't even a soldier, just a teacher – a whole school bombed out of existence. We never even had a body to bury. Because of you.'

Ty could feel the moist warmth of the man's breath on his face. 'I don't know how long they're going to keep you here,' Weil continued, 'but it makes me sick to have to wait on you. Part of me wants to kill you right now,' he added, the knife moving infinitesimally closer to Ty's jugular, the pressure of its blade like a line of fire against his skin. 'Do you understand what I'm saying?'

Ty realized the other man was waiting for an answer, and he nodded under the palm of Weil's hand.

'I warned my superiors. I told them who you were, but they refused to let me execute you. All because of something on that frigate.' Weil leaned in a little closer.

'Fuck that. The instant I think you're going to walk out of here, I'll be back. Me and my friend here,' he added, twitching the knife a little. 'Are you scared? Because you'd better be fucking scared, Whitecloud. I'm not finished with you yet.'

Suddenly the pressure was gone and Ty sat up abruptly, hyperventilating, grabbing at his throat even as Weil lurched out of the door and slammed it shut.

Ty stumbled off the bed and over to the armchair, pulling himself into a tight ball and moaning with terror.

Gradually his eyes fixed on the darkened city beyond the window. He had been a fool to hesitate for so long; anything was better than staying here a second longer than necessary.

He leaned against the glass with his right hand, and peered down, just able to see the ramp directly below him. Even if he could break through the glass, even if he had a breather mask handy, he would be dead as soon as he hit the ground.

Instead he lifted his left hand straight up, sweeping it in an arc several times from left to right.

Would they be watching even now, in the middle of the night? Perhaps not.

But if they were, there was only one way to be sure.

A short while later – he estimated no more than twenty minutes had passed – Ty watched a set of headlights approaching the residency up a long street before driving down the airlock ramp. On closer inspection, it proved to be nothing more than a standard unmanned supply truck.

He sat back down, feeling obscurely disappointed. Then there was a distant, muffled clang as the airlock door opened and closed again. He swallowed and stared once more at the sprinkle of lights outside, wondering who was looking back, and what they were thinking.

An earth-shattering roar shook the building. Alarms began to clang discordantly both inside and outside.

There were shouts and footsteps in the corridor outside, and he realized with a shock that the window of his room had become badly starred. Already smoke drifted up past it.

Ty lurched upright and headed quickly to the door. The message had instructed that he should be ready to move. But did that mean he should simply wait here, or instead try and see if he could find a way out of the damaged building?

He remembered Weil's promise, and decided not to stay.

Sliding the door open quietly, he risked a glance outside, towards the bank of elevators. Weil was gone from his post. He eyed the elevators hopefully, but hesitated while deciding it might be too dangerous to use them.

Instead he stepped out into the corridor and headed quickly in the opposite direction, making for a door leading into a stairwell. Smoke drifted up from several floors below.

He took the steps downwards three or four at a time, the air growing denser with smoke as he descended. He could distinctly smell burning plastic, but also something else he could not quite identify.

After a moment he realized this was the unique odour of Redstone's air, which meant the building's atmospheric seals had been breached.

He continued down several levels until he came to a glass-fronted box mounted on the wall. It was filled with cheap emergency breathers, so he punched out the glass and quickly pulled on a mask.

Heavy footsteps, approaching from above.

Ty leaned out over the banister and peered up in time to see Weil glaring straight back down at him from several levels above.

Ty bolted down the remaining steps, then burst through a door that led into a ground-floor atrium-style lobby with a reception desk at one end. The bank of elevators was on the opposite side from the desk, and the door of one of them was jammed halfway open. Thick dark smoke billowed from inside it towards the ceiling.

He ran to the centre of the lobby, looking frantically from left to right, but no one else appeared to be around.

Voices sounded somewhere nearby just as his breather gave a beeping sound to warn that the smoke was clogging its filters. He crossed the lobby quickly to where several floor-to-ceiling windows had been shattered, the glass crunching under his feet. He slipped outside through one, and heard sirens in the distance.

He paused there, momentarily indecisive, as the freezing cold wind cut into him like a knife. Where next?

Suddenly a small unmanned taxi pulled up next to him. Ty stared at it uncertainly, then climbed in.

The vehicle performed a U-turn and accelerated back the way it had come. Ty glanced through the rear window in time to see Weil emerge on to the street. He ducked out of sight and prayed he had not already been spotted.

The taxi headed for the city centre, where the buildings rose higher, manifesting the same blocky and severe architectural style as found in any other Freehold settlement. Perhaps ten minutes after picking him up at the Residency, the taxi cut down a ramp into the underground parking area of a building that was just one of several identical monolithic slabs arranged in a row.

He quickly disembarked and pulled the cheap breather off his face just as an elevator opened, chiming softly. He guessed he was meant to get inside.

It delivered Ty a minute later to an apparently deserted floor several levels up. The walls were bare concrete, with gaping holes where electrical and communications systems still had to be installed. He proceeded down a long corridor, checking through door after door until he at last found an office space containing some furniture: a large leather seat and an expensive-looking imager and tach-net data combo. A mound of packing material was still scattered around.

The imager came to life even as Ty stepped towards the chair. It briefly displayed the manufacturer's logo in iridescent 3D, before that was replaced by the head and upper shoulders of what was obviously a software-generated avatar.

'Mr Whitecloud,' began the avatar. 'Thank you for coming. Please take a seat.'

The voice, too, was synthesized, since there was a discernible pause between each word: as if whoever was speaking to him via the avatar was punching the message into a keyboard rather than allowing his own voice to be processed by the machine's inbuilt privacy circuits.

'I represent the Consortium Legislate's intelligence division,' the avatar continued. 'We have brought you here to discuss the artefact you recovered.'

Ty sat down. 'How do I know you're who you say you are?' he demanded bluntly. For some reason, he was not surprised that whoever he was talking to knew his real identity. 'For that matter, why not just send someone real?'

The avatar ignored his questions. 'We believe Dakota Merrick and Lucas Corso intend to instigate a new expedition, one aimed at penetrating deep inside Emissary territory.'

Ty stared at the image, stunned. 'Why are you telling me this?' he asked.

'They're going to recruit you for the expedition. We want you to accept their proposal and report back to us, as and when required.'

Ty licked his lips and glanced around him. 'Why the hell would I do any such thing? Is that why you brought me here?'

'If you prefer, I'd be happy to transmit your current whereabouts to the Freehold authorities, Mr White-cloud, along with details of your true identity and your war-crime charges.'

'Wait!' Ty was halfway out of his chair. 'Just wait a minute.' He reached up to clasp his brow with one shaking hand. 'All right. But how am I supposed to contact you?'

'We can maintain contact with you via an encrypted tach-net link, the details of which are stored on the data-ring on the imager before you.'

Ty glanced at the imager's plate and for the first time noticed a silvery data-ring sitting there, but made no move towards it. Not for the first time, he had the sensation of teetering on the very edge of a steep precipice.

'Mr Whitecloud,' the avatar repeated. 'Please pick up the ring. The data contained within it uses an extremely robust form of encryption, which can be used to establish a secure communications link while disguising its own activities.'

Ty didn't move. 'You're serious? They're going on some kind of expedition . . . to the Emissaries?'

The avatar didn't reply.

Ty let out an angry sigh. 'I'm grateful you got me out of there, but there are going to be people out looking for me now. Where am I supposed to go?'

'Go back to the residency. Tell them you escaped because you believed it was under attack; that much is certainly true. The explosives used will be traced to a Uchidanist undercover tactical unit currently operating out of Unity. In your desperation to escape, you got into the first vehicle you saw. But,' the avatar added, 'you must take the ring with you. That much is vital.'

Ty glanced at the ring. 'It's not safe back there,' he complained. 'There was a man there – Marcus Weil, one of the men guarding me. He said he knew who I was and he'd kill me before he'd ever let me leave.'

The avatar gazed at him, unblinking, for so long that Ty began to wonder if whoever was on the other side of this transmission was in fact still present.

'Go straight back down to the taxi that brought you here, and it will take you to a police station not far from here,' the avatar finally replied. 'Tell them that you got in the taxi outside the residency, asked it for help, and it brought you to them. Mention nothing about coming here, Mr Whitecloud. You will of course give them the name Nathan Driscoll.'

'And what about Weil?' Ty asked.

'With any luck, you won't have to worry about him any more.'

'But . . .'

Shut up and just be glad you're alive, Ty told himself. Anything was better than being trapped in the same building as that knife-wielding madman.

He stared at the ring still sitting on the plate, and impulsively reached out for it.

At the exact same moment as his fingers came into contact with the ring, Ty felt a sharp spike of pain in one temple and squeezed his eyes shut, glimpsing a tiny spark of light in the corner of one eye.

Panic gripped him. How could he have been so stupid? How could he have been so . . .

The next thing he knew, he was still sitting in the chair, but the avatar was gone and the comms unit had shut itself down.

There had been something that worried him terribly, but he was damned if he could remember what it was.

Ty stared at the ring nestling in his palm, then slid it on to one finger. He felt it contract slightly until it was snug against his flesh.

He then made his way back through the deserted offices the way he had come, disturbed by what he realized was an entirely irrational terror that Weil might suddenly appear from around some corner, blade raised to slash out at him. Ty pushed the fear back, thinking: *For one more day I'm still alive. And I'll be alive tomorrow and the day after that, and the day after that* . . . It was like putting one foot in front of the other, or even breathing, drawing down each swallow of air and then exhaling it. You did what you had to in order to stay alive, to stay ahead of your enemies.

So he made his way to the elevator, and returned to the taxi.

SIXTEEN

The *Mjollnir*'s bow was blunt and rounded, with a thick bulge one-third of the way back, concealing an internal centrifuge that could be spun up to provide artificial gravity. She tapered slightly towards the stern, before flaring out again to accommodate fusion drives powerful enough to push her halfway across a solar system in just days, at maximum burn. At the moment, however, she floated peacefully in orbit above Redstone, caged by a spider's web of pressurized maintenance bays that would be dismantled once the hull repair crews had finished their work.

'Bridge of *Mjollnir* to the approaching shuttles,' spoke a voice in Corso's ear. 'We need to confirm the details of your manifest. Who am I speaking to?'

Corso glanced at the three other figures seated behind him in the supply shuttle. Like him, they all wore bulky armoured spacesuits, although for the moment they had left their helmets off. He saw Leo Olivarri, Eduard Martinez and Dan Perez. Perez had been the *Mjollnir*'s head of engineering until, like Nancy Schiller, he had been removed from his job for remaining loyal to Martinez.

Olivarri's boss, Ray Willis, was on a second shuttle following a parallel course to their own, which also carried Ted Lamoureaux, Nancy and Ty Whitecloud. The three members of the frigate's crew remained completely unaware that the man they knew as Nathan Driscoll was operating under an assumed identity.

Perez signalled with one hand, and Corso put the *Mjollnir* link on standby.

'Your name is Herera,' Perez instructed Corso. 'Victor Herera.'

'Why the hell is he asking?'

Perez shrugged. 'It'll be nothing more than a standard security precaution. And it's probably just shitty luck they picked on us.'

Corso reopened the comms link. 'Sorry, bridge, we're getting random system glitches. You're talking to Captain Herera, manifest five alpha zero.' He then added, 'Any problems up there?'

'No problems,' replied a bored-sounding voice at the other end. 'Security's been moved up a couple of notches this morning.'

'Any idea why?' Corso kept his voice casual.

'Damned if I know, but we're requesting you to dock at Bay Three, not Four. Sorry about that. Over and out.'

Corso cut the link and turned to look at the men behind him. 'Do you think they've worked out who we are?'

Perez's reply was blunt and to the point. 'If they had, Senator, we'd already be dead.'

Corso nodded and turned to face the viewscreens once more, while trying to ignore the tension growing in his chest.

Whatever lingering doubts Corso still harboured about the Senate's intentions had vanished a few nights earlier, when Marcus Kenley had appeared at his Senate lodgings in a stolen taxi, its electronic brain hacked in order to prevent it from revealing either its occupant or its whereabouts. He brought with him the news that several of Corso's supporters in the Senate had been arrested during the past hour.

Corso had dressed in a hurry, and then discovered Kenley had also hacked the taxi's speed limiter, as the little vehicle accelerated with frightening speed, almost flipping on to its side at a sharp turn.

Following Jarret's defeat in the challenge, Kenley had been instrumental in setting up safe-houses around Unity, and before long they arrived at a colonial-style building on the outskirts of town. It was a huddle of old-fashioned pressure-domes like something out of a historical 'viro.

Griffith and Velardo were already there, using secure data-net connections to organize more extractions. Olivarri and Willis arrived with the morning, along with some late arrivals who had their own stories of close escapes from the Senate's police.

At first the public news networks told of chaos in the streets surrounding the Senate, but when the networks went offline Corso knew his worst suspicions had come true, and a counter-coup was under way. He kept himself awake throughout the next few nights with a steady diet of coffee and amphetamines, throwing himself into finalizing the details of a plan to take control of the *Mjollnir* before it could be removed from Redstone's orbital space.

Kenley went off and returned a few hours later with Dan Perez in tow; both men departed once again, this time accompanied by Ray Willis, on a mission to retrieve the *Mjollnir*'s commander. They reappeared with Martinez some hours later, looking dirty and exhausted, Willis's face streaked with blood that was clearly not his own.

By then Whitecloud had been tracked down to a secure government building, but by the time someone went out to try and extract him, the residency building had been bombed and Whitecloud had vanished.

His subsequent reappearance in a Unity police station, kilometres away from the residency, raised questions that Corso did not have the time to try and answer. Sympathetic contacts within the Senate's own security services arranged for Whitecloud to be transferred to a less secure facility, where falsified documentation was all that was needed to extract him and bring him to the safe-house, to join with the rest of them.

But of far greater concern to Corso was Dakota's failure to show, even as the time to launch for the *Mjollnir* approached. He felt her absence like an ulcer throbbing in his guts, because without her everything he had planned was for nothing. He found his mood swinging between fury and despondency, and yet there was no way to contact her, not even through Lamoureaux after he also arrived at the safe-house.

At one point, looking up from where he had fallen asleep in front of a screen, Corso realized that more than seventy-two hours had passed since his narrowly escaping arrest. He looked around at the people sitting before other screens, or talking quietly on secure links, or sleeping on mats on the floor.

During the next twenty-four hours most of them would scatter, through Kenley's underground network, to other safe-houses, while a very few, himself included, would board a couple of shuttles in place of the team of engineers detailed to check final repairs to the *Mjollnir*.

That, at least, was the plan. But if Dakota didn't show, that could still undo everything they had worked towards.

Corso activated the shuttle's interface, and saw they were only a few minutes away from docking with the frigate. He tapped on a screen before twisting around to face

Martinez. 'I'm updating the other shuttle on a course change. But not the one the *Mjollnir*'s expecting.'

'Senator?'

'If they're already on to us groundside, they could be diverting us into a trap. The last thing we need is to find ourselves facing an armed welcoming committee. Am I right in thinking each docking bay has an emergency override that can be triggered by an outside signal?'

'If you have the right signature code, yes,' Martinez allowed, 'but it's bound to tip them off that we're up to something.'

'It might be too late for that already. Give me the code anyway.'

Martinez sent him the code through their linked suit comms, while Corso glanced at the screen in front of him to watch the frigate growing larger by the second.

He punched in the course correction. 'Bay Five it is.'

Sunlight broke over the rim of the planet below, filtered down to a soft glow by the shuttle's external sensor arrays. A screen showed clouds drifting over the Mount Mor peninsula, while the broad curve of coast along which Port Gabriel was located could be seen to the west. Approach warnings began to blink as the two shuttles neared a row of bay entrances close to *Mjollnir*'s bow.

'*Mjollnir* to lead shuttle,' declared the voice from the

frigate's bridge. 'You're heading the wrong way. Please get back on your original course.'

'We're having problems with our automatic guidance systems,' Corso improvised, 'and it can't lock on to your docking signal. We're trying to compensate for that, but it's tricky.'

He heard the officer at the other end of the link move away from the microphone to speak to someone else, but he couldn't make out any of their mumbled words before the first voice came back online. 'We've just queried your shuttle's on-board systems and they seem to be working fine. This is your final warning, Captain Herera. Now head for Bay Three.'

Corso put the link on hold and twisted around to look at his fellow passengers. 'Any ideas?'

Martinez shrugged. 'Fuck it, we're just thirty seconds from docking. Use the override to get the bay doors open and don't even bother replying. If they don't know who we are yet, they're sure as hell going to realize pretty damn soon that we're not the engineers they were expecting.'

Corso nodded, and punched in the override. A moment later the bridge of the *Mjollnir* came back online.

'Bridge to shuttle, rendezvous without boarding. Repeat, rendezvous without boarding, Captain Herera. Is that clear? Dock with the external maintenance bays, but not with the *Mjollnir* itself. If you board, we'll consider it a hostile action.'

Corso reached out and terminated the link. The *Mjollnir* seemed to rush towards them, blotting out the stars beyond. Now all that could be seen on the displays was a wall of grey metal expanding towards him.

A thin line of light appeared directly ahead, quickly growing wider as massive steel doors swung open to reveal the brightly lit interior of Bay Five.

Corso felt his body forced back into the seat as the shuttle decelerated hard, and he wondered if they were cutting it too fine. But before he had completed this thought they were already inside, automated grapples seizing the tiny ship and lowering it into a docking cradle.

The next step was critical: they had to disembark from the shuttle and get inside the frigate proper, before the crew on the bridge had a chance to react. Long, precious seconds passed while an airlock docked with the hatch in the shuttle's belly. They spent this time pulling on their helmets and securing them.

Corso knew there was a risk that Simenon might decide to dump the internal atmosphere and flush them out into space. Despite this concern, for the moment they kept their visors raised. It was easier to communicate face to face, and besides the helmets were designed to self-seal in case of a catastrophic loss of pressure.

Corso himself went through the airlock last, dropping only slowly in the zero gravity before emerging into a disembarkation lounge located right next to the bays.

Behind him the bulkheads rumbled and shook as the second shuttle docked.

Martinez and the rest were already checking the seals on each other's suits. Corso checked Perez's suit, then Perez did the same for him. There was a clanging sound nearby, before, one by one, four passengers from the second shuttle dropped into the lounge, through a separate airlock.

Olivarri meanwhile deposited an oblong case on the shelf running along one wall, and opened it to reveal several lightweight pulse-rifles. He passed these out to everyone but Lamoureaux and Whitecloud.

Martinez picked up a rifle, before stepping over to Corso and clapping him on the shoulder. 'You did a nice job getting us this far, Senator. But I think I'll take it from here.'

Martinez turned and called for everybody's attention.

'First, a reminder of what we can expect. *Mjollnir* is currently undergoing last-minute checks before departing for the Sol system, a day from now, with a full complement of crew that's expected to arrive here in no more than another three hours. In the meantime there's a minimal presence on board – I reckon a skeleton crew of no more than a dozen.'

'Why so few?' asked Lamoureaux.

'Because the main security contingent charged with guarding the frigate headed back down to the surface just under an hour ago. That leaves us a fairly narrow window of opportunity to take control and break from orbit. Mr Driscoll,' he turned to Whitecloud, 'you're going to head straight to the labs. Leo, escort him there and keep your eyes peeled. Don't engage anyone you run into if you can avoid it. Make sure first of all that the artefact's where it should be and report back if there's any problems or likelihood of delays.'

Corso watched the two men depart and felt his lips tighten in disapproval. He did not enjoy having to maintain this pretence regarding Whitecloud, or even having to act civilly towards him, and yet it was clear from his own research into Whitecloud's career that the man was quite brilliant. It was hard to believe someone with such a remarkable mind could have used it to perpetrate such terrible acts of inhumanity, but history was littered with just such men.

The rest of them then moved out of the lounge, and floated in pairs down a long shaft. Dan Perez and Nancy Schiller took point, while Ray Willis came last, guarding their rear. The ship was running at low power, so they proceeded through a strange half-twilight, their shadows racing in front of them like black ghosts whenever they passed a dimly glowing light fixture.

Corso swallowed and tried to ignore the fits of light-headedness that sometimes blurred his vision. He was still running on chemicals, and the last occasion he had actually slept seemed like part of another lifetime.

So much of what they had planned hinged on various assumptions, particularly that the frigate's security overrides would have remained unaltered in the wake of

Martinez's arrest. If they had been changed, however, the extra time taken up by burning or blowing their way through various sealed entrances might allow the security services enough time to muster a serious response.

Before he could ponder any further, they arrived at a transport terminal and boarded a cylindrical windowless car that carried them swiftly along a tunnel running the entire length of the frigate, and headed towards the centrifuge's hub.

They had managed to get this far. Surely, thought Corso, fate wouldn't be so cruel as to prevent them from reaching the bridge.

The group disembarked shortly after, and found themselves in a cylindrical chamber six metres across and twice as much in length. It was situated at the axis of the centrifugal wheel that spun constantly to provide *Mjollnir*'s bridge and main crew quarters with artificial gravity.

Four colour-coded doors were set into the central third of the chamber, which revolved independently of the rest. These doors opened on to shafts radiating outwards from the chamber, each one leading into the centrifuge's inner rim. No one was surprised to find the emergency locks on all four doors had been engaged.

Corso watched as Nancy Schiller floated forward to grab a handhold next to one door, pulling herself in close as it dragged her around. She used her teeth to pull off a glove, then reached out to tap at a screen set into the door itself.

'Fuck, it's not responding,' she announced. 'My codes are no good.'

Icy fingers twirled inside Corso's belly.

'I'll give it a try,' said Martinez.

He grabbed a handhold next to another door, as it swept by, and tapped at this door's screen. After a few moments the outline of a hand appeared, against which Martinez pressed his palm, and the door hissed open in response.

We're in, thought Corso, and realized he had been holding his breath the whole time. There were sighs of relief and whispered prayers from the others.

He floated forward, grabbing another handhold next to the door Martinez had opened, and suddenly it was the station that was spinning while he remained stationary.

'I thought there were supposed to be elevators,' he grumbled to Martinez. He could feel the tiniest pull of spin-g by now, and it would only get stronger the closer they came to the centrifuge's outer rim, seventy metres away.

'Blame our friends on the bridge,' said Martinez. 'Looks like we're going to have to climb all the way down.'

Martinez let go of his handhold and pushed over to

the door Nancy had tried to open. Twenty seconds later this door also slid open, to reveal a second shaft.

'Dan, take the other shaft,' instructed Martinez, turning and lowering his legs past the open door. 'Nancy, Ray, you're going with him. When you get to the ring, approach the bridge from the spinward direction, and we'll come at it from the other side. But wait for our signal before trying to enter it. Senator, you're with me and Ted.'

Martinez took the lead, followed by Corso, with Lamoureaux coming last. The machine-head, Corso noted, now had a perpetually distracted look on his face, like someone who had forgotten something but couldn't quite remember what.

'Ted.'

Lamoureaux finally seemed to snap out of it. 'What?'

'Something worrying you?'

'No.' Lamoureaux shook his head, then shrugged. 'But I'm getting some weird distortion noise coming through my implants.'

'Anything we need to be concerned about?'

Lamoureaux thought for a moment. 'I don't know. Maybe not.'

The inside of the shaft was studded with handholds, but Corso wasn't used to heights, and he had to fight off tendrils of panic that accompanied the slow increase of the wheel's spin-g as they approached the ring. He focused instead on the steady rhythm of his movements, while keeping his eyes fixed on the wall directly before him.

By the time they arrived at the ring, the gravity was close on two-thirds standard. Their way was now blocked by the roof of the shaft's elevator car. Martinez used a single shot from his pulse-rifle to blow out an emergency hatch in the car's roof, before climbing down inside it.

Corso dropped down on top of the car and peered inside to see Martinez studying a panel next to the closed elevator doors. The panel looked blackened and melted.

Martinez looked up at him and shrugged. 'It's been shot to pieces, and we're going to have to go through the hard way. Got the explosives?'

'Can't you just yank the doors open?'

Martinez shook his head. 'These aren't your standard-issue elevator doors, Senator.'

Corso nodded, reached into his suit's thigh pocket and withdrew the dark, slim oblong of a putty-like material before passing it down to Martinez. Corso next motioned to Lamoureaux to climb a little way back up the shaft, before following him a moment later. A minute passed before Martinez himself clambered back out of the car and crouched as close to the wall of the shaft as he could get.

A dull crunch sounded, and a sharp, rattling vibration set Corso's teeth on edge.

A trail of thick, oily smoke drifted up from inside the elevator car. Martinez dropped back down inside and braced his shoulder against the doors, which were now bent and twisted out of shape. He thumped against them several times before they suddenly slid half-open with a discordant screech.

Light flashed from beyond the opening, sparkling on Martinez's shoulder and burning a dark circle into the fabric of his suit.

Corso yelled and dropped down through the roof of the car, as Martinez staggered backwards. Corso squeezed into the tight space and managed to fire off a couple of blind shots through the half-open door.

He heard a muffled thump, then silence.

'That was stupid of me,' gasped Martinez, who had fallen back, one gloved hand pressed against his shoulder.

Corso smelled burning flesh, and forced a surge of bile back down his throat. 'Shit, I think I might actually have got him,' he said, listening carefully.

He moved forward cautiously, turning sideways to squeeze between the two buckled doors and peer through the rank, oily smoke.

The lights inside the centrifuge ring were much brighter than throughout the rest of the ship. Corso edged forward until he almost stumbled across the body of a young woman slumped forward on the gently curving deck. One side of her face was burned and blackened, and her weapon lay nearby. Headshots from a pulse-rifle such as his own were invariably fatal.

He stood up and pulled his glove back on, but found

to his surprise that his hands were shaking so hard it took a couple of attempts. He drew in a couple of deep breaths, and ignored the welter of regret and shame floating just under his thoughts. They still had to get to the bridge.

Hearing a grunt from behind, he turned to see Lamoureaux helping Martinez out through the elevator doors. Martinez spared the dead girl only a brief glance, but Lamoureaux stared at her corpse in open-mouthed horror.

'Let's get moving,' said Martinez, stepping on past the body.

Corso put a hand on his chest. 'Wait a second, you're not going anywhere. You've just been shot—'

Martinez met his gaze. 'Right now our priority is to get to the bridge. Soon as we're in control there, I can go to the med-bay. But not before.'

The *Mjollnir* felt deserted without its full complement of crew. Like a ghost ship, Ty thought, as he and Olivarri moved along echoing passageways and down connecting shafts made eerie by silence and shadows.

They passed storage bays filled with towering steel racks that had clearly been newly installed while he had still been held inside the Senate Residency. He saw new computer equipment, and observed that dozens of med-boxes had been slotted into some of the racks. Many more were piled on giant pallets that filled up much of the remaining space within the bay.

They moved on, soon reaching the laboratory complex, which was sealed off from the rest of the ship by its own airlock system. The labs were designed primarily for assessing planetary biospheres, and Ty was not surprised to find that they too had been overhauled and upgraded since he had last been there.

'Why all the precautions?' asked Leo, casting a wary eye around him. There were new cryogenic facilities that could be used for storing biological specimens, as well as for incubation and dissection. There were also airtight isolation booths for storing live samples, their interiors visible in a bank of monitors set into one bulkhead directly above the main interface.

Ty took a seat next to a console and pulled off his suit's gloves to log on. 'Remember the *Mjollnir* was primarily used as a colony ship,' he said without looking up. 'These labs were built so they could analyse alien flora and fauna. That means keeping them in strict isolation in case of any potential biohazards.' He nodded over his shoulder at the main airlock. 'You don't want to take the chance of the rest of the ship getting contaminated, if something nasty gets loose.'

'But a lot of this looks brand new.'

'Just like in those bays we passed,' Ty agreed. 'Hang on . . .'

A screen took up most of the wall directly above the console. A grid of images now appeared on it, each showing identical views of metal-grey rooms. All but one of these was empty.

'What are they?'

'Those are the isolation booths for storing larger samples,' Ty explained. 'The body I brought back is held in one of them.'

He looked around suddenly. 'What's that?'

'What?' said Olivarri.

'That noise.'

'I don't hear anything.'

'It sounds like . . . I don't know. Almost like singing.'

Olivarri just looked dumbfounded. 'I have no idea what you're talking about.'

Singing wasn't the right word for it, exactly. That would imply there was something pleasant about it, when in fact it was horribly abrasive. It was more like static, he decided, but barely at the edge of perception. After a moment it began to fade.

'You really didn't hear that?' Ty said, after it had passed.

Olivarri shrugged and shook his head. 'I really didn't hear anything. Maybe a problem with the comms?'

'Maybe.' Ty tapped at the interface once more and the empty booths disappeared, all except for the one containing the Atn's remains, which now expanded to fill the screen.

'That's it.' He turned to Olivarri. 'That's the reason we're here.'

Leo let out an incredulous laugh. 'You're fucking

kidding me. *That's* what we've been fighting for? It looks like a pile of junk.'

'Appearances can be deceptive.'

A pile of junk was a fair description, Ty realized. But inside it might just be found the one thing that could bring down an entire civilization.

Corso and Lamoureaux supported the wounded Commander and helped him along the passage. As they walked, they passed archways leading aside into mess halls and recreational areas, all of them now deserted. Thick, lush vegetation grew from pots placed at every metre or so, all tended by small, delicate-looking machines that climbed in between branches or vines.

They kept their weapons at the ready, but met no further resistance. Before very long they reached the door leading into the bridge itself and found that it was, of course, sealed.

Martinez let go of them and slid down against one side of the passageway.

'Lucas,' he instructed, his face pale and slick with sweat, 'radio the others now. Don't worry about breaking silence. We just need to know if they're in position yet.'

Corso established contact with Nancy Schiller and she delivered a brief report. He then asked her to send Ray Willis to join them.

'They had a clear run all the way around the far side

of the wheel,' he told Martinez and Lamoureaux. 'The bridge is sealed around the other side as well.'

'Why do we need Willis here?' asked a puzzled Lamoureaux.

'In case you hadn't noticed, we're one man down,' Corso explained. 'Otherwise I'd be the only one on this side who's both armed and uninjured. There's three of them around the far side of the bridge, so they can easily spare Ray.'

'For what it's worth,' said Martinez with effort, 'I'm beginning to think there's a lot fewer people on board than we thought.'

'Maybe,' Lamoureaux suggested, 'they've got other people scattered throughout the rest of the ship. There's plenty of room to hide.'

'No, I think everyone left is on the other side of that door,' Martinez grunted, pushing himself a little more upright. He looked increasingly pale and frail. 'I'm going to try and persuade them to let us in.'

Martinez opened a command frequency to the bridge. As he spoke, his voice took on a deeper, solider timbre.

'This is Commander Eduard Martinez hailing whoever is currently on the bridge of the *Mjollnir*. Please respond.'

An unfamiliar voice burst out over their shared comms. 'I hear you, *Mister* Martinez. This is Luis Simenon, acting commander, addressing the boarders. You are committing an act of piracy and I demand you surrender your weapons.'

'Luis, I need you to open up the door. You're out-numbered, and you're already one woman down.'

'The last I heard, *sir*, you were under arrest for sedition. That means you don't have the authority any more to—'

'Mr Simenon,' Martinez thundered, 'the *Mjollnir* is still my commission. It'd take a special plenary meeting of the Senate to change that fact, and I don't recall hearing anything about one taking place. That means I have every right to board my own command, and yet *your* people actually fired upon me and my men. Whatever explanation you have, I'm sure it's bound to be fascinating.'

Simenon didn't respond for at least another thirty seconds, and when he came back he sounded cold but subdued, even apologetic. 'My orders come directly from the Senate security services, Commander, just as they did when I relieved you of command. There are fast-response teams on their way here, so I suggest you and your men surrender your weapons now, or suffer the consequences.'

'He's cut comms,' Martinez said a moment later.

'Is he telling the truth?' asked Corso.

'About the reinforcements? Sure. There's a couple of orbital platforms that can launch police boats in a hurry, plus there are tactical teams on permanent standby on the ground.' He nodded towards a screen flush with the door's surface. 'Help me over there and let's see if I can get us through that entrance.'

Corso got an arm under Martinez's shoulder and helped him over to the door just as Ray Willis arrived, his rifle slung over one shoulder. He was panting heavily, having just run the entire way around the centrifuge from the opposite side of the bridge.

'I saw a body,' Willis gasped. 'Was there any . . . ?' He stopped when he saw Martinez.

'We ran into some trouble,' said Corso.

Willis nodded, his chest still heaving. 'Door's locked round the other way as well,' he said, 'though we didn't run into anyone. Nancy's ready to blow it open on your signal.'

Corso nodded and checked his pulse-rifle. Its battery was at half capacity. Weapons such as these were only good for about a dozen shots before their batteries were completely drained, but they were cheap and easy to manufacture.

He nodded to Willis, who moved to one side of the bridge entrance, his back to the wall and his rifle held close to his chest.

'Visors down, everyone,' said Corso, taking up position opposite Willis. 'Ted, get the Commander safe to one side as soon as he's done.'

Martinez finished entering his code into the screen, but didn't activate the door. Corso warned Nancy to be ready, then waited until Martinez was out of harm's way before leaning over to touch a panel on the screen that read CONFIRM.

The door slid open a moment later, to the sound of shouting from inside.

'Now,' Corso barked into his comms.

Willis twisted at the waist, aimed the barrel of his rifle through the open door and fired off several shots. Almost at the same moment there was an enormous thump from somewhere inside, followed by more yelling and scuffling.

Willis ran inside, Corso following a moment later.

The first thing Corso noticed was the buckled remains of the door on the far side of the bridge. One of the *Mjollnir*'s crew lay face-down near the interface chair positioned at the bridge's centre, a pulse-rifle just beyond his outstretched hand.

Willis was barking orders at a uniformed man and woman who had sheltered behind a comms console. They stood up uncertainly and dropped their weapons, clearly shaken.

The noise and confusion was tremendous, as black smoke rose up to collect under the smooth dark dome of the bridge's ceiling.

Nancy kept her rifle levelled at an unarmed man, dressed in the clothes of an orbital dock-worker, who was hiding behind another console, while Perez had his aimed at a man in the uniform of a deck officer, his shoulder and one side blackened from a pulse-rifle shot. The officer was sitting next to a console, a pistol gripped in one hand, but pointed at the deck as if momentarily forgotten.

Simenon, Corso guessed. He looked dazed, as if he wasn't sure where he was.

Corso trained his own weapon on Simenon's head, while Perez inched forward, barking at him to drop his pistol and get down on the deck. Instead Simenon seemed to remember where he was and took a two-handed grip on the pistol, but without raising it.

'Drop the fucking gun!' Perez screamed.

Simenon breathed hard through his nostrils and shook his head emphatically, even though Corso could see he was completely terrified. 'You won't stand a chance when the response teams get here,' he replied, his voice cracking.

'It's over, Luis,' Perez yelled. 'Drop the gun, and you can take these people back down. Do you understand? Drop the fucking gun *now* or—'

Simenon shook his head emphatically, the motion almost like a tic, and he brought his pistol up quickly to aim at Perez.

Corso fired off a single shot that hit Simenon square in the side of the head. There was a distinct *crack* as his brain boiled, the pressure fracturing his skull.

He tumbled to the deck, his legs folding under him as if a puppet's strings had been cut.

Corso put his rifle down and pulled off his helmet. The air now smelled a lot worse than when wearing it.

'You okay?' asked Schiller, eyeing him. She'd herded the dock-worker over to join the rest.

'You know what Simenon just did?' Corso replied. 'He killed himself.'

Schiller looked confused.

'With all due respect, Senator,' said Perez, 'what the fuck are you talking about?'

'He was put in charge of a major military asset, and lost it,' Corso explained. 'He's probably got family, and they'd have been left with nothing if he'd just surrendered.'

Perez shrugged. 'So?'

So it's wrong. So it's completely, utterly fucked up, Corso wanted to yell. But Perez was still a Freeholder born and bred, so he just shook his head and dropped the subject.

Corso went over to the three survivors, now lying face-down on the deck, guarded by Schiller and Willis. Perez activated the bridge's comms console, and a moment later Martinez and Lamoureaux entered and surveyed the scene.

'You,' Corso demanded, nudging the prisoner in overalls with one booted foot. 'What's your name?'

The man in overalls twisted his head around slightly to face Corso. 'Inéz Randall,' he muttered. 'I'm an engineer,' he explained, 'for the—'

'Listen up, Inéz,' Corso instructed him. 'Take your two friends here, head for Launch Bay Five, take one of the shuttles there, and get off this ship as fast as you can. Don't do anything stupid or heroic, because you'll only wind up dead, do you understand me?'

Randall nodded.

'All right,' said Corso. 'Get up, all three of you. Move.'

They stood hesitantly and Corso finally got a good look at them. These were nothing more than raw junior officers who had just happened to be in the wrong place at the wrong time. They had obviously been brought on to the frigate to run the final checks on the ship's primary systems.

'Is there anybody else on board?' Corso asked them.

They exchanged nervous glances. 'Just us,' said Randall.

Corso studied the man and decided he was telling the truth. 'Then get moving.' He waved the barrel of his rifle towards the blown-open entrance. '*Now.*'

Once they were gone, Corso sat down heavily in a chair and pulled off his glove to run one hand through his sweat-soaked hair. He watched as Schiller and Willis carried the two corpses out of the bridge, dumping them on the deck just beyond the undamaged entrance. Lamoureaux meanwhile helped Martinez on to a low couch set against one wall, then himself stepped over to the interface chair.

'Ted,' he began. Lamoureaux glanced over at Corso, as the chair's petals folded down to allow him access. 'Keep an eye on those three, and make sure they head straight for the shuttles. Also get in touch with Leo, and check if he made it to the labs okay.'

Lamoureaux nodded, peeling his suit off and

dropping it to the deck before taking his position. Corso pulled his own suit off and draped it over a console.

'There's an evac order going through the maintenance bays around the frigate,' Perez reported from the comms console. 'I heard from Leo already: everything is right where it should be, according to Driscoll.'

Corso nodded and turned to Martinez. 'Okay, Commander,' he said, taking the other man's arm. 'Med-bay for you. Nancy, will you help him there?'

Nancy Schiller nodded and helped Martinez slowly out of the bridge.

'There are some fast boats moving into orbit,' Lamoureaux reported. Corso glanced over and noticed how he'd left the chair's petals unfolded, and was now staring at somewhere far away. 'I don't know if we can manage to break orbit before they get within range. Maybe I can . . . oh shit.'

Corso stood up, alarmed. 'What is it?'

Lamoureaux licked his lips, drumming his fingers on the armrests of the interface chair. 'It's Dakota . . . or her ship, at least. It just showed up out of nowhere, coming in fast. She's . . . hang on.'

Corso waited, suddenly tense. 'I just heard from her,' Lamoureaux continued. 'She'll be on board in the next couple of minutes.'

'That doesn't solve the problem of those boats coming our way,' said Perez. 'Those things have some serious fucking firepower, Senator, and we haven't even had a chance to break orbit.'

'Ted—' Corso began.

'I already initiated a hard burn,' Lamoureaux replied, 'but it takes time to get a ship this size moving.'

'Just how long?'

Lamoureaux leaned back against the headrest, his eyes squeezed shut. 'The drive-spines are currently only at half-charge. That means it's going to be at least a couple of hours before we'll be able to jump out of this system. Ah shit, that's no . . . hang on.'

He leaned forward suddenly, shook his head and blinked his eyes wide. 'We've got two armed corvettes approaching on an intercept course,' he said. 'They must have already been in orbit.'

It hit Corso like a punch in the stomach that, without Dakota's help, they were going to die. Lamoureaux couldn't save them but, with the aid of her ship, Dakota could. Suddenly their hastily assembled plan to hijack the *Mjollnir* looked as precarious as a house of cards in an earthquake.

Then he realized something was wrong with Lamoureaux. He sat bent forward in the interface chair, clutching at one side of his head with a pained expression.

Corso stepped forward quickly, catching him before he could fall out of his seat. The navigator's skin had turned pale and waxy.

'What the hell is going on?' said Perez.

'I don't know,' Corso snapped, pulling himself up on to the dais to help Lamoureaux back properly into the seat. 'Ted, what is it?'

When he replied, Lamoureaux sounded groggy, unfocused. 'I don't know. It was like there was this enormous pressure inside my head and . . . oh, damn.'

The bends, thought Corso; his Magi-boosted implants were finally burning out his cortex.

Corso moved out of the way as Lamoureaux leaned forward, and to one side, and vomited noisily on to the deck. Corso held him by the shoulder and ignored the shocked expression on Perez's face.

'Where's Olivarri?' Corso demanded.

Perez stepped over to another console, and Corso watched Perez's face change from orange to blue as the console's display flickered with bright colours. 'He's on his way here,' Perez replied after a moment. 'I'm reading him as just entering the wheel.' He reached out and tapped at the screen again. 'I can activate the external feeds from here.'

A moment later the dark bowl of the bridge's ceiling filled with stars and with the broad curve of the planet below, along with a simulation of the *Mjollnir* as it would appear at a distance of a few kilometres. Smoke from the explosion had already been sucked away by the ventilation system.

Corso could see the fine network of work-bays and pressurized cabins surrounding the frigate, and several tiny craft moving steadily away from it. One was a shuttle carrying Simenon's skeleton crew, while the rest undoubtedly contained the engineers and repair specialists who had been working on the hull until the order to evacuate.

According to a string of data floating next to the frigate it was indeed under way, but its speed was still relatively incremental despite the enormous amount of energy flowing out of the fusion drives.

'Any sign of Dakota's ship?' asked Corso, still holding Lamoureaux upright. He appeared to be barely conscious.

'I think she's on the frigate's far side,' Perez replied. 'One moment.'

The starscape overhead wheeled suddenly, spinning around by a hundred and eighty degrees. Now Corso could see a Magi ship rapidly approaching. It looked, as ever, like some creature born to live between the stars, its forward-reaching drive-spines like the grasping tentacles of a monstrous sea-creature.

Lamoureaux's head flopped against Corso's arm, and he grasped the machine-head under one shoulder and guided him down from the interface chair. Perez helped drag him over to one of the couches lining the walls of the bridge.

Leo Olivarri suddenly appeared, looking breathless. He glanced from Lamoureaux to Corso with a questioning expression.

'Leo,' said Corso, 'I need you to get Mr Lamoureaux here to the med-bay.'

Olivarri nodded and came over, clearly recognizing this was no time for questions. Lamoureaux's skin was clammy but together they managed to get him back on to his feet. He gradually seemed to become a little more aware of his surroundings, and then Olivarri helped him out of the bridge.

Perez looked worried. 'Senator, without someone manning the interface chair, we're going to be at a very serious disadvantage.'

Corso sucked in a breath and turned back to study the overhead projection. By now the *Mjollnir* had mostly passed out of the orbital dock, while the Magi ship had drawn abreast of it. The two hostile corvettes, identified by icons floating beside them, were still a few thousand kilometres distant.

Another string of data appeared directly between the Magi ship and the frigate, marking a single blip moving quickly across the gap between the two craft.

That's her, Corso thought. But why was she leaving her ship? Surely she was intending to accompany the *Mjollnir* from inside her own vessel?

'Senator.' Corso turned to Perez. 'We have pulse-weapons mounted on the hull, but we've had to divert most of their power to the fusion drives. Unless you can come up with something very soon, we're going to be sitting ducks for those corvettes.'

Corso nodded, and stepped forward until he stood directly underneath the projection of the *Mjollnir*. It looked real enough to make him feel he could reach up and touch it. He watched as the blip representing

Dakota reached one of the frigate's external airlocks, and disappeared from sight.

'Dan, patch me into the frigate's general address system. Dakota just came on board, and I want to be sure she hears me.'

'Patching you in now,' Perez replied, his hands sliding rapidly across the surface of his console. 'One moment and I'll have a visual on her.'

The *Mjollnir* and the surrounding starscape began to shrink overhead, as if receding at enormous speed. In its place appeared a larger-than-life image of Dakota, now inside an airlock already halfway through its opening cycle.

She was naked, but her skin was coated in what looked like thick black oil, her eyes gleaming and alien-looking. She had a bag slung across one shoulder, out of which she pulled a jumpsuit.

Corso glanced over at Perez and saw a censorious look on his face. It was hard to remember that he too had been that buttoned-down before he first left Red-stone.

Overhead, Dakota pulled on the jumpsuit, the black slick coating on her skin draining away. She glanced briefly towards the microscopic lens buried in one wall of the airlock with a sardonic smile, and Corso felt his face redden.

'Dakota, if you can hear me, we need you on the bridge *right now*. We've got a couple of corvettes approaching and Ted's—'

She had stepped out of the airlock and was now pushing her way down a connecting shaft towards the centrifuge hub. 'I know about Ted,' she replied, as if addressing the air. 'Just hang on. I'll be there soon.'

Dakota disappeared from the overhead display, replaced by the previous view of the local starscape. The corvettes had by now resolved into distinct shapes.

'We're being signalled by one of the corvettes,' Perez announced. 'They're warning us to shut down the engines or they'll start shooting.'

'Bullshit,' Corso heard himself say. 'They're bluffing. This is the only colony-class ship the Senate has left.'

'Maybe so, Senator, but if whoever ordered those corvettes to come after us lets us get away, he's going to face a firing squad, or at least a challenge from a queue of subordinates. Blowing a hole in our side might look like a safer bet, with that in mind.'

Damn you, Dakota. How long could it take to get to the centrifuge hub, then to the bridge?

'They must know there's no way we can just stop the acceleration. Even if we shut down the fusion drive, and used the manoeuvring systems to push us back, it'd be hours before we could come to a halt relative to the docks.'

'Look, Senator,' said Perez, 'I'm not necessarily coun-selling surrender, but if they *do* fire on us, they could cripple us, or a lot worse.'

Corso shook his head and licked suddenly dry lips. 'No. We keep going. Don't respond to their messages.'

'They're getting ready to fire on us,' Perez retorted, growing visibly angrier and stepping out from behind the console, with bunched fists. 'They're letting us see their targeting systems to make sure we know exactly what they're intending. Senator, if we don't signal them now and agree—'

Perez stopped abruptly at a sudden bright flare of light from the overhead display. Corso looked up to see that several pale spheres had now appeared between the frigate and the two approaching corvettes.

Except the corvettes weren't there anymore.

'What—?' Perez stopped and turned back to the console, staring down at its softly glowing surface as if he couldn't believe his eyes. 'They just . . . hang on.'

Perez replayed what had just happened. They both watched as bright beams of light flickered out from the spheres, tearing the two ships apart.

Dakota entered the bridge at that same moment, looking breathless. Perez stared up again at the overhead display, then at her, clearly putting two and two together.

'Tell me everything I need to know,' she said, stopping briefly to draw breath at the edge of the dais supporting the interface chair.

'We're breaking orbit,' Corso told her. She dropped her bag on the floor next to the dais and pulled herself up and into the interface chair. 'But it's taking too long,' he warned.

Dakota nodded, and Corso watched the intense way her small white fists gripped the chair's armrests.

She closed her eyes and for a few moments fought to steady her breathing, then nodded tightly. 'I'm going to ramp the drive up for a premature jump. If we can get out of range of the orbital defence systems, we might be able to take our time before making a longer jump.'

Corso watched as the petals surrounding the interface chair began to fold up around it, surrounding Dakota in silent darkness. He could feel the frigate's acceleration beginning to bite. Much like the *Mjollnir*'s sister-ships, its centrifuge could be spun down during periods in which it was performing an extended hard burn, when each of the living spaces contained within it rotated on massive hydraulics so that the acceleration provided a comfortable level of gravity. When the acceleration ceased and zero gee returned, the centrifuge could once again be spun up.

He glanced back up at the projected starscape. The Magi ship that had brought Dakota to the frigate was slipping out of range. It was also beginning to slowly spin as if out of control, edging towards the delicate filigree of the orbital dock the *Mjollnir* had now left behind.

Something was wrong.

Dakota.

Her eyelids trembled, then opened on to nothing.

'What is it, Lucas?' she asked, the sound of her own voice close and flat within the confined space.

Your ship, what's happening to it?

'I don't have any choice,' she replied in a half-whisper.

Don't have any choice about what?

'About leaving it behind.'

SEVENTEEN

Even as she locked into the *Mjollnir*'s sensory dataspace, Dakota could still hear the Mos Hadroch whispering to her.

It was so close to the edge of perception that she might have dismissed it as only her imagination had she not been able to filter it through the rapidly receding Magi ship. There was something alive nestling within the carapace of the dead Atn – and it, in turn, could sense her.

Until that first moment of contact, as she made her way across the empty space that had separated the now rapidly receding starship from the frigate, she had assumed the Mos Hadroch would prove to be some inert device, a tool and nothing more.

But instead she was beginning to suspect it was something much more akin to the Magi's highest levels of technological achievement, so that to say it was merely sentient would be to do it a severe injustice. What she was now picking up through her enhanced senses was more akin to an artificial god, though not much bigger than a human skull, and fashioned to one very specific purpose.

Dakota closed her eyes tightly, sensing faint tendrils of enquiry from the dead minds that lived inside the Magi ship. So far, she was pretty sure they had no inkling of the act of betrayal she was about to commit. There had been a time when she had been greatly worried about their ability to see inside her mind, but since those early days she had learned how to mask her thought processes from their attention.

We've got fresh contacts, she heard Perez say, panic edging into his voice. *Missiles. Approaching fast, launched from the surface. I'm reading a hundred and eighty seconds to impact.*

She had seen them already. She felt her subjective experience of time shift, so that seconds seemed to take minutes to pass, as she locked completely into the *Mjollnir*'s data-space.

There was none of the pain or confusion she had endured in every attempt to interface with the Magi ship at anything more than a very low level following her resurrection. The frigate's data-space was tragically primitive by comparison . . . but it worked.

The Meridian drones had emerged in their hundreds from the Magi ship, and now some of them darted towards the missiles which were accelerating towards the frigate at more than twenty gee. The drones blazed with intense heat in the instant just before they sent out a pulse of fire bright enough to be visible from the planet surface below.

Alarms blared throughout the *Mjollnir* as this flash of energy overwhelmed its external sensor arrays. Down on the surface of Redstone, technicians and officers in both the Freehold and Uchidan territories were roused from their sleep inside armoured subsurface bunkers, as early-warning systems mistook the sudden flash for an attack.

The missiles meanwhile were reduced to spatters of molten metal that registered on the bridge's overhead display as fuzzy-edged splashes of colour rapidly fading from white to orange.

Dakota opened her eyes and let her breath out slowly.

She had saved their skins, and she had not needed the Magi ship to do it. The Meridian drones had responded to her commands with deadly efficiency, whispering to her of attack and defence, strike and counter-strike.

For the first time, she began to believe they might actually be able to take on the Emissaries.

Dakota

The air inside the petals tasted warm and slightly metallic. She sat motionless, alone in the darkness, and enjoyed a brief moment of silence.

Dakota can you

She let the last of the air out of her nostrils and waited for her heart to stop thumping.

hear me?

'Dakota! I . . .'

Corso paused in mid-sentence as the chair's petals

folded back down. Dakota surveyed the bridge, full of light and sound and motion.

'I took care of it,' she said, slowly lifting herself out of the interface chair and stepping carefully down from the dais. 'There won't be any more missiles.'

'How?' Corso demanded, his face damp with sweat. 'I mean, I saw it on the overhead. It was incredible. But . . . how?'

She looked past his shoulder to see a man she didn't recognize standing by one console. He studied the data scrolling in front of him so intently it was obvious he was deliberately trying not to look at her.

'I told you,' she said. 'I got my hands on some weapons – very old, very powerful weapons left behind by a dead civilization.'

'We're being hailed from the ground, Senator.'

Corso turned to the man by the console and nodded distractedly. 'Any news?'

'There are more missiles on their way. They say they won't pull them back unless we stop and surrender.'

Dakota walked past Corso to join the other man sitting at the console. 'What's your name?' she asked.

'Dan Perez.'

She nodded to the console. 'Please.'

He shrugged and stepped aside. She studied the data displayed there and frowned.

'These missiles aren't tacticals,' she announced, looking over at Corso. 'This is the kind of ordnance that could vaporize the frigate. It doesn't make sense.'

'Why not?' asked Perez, still standing beside her.

'Because they've lost,' she replied. 'There's nothing to be gained in destroying the frigate.'

'You haven't spent a lot of time around Freeholders, have you, Ma'am?' suggested Perez. 'Apart from the Senator here, that is.'

She turned to face him. 'What's that supposed to mean?'

'Just that if you had, you'd know they'd rather blow the frigate out of the sky than let her escape. The consequences don't matter. To them it's all about honour.'

She glanced at Corso, who affected a weary shrug. 'He's right, Dakota.'

She shook her head in irritation. 'Then they're a bunch of fucking idiots. All right, we could hang around here and take all those missiles out with the drones, but we'd just be wasting valuable time.' She headed over to the interface chair. 'I'm going to jump us out of here now.'

'The drive batteries are low,' warned Corso. 'It's not enough to even get us out of this system.'

'We're not going to jump out of this system,' she replied, pulling herself back into the chair's embrace. 'Remember I said I wanted to make a premature jump? Well, we're going to take a hop and a skip, just a couple of million kilometres here or there. It doesn't really matter where we come out, as long as it puts some distance between us and Redstone.'

Corso had followed her back over, and Perez watched

them carefully as Corso stepped up on to the dais and gripped the side of the chair.

'How sure are you that you know what you're doing?' he demanded, keeping his voice low. 'You disappeared for a hell of a long time, and I can't tell you how difficult that made things for me. And what the hell's going on with your own ship?'

'I ⸺ frequently ⸺ far indeed from knowing just what I'm doing, Lucas. I just take each minute as it comes. And as for my ship,' she added, 'just wait and see.'

She closed her eyes, shutting out the bridge and dipping back into the data-space. The new batch of missiles – built for hard acceleration and tipped with antimatter warheads – wouldn't get in range of the frigate for at least another thousand seconds.

She looked up at the overhead projection and saw that the drones were now spiralling back in towards the Magi ship. Clearly some of its minds had finally realized what she intended, and it had already begun to accelerate away from Redstone – but still not fast enough.

Some of the drones began to burn with a furious incandescence, focusing this energy into highly destructive beams that played across the hull of the Magi ship. Corso watched with slack-jawed horror as it began to disintegrate under the intensive fire.

Corso grabbed Dakota by the shoulder, almost pulling her out of the interface chair. 'What the hell are you *doing*?'

'Fixing a problem,' she replied, before closing her eyes and ignoring him.

The petals began to fold around her once more, and Corso began yelling and cursing as he moved out of their way. She knew he wouldn't meanwhile try to take control of the frigate away from her; if he did, he'd only be making it into an easy target.

Once the petals had enclosed her, she opened her eyes to see the universe unfold around her.

She could feel the different parts of the frigate as if they were parts of her own body. The mass of electronics and machinery linking the frigate's drive-core to the external drive-spines was a tangled nightmare, but at least it was functional.

Dakota took one last glance at the Magi ship. It was now spinning out of control, its drive-spines shattered, unable to leap out of local space. She queried it tentatively, but there was no reply.

The drones struck again. They finished the job, and the Magi ship began to descend towards the upper reaches of Redstone's atmosphere, where it would start to burn up. Hot salt tears ran down her face, and she gripped the armrests so hard she thought she might break them.

The drones were already racing back towards the *Mjollnir*. She waited until they got nearer, drew them close against the hull and activated the drive-core.

Redstone vanished instantly from the overhead display. They had crossed more than sixty-five million kilometres in a fraction of a second.

It was going to take time to power the drive up for the next, hopefully much longer, jump, but for the moment they were far away enough to be safe.

She let the petals fold back down, and slumped forward in her chair. The sweat was literally dripping from her. She found Corso waiting for her, his expression furious.

'What the fuck just happened there?' he demanded.

'There are things I know,' she replied, 'that you don't, but I'm not ready to talk about it yet.'

'You destroyed your own ship and you don't feel like talking about it right now?' he bellowed.

Perez sat tight-mouthed, and clearly unsure of what was going on. Dakota stared back defiantly at Corso. 'We're out of range of Redstone, and we're going to jump again in a couple of hours. That's all you need to know right now.'

'And what happens when we get within range of the Emissaries?' he grated through clenched teeth. 'What the *fuck* are we supposed to do without your Magi ship? How are we going to get past their defences—?'

'We'll do fine with the weapons I brought with me,' she snapped. 'I know what I'm doing.'

She met his eyes and saw for the first time how frightened he was. She nodded towards Perez. 'Who else is on the ship?'

Corso glanced over his shoulder at Perez before

replying. 'Eight of us came on board, but one got wounded when we tried to take control of the bridge. He's currently in the med-bay. We also brought an Atn specialist who seems to know something about the Mos Hadroch. He went with some others to make sure it was still on board. It is.'

'I spoke to Ted on the way in, but what happened to him? He was there one second, then gone. Is he all right?'

'He's in the med-bay too. Whatever it is that's been happening to other machine-heads, it finally got him, too.'

As Corso started to step down from the dais, Dakota reached out and touched his elbow. He paused, looking back at her.

'I wouldn't have been able to do anything with the Magi ship, even if I wanted to, Lucas. It's not like it was before, when I had real control over it. That's all gone for me now, and it will be for Ted, too. The ship was more like a prison at the end, and destroying it was the only way I could get free of it.'

Corso shook his head as if in disbelief, and headed over to the bridge entrance.

'I think it's about time,' he said, turning back to her, 'to head down to the labs and see just what it is we went through all this for. But first we're going to the med-bay.'

EIGHTEEN

Once they had exited through the hub, they stopped frequently so that Corso could consult the map-projections that hovered over major intersections. Localized micro-relay systems, tied into the frigate's central stacks, showed Dakota exactly where they were at every step, yet one look at Corso's grim expression made her reluctant to point this out.

He pushed ahead of her without looking back once, and she wondered if he had experienced the same powerful sense of déjà vu she herself had felt from the moment she had boarded the frigate. It seemed very much like being back on board the *Hyperion*, except this time they were the ones in charge. It was a strange feeling because so very much had changed since then, but perhaps nothing quite so much as Corso and herself.

They boarded a car at a transport station, and sat in uncomfortable silence for several minutes until Corso finally broke his silence. He leaned towards her, his face red and angry.

'Why did you wait this long, before just appearing out

of nowhere?' he demanded. 'Did you have all this planned before you turned up on Redstone?'

She cleared her throat before replying. 'Some of it,' she admitted.

'But you just couldn't be bothered letting me in on it.'

'Of course not,' she replied.

'Why the hell not?'

'Because . . . I was afraid you might try to stop me.'

He waited several more seconds, clearly expecting her to continue. When she didn't, he just shook his head in disgust and stared away from her until they reached their destination less than a minute later. Corso took the lead again once they disembarked.

The med-bay was much more up-to-date than the *Hyperion's* had been. Even though the *Mjollnir* had been constructed centuries ago, she had clearly undergone a thorough refit.

Dakota gazed down at Lamoureaux through the transparent lid of a medbox. Another medbox nearby contained a distinguished-looking man in late middle-age.

She heard a soft hum and looked over to see that Corso had activated the examination table. Its bottom edge slowly tilted towards the deck, while a tangle of ceiling-mounted diagnostic equipment whirred and clicked as it dropped into place above the table's head-rest.

'Who is *he*?' asked Dakota.

'That's Eduard Martinez, who led the expedition to find the Mos Hadroch. On the table, please, Dakota. I want to run a full scan on you.'

'Why?'

'Because we can't afford you keeling over the way Ted Lamoureaux did.'

'You don't actually need a machine-head navigator to make a superluminal jump,' she pointed out. 'You could just set the parameters yourself.'

'Yes, but we still need you to tell us which way we're heading, and you can't do that if you wind up in a coma or worse.'

Conceding this point, Dakota reluctantly climbed up on to the examination table and lay back, sliding her fingers around thick moulded plastic handholds on either side. She watched the diagnostic gear move slowly down the length of her body, imaging her internal organs while simultaneously mapping her nervous system.

'I don't suppose there's a real doctor anywhere on this ship?'

Corso didn't reply, instead pushing himself away from the table and towards the desk and chair that formed the nurse's station. He grabbed hold of the back of the chair as he studied whatever analysis the med-bay's computers were now coming up with.

'Okay, Dakota.' He turned and glanced at her. 'I think it's time we talked. What did you mean when you said you destroyed your ship to get free?'

'I told you, I wasn't ready to—'

'Bullshit. You just don't *want* to talk about it, full stop. I don't care, but I want an explanation. I *deserve* an explanation.' He nodded towards the two occupied medboxes. 'Those two wouldn't be in there if they didn't believe in what we've been trying to achieve over the last couple of years. People got killed when we boarded this frigate. Most of them weren't bad people either, Dakota. They were just doing their job, and now they're dead. So don't try and feed me any more crap about not being ready.'

Dakota realized that the corners of her eyes were damp, and blinked the incipient tears away. 'I told you things were different after the Magi brought me back from the dead.'

'Different in what way?'

'In that now I only ever go where the Magi ships want me to go. I don't get to have a say any more, not since I was resurrected. They made me, rebuilt me, and that makes me *part* of them. But I'm still useful to them, whether I like it or not.'

'So you decided to do something about it.'

'The thing you have to understand,' she said, 'is that the Magi ships are hardwired to track down and destroy caches, and to find the entity that made those caches – the entity we know as the Maker. Right?'

Corso nodded.

'*Hardwired*, Lucas. That means finding the Maker has a higher priority than anything else where the Magi ships are concerned, even higher than obeying their navigators.'

'So their original navigators weren't really in charge of their ships either?'

'It's more complicated than that. The original navigators were bred to their purpose, and because of that they shared the same obsessive goal as their ships did – there could never be a conflict of interest. But *they* were all wiped out, and when we came along, instead of making everything better again, it presented the Magi ships with a conflict. On the one hand they're programmed to obey our orders, but on the other they're overwhelmingly programmed to track down and destroy any caches and ultimately find the Maker.'

'So what can they do?'

'They can try to change their human navigators: remould them into something more compatible with their own mission. Except, instead, it's turning them into vegetables or – if they're lucky – just leaving them with permanent brain damage.'

'Jesus and Buddha,' Corso exclaimed. 'You're talking about the bends?'

There was a soft electronic chime and then the whirring diagnostic equipment slid back up towards the ceiling and fell silent. Dakota pulled herself upright and clasped her hands over her knees.

Corso glanced towards Lamoureaux's medbox, then back again, with an appalled expression on his face. 'You're seriously telling me the Magi ships are trying to turn our navigators into something that isn't human?'

'Trader once told me he didn't regard me as human anymore. I didn't really believe him at the time, but I understand what he meant a lot better now.'

She could see Corso was still struggling with this revelation. 'But it's not working, is it?' He nodded at Lamoureaux.

'No, it's not,' she admitted. 'At least not for most of us. But I can't say for certain they haven't already succeeded in turning other machine-heads into the image of their original navigators. Maybe we won't find out until something happens.'

'Like?'

'I think their first priority would probably be to destroy the cache at Tierra.'

She watched Corso try to assimilate this. 'What?'

'Remember their original mission, apart from tracking down the Maker, was to destroy caches wherever they could find them. They don't make exceptions.'

'But the Magi ships don't have weapons,' he pointed out. 'How could they . . . ?'

She smiled as Corso reached the obvious conclusion on his own, his eyes widening in horror. 'By destroying whichever star the cache is orbiting, of course,' she said, finally pushing herself off the examination table.

'We have to warn them,' he said, in a half-croak.

'Sure, you could,' she replied, stepping over to the screen to study the details of her diagnostics, noticing the dark patches inside her skull where her implants were located. 'But think about it, Lucas. I heard the news about Consortium forces moving in and taking over the Tierra cache by force. They're not going to listen to anything you have to say. But, if it came to the worst and we did lose the Tierra system altogether, there are other caches out there, and we still have other ships we can use to find them.'

She watched him think this over. He'd try to warn them anyway, she had no doubt, because that was the kind of man he was: endlessly drawn to hopeless causes.

'So you destroyed your ship . . . ?'

'Because I couldn't trust it any more.'

Corso gaped at her, dumbfounded.

There was another chime, and the diagnostics display flashed a couple of times.

'What does it say?' she asked.

'That there are lesions in your brain,' Corso told her. 'The med-bay thinks you've suffered a *grand mal* seizure.' He reached out and touched the screen, and more information appeared. 'It's the same thing as Ted,' he observed.

'I *feel* okay. And whatever changes the Magi made to my brain or Ted's, your med-bay isn't programmed to factor them in.'

'Well, one way or another, there are changes.'

'Will Ted be okay?'

Corso shrugged. 'We won't know until the medbox is finished with him. How are you feeling?' he asked, looking at her with a curious expression.

'About what?'

'I know you were . . .' he struggled to find the right word '. . . *attached* to your ship; to the experience of being joined with it.'

'I'll deal with it,' she said abruptly. 'I'm not going to crack up like I did before.' She nodded towards the medbay entrance. 'You said we should take a look at what we've gone to all this effort for. How about now?'

Ty Whitecloud looked up at the sound of the lab's airlock cycling, and realized he still had no idea if the Senator's plan to hijack the frigate had been successful. He sat at the lab's primary console, sudden tension knotting the muscles of his back.

The inner airlock door finally sighed open and Senator Corso entered the lab in the company of a woman he felt certain he had never seen before, but who looked familiar. After another moment, he recognized her from news archives as Dakota Merrick.

Her eyes were wide and dark, and she hardly seemed to blink. Her hair stood up in spiked tufts, giving the impression of someone who didn't get much sleep, and she was attractive, in a half-starved-looking sort of way. Had she, he wondered, already been on board the frigate when they arrived?

'Dakota, this is Nathan Driscoll,' said Corso, fixing Ty with a peculiar stare, as if to put particular emphasis on Ty's *nom de guerre*. Corso had so far spoken to Ty only when absolutely necessary, and as on those occasions the Senator's distaste for him remained entirely evident. 'Nathan's responsible for the original research that led us to the Mos Hadroch. Without his help, we wouldn't have got this far.'

Ty nodded wordlessly to Dakota, and crossed his hands on his lap so that the ring he had been given by the Consortium agent, and which he wore on his right hand, was hidden under the left palm.

He heard that high-pitched static-like sound again, but it rapidly increased in pitch until it passed beyond his ability to hear it. He saw Merrick wince in that same moment, pressing the fingers of one hand against her temple.

She heard it too, he realized. A glance at the Senator confirmed that he appeared unaware of her distress.

'I think it's time we had a look at exactly what we came here for,' said Corso. 'Mr Driscoll?'

Ty nodded and stood up. 'This way,' he said.

They passed through another room, then came to the isolation chamber containing the Atn's remains.

Ty tapped some commands into a terminal mounted next to a sheet of polycarbonate armoured glass, through which the alien remains were visible. A moment later a long robot arm slid out from a recess in the chamber's ceiling, turning this way and that as it reached downwards, its machine-fingers spreading wide, each one of them tipped with a different kind of probe or instrument. It came to a halt just a few inches above the dead alien's carapace.

Ty inhaled deeply and stared at the alien body through the glass. *I've waited a long time for this*, he thought, then he exhaled slowly.

He quickly typed more commands into the terminal, and in response the upper right corner of the window darkened to show an image of the Atn's remains as seen from directly above. After another moment, this image was replaced by a series of vague outlines rendered in grey, which constantly shifted and altered.

Ty pointed to the monochrome images. 'This is from a multi-system scan I managed to run on the thing's body before they locked me out of the lab,' he explained. 'X-ray, muon, the works. Look here.' He pointed to a black shadow at the core of the image. 'There's something lodged inside the Atn's carapace, but it's completely opaque to everything I can throw at it.'

'And that's the Mos Hadroch?' asked Corso.

'I'm rather hoping it is, yes,' Ty replied, glancing at the Senator.

Merrick was frowning, clearly distracted by something. 'It's the Mos Hadroch, all right,' she said. 'It's been scanning me from the moment we walked into this lab.'

The two men stared at her.

'I'm serious,' she continued. Her eyes lost focus for a moment, and Ty thought she might faint. 'I think it's trying to find information about the swarm.'

'Maybe bringing you here wasn't such a good idea.' Corso began moving towards her.

She put up a hand. 'Wait, Lucas.'

'What does it want to know?' asked Ty, deeply fascinated.

She moved back against one wall, pressing a hand against the bulkhead behind her. 'The swarm's purpose,' she replied. 'Its reason for being.'

'Do you actually know that?' Corso asked, just beating Whitecloud to it.

'Sure.' She shrugged. 'There are millions of swarms scattered all across the face of the universe, all in long-range contact with each other via tach-comms. They want to manipulate the underlying structure of reality.'

Corso laughed dismissively. 'Come on, that's ridiculous. Who ever—?'

'It's not ridiculous,' Ty interrupted him. 'Not if they're Wheeler-Korsh engines.'

Corso shook his head. 'Wheeler *what*?'

'A hypothetical technology that manipulates the fundamental properties of space at its lowest possible level, where matter and information cease to be distinguishable,' Ty explained, glancing back into the chamber. He touched the terminal and several tiny cutting tools swung down until they almost touched the carapace. *Wheeler-Korsh engines? Incredible.* 'And if matter is only an expression of information,' he continued, 'then the universe itself is ultimately programmable, an infinitely complex computational system. Subatomic particles aren't really anything more substantial than a collection of data concerning spin, angle of momentum, location . . . that kind of thing. Some might say that this means there is no such thing as death, only iterations of a program that started running at the beginning of time.'

'That sounds almost like religion,' said Dakota.

Ty froze for a moment, realizing how close he was coming to describing Uchidanism. 'It's pure speculation, of course,' he said, turning and forcing a smile. 'Unless one actually finds a Wheeler-Korsh engine, in which case it ceases to be just speculation.'

'It sounds pretty far-fetched,' said Corso, glaring.

Ty ignored him. 'How did you find this out?' he asked Dakota.

'I tapped into the swarm's collective mind when I went out to investigate it,' she explained. 'It's how I found out about the Mos Hadroch.'

'Wait a minute,' said Ty. 'You said they communicated by tach-comms, but if they're spread all across the universe, how could they power the signals to reach that far? You'd need power on an astronomical level to pull off something like that.'

'I watched them use the energy of a nova,' she

explained, 'just to power a signal to a swarm located in another galaxy.'

Both men stared at her in silence for several moments.

'I should be used to having you completely fuck with my head by now,' the Senator finally grumbled, then turned to look at Ty. 'Mr Driscoll, I think it's time we cut that thing open and looked inside, don't you?'

Ty nodded and set to work. Tiny precision plasma jets began to cut into the Atn's carapace with smooth efficiency. Multi-jointed manipulators reached down, securing pieces of metal shell as the jets sliced through them.

The internal biological components of the Atn had long since turned to dust, though Ty made a mental note to analyse the remains of the brain when he had the time and opportunity. There was a chance that useful data might have survived.

'I can't tell you,' he muttered, 'how much I've been looking forward to this.'

Once a large enough hole had been cut, Ty stepped away from the terminal, and the entrance to the isolation chamber slid open. 'Let's take a look,' he said, stepping through.

The three of them crowded inside the small space, which smelled of burned dust and hot metal. The Senator's earlier antipathy towards him appeared to have shifted into something like a grudging respect. It was Merrick that Ty could not make his mind up about: the news archives had carried accusations of murder and thievery. She struck Ty as someone who worked hard to keep her emotions under control, but certainly not the cold-blooded killer she had sometimes been made out to be.

'They're amazing creatures, the Atn,' said Ty, pulling on a pair of insulated gloves. The edges of the hole cut in the carapace still glowed faintly with trapped heat. 'There's strong evidence they've been around for longer than any other species we've come into contact with. Perhaps longer than even your Magi, Miss Merrick,' he added. 'And when we've shuffled off the galactic stage, they'll come wandering back through the empty ruins of our cities.'

'I wondered if maybe that was why they were entrusted with the Mos Hadroch in the first place,' said Dakota, watching as Ty squatted by the carapace. 'They operate on a timescale that pretty much beggars the imagination.'

'I think maybe we'd better get on with this, don't you?' said Corso with faint annoyance.

'Yes,' Ty agreed, reaching into a pocket and pulling out a slim torch.

He shone the light into the cavity and discovered that, as he suspected, the creature had been thoroughly gutted. The light played over something smooth, and he reached in past the jagged edges of the hole and touched it. To his surprise, it was very slightly warm to the touch. He shoved the handle end of his torch inside his mouth, to free his hands, then pushed both hands deep inside the cavity.

The object nestling inside the carapace was roughly conical in shape, its blunted point facing up towards him. Two bars like handles extended out and then upwards from the base of the cone, which at least gave him something to grab hold of.

Ty got a good grip on the object and lifted it out. Then Corso grabbed one handle, and together they lowered it to the deck. It was a pale cobalt-blue colour, and seemed to glow with a faint iridescence. There was something undeniably alien about the device, some nameless quality of otherness that sent a tingle of fear and excitement racing down Ty's spine.

Corso peered at it with clear alarm. 'It's not radio-active, is it?'

'Not according to the instruments,' replied Ty. 'If it was, we'd have known long before we even brought it on board. I don't know what could be causing that glow.'

Suddenly Ty heard a sound, like whispers mixed with static, cutting through his thoughts and once again rising to a high-pitched whistle before fading to nothing. He glanced over at Dakota and saw her wince and cover her eyes with one hand.

'I can hear it again,' she murmured. 'The Mos Hadroch, I mean. I think something's just happened.'

Corso put up one hand to touch the comms-bead in his ear.

'That's fine, Dan,' he said after a few moments. 'Thanks for letting me know.'

He turned back to face them. 'Perez says half the primary data stacks just spontaneously rebooted themselves without explanation. It could be there's someone still hidden on the frigate and trying to sabotage us before we can jump out of this system.'

Dakota shook her head. 'No, it's the Mos Hadroch. I'm certain of it.'

'Then what the hell is it doing *now*?' Corso demanded.

'I think,' she replied carefully, 'it just wants to know who we are.'

NINETEEN

Two hours later, the primary stacks had recovered, whereupon Dakota jumped the *Mjollnir* half a light-year outside the Redstone system. A day later the frigate jumped more than a hundred and fifty light-years, to a point deep inside the Hyades Cluster.

The frigate's astrogational systems started matching the local stellar population against maps of known stars, quickly identifying a reddish-orange star no more than two or three light-years distant as Epsilon Tauri.

Dakota left the bridge and made her way to a nearby meeting room, where the others were waiting. She smelled food as she entered, unfamiliar spices and odours that made her stomach growl. An image of Epsilon Tauri, the surrounding cluster spread out around it like a sprinkle of multicoloured diamonds, floated above a low table in the centre of the room. The room itself was oval-shaped, with low couches set against curving bulkheads and facing inwards towards the table. The only faces not present were Martinez and Lamoureaux, but Corso had told her they could expect to be decanted sometime in the next twenty-four hours.

Corso himself looked dog-tired and haggard. While Dakota had been busy prepping the *Mjollnir* for its jump, he and Schiller had got busy moving the bodies of the dead to the ship's morgue. Then they had a go at scrubbing the bloodstains off the deck.

Corso looked at her with raised eyebrows as she lowered herself on to a couch opposite him.

'I just put us about halfway across Consortium territory,' she told him, leaning back, her shoulders cramping with fatigue. 'We can jump again in another day or so, which should take us a long way outside the Consortium.'

Corso handed her a bulb containing some dark liquid. 'Here, Redstone coffee – guaranteed to wake you up.'

She took it and sniffed at it warily, then noticed Perez and Schiller were watching her carefully. She sucked at the straw for a moment, then her eyes widened and her face turned pale.

She dropped the bulb and succumbed to a coughing fit. Someone laughed. When her eyes had stopped watering, she could see that Corso was grinning at her.

'What,' she asked, 'the *fuck* is that?'

'There's this weed, see, grows in water-pipes and plumbing back home,' said Nancy Schiller. 'They've been brewing it up since the days of the first settlers. They made me drink a gallon of the stuff in one go when I first joined up.' She shook her head sadly and gazed at Corso. 'This girl wouldn't last an hour in any regular crew.'

Dakota started coughing again, and Corso passed her a glass of water. She swallowed it all in one go, to clear a little of the sour, gritty taste from her throat. When she looked up, Corso wore a conciliatory grin.

'So,' began Perez, looking around them, 'down to business. First question: do we get to fly a pirate flag on the ship? And second question: who wants to make it?'

'Don't be ridiculous,' said Schiller 'I say we paint FUCK YOU on the side and just fly the damn thing into the sun of the first heavily populated Emissary system we find. Besides . . .' she added, pausing to take a long suck at a bulb, 'I can't sew. Can you?'

Perez shook his head sadly. 'They've got lots more suns where we're headed. I fear they won't miss just the one, Nancy.'

Schiller shrugged. 'Well, that's the flaw in my plan right there. Maybe you could wear an eyepatch, Dan.'

'If *you* wear a bag over your head, I'll think about it. What do you say, Senator?' Perez looked over at Corso. 'Should we pass a resolution that Nancy has to wear a bag over her head for the rest of the trip?'

Corso shook his head. 'I'd rather wait for Eduard to get better, as I think any bag-wearing decisions should stay strictly with him.'

Perez chuckled, and an awkward silence fell.

Corso put down his bulb – now half empty, Dakota noted – and leaned forward, hands resting on his knees, while making sure to catch each of their eyes in turn. Dakota watched as Driscoll drained a bulb of the foul concoction, and put it down empty with apparent satis-faction. *Guy looks like he drinks it every day for breakfast.* Maybe he was from Redstone, like the rest of them.

'All right,' said Corso, 'this meeting is about making sure we're all on the same page. That means us talking about what's up ahead.'

'But we're not all here,' said Nancy. 'The Comman-der's still on ice and your other guy's still in recovery. Don't you think maybe we should wait until they're out of the med-bay?'

'Martinez'll be out of there sometime in the next several days, and Mr Lamoureaux isn't going to be tak-ing up any duties until at least then either. So we'll fill them in when the time comes,' said Corso. 'Look, we're all from different places, some of us from Redstone, some not. The only thing we've really got in common is our reason for being here, and that's the Mos Hadroch.'

He glanced over at Dakota. 'Nathan's filled everyone else in about what we found inside the Atn, while you were still up on the bridge. I can't think of a better time than the present for you to tell us just exactly what it is the Mos Hadroch can do.'

They all looked at her expectantly.

'Okay.' She cleared her throat. 'The main thing you need to know is that every new superluminal drive-core produced by a cache is quantum-entangled with that same cache. That entanglement means any changes you make to the cache can affect any ships carrying those superluminal drives, regardless of how distant they may be.'

Dakota looked around them and noticed that, apart from Driscoll, their expressions ranged from uncomprehending to suspicious.

'Where did you *get* all this?' asked Schiller.

'From the swarm,' she lied. 'What you need to understand is that the Mos Hadroch is like a key. Take it into a cache and plug it into the cache's drive-forge – that's the device you need to manufacture a superluminal drive – and it gives you control over every one of the superluminal drives that ever came out of it.'

'And what happens then?' asked Willis.

'My understanding is it's possible to trigger a destruct sequence that will destroy not only the drives seeded from the forge, but also the ships carrying them.'

She watched them absorb this information for a moment.

'How quickly does it act?' asked Driscoll.

'Given the entanglement, I'm guessing it's as near as damn instantaneous.'

'What about the Tierra cache?' asked Perez. 'Couldn't the Mos Hadroch be used on that, too?'

'It could,' said Corso, leaning forward. 'That makes it particularly important not to allow it to fall into the wrong hands.'

'And the Shoal?' asked Olivarri. 'Surely it's a threat to them as well.'

'If you can find the cache from which the drives for

the majority of their starships were manufactured, then, yes,' said Dakota.

'What concerns me,' said Schiller, 'is how well defended this Emissary cache we're heading for must be. If it's as old as I've been told it is, then they're going to want to keep it safe.'

Dakota shook her head. 'Not necessarily, because they have no idea that a threat of this nature even exists. Our destination is a relative backwater close to what used to be the heart of their empire, but the main centre of activity moved on a very long time ago. They rely far more now on much more recently discovered caches.'

'Then why don't we try and destroy *those?*' asked Schiller.

'Because, historically, the vast majority of their fleets use drives that were created in that less well-defended, older cache we're heading for. Any ships using drives taken out of those newer caches won't be affected, of course, but we'll still be able to shut down or even destroy over eighty per cent of their existing fleets.'

'But that still doesn't tell us how the hell we're going to get close enough to the cache without being blown to shit!' Schiller insisted. 'I've seen footage of the battle with the godkiller in Ocean's Deep. How the *fuck* do we defend ourselves against something like that?'

Dakota nodded towards the star-simulation hanging just above the surface of the table. It faded and, then, for the next few minutes it played back the destruction of the corvettes and missiles by Meridian drones.

She made sure, however, to leave out the part where she destroyed her own ship.

'Those things . . .' Willis started, as the images faded.

'Are weapons created by a race called Meridians,' Dakota said. 'They're long gone, but these drones are self-maintaining and extremely powerful. They're going to be our defence while going in. Believe me, I was barely using a fraction of their total power.'

'Any other questions?' asked Corso, looking around.

Dakota studied their faces. Some looked fearful, but most of them appeared awestruck by what they had just been told.

'All right,' said Corso, standing. 'We have preliminary reports of drive-spine failure in three separate areas of the hull. We're going to be spending most of our journey time repairing this ship, and none of us gets out of working on those repairs.'

He turned to Schiller. 'Nancy, we're going to have to do the repair work in shifts, so draw up an initial rota and I'll check it over with you in an hour from now. Put Ted and the Commander in there as well – soon as the med-bay says it's okay, they're going to be doing the same work as the rest of us.'

He turned to fix Dakota with a stare. 'I'd like a word with you in private.'

She nodded and followed him out of the meeting room. He kept going, following the deck as it curved upwards. He didn't stop until they were almost at one of the spoke-shafts, before turning to regard her with his arms folded.

'Whatever it is you're up to, it's time to start talking,' he said. 'You didn't tell me everything I needed to know back in the med-bay, did you? Those weapons didn't just materialize out of nowhere. It's not just that you obviously know the exact location of the cache we need to hit, or even that you've got a shitload of intel about the swarm and the Mos Hadroch, but how the hell could you know all this about the Emissaries?'

He raised a silencing hand as Dakota opened her mouth to speak. 'Stop,' he said. 'You can't try and fob me off by telling me you got all this from the swarm, because I just don't buy it. Do you remember when we were stuck together in that tower on Night's End?'

Dakota nodded. 'I remember.'

'You said you knew whenever I was lying: you could see it in my eyes, the whole way I acted. Well, here's back at you.'

Dakota folded her arms around her chest, hugging herself as if she was cold. 'I'm sorry I haven't been more straight with you,' she mumbled. 'I guess this is as good a time as any.'

He leaned in towards her. 'For what?'

She drew in a breath, then exhaled, letting her shoulders sag. 'Trader's coming along with us. I got the information about the Emissaries from him, and he also led me to the Meridian drones. He's also the reason I know exactly what the Mos Hadroch can do. He'll rendezvous with us just before our next jump.'

Corso's mouth worked helplessly for a couple of seconds before he could get anything out. '*What?* Are you fucking *crazy?*'

She stared back at him defiantly. 'See, this is why I didn't tell you straight away.'

'No, why would you not want to do that?' he yelled, throwing his arms wide. 'Because I'd have said you were out of your fucking *head*!' He was shouting, and the sound of his voice reverberated from the bulkheads around them.

'At least hear me out,' she said quietly. 'I haven't failed you yet.'

Corso stood, staring off down the long corridor, then shook his head before looking back at her directly. 'All right, then, go ahead. Tell me why that murderous fucking fish is coming along with us.'

'Remember how I told you I could only go where the Magi ship wanted me to go?'

Corso nodded.

'It took me to Trader. I didn't have any choice.'

'Why him?'

'Because he has the key to awakening the Mos Hadroch. Without that key, it's useless, like a bomb without any explosives.'

'Everything he says is a lie, Dakota.'

'That's not true,' she replied sharply. She could feel her nails digging into the flesh of her palms, where she'd balled them into fists. 'He merely twists the truth to get his own way.'

Corso gave her a pitying look. 'Got you right over a barrel again, hasn't he? What does *he* get out of this?'

'If we pull this off, he'll have helped turn the tide of the war. I think he's hoping the Shoal will decide to forget he's the one who started it.'

Corso laughed. 'In other words, he can't even get his own people to back him up. I can't tell you how much I don't like this.'

'So what do you want us to do?' she demanded. 'Go ahead without him? Take our chances and hope for the best? I mean *what*, Lucas? It's not like the artefact comes with a fucking manual. I've got no idea how to make it work. Do you?'

'We've barely got this far, and already it feels like everything's getting out of control.'

Dakota stepped forward and laid a hand over one of his. 'You've changed a lot, Lucas. The man I first met on board the *Hyperion* could never have got us this far. We need to try to find some way to control the Mos Hadroch that doesn't involve Trader. If it's at all possible, maybe Driscoll can work it out before we reach our goal.'

'And if it isn't?'

'Then at least what Trader wants is what *we* want, for a change. And if he's lying about that . . . Well, we'll watch him, Lucas, and we'll be ready. It's really all we can do.'

TWENTY

A little more than a day later, Dakota made her way to the *Mjollnir*'s stern and towards the main hold, an enormous drum-shaped vault that took up nearly a fifth of the frigate's overall internal space. Taking a seat in an observation blister overlooking its airless interior, she saw the Meridian drones nestled amongst the drop-ships and cradles, and clinging to various bulkheads as if glued to them. Their perfectly reflective surfaces rendered them nearly invisible.

She watched the main doors of the hold swing slowly open, splitting into four quarter-circle slices and revealing a widening cross of starry black. Trader's yacht hung at the void's centre, growing slowly larger as it slowly manoeuvred itself inside the hold.

The yacht was the colour of parchment. Its drive-spines sparkled under the hold's powerful lights. It moved to one side as the doors began to swing closed again, waiting until the grapples took hold of it, pulling it in towards an empty cradle.

Dakota touched a comms terminal, and a moment

later a soft chime told her a link had been established with the craft.

'Welcome aboard, Trader.'

'Greetings and felicitations, dear Dakota. Awareness comes upon me that the frigate is refusing to extend an airlock connection to my yacht. May I ask why?'

'You're going to have to stay where you are for the duration of the voyage. Senator Corso made himself very clear on that point.'

'Ah, Lucas Corso. I have heard news of his hard journey up life's stream these recent years. His teeth have grown; now become a predator rather than prey. I gather you've had an opportunity to use the Meridian drones already?'

'I did, yes. Are you sure you trust me with that kind of firepower?'

'I think of our relationship as symbiotic, Dakota. Our need for each other assures mutual trust. But even those drones aren't quite enough for our purposes. This frigate remains extremely vulnerable to direct attack, so I propose we acquire shielding of a far more advanced type than that currently available to you.'

'Where from?'

The *Mjollnir*'s primary stacks alerted Dakota to new data, squirted over from the Shoal-member's yacht. She tested the data for traps, and, on finding none, dropped it behind a firewall within the terminal's memory. It turned out to be a set of coordinates for a system located a few thousand light-years further along their projected trajectory, close to the edge of the spiral arm and not far from the region of the Long War.

'The system in question requires a slight detour, but that shouldn't add more than a few days to our journey time,' Trader explained. 'And Dakota . . . please reconsider allowing me on board, as I would very much like to see the Mos Hadroch. I have waited a long time for that, and I want to demonstrate that I can be trusted.'

It was surely just her imagination that she detected a strain of wistfulness behind the machine-tones of his translation system.

'Not a chance in hell,' she replied. 'I had enough trouble persuading Lucas to let you even get this near.'

'No one enters the arena of battle without making sure their weapons are fully operational, Dakota. If the Mos Hadroch is a gun, only I have the trigger. We need to test it before we can implement it.'

The damn fish had a point, she realized. 'I'll talk to him,' she replied. 'That's all I can do. But he's still not going to go for it.' She shifted in her seat and waited for Trader's reply.

Corso had ramped the security systems up to full alert in preparation for the Shoal-member's arrival, and put Nancy Schiller to work at rejigging the primary command systems to make them even more hack-proof than they already were.

'Then it appears I am trapped between the crushing depths and the deadly air,' Trader finally conceded. 'You should be aware that when we reach our final destination, I won't be able to control the Mos Hadroch at a distance. Will you keep it from me even then, Dakota?'

'No,' she replied. 'Not when that time comes. Of course,' she added, 'you could just tell us how to activate it ourselves. Then you wouldn't need to come along at all.'

Dakota smiled to herself as a long pause followed.

'I believe we understand each other,' Trader finally replied. 'Goodbye for now, Dakota.'

'Wait.' She put out a hand, forgetting Trader couldn't see her. 'There's something I want to ask you.'

'Yes?'

'On my way to the swarm I came across hundreds of destroyed Atn clade-worlds. But most of them were destroyed long before the Mos Hadroch was supposedly created.'

'Your point?'

'At first I assumed the swarm attacked those clade-worlds because it suspected the Mos Hadroch could be hidden on one of them, but clearly the Atn and the swarm have been at war for much, much longer than that. Why is that? Or is the Mos Hadroch older than I thought?'

'We all live amongst the ruins of our predecessors, Dakota. There are wars that began when the first stars were young, and will not end even with the death of the last star. Both the swarms and the Atn began their own existence as weapons on either side of a long-forgotten war – but the Atn forgot their original purpose. Does this satisfy your curiosity?'

'Yes.' Dakota pushed herself out of her chair and took one last look out into the bay. 'Goodbye, Trader.'

'I have been monitoring communications traffic from Redstone, Dakota. I know that you destroyed your own ship.'

Dakota gripped the back of the seat she had just vacated. 'Yes, I had no choice. You already know why.'

'It is always better to be the master of your own destiny, is it not? And yet I imagine it must have been a painful decision. I imagine it must make you feel very lonely.'

She let go of the chair and drifted over to the window, suddenly breathing hard. She could just make out her reflection, floating like a ghost over the interior of the bay, and she fought an urge to activate the drones again, to burn Trader's ship in its cradle.

'More than you can imagine,' she replied, and left.

TWENTY-ONE

Not long after Trader rendezvoused with the frigate, Corso paid a visit to the labs.

'Figure out how the hell the thing works, Whitecloud. Or at least how it *might* work. That's your job as long as you're on board the *Mjollnir*. You'll eat here and sleep here in the lab, as well. Is that understood?'

It was the first private conversation they had had, and Corso clearly had not been in the mood for making friends or wasting time with pseudonyms when no one else was around. There were dark rings under the Senator's eyes, and Ty had been aware of the frenetic level of activity following their departure from Redstone, while he himself had been safely ensconced in what had now become the familiar confines of the frigate's laboratory complex.

Ty gazed around the low-lit lab as if he might find the right answer there. 'But won't people ask questions if I don't take quarters with the rest of them? I mean, there's plenty of room in the centrifuge—'

'No.' Corso stabbed a finger at Ty's chest. 'I don't want you mixing with the rest of my people.'

'All right, but what about the hull repairs? There are only nine of us apart from the alien, and drive-spines deteriorate badly over long jumps. If I don't join the repair rota with the rest of them, they're going to ask why.'

Corso clearly did not enjoy having to concede this point. 'Fine, I'll make sure you're on the rota so no one asks questions. But you stay put here the rest of the time, regardless. If anyone asks, it's because you're a selfless scientist who just can't tear himself away from his work. Just remember, Mr Whitecloud, the only reason you're still alive is because my people intervened on your behalf back at Ascension. That still doesn't mean you didn't deserve a bullet in the back of your head. So, while you're on this ship with me, you do exactly as I say or I *will* make life seriously fucking unpleasant for you. Am I clear?'

Ty again looked around the laboratory. 'But what if I can't figure out how the Mos Hadroch works?' he stammered. 'What then?'

Corso came up close, grabbing a fistful of Ty's shirt.

'Think of it this way, Ty. This is a chance for you to exonerate yourself. The fact is, we're all fugitives here, and chances are none of us is ever going to see home again. But if we *do* get out of this . . .' Corso let go, putting one hand on Ty's chest and pushing him away. 'If we do, then you'll still be Nathan Driscoll.'

'So you're saying you'll let me go when the time comes.'

'I'll give you a chance to disappear. But God help you if Dakota or any of the others ever work out who you are before then.'

Corso pushed himself towards the airlock and grabbed a handhold next to it. 'Let's face it,' he added, looking back over at Ty, 'it's not like you'd have anywhere to hide if they did.'

Ty laughed, and Corso stared back at him, speechless.

'Did you know I was conscripted, Mr Corso? The Uchidans put me into military R&D and ordered me to work on one tiny part of a project that employed dozens of researchers. I'm not denying I had at least some responsibility for what happened back on Redstone – it was easy to guess the strategists were planning something big in advance of the Consortium forces arriving, but my rank was much too low for me to be told anything more than what was strictly necessary. The people who actually planned and implemented the counter-attack were never required to face a Legislate tribunal, only the technical staff. We were scapegoats, nothing more.'

Corso pushed himself back over towards him. Ty flinched, but the Senator came to a halt a few metres away by placing one hand against a bulkhead.

'I've read your file, Ty. You can't tell me you were only following orders. It's not an excuse, never has been. Hundreds died.'

'If I could go back in time and make things different, I would. I used to fantasize about how things might have been if I'd made different choices. You said I had a chance to exonerate myself, and that's all I've wanted, all these years. I'm not a monster, Mr Corso. I just want you to understand that.'

Ty drew in a breath, and waited. The other man's expression was unreadable.

'Actions count more than words, Ty,' Corso said finally, twisting around until he faced the airlock once more. 'Find out how the Mos Hadroch works, and you'll help save a lot of lives. Maybe that'll give you the peace you're looking for.'

I hope so too, thought Ty, and watched as Corso turned and left.

Ty spent the next couple of hours taking his mind off this encounter by familiarizing himself with the upgraded lab equipment before moving the Mos Hadroch out of the isolation chamber and into the main lab. Its faint iridescent glow had long since faded, along with the aural hallucinations that only appeared to affect people with some form of cerebral implant. Now it sat amidst an array of technology that could carry out a much finer analysis than the isolation chamber could possibly manage.

The artefact now sat in a cradle which had, in turn, been mounted in the heart of a gigantic multi-phase imaging unit intended for carrying out almost every conceivable type of material analysis the *Mjollnir*'s scientific and technical staff could hope for. For the moment, some methods were out of the question: for instance, ultrasonic spectroscopy meant hitting the thing with a laser, and Ty was far from sure the Mos Hadroch would not interpret this as a form of attack and thus retaliate.

The lab even contained its own dedicated manufactory for creating yet more gadgets, should they be required; so its dedicated stacks were filled with thousands of blueprints whose components could be manufactured within a matter of hours or days.

And yet Ty hesitated, unsure where to even start. He retreated to a chair and sat staring at the artefact for the better part of an hour, quietly brooding.

I have absolutely no idea what I'm doing, he finally admitted to himself.

The Mos Hadroch was, according to Dakota Merrick, alive; it was certainly more than a machine, and clearly something *intelligent* lurked within its outwardly inert form. But, for all the high-tech tools he had to hand, Ty rather suspected they would be about as much good as trying to reverse-engineer stack circuits by hitting them with a lump of flint.

So instead he sat and reflected, and wondered if that strange intelligence might manifest itself a second time. He settled back, aware that his adrenalin rush of the past few days was finally beginning to tail off.

He only realized he'd fallen asleep, when, several

hours later, he woke to the insistent buzz of a comms panel.

The lab complex had a small kitchenette, which Ty had stocked with self-heating ready meals from one of the frigate's vast and echoing mess halls. He drank water while he waited for one of them to heat, then swallowed it in a hurry before making his way to the airlock bay where Nancy Schiller and Ray Willis were already getting suited up.

'You're late,' said Nancy, who looked like she hadn't slept since they had left orbit around Redstone. He also noticed she was careful not to meet his eye. 'Where've you been, the last couple of days? Haven't seen you anywhere on the centrifuge at all.'

Ty had been wondering when a moment like this might arrive. He had expected the lifespan of their affair to last only as long as their previous voyage together. It was a matter of some consternation when he had come face to face with her inside the safe-house, after expecting never to see her again.

'In the labs,' he replied, heading for one of the racked suits and lifting it down. 'I had a lot of work to do.'

Nancy and Ray were soon ready, and they stood there with helmets in hand while Ty struggled with the lower half of his suit.

'So what exactly is there to do?' Ray asked him. 'If you're talking about the Mos Hadroch, that is.'

As it recognized that someone was wearing it, Ty's suit automatically began to adjust itself to his body, the shoulders tightening here, the legs growing a few inches longer there.

'Well,' Ty replied, 'for all we know, it might be giving out some kind of signal. Or it might contain readable data, if only I can figure out how it's encoded. But it's definitely not inert. It came to life, just briefly, when we pulled it out of the Atn's body.'

'I remember you said so at the meeting,' Nancy commented, 'but you didn't tell us exactly what happened.'

He shrugged. 'Mostly it just . . . glowed a bit. And Merrick seemed to be able to pick up some kind of signal coming from it through her implants.'

Nancy and Ray eyed at each other at the mention of Merrick. 'Now there's a weird fish,' commented Ray. 'How much do you know about her?'

'I know she was implicated in that whole, ah, thing that happened on Redstone,' he replied, trying hard to sound casual. 'But shouldn't we be heading out?' he asked, nodding towards the nearby row of pressure doors.

'Not just yet,' said Nancy. 'We're going to be—'

A rumbling alert sounded, three quick blasts like a horn; signifying a jump alert.

'Jumping in just a minute,' Nancy finished with a grin. 'Then we can go out.'

Ty nodded, relieved at the fortuitous change of conversation.

When they finally got outside, several specialized spider-mechs were already waiting for them, with toolkits attached, floating a few metres above the hull. The Tⁿⁱⁿⁱⁿ Oⁿⁱⁿⁱⁿ ⁿⁿⁿ ⁿⁿⁿⁿⁿ ⁿⁿ ⁿⁿ ⁿⁿⁿⁿ ⁿⁿ ⁿⁿⁿⁿⁿ ⁿⁿ frigate, a distant burst of fireworks caught in one eternal instant.

Ty found he wasn't feeling as nervous as he had expected. In fact, being outside the hull felt no worse than standing on the surface of some clade-world. All he had to do was make sure he didn't make the mistake of thinking of the ship as a huge metal tower with him clinging to its—

Whoops. Vertigo hit Ty, and he focused hard on the hull itself, taking several deep breaths and holding on to them.

Flat ground. That's flat ground underneath you, he told himself, over and over.

Once the attack subsided, he gazed back along the hull, towards the flat dome of a shaped-field generator, only a few metres away. Apart from defensive purposes, these devices were primarily used to deflect interstellar debris that might otherwise tear through the hull. If he relaxed his eyes just a little, he could even pick out the faint sparkle of the combined energy fields surrounding the entire frigate.

Just beyond the field generator rose the first of a forest of drive-spines, curving up and outwards from the hull itself.

'Will you look at that,' said Willis, his voice sounding flat and close inside Ty's helmet. 'All that way in less than a second.'

'It's not such a big deal,' Nancy replied. 'Coreships did it all the time.'

'Well, yeah, but . . .'

But Ty knew what he meant. You didn't see or feel anything when inside a coreship; it was the same rocky sky held up by pillars you looked at, wherever in the galaxy you might actually happen to be. Being able to step outside and see where you were could be an awe-inspiring experience.

'All right,' said Nancy, suddenly all brisk efficiency. 'I had to lead a bunch of repair crews the last trip out, so just follow my lead and do what I tell you, and it'll all be fine.'

'What about the spiders?' asked Willis. 'Couldn't we just run them from inside the frigate and get *them* to do the work?'

'We tried that,' Nancy replied, 'but there's always something finicky that needs a pair of hands to deal with. But, with any luck, the spiders will still end up doing most of the work. Now check your HUDs for the schedule.'

Ty dutifully brought up his suit's display, which indicated a list of repairs to be made, ordered by priority.

'That's three drive-spines in need of immediate repair, all on this section of the hull,' said Nancy. 'Follow me.'

Ty used lanyards, coiled silver lines that shot out of the rear of his suit just below the air tanks and attached themselves to the hull. All he had to do was lean one way or the other and the lanyards would carry him along at a couple of kilometres an hour, rapidly retracting or reaching out to grip the hull in a steady rippling motion. As Willis and Nancy did the same, Ty was reminded of how comical the lanyards looked, as if each of their suits had suddenly grown spindly cartoon legs.

Nancy had slaved the spiders to her own suit, so that they followed a short way behind her, propelled on tiny puffs of gas.

They soon reached the first drive-spine. In that brief, barely measurable moment when a craft passed through superluminal space, electrical systems often failed and the molecular bonds of the hull began to crumble at the extremities. Nobody knew what would happen to a ship if it stayed in superluminal space for a few seconds longer, but Ty strongly suspected that it would disintegrate entirely.

At the base of the first drive-spine was a tangle of power cables leading inside the hull, ultimately terminating at one of the plasma conduits. Some of the cables had worked loose, which was easy enough to fix.

The drive-spine arching above them looked grey and dusty towards its tip, like it had become badly corroded.

Ty could see where a panel had come loose about halfway up, exposing naked circuitry beneath.

'Ray, will you go ahead and take a look at the other spines?' suggested Nancy. 'We only need two pairs of hands for this one, and it might speed things up if we know what else we're going to have to deal with, okay?'

'Uh . . . sure,' said Willis, after a moment. 'Are you sure you wouldn't rather—'

'No, I wouldn't,' she replied, just a little bit too sharply. 'Besides, myself and Nathan need to talk over some of the . . . some of the technicalities.'

Uh-oh, thought Ty.

'Yeah,' said Willis, sounding far from pleased. 'Yeah, I'll do that.'

'Thanks,' said Nancy.

'Yeah. You kids have fun,' Willis grumbled.

Ty watched as he moved away across the surface of the hull, dragged along by his suit's smart lanyards, whipping in and out.

A moment later a one-to-one channel request was transmitted to Ty's suit, and he accepted it with a sinking feeling.

'Quite something, isn't it?' asked Nancy. 'The view, I mean.'

'Yes, quite so,' Ty replied. 'How have you been, Nancy?'

Things had been cordial in the safe-house, but it was best, he felt sure, to nip this in the bud. Corso had warned him to stay away from the rest of the crew, and he had little doubt how the Senator might react if he discovered Ty had once been sleeping with the *Mjollnir*'s head of security.

'Good enough,' Nancy replied. 'Kind of crazy how we both wound up here, yeah?'

'I guess so,' he replied, finding himself suddenly stuck for words.

A silence followed, seeming deeper and wider than the void around them. Ty felt an urgent need to fill it. 'I think it was a surprise for both of us,' he said, and then laughed.

Nancy's own laugh sounded more than a little forced. 'Yeah,' she said. 'About that.'

'About what?' Were they ever going to get these repairs done?

'About us. Back on the . . . back on that last trip. That whole thing.'

'It's all right, Nancy,' he said. 'I don't think either of us was looking for much more than—'

'No, it's not that. I mean, that's what I *was* going to say, right? There's no expectations, since I don't think we thought we'd ever see each other again.'

'No,' he replied, 'I guess not.'

'But . . . we *are* here, and maybe we won't make it back. Yet I don't know if there's any of us wouldn't rather be somewhere else.'

But you still have a choice, Ty almost said. Every step he had taken was either due to a gift from providence or through a desperate clutching at life. The alternatives had been stark: stay in Unity and risk execution, or board the *Mjollnir* and take his chances with the Emissaries. So here he was.

'I guess not,' he replied. 'I won't bother you, Nancy, if that's what you're afraid of.'

She came closer. 'That's not what I meant.'

Something in the tone of her voice made it clear she was struggling to find the right words. Nancy was, Ty had found, not the type to reveal her feelings except in the most intimate of circumstances.

'I don't know what we're going to face out there,' – she waved one gloved hand towards the stars, – 'an . . . when I think about it, I don't want to be alone.'

Something made him reach out and touch one gloved hand to the arm of her suit. He stared at his spread fingers, contemplating this unexpected betrayal by one of his own limbs.

'You won't be,' he said finally.

'I'm glad, Nathan.' She then moved away, sounding more subdued now. 'I . . . you know where I am. Just drop by sometime.'

'I'll do that,' he heard himself reply.

Ty watched her go, suddenly back to her brisk efficient self.

He had actually meant to cut things short; that being the easiest way to deal with such things. He had opened his mouth intending to say one thing, but something else entirely had emerged.

He summoned one of the spiders and started to

rummage inside its toolbox, feverishly thinking all the time. What, he wondered, could Corso actually do to him by way of punishment? Very little, he suspected.

Ty called up his suit's menu and put in a call to Nancy, and she replied almost immediately.

'Tonight,' he said. 'Ship time. Come down to the labs.'

'You . . . need help with something?'

'Yeah,' he replied with a grin. 'Something like that.'

TWENTY-TWO

'This is where we are just now,' indicated Lamoureaux.

Dakota leaned back in her seat on the bridge and stared up at the overhead simulation: a view of the Milky Way as it might be seen from roughly twenty thousand light-years above its ecliptic plane. A small point of light representing the *Mjollnir* blinked constantly from deep within the Orion Arm.

From the perspective Lamoureaux had chosen, it was clear the Orion Arm was not so much a true spiral arm in its own right, but more a broad streak of stars caught midway between the Sagittarius and Perseus arms.

'And this,' Lamoureaux continued, from the interface chair, 'is our first stop. After that we're in for the really long haul.'

A line reached out from the icon representing the *Mjollnir*, and came to an end at a star fifteen hundred light-years from their current position. A second line grew from there, stretching across a relatively starless gulf before terminating at a point deep within the Perseus Arm.

Dakota studied Lamoureaux, who had tipped the

interface chair all the way back to a forty-five-degree angle, until he was looking almost straight up at the simulation. He still seemed frail, and when he glanced at her she could sense the pain and loss he was feeling. Sometime soon, she was going to have to explain to him just why she had destroyed her ship.

Corso sat close behind Dakota, while Nancy, Ray and Nathan were still outside working on the drive-spines Martinez was not expected out of the med-bay for another couple of days, Olivarri was asleep in his quarters, and Perez was somewhere halfway across the ship, checking over the plasma conduit systems and prepping the onboard fabricators to produce replacement drive-spines.

'Ted, can you put up that information I gave you about our first target system?' asked Dakota.

'No,' said Corso from behind, his tone hostile. He had barely spoken to her since she had told him about Trader. 'That can wait a minute. Ted, you said you had secured some updates on the war.'

Ted flashed Dakota an apologetic glance before he nodded assent to Corso. Moments later dozens of bright red points appeared in clusters along one edge of the Orion Arm, with a few scattered deeper within it.

'These are the current confirmed sightings of Emissary forces,' Lamoureaux explained. A few dozen more points now appeared, coloured yellow. 'And these,' he continued, 'are stars that have gone nova since the war escalated. You can see they're mostly centred on the region of the Long War, but there's been more detonations deeper inside our arm, and getting closer to Consortium territory.'

'Any word from Ocean's Deep?' asked Corso.

'They're in total disarray, Senator. The Legislate's taken up a large military presence in the orbital station and rounded up a lot of the key Authority staff for questioning. Most of this news comes through Bandati contacts, rather than from our own people. It's the same at Tierra – no news coming in or out.'

'I think,' declared Corso, 'it's time everyone stopped calling me "Senator". From now on "Lucas" will do just fine, don't you think?'

'Then I guess you'd all better start calling me "Eduard".'

They all turned to see Martinez standing at the entrance to the bridge. Corso started to rise, but Martinez gestured him to sit back down.

'I'm fine. Leave me be,' Martinez insisted, shuffling forward. He was walking with a stick, Dakota noticed. He stopped when he spotted her, staring at her like she was a ghost.

'Sir, are you absolutely certain you're ready to be out of treatment?'

'Why, yes I am, Lucas,' Martinez replied, still without taking his eyes off her. 'I just have to go easy. Maybe spend another night in the medbox to speed up the healing.'

He moved closer to her. 'So you're Dakota Merrick.

When the hell did you get on board? And where the hell were you when we were getting ready to . . .'

'Commander,' Corso interrupted. He had come to Martinez's side and put a hand on his shoulder. 'As soon as we're finished here, we'll go to your quarters and I'll explain everything.' He gestured towards a couch. 'Please.'

Martinez looked like he was struggling to control his temper. 'Then you'd better make your reasons good,' he replied tautly, and headed for the seat.

A priority comms icon appeared, floating just to one side of the galaxy simulation. Corso reached up to his ear and spoke quietly into the air for a few moments.

'Nancy just reported in,' he explained, once he had finished. 'If we're going to make a significant jump any time during the next couple of days, we're going to have to leave up to a quarter of the drive-spines offline.'

'That's not good,' said Martinez.

Corso shrugged. 'Not much we can do about it. The engineers hadn't finished work on the hull when we boarded. Dan's ready to start running out replacement drive-spines as soon as he's got the fabricators back online.'

He paused for a moment, then turned to face Dakota, with visible reluctance. 'How many jumps do we need to reach our first destination?'

Martinez frowned, looking back and forth between them. 'First destination?'

Of course, Dakota realized, he didn't know about Trader yet.

'We're taking a detour,' Dakota explained, 'so we can salvage weapons systems left behind by an extinct alien race. It means stopping off at another star system on the way.'

Martinez regarded her warily before turning back to Corso. 'And you concur with this?'

'We're just one ship, so we're going to need every advantage we can get. A couple of days' detour shouldn't make any difference in the long run.'

Martinez nodded wearily and looked back at Dakota. 'Lucas asked you how many jumps to get there.'

'At least three,' Dakota replied. 'Possibly more, given the issue with the drive-spines.' She stood up and nodded to Lamoureaux. 'Ted, if you don't mind, maybe I'd better run the next part myself.'

'Sure.' Lamoureaux stepped down from the interface chair, moving with elaborate care. Dakota felt his implant-mediated senses brush against hers.

'Okay.' She climbed into the chair and locked on to the ship's data-space. A moment later the great swirl of the galaxy faded, to be replaced by a model of a single star system.

'This is where we're headed next,' she explained. 'You're looking at a star towards the cooler end of the main sequence. It has eleven planets altogether, but our main point of interest is coming up in a moment.'

The system expanded rapidly until they had a view of

a lifeless world no more than a few thousand kilometres in diameter, its surface dotted with ancient impact craters. A broad, artificially flat plain, at odds with the surrounding landscape, surrounded what seemed at first to be just another crater.

'That's the cache entrance you can see there,' Dakota continued. A cutaway view of the planetoid now appeared next to its photorealistic image. 'Same layout as the Tierra cache, in fact and, like the Tierra cache – and every other cache in existence, from what I gather – it's located on a dwarf planet too small to be geologically active.'

The cutaway showed that the cache primarily consisted of a borehole extending more than thirty kilometres beneath the surface, with hundreds of passageways of varying length extending out from this central shaft and into the remaining body of the planetoid.

'How the hell could you know all this?' asked Martinez, switching his gaze between her and Corso.

'This all comes from a renegade Shoal-member—'

'A renegade *what*?' said Martinez, looking like he was about to throw his walking stick at her.

'Eduard,' intervened Corso, 'as soon as we're done here. I swear.' He nodded to Dakota for her to continue.

Martinez looked far from happy, but held his silence.

'It's a dead cache,' Dakota continued. 'I learned that it was discovered by a race called the Meridians, who're long gone. They had a colony here, but they wiped themselves out while fighting over it. The physical structure is still there, but everything inside was destroyed. If we get the opportunity or the time, I think it would be a very good idea to take a look down inside the cache. Apart from the fact I want to see what it looks like, it'll give us a much better idea of exactly what we're going to be facing once we reach our final destination.'

'And these weapons we're looking for,' said Corso. 'They're inside the cache?'

Dakota tilted the interface chair a few degrees upright so she could see his face more clearly. 'No, but apparently they're close to the mouth of the cache,' she explained. 'And, strictly speaking, they're not weapons. They're a form of field technology – same idea as our own field-generators but whole orders of magnitude more powerful – according to . . .' *according to Trader*, she almost said, until she caught Corso's eye.

'The point is,' said Corso, now picking up the thread, 'there's something there that can give us an even better fighting chance against the Emissaries.'

'According to who?' asked Martinez. 'Some . . . Shoal-member?'

'I think maybe we should go and have that talk,' said Corso, looking as if he would rather do almost anything else. 'And maybe a good stiff drink, if your meds will allow it.'

TWENTY-THREE

'Let me get this straight,' said Ty. 'I thought no time passed *at all* during a jump?'

They had come outside again as soon as the latest jump had been completed. Star-tangled nebulae hung in the void behind Olivarri. He had the whitest teeth Ty had ever seen in another human being; they positively shone when he grinned, and right now they were just about the only thing Ty could distinguish through the other man's visor.

Their three-person repair team was completed by Nancy, who was mending a spine-clamp prior to lowering a new spine into place. Ty could see her over Olivarri's shoulder, busily working away.

What lazy creatures we men are, he thought, *standing here while the woman toils.* The reality, of course, was that Nancy didn't trust anyone but herself to fulfil certain jobs. He found himself recalling the way her hands had gripped his hair the night before, her small lithe form arching above him, her mouth round and wide as she noisily climaxed.

'*Virtual* time passes. Jump-space has to find a way to

deal with the sudden appearance of physical matter from our universe. So it wraps the *Mjollnir* in a bubble of virtual time.'

'Because time doesn't actually exist within super-luminal space?'

'Exactly.' That toothy grin again. 'It's the virtual time that allows the physical matter to begin degrading.'

'But that's purely theoretical, isn't it? We don't know this for a fact.'

Olivarri was standing with one gloved hand resting on the lower curve of a drive-spine. He raised his other hand and waggled it from side to side. 'No, but it's the current best explanation, unless the Shoal have a better idea, and they weren't telling us even before they pulled a vanishing act. But virtual time at least explains why the degradation starts from the outside' – he lifted his helmeted head to look up towards the tip of the drive-spine – 'and works its way in towards the hull, rather than affecting every atom of the frigate at once. You need to introduce time, even if it's just virtual time, to explain that.'

'Like the little bubble of virtual space-time we're caught in had started to shrink.'

'Exactly. And because the virtual time that passes is vanishingly small—'

'We come out with relatively minor degradation.'

'Got it.' That brilliant toothy smile again.

Ty turned to look behind him towards the stern. He couldn't even pick out the Hyades Cluster any more, and it was only six days since they had left Redstone. A hundred metres away, a couple of spiders were hovering around another drive-spine, getting ready to repair some of that very same degradation.

He and Olivarri had decoupled the failed drive-spine, and half a dozen spiders were ready, their extendible arms gripping it at various points, to lift it away from the hull once the clamps that attached it in place were released.

Its replacement waited nearby, held in place by its own separate retinue of spider-mechs. It was a tricky and dangerous procedure, so all three humans kept a safe distance for the moment, letting the spiders do most of the work, and stepping in only where absolutely necessary.

Despite the precautions, there had already been some near fatalities. Lamoureaux had nearly fried himself getting too close to some frayed power-conduits; a hull-plate had swung loose while being detached, totalling a couple of spiders and very nearly taking Corso with it. And that wasn't even taking into account the greater risk of replacement drive-spines blowing up once they were plugged into the frigate's plasma flow, if they weren't configured in *just* the right way.

Given those risks, using the spiders generally, with a few human beings at hand to step in if absolutely necessary, was a fine idea in principle, except that in practice the team had to take over from the spiders on pretty much every occasion. The mechs were fine for grunt work, but the more delicate aspects of the job required human hands and minds.

'Okay,' said Nancy, 'releasing the clamps *now*.'

The restraints holding the drive-spine in place slid back into the hull, and the spiders arranged around it began emitting tiny jets of gas. Slowly, ponderously, the spine rose away from the hull, tilting to one side as the spiders coordinated with each other. The new drive-spine began to move forward as its own retinue of spiders pushed it towards the slot.

The work was so tedious that it was easy to fall into lengthy conversations. Nancy and Leo had spent most of this shift talking politics, and they quickly picked up the same thread again as the spider-mechs dragged the two drive-spines in different directions.

'Am I right in thinking,' asked Olivarri, 'that the only people who're allowed to vote or hold political office in the Freehold are those who've seen military service?'

'Well, mostly,' Nancy replied. 'Senator Corso's one of the exceptions, but for most of the Senate members, yeah. It's a sane principle.'

'Sane how?' asked Olivarri.

'Well, think about it,' Nancy replied. 'Why should someone who isn't prepared to pick up a gun to actively defend his or her society get to have a say in how that society is run?'

'Well . . . I'm not sure that the kind of people who *are* prepared to pick up a gun, based on an argument like that, are the ones I'd want running things for me.'

'Why?'

'Because they usually turn out to be exactly the kind of people I need protecting from in the first place.' Olivarri guffawed.

Nancy made a sound of disgust. 'You just don't understand.'

'What's not to understand?' Olivarri shot back. 'That's *exactly* why the Freehold were booted from world to world.'

'Leo, seriously. You have no understanding of the historical context. Our ending up on Redstone had nothing to do with our relations with the Consortium. The Freehold is about self-determination. It's about the right of the individual to defend herself and not to have to answer to any authority that wants to take away her basic human right to self-determination.'

Ty sighed quietly. Leo appeared bent on needling Nancy, and she appeared unable to resist rising to the bait every time.

'Okay,' said Olivarri, 'so what happened to all those ideals? That's – what – two coups you've had in a little over two years?'

'Because . . .' Nancy sighed. 'The wrong people are in charge, that's all.'

'Those people with the guns, you mean.'

Ty was deeply grateful when they all received an automated alert that the new drive-spine was ready to be locked into place. Nancy moved in close, obsessively rechecking the hull clamps and running a final systems scan. After a few minutes she stepped back, and they watched as the spiders slowly lowered the new drive-spine into its slot, the clamps snicking smoothly into place.

'Nice,' said Leo approvingly. 'Everything went right, just for once.'

But Ty reflected on how often the drive-spines were failing, and how many of them would need replacing before they reached the end of their journey. They were making long and frequent jumps that would take the *Mjollnir* a lot further and faster than it had needed to go on its maiden superluminal flight. At the rate they were going, they would end up having to cannibalize the ship itself for the necessary raw materials.

Nancy was in an ebullient mood once they got back inside.

'C'mon, Nathan, come back up to the centrifuge with us. You can't hide away from the rest of us for ever.'

Ty stowed his helmet on a rack in the changing room and climbed out of his pressure suit, wrinkling his nose at the smell of his own stale sweat. He twisted his head around in a slow circle, hearing the crunch of tired muscles as he locked his hands together behind his head and stretched a little.

'Maybe,' he replied. But Nancy understood that *maybe* within the context of their developing relationship really meant *definitely*.

Ty glanced at Olivarri, who was pretending not to listen. He had no idea what the other man might report to Corso, though perhaps it was better to play safe. 'But not this time,' he added, for Olivarri's sake. 'Maybe next time.'

'*What* next time?' Nancy jeered, smacking him in the chest with a glove she had removed before tossing it into a bin below the helmet rack. She was grinning, but Ty recognized the uncertainty in her smile.

'Soon,' he mouthed at her, then glanced again at Olivarri to make sure he hadn't noticed. He would sneak up to Nancy's quarters only when he thought he was less likely to run into anyone else.

'Shower!' Olivarri shouted, pushing away from them and heading towards the washing facilities. 'I *need* a fucking shower.'

With a thin, permeable mask covering his nose and mouth, Ty groaned with pleasure as needle-thin jets of hot water washed away the tension that had gathered between his shoulders. The water shut off after two minutes, and was rapidly vacuumed out of the sealed shower cubicle while he leaned against its door.

He looked down at where his skin was red and chafed from wearing a pressure suit for hours at a time. When he closed his eyes, all he could see was stars scattered across the void like diamond dust.

Ty glanced down at the ring he still wore on his right

hand, as the cubicle door clicked open. That encounter with the avatar back in Unity felt more and more surreal, the further the *Mjollnir* got from home, and yet the ring was always there to remind him he hadn't just imagined it.

He grabbed a towel and pushed his way out, hastily drying himself before pulling on a set of clean clothes from the locker. How, he wondered, might he have gone about arranging that strange encounter, if he had been in the shoes of whoever was behind the avatar? What resources would he have needed?

Access to explosives, for a start. Ty brushed his fingers through his damp hair as he thought. Explosives wouldn't be too hard to get hold of, for someone determined enough. His time with Peralta had taught him how cheap fabricators could be hacked to mix the right chemical compounds. Unmanned taxis were equally notorious for being easy to hack. The imaging equipment the agent had used to speak with him was expensive, but standard; all that was necessary was to pay someone to install it in an empty office, no questions asked. One man could do it. In fact, given modern tach-net comms technology, one man could organize it all and not even have to be on the same planet.

Ty paused, his eye catching the glint of the ring. The avatar/agent had threatened to expose him if he didn't take the ring, but in reality he had already been exposed. For a start, Marcus Weil had recognized him, and he hadn't been quiet about it. Quite possibly Martinez and the other members of the frigate's crew were the only ones who did not know his true identity. All in all, it made a mockery of the avatar's threat.

Filled with a sudden decisiveness, Ty grasped the ring and started to pull it off. He would fling it into the void the next time he was outside the ship.

He tugged it as far as his knuckle and then froze, gripped by a sudden conviction that something terrible would happen if he took the ring off. He just stood there, bewildered by his own sudden reluctance.

'Hey.'

Ty spun around, his heart in his throat. It was Olivarri, and he had been so sure he was alone.

'Are you all right?' asked Olivarri. 'You were standing there staring into space like you'd seen your own ghost.'

'I'm fine. I was just . . .' Ty reached up and realized with some confusion that his hair was now bone-dry. How long had he stood motionless? 'I must be more exhausted than I thought,' he stammered.

'Yeah, I guess.' Olivarri nodded warily. 'Takes it out of all of us. Some of us haven't clocked this much time doing EVA in more than ten years.'

Ty realized all he wanted to do was get out of there. 'I guess so,' he replied, and stepped past the other man.

'Wait.'

Ty turned back in irritation.

'There's something we need to talk about,' said Olivarri.

He stepped over to open a locker, withdrawing a slim

black box. He placed this on a shelf under a mirror, then touched a hidden switch on top. A single orange light on one side blinked into life.

Ty stared at the device in confusion. 'What is that?'

'It's a jamming device. I'm just making sure our conversation stays private, in case anyone's listening in.'

Ty looked around. 'What exactly is it you want, Leo?'

'You're going to help me make sure the Mos Hadroch gets into the right hands, Mr Whitecloud.'

Ty stared back at him. 'Who exactly are you?'

Olivarri spoke low and fast. 'I work for the Legislate, Ty. I can make sure you're safe when you get back to the Consortium. Nobody will ever find you, and that's more than Senator Corso could ever guarantee. As far as anyone's concerned, you'll disappear. If you cooperate, we'll give you a whole new life, and you'll never have to worry about anyone tracking you down again. All you have to do is agree to help me.'

'So . . . you're, what? A spy?'

'I work for the Consortium Security Services. I was meant to bring you into custody along with the Mos Hadroch. Then the Senator decided to take the frigate by force and, by the time I learned about it, it was too late to come up with an alternative plan.'

Ty shook his head. 'Just what is it you want from me?'

'Nothing just yet,' Olivarri replied. 'Right now I'm just establishing contact. We wanted the artefact where we could run our own tests but, by the looks of it, Merrick and Corso have access to information we don't.

For the moment, we're going to let them run things the way they want to.'

Ty stared back at him. 'Then what the hell do you need *me* for?'

'We're concerned about what happens to the artefact *after* it's been implemented. It's a powerful weapon that could conceivably be used to shut down the Tierra cache once the *Mjollnir* returns to the Consortium – or any other cache, for that matter. That makes it too valuable to allow it to remain in anyone else's hands.'

So that's it. 'But why didn't you tell me any of this before – when you first contacted me? And what about this ring?' he asked, bringing his hand up and displaying it to Olivarri. 'What the hell is it for?'

'What?' Olivarri glared at him. 'Ty, what the hell are you talking about?'

'What am *I* talking about?' Ty laughed. '*You're* the ones who contacted me.'

'Ty, no one else in the security services has been in contact with you, apart from myself, believe me.'

'But . . .' *The explosion, the taxi, the meeting with the avatar.*

'Wait,' continued Ty. 'This doesn't make sense. There was that Consortium agent back in Unity. Who was he?'

Someone who merely *claimed* they worked for the Consortium, Ty reflected. He stared at the ring on his finger as if seeing it for the first time. He had a sudden, overwhelming sense that there was something he needed to remember.

'Ty, I swear, *nobody* from my side has approached you before now. I can guarantee that.'

Then who the hell . . . ?

Ty suddenly felt a deep terror grip hold of him. He pushed roughly past Olivarri, the sudden motion sending the other man sprawling.

Ty collided with the door, and clumsily pulled himself through, and kept going, caroming from side to side as he made his way down a passageway leading towards the nearest transport station. Only once he had reached it, and climbed inside a car, did he finally come to a halt, lungs aching breathlessly.

He glanced frequently out through the car's open door towards the hub entrance, but there was no sign yet that Olivarri had followed him.

Ty was seized by a crippling pain in his head and he doubled over, gripping his skull and crying out at the unexpectedness of it. As he squeezed his eyes tight shut, he saw a tiny but intense flash of light in his peripheral vision, and . . .

The next thing he knew, he was still inside the transport car, but his hands were grimy and his body stank of sweat like he had never once taken a shower.

There was something he had to remember . . . something important.

But, however hard he tried, it wouldn't come back to him.

TWENTY-FOUR

The *Mjollnir* jumped again only seven hours later, before dropping back into space several hundred light-years closer to the edge of the Orion Arm. Ahead lay the region of the Long War, the main battleground of the Shoal's fifteen-thousand-year conflict with the Emissaries, and beyond that the Perseus Arm.

Once the all-clear had sounded, Lamoureaux climbed back out of the interface chair and nodded to Corso.

'We're pushing it with these jumps, Lucas. Too many and too often. This ship wasn't designed for that kind of stress.'

Corso glanced towards him. 'Objection noted,' he replied, and returned his attention to the console before him.

Lamoureaux thought of saying something more, then changed his mind and left the bridge: there was no point telling Corso what he almost certainly already knew. More than twenty drive-spines had failed this time. New ones were already being manufactured, but if they kept failing at this rate the *Mjollnir*'s jump capacity was going to be seriously compromised.

*

Ty had paused in his work when the jump alert sounded, waiting quietly until the all-clear followed a minute later.

He dreaded the next time he might be assigned to a repair crew with Olivarri. Following their encounter, he had buried himself in his work, running ever more in-depth and increasingly aggressive scans of the Mos Hadroch, trying to get some idea of its internal structure. And yet, despite all his efforts, it remained as frustratingly opaque as ever.

He thought frequently of Nancy, of drowning himself in the taut muscular curves of her body. The more rational part of him would then like to catalogue the risks inherent in their affair, or remind him of the impossibility of it continuing after their return home. To his eternal surprise and consternation, the thought of the relationship coming to an end left him desolate.

He was still sitting there brooding half an hour later when the *Mjollnir*'s primary control systems and life-support suffered a catastrophic failure, and another, more urgent, alarm began to sound.

Dakota had picked a cabin located outside the centrifuge, having spent too many years working and living in zero-gee conditions to ever really be able to sleep comfortably in gravity, simulated or otherwise. She was still lying there awake when the alarm sounded.

She instantly sat up and locked into the data-space, only to find that large parts of it had gone offline. It was like walking into a deserted house and finding that most of the doors had been locked.

A moment later she felt Lamoureaux pinging her from within the centrifuge.

<Something bad's happened,> he sent. <Most of the physical systems just shut down, from what I can tell. Life-support, fusion reactors, bays and fabricators – none of them are responding even to basic queries.>

Do we have any idea what's going on?

<Not yet, but I'm heading back to the bridge. Lucas was there when I left, so maybe he'll know something.>

To her considerable alarm, the lights suddenly flickered and went out. Emergency lighting kicked in a couple of seconds later, bathing her in a blood-red light. Some data trickled in from the exterior sensor arrays: nothing out of the ordinary was taking place outside the ship, which at least ruled out an external attack.

If we can't get the life-support back online, we're in deep shit, Ted. This is starting to look like—

<Sabotage. I know. But don't jump to any conclusions just yet. This isn't the kind of thing you can pull off by just crossing a few wires here or there. Shutting down systems like these one at a time is one thing. But all at once? That takes some serious skill.>

Dakota pulled herself over to the door of her cabin and pressed her palm against its access panel. Nothing happened. She slammed the flat of her hand against it, then remembered there was a manual override accessible through a side panel.

She pulled it open and tugged at the lever behind it. Something clicked loudly and the door slid partway open to reveal a sliver of red-lit passageway beyond. Dakota prised at the open edge of the door with the fingers of both hands until it finally slid all the way open with a protesting whine.

She headed straight for the bridge. The quickest way there was to board a car at the nearest transport hub, about a minute's walk away, but they all proved to be out of action as well. Dakota peered in through the window of one car and saw red failure lights blinking spasmodically on its dashboard. She turned back and made her way to a corridor that led directly towards the hub.

Once it was clear that the *Mjollnir* had suffered a sudden catastrophic systems failure, there was a part of Corso that was not surprised, and his first thought was of Trader.

Ever since Dakota had brought the Shoal-member on board, Corso had made sure that a discreet but constant eye was kept on his yacht. Although the frigate's internal surveillance system had been directed to survey the main hold at all times, Corso wasn't taking any chances. Both Willis and Schiller made frequent trips to the bay to check on Trader's ship in person. Corso couldn't say exactly what he was hoping they might find, but he wanted to send the alien a message that he was under constant surveillance.

He shut the alarm off, and the silence that followed fell across the bridge like a heavy, smothering blanket. He next used a console to project a highly detailed schematic of the *Mjollnir* overhead. Red dots blinked on and off up and down its length, identifying the depressingly numerous systems failures.

A groggy-looking Martinez entered the bridge, pulling a jacket on. 'What the hell just happened?' he demanded, striding over to join him.

'Take a look for yourself.' Corso waved towards the console.

Martinez leaned over its glassy surface and quickly scanned the data Corso had just pulled up. His eyes widened, and then he glanced upwards at the schematic floating above their heads.

'I've never seen anything like this,' Martinez muttered, then peered over at the recently vacated interface chair.

'You're wondering if a machine-head could pull something like this off?' suggested Corso.

'Could they?'

'You told me yourself that the new security measures make it just about impossible for anyone with implants to take covert control without being directly plugged into the interface chair. And if either Ted or Dakota was responsible, the other would know.'

'That's the idea,' Martinez agreed. 'But the system's never really been tested properly, and I wasn't around when they carried out the most recent modifications. Do we have any idea where either Merrick or Lamoureaux are?'

Corso sighed. 'Right now I couldn't tell you where *anybody* is, Commander.'

'You do realize they're the first and most obvious suspects, regardless?'

Corso nodded irritably. 'Don't forget how hard we've been pushing the *Mjollnir*. We don't know what problems that might have caused. First that expedition to find the Mos Hadroch . . . then off again not much more than a week later. We're making longer, more frequent jumps than any human-built ship has ever performed before. We're having to carry out almost constant maintenance as it is.'

'No,' Martinez snapped. 'This is deliberate sabotage.'

'How can you be sure?'

'For God's sake, Lucas.' The Commander nodded towards the overhead schematic. 'Each and every subsystem has been targeted separately. Something like that takes conscious effort. Did you check the surveillance records yet?'

Corso opened his mouth and paused momentarily. 'No, not yet.'

Martinez leaned over the console, and Corso watched as he pulled up screeds of data, muttering while he worked.

'Take a look at this,' he said, moving to one side. Corso glanced at the data and saw that it was a series of logs.

'The past twelve hours of visual records,' explained Martinez. 'All of them wiped. You need high-level access to be able to pull off a trick like that – the kind of access only an interface chair gives you.'

Corso stared at the data. 'Before you start pointing fingers at the team, remember our passenger in the hold. Besides, the Mos Hadroch might have triggered some glitches early on as well.'

Martinez frowned. 'Trader's stuck inside his own ship. He surely can't pull off a trick like this from inside there, can he?'

'I don't know,' Corso replied. 'But then, I don't know if Ted or Dakota could have pulled this off either.'

Just then, Lamoureaux came on to the bridge, looking distinctly out of breath. 'I came straight back here as soon as I heard the alarm. What's happened?'

Corso ignored the look on Martinez's face as he turned to face the machine-head. 'We don't know yet,' he told Lamoureaux. 'I was hoping you might know something.'

Lamoureaux shook his head. 'Most of the data-space is down. Dakota would tell you just the same.'

'Where is she?' asked Martinez.

'She's on her way here.'

'Just to be clear about it, even with the ship's networks down, you can still talk to each other?'

'Sure.' Lamoureaux nodded. 'Machine-head hardware creates its own spontaneous networks, as long as you're reasonably close to each other.'

363

'Could you get in touch with any of the others by using your implants?' asked Corso.

Lamoureaux thought for a moment. 'Like use them to reroute some of the low-level comms? Yeah, maybe. The primary systems are down, but secondary and back-up seem to be rebooting spontaneously.'

'Go to it,' said Corso.

Lamoureaux headed back to the interface chair.

'All right,' said Martinez, just as Schiller and Perez entered the bridge, 'here's what we're going to do. We've got no idea if this is hostile action, but until we know otherwise we have to assume it is. We need to find out where everyone is and start piecing together how all this happened.'

'And if we can't find them?'

'Then we go looking,' Martinez replied.

Dakota reached the hub twenty minutes after the alarm had shut off and found Nancy Schiller and Dan Perez already waiting there. Both were armed with pulse-rifles.

'That leaves just Driscoll and Olivarri,' Schiller observed to Perez, as Dakota approached.

'Any idea what's going on?' asked Dakota, grabbing a wall rung.

'We're assuming it's sabotage until we know otherwise,' said Perez. 'We're just keeping an eye out.'

'What for?'

'Can't rule out a third party,' Schiller growled, patting

her rifle. 'Lots of places on board for a saboteur to hide in. That means we've got to be ready for any surprises.'

'But no word from Driscoll or Olivarri?'

Perez shook his head. 'Not yet.'

'Look, you're forgetting about Trader. I'll go back down to the stern and check he's still where he should be.' She started to head back the way she had come.

'No,' said Schiller, raising her rifle towards Dakota. 'You stay right here where we can see you.'

'Okay,' said Dakota, turning back slowly. 'If that's what you want.'

Perez put one hand on the barrel of Schiller's rifle and pushed it back down. 'Nancy, let's first work out what happened before jumping to any conclusions, okay?'

Schiller's mouth worked like she wanted to say something in response, but then she relented, lowering her rifle and muttering something foul under her breath.

'Look, right now we're just trying to figure out where everyone is,' Perez explained. 'Most comms are still down, so we've been sitting tight and waiting to see who makes it back here, assuming they've got the sense to head for the bridge. If Olivarri and Driscoll don't show, we're going to go looking for them.'

'In that case,' said Dakota, 'you're going to want to break out the spider-mechs, especially if you think there might be saboteurs on board. They're independent of the *Mjollnir*'s control systems, so they probably won't have been affected by whatever's happened. Plus, they can move around the ship and report back a lot faster than any of us can. In fact, I could run a couple of dozen of them at once single-handed. That'd free you up to—'

'Goddammit, no,' snarled Schiller, clearly working up a temper. 'How do we know she's not the one who did all this?' she said, gesturing towards Dakota. 'Maybe if we lock up her and Lamoureaux, we won't have to worry about either of them sabotaging anything else until we have some idea just what the fuck is going on.'

'You have no idea what you're talking about,' Dakota snapped, now losing her own temper. 'I'm sick and tired of you thinking everyone with an implant is some kind of devil out to—'

'Stop it, both of you!' Perez yelled. 'Keep this crap up and we won't even deserve to survive what's up ahead. We either work together or we give up now. Standing around pointing fingers solves nothing.' He looked at Dakota. 'It's a good idea, Miss Merrick – but I'm coming with you.'

Ty panicked when at first he couldn't raise anyone over the comms system, then nearly convinced himself he was trapped there in the lab as the doors failed to respond. But he soon located the emergency overrides and made his way out into the passageway beyond.

When the alarm finally shut off, his ears still rang in the sudden silence. He pushed himself cautiously along through the ship, unnerved by the eerie red emergency lighting, which made the frigate seem somehow unfamiliar and threatening.

He worked his way onwards until he reached a hydroponics deck filled with lush scents, the air warm and humid. There was also a transport station there, but when he tried one of the waiting cars it didn't respond.

He was going to have to get himself to the bridge the hard way.

Ty retraced his steps, pushing himself along a wide passageway until he found his path blocked by an enormous pressure door that must have slid into place when the alarm went off. He stared at it, dismayed, wondering if the ship had lost atmosphere in some areas. He tried the overrides, but this time they didn't work.

He doubled back and tried another route. Once again, he found his way barred, but this time the overrides did work.

He passed through three more such doors on his journey towards the centrifuge, before he sighted several bright points of light moving towards him from up ahead. He waited until they drew closer, finally resolving into half-a-dozen spider-mechs propelling themselves forward on gentle puffs of gas.

'Hey! Driscoll! Is that you?'

Ty recognized Dan Perez coming along the passageway a short distance behind the spiders, accompanied by Dakota Merrick. Ty moved to one side to let the spiders pass. Two of them cut off down a side passage, while the rest kept on in the same direction, heading back towards the hydroponics deck.

'Where were you when the alert sounded?' asked Dakota, as she and Perez drew abreast of him.

'In the labs,' Ty replied. 'I had trouble getting out.'

'And the Mos Hadroch? It's still where it should be?'

The question surprised Ty. For some reason, the possibility that it might be in danger had simply never occurred to him. 'It's fine,' he replied. 'But who would want to take it?'

Dakota got a strange look on her face. 'One of us should go back and stay there, keep an eye on things.'

'Then, in that case, I might as well go back myself,' said Ty.

Perez nodded. 'Yeah, good idea. We just needed to make sure everyone was all right while the comms are down. The others are up on the bridge trying to figure out what happened. I'll send a couple of spiders with you as well, just in case.'

'Just in case what?'

'We can keep an eye on you through the spider's sensory systems,' Perez explained. 'Until we have a better idea what's going on.'

'I guess I don't have a problem with that,' Ty replied.

'One other thing,' said Dakota. 'We haven't heard or seen from Olivarri yet. Have you?'

Ty shook his head. 'No, not . . .' *Not since he*

approached me to tell me he was spying on all of us. 'Not since our last shift together, no.'

Perez glanced at Dakota. 'I guess we keep on looking then.'

'Yeah. Listen, Nathan. Since we can stay in touch through the spiders, if you see or hear anything, let us know straight away. *Especially* if you see Olivarri.'

A couple of hours later Dakota hauled herself back up to the bridge and collapsed on to a couch. Corso and Martinez stepped over to join her, while Willis worked away in the background at mapping the areas of the frigate that had already been checked out.

'I've had time to think about this now,' she told them. 'There are about a dozen key vulnerabilities at different points on the ship, based on what I've seen with my own eyes as well as via the spiders, and every one of them was hit individually.'

'Ted said pretty much the same thing,' said Corso, who had taken a seat next to a console and swivelled it around to face her. Martinez stood beside him, eyeing her like she was something you would grow in a Petri dish. His attitude towards Corso had clearly become somewhat strained ever since learning about Trader. 'So it's definitely sabotage?'

She nodded, and tried to blink away her fatigue. 'I think someone spent a lot of time setting things up. The data-space has recovered enough that I managed to track down software routines in the primary stacks which I can't even begin to explain. They might be viruses, or they might be something else. I'm guessing the former, but they've now been cleaned out or isolated.'

'And that's what caused the ship to shut down?'

Dakota shrugged. 'That's my guess.'

Martinez folded his arms and looked from one to the other. 'But still no sign of Olivarri?'

'Nope.' Dakota shook her head. 'The spiders are still out searching through the whole ship, but there's just too much space to cover. It could take us weeks to investigate every nook and cranny.'

'All right, what about Trader?' asked Corso.

'Look,' she said, 'disregarding just for the moment the fact neither of us trusts him in the least, I just don't see any way he could have pulled this off.'

'But it's not like there isn't precedent,' Corso insisted. 'We know he's lied in the past, and we both know how machine-heads like yourself are vulnerable to—'

Dakota sat up and glared at him. 'Listen, I'm getting really sick of being treated like I'm some kind of bomb about to go off. Why don't you—'

Something beeped loudly, cutting her off mid-sentence.

'That's Dan on the emergency frequency,' said Willis, stepping over to an adjacent console. 'I'll put him through the overhead.'

Dan Perez's face appeared on a screen next to the

couch. Nancy Schiller was visible just behind him, floating in a stretch of red-lit passageway.

'It's Olivarri.' Perez sounded out of breath. 'We just found him, down near one of the fusion-maintenance bays. He's dead.'

TWENTY-FIVE

By the time Corso and Martinez reached the maintenance bay, Perez had found some opaque plastic sheeting to cover Olivarri's body. Schiller had meanwhile headed back to the bridge.

Corso winced when Perez pulled the sheet back from Olivarri's head and upper torso, because the back of his head had been caved in. Dried blood had crusted around his mouth, and his nose was crushed flat against his skull.

He was barely recognizable, Corso thought.

Martinez leaned in close to the body and looked up at Perez. 'Where exactly did you find him?'

'Over there.' Perez nodded towards where a large steel panel had swung away from the wall. 'Whoever did this wedged him behind that maintenance panel, but it then set off an alert on one of the control boards. I got the shock of my fucking life when I pulled the door open to check it out.'

'Question is,' said Corso, 'why hide him here? Why not just drag him to an airlock and push his body outside the ship? That way we'd never have known what happened to him.'

Martinez shook his head. 'Too much chance of getting picked up by the hull's sensor arrays. They run on their own power and control systems, so whoever did this presumably knew they'd be spotted if they tried to do so. To be honest, we're lucky we found him at all. This ship is big enough that, apart from an alert being triggered, it might have taken a long time before we eventually found him.'

Perez looked up from Olivarri's pulped features. 'Look, this is pure speculation, but is it possible all this – the sabotage, the systems failures – was intended just to cover this up?'

The three men exchanged looks. 'The same thought did cross my mind,' said Corso. 'We've already got most of the primary systems back online. At first we thought we were looking at a catastrophic system failure, but in the end it proved to be not much more than an inconvenience.'

'A distraction, in other words?' said Martinez.

Corso stared down again at the dead man and felt a flash of resentment, as if this new crisis were somehow the victim's fault. It was hard to connect this crumpled ruin with the living, breathing human being Olivarri had been.

Martinez sighed and turned to Perez. 'Any sign of the weapon?'

'Not that I could find,' Perez replied. 'But I'd say it was a wrench or something similar. There are diagnostic programs we can run to figure out how it was done, within a fairly narrow margin of error. Same thing goes for any DNA or other chemical traces left behind – assuming we find them.'

'We're going to have to search everyone's quarters,' decided Martinez. 'These labs, the bridge, and anywhere any of us have spent much time.'

'Surely whoever did this wouldn't have been stupid enough to leave a murder weapon lying around their own quarters?' Corso protested.

'We don't know, do we?' said Martinez. 'Any idea who was the last of us to see him before he was killed?'

'He was outside doing hull repairs with Nancy and Nathan,' said Perez. 'But that was several hours before the outage.'

Corso recalled that Olivarri had spent a lot of time visiting remote parts of the ship, checking up on various life-support and maintenance systems in areas where the surveillance coverage was often less than adequate. There might have been any number of opportunities for someone to track him down and kill him.

Martinez glanced over at Perez. 'Dan, would you mind giving me and Lucas a minute alone?'

Perez looked warily at the two of them, then walked out into a passageway adjoining the bay. Martinez turned to Corso, his expression grim.

'I was still in the med-bay when that Shoal-member came on board,' he said, sounding heated. 'And since then I've listened to all your arguments about why he's here, but I don't get the sense you're anywhere near as much in control as you seem to think you are. Merrick didn't show herself until we were already on board, even though we needed her around well in advance of the launch. The way it seems to me, she doesn't give a damn what anyone else on this ship says or thinks, and now we're one man down, which means we've got a killer somewhere on board. Let's just say you're not inspiring my confidence in your leadership skills.'

Corso felt his jaw muscles tighten. 'I told you already why things are the way they are.'

'And yet I keep asking myself the same question again and again: who's in charge of this expedition? You or Dakota?' Martinez raised his eyebrows a fraction. 'Or maybe Trader's the one who's really running things?'

'You're saying you could have done things better?'

Martinez sighed. 'Once word about this gets around, everyone's going to be wondering if they'll be next. What you need to do now is make them feel like you're in control of things, because *you're* the reason we're all here. And if you thought your job was hard before, it's about to get an awful lot harder. I mean, you do realize Dakota's going to be top of everyone's shit list when they start looking for someone to blame for his death? Assuming,' he added, 'that she didn't do it herself.'

Corso let his shoulders sag. 'All right,' he conceded, 'what do you suggest?'

'Talk to Dakota – Lamoureaux as well. See if their stories add up, and if they do we can get on with finding out who actually *did* do this.'

'Fine. I'll talk to Dakota first.'

'We'll both talk to her.'

'No,' Corso shook his head fiercely, 'I'll talk to her alone. The rest we can interview together.'

Martinez fixed him with a look that made Corso wonder if he was asking for too much this time.

'All right.' Martinez nodded at Olivarri's corpse. 'We'll play it your way for now, but just for now. Just show me you've got a handle on things.'

'Thank you, Eduard. Right now she needs to work with Ted to get the rest of the data-space back online, but I'll talk to her as soon as they're finished.'

'No.' Martinez shook his head slowly. 'Don't try to thank me. Just figure out what the hell's going on before anyone else ends up like this.'

'Are you serious?' Dakota looked offended. 'You think *I* had something to do with Olivarri's death?'

Corso leaned against a bulkhead and closed his eyes for a moment. They were back in the debriefing room located on the centrifuge. Dakota slumped back in her chair, her eyes puffy and red from too much stress and too little sleep. They had all been working long and hard at getting the last of the systems online.

Tension had hung heavy in the air since Olivarri had been found dead less than twelve hours before, and large parts of the frigate had been declared off-limits. People got on with their jobs, or talked over food in one of the canteens, but it was impossible to miss how they all kept glancing over their shoulders, or the careful way they looked at each other. Corso could feel it too: the sense that nowhere was safe.

'You know that I *have* to ask, because no one but you and Ted has the kind of high-level access needed to pull something like this off.'

She gave him a withering look. 'Nice to know you've got my back, Lucas.'

'Jesus and Buddha, Dakota, I only just managed to convince Martinez to let me talk to you on my own.'

'Why? What is it you don't want him to hear?'

'For a start, he's better off not knowing about some of the things that happened at Nova Arctis. It's a matter of public record that the Uchidans mind-controlled you at Port Gabriel, but if he knew how Trader did it to you a *second* time, he'd lock you up or throw you out the nearest airlock, and to hell with me or the Mos Hadroch.'

'And that's what you think is happening to me?'

Corso felt his face grow hot. 'I'd be an idiot if I ruled it out.'

She stood up and leaned against the table, facing him obliquely, her arms folded defensively over her chest. 'Then I'm ruling it out *for* you. And, in answer to your next question, I've barely even spoken to Olivarri, except for the one time we were out on the hull working on some repairs along with Dan.'

'There's no possible way Trader could have got to you somehow, without your being aware of it?'

'Look, what Trader did to me back then was a kind of rape. But he had to get physically close before he could do it. I'd know if he tried anything like that again, and he knows that I'd know.'

'And yet you said you met him in person, the time he gave you control over the Meridian weapons.'

'That's true,' she nodded, 'but there still wasn't any direct or even indirect contact of any kind. Certainly nothing physically passed from him to me in any way.'

'But it doesn't always have to be physical, does it?'

'No, but this time I'd have *known* it. If I'd been affected in any way, the Magi ship would have told me.'

'Except that your Magi ship isn't around any more.'

'Yes, but . . .' She hesitated. 'Look, I see where you're going. But if I was compromised, Ted would know.'

'All right.' Corso moved away from the wall and came closer to her. 'Can you think of a reason why anyone might want to kill Olivarri? Even Trader?'

'Hell if I know,' she replied. 'Have you talked to Trader?'

'I did. He says he knows nothing about it. But even if he's lying, what can we do?'

Take his yacht away, for a start. Dakota wasn't ready to tell Corso or anyone else just what Moss had given her at Derinkuyu. She had thought more than once of trying a gentle infiltration of the Shoal-member's ship, but had held back for fear such an intrusion might be detected.

'I can't make any suggestions when it comes to the rest of the people on board,' Dakota replied. 'They tend to . . . keep their distance.'

'They do?'

She shot him a look of annoyance. 'Come on, Lucas, of course they do. I'm a machine-head and, worse, I'm the one they've all heard of, the one who gets blamed for just about everything that's gone wrong in their lives since Nova Arctis, right? I mean, apart from me and Ted, who the hell else has some kind of implant?'

A strange look passed over Corso's face, as if he had suddenly remembered something.

'What?' asked Dakota, peering at him.

'Nothing,' said Corso, a little too quickly. 'Look, it's true the rest of them can't help but remember what happened at Port Gabriel every time they see you. But that just makes it all the more important to prove you've not been compromised in the same way again.'

'And how do you propose to do that?' she asked, tightening her lips into a thin, bloodless line.

'Remember how I tracked down and destroyed the routines that Trader placed in your head back at Nova Arctis? Well, the med-bay should be up to the same job, and a deep scan on your implants would show if they're clean or not.'

Dakota's expression turned defiant, but Corso could detect the faint dampness at the corners of her eyes.

'All right,' she said, standing up. 'If that's what it takes. But you're going to have to persuade Ted to do the same.'

'I've already talked to him,' said Corso, straightening up once again. 'He's going to meet us there.'

They found Ted Lamoureaux waiting at the entrance to the med-bay. He was looking distraught.

'You'd better take a look inside,' he said. 'I've already alerted the bridge.'

Dakota and Corso entered and immediately saw that the diagnostic equipment had been badly vandalized. Every unit above the examination table was blackened and burnt with scorch marks.

Lamoureaux came in behind them. 'I got here about twenty minutes ago,' he said. 'Everything's fried except for the medboxes.'

Dakota surveyed the damage, feeling suddenly numb. The labyrinth of bays and corridors that contained the med-bay was one part of the ship they had not searched during their hunt for Olivarri earlier.

Lamoureaux pushed past them, bringing himself to a halt by grabbing the edge of the examination table and pulling himself close to it. He reached up and levered open a panel on the side of one of the diagnostic units, revealing the scorched and blackened circuitry.

It occurred to Dakota that the easiest way to go around destroying the diagnostic gear would have been by using a handheld plasma cutter, just the kind of thing you would expect to find lying around a ship like the *Mjollnir*.

'The Commander told me to get here as fast as I . . . shit.'

Dakota turned to see Nancy Schiller appear in the doorway. She stared at the ruined scanner, then turned to look at Dakota, her knuckles turning white where they gripped the plasma-rifle that had barely left her hands since the start of the outage.

'We *can* manufacture new units, can't we?' asked Corso.

Lamoureaux pushed himself away from the table. 'I don't know if we can. It's going to take time to get the rest of the fabricators back online and up to full capacity, and we're pushing them to the limit as it is in manufacturing the new drive-spines. Full-body imaging gear like this is pretty advanced even for the fabricators we've got on board. It's not like knocking out gun-drones or spider-mechs.'

Corso gestured to Nancy to follow him out into the corridor, where they began conversing together in quiet tones.

Lamoureaux touched Dakota's elbow and she moved closer.

'This is going to make things harder for us both,' he said, keeping his voice low enough not to be overheard. 'It's going to seem like one of us did this so we couldn't be scanned.'

'Don't take this the wrong way, Ted, but *you* were in charge of the ship when everything shut down. And you were also the first one here.'

'I've been up on the bridge the whole time until now, and I'd also say this damage was done during the outage.'

'All right,' she said. 'Does it feel to you like someone's trying to set us up?'

'If they are, they're doing a very good job – not that we were winning any popularity contests before this.' As he said it, he glanced towards Nancy.

'You know,' said Dakota, 'I came down here and ran a scan on myself the first chance I had after coming on board. Just to be sure. Anyway, I'm clean.'

The corner of Lamoureaux's mouth twitched slightly. 'I did the same thing. Also clean. Did you tell the others that?'

'You think they'd just accept our word for it?'

They pulled apart as Schiller and Corso re-entered the med-bay.

'Commander Martinez is on his way here,' Nancy announced, still glaring at them both. 'Nobody moves until he gets here. Got that?'

The several minutes before Martinez arrived were some of the most uncomfortable Dakota had ever experienced.

She could have communicated with Lamoureaux via their implants, but her gut told her that Nancy would only become even more paranoid if she guessed what they were doing. So they waited in silence, trying to avoid looking directly at Nancy, while Corso checked data-files on the med-bay's terminal.

Martinez, when he arrived, studied the ruined equipment with a defeated expression. 'Well, looks like nobody's getting scanned any time soon,' he muttered.

'Oh maybe one of *them* did it,' said Nancy, her eyes burning into Dakota's. 'It's what we're all thinking, isn't it?'

Dakota did her best not to flinch from her gaze. 'Or maybe *you* did it, Nancy,' she suggested. 'It's not like anyone doesn't know you've got a problem with me and Ted.'

'Oh, come *on*,' Nancy snapped, gripping her weapon closer to her chest. 'Nobody's going to smash this stuff to pieces unless they were scared of what it might reveal.'

'Shut the hell up, Nancy,' growled Martinez. 'I don't want to hear one more word of idle speculation.'

Nancy fell silent, but still looked defiant.

'Lucas,' Martinez continued, 'how long would it take for us to build some new diagnostic units?'

'We can't,' Corso replied wearily. 'I just checked the fabricator databases and the med-bay blueprints have all been wiped as well.'

Nancy's gaze once again settled on Dakota, as if she had just heard a piece of particularly damning evidence. 'Well, what do you know,' she murmured, and stepped back out of the room.

Corso stared after her with an alarmed expression. 'Eduard—'

'Don't worry about her,' Martinez interrupted quietly. 'She's not going to do anything stupid. She's just scared – like the rest of us.'

Scared people do dangerous things, Dakota almost observed, but thought better of it.

Martinez declared the bay off-limits and sealed the room with Schiller's help, placing a couple of dedicated sensors on the door that would sound a full alert if anyone tried to enter without permission. Corso and Lamoureaux made their way back to the bridge together.

As soon as they were out of earshot, Lamoureaux pulled Corso to a halt. 'We have to talk about White-cloud,' he said urgently.

Corso nodded, and rubbed the bridge of his nose. 'I think I know what you're going to say. He's the only other one on board with an implant, so maybe he can also be compromised.'

Lamoureaux nodded. 'Uchidan implant technology isn't so very different from what I've got in *my* head.'

'I thought the Uchidan technology was a lot more limited?'

'Sure, extremely limited,' Lamoureaux confirmed. 'No localized environmental data, no ability to interface with any machinery outside of a dedicated transceiver, and even then only in the crudest possible way. I could stand right next to him and I wouldn't be able to tell if there's anything lodged in his brain, but that wouldn't necessarily mean he isn't vulnerable to outside control. I mean, I don't know whether it can be done, but that's not the same thing as saying it can't.'

'You've got to admit,' said Corso, 'it'd be kind of ironic if that did turn out to be the case.'

'Ironic how?'

'He's at least partly responsible for what happened at Port Gabriel, so it'd be a kind of karmic justice, don't you think?'

'Maybe.' The corner of Lamoureaux's mouth twitched slightly. 'I'll have to admit I hadn't thought of that.'

Corso nodded in the direction they'd been heading. 'We should get back to the bridge now,' he said, pushing away from the bulkhead they had paused to rest against.

'Lucas, wait. I didn't just want to talk to you about Whitecloud.'

Corso grabbed a rung, before he could drift too far ahead. 'What then?'

'I mean Olivarri. Your aides asked me some questions about him when we were back at Ocean's Deep.'

'What kind of questions?'

'About who I might have seen him talking to.'

Corso frowned. 'Ray Willis was Olivarri's boss. He'd have told me if something was wrong.'

'I had the impression they were just feeling something

out, like there was just the merest *suggestion* of irregu-larities. That's what Nisha said to me.'

'Why are you telling me this now?'

'It's not too late to send a signal back to Ocean's Deep. I don't know what's happened to Nisha or Yugo since the Legislate took over, but maybe one of them might still be in a position to help us run a deeper background check on him.'

'I don't know,' said Corso. 'It's going to use a lot of power to boost a signal that far.'

'Sure,' Lamoureaux agreed. 'But on the other hand we might find out why someone wanted him dead.'

TWENTY-SIX

Over the next few days, Ty was surprised at how quickly normal routines reasserted themselves. When Nancy made an unexpected visit to the lab on the evening after the discovery of Olivarri's body, he had asked her questions even as he undressed her, until finally she pressed a finger against his mouth to forestall any further interrogation.

By the following evening, the last of the disrupted systems were back to normal, and Ty found himself scheduled to take part in the first of a series of hull-maintenance shifts, in the company of Martinez and Perez. As soon as they were outside, Ty made an excuse to head off in the direction of the stern, and a failing drive-spine, accompanied by a half-dozen spider-mechs.

He set the hull-clamps to retract, and waited until they had unlocked from around the spine, before setting the spiders to work in lifting it out of its socket. He then left them to it, making his way quickly to an emergency airlock close by.

Ty clambered inside and yanked the hatch shut after him, pulling his helmet off as soon as the air had finished cycling. Then he activated the airlock's inbuilt comms terminal.

This, he knew, was where he ran the greatest risk of being caught. Although he had been careful to pick out an airlock equipped with an imager-enabled terminal, the unscheduled tach-net link he was about to open might drain enough power to trigger an alert on the bridge, one that could in turn be traced back to his current whereabouts. But it was still a risk he was prepared to take.

He pulled off his right glove and reached out to the terminal screen, then paused. He could stop now, go back outside, and get on with his scheduled task. He could simply forget about his encounter with Olivarri.

No. He took a deep breath, shook his head as if to dispel his fears, and pressed his palm flat against the screen – making sure the ring given to him by the avatar came into full contact with it.

The panel flashed twice, to show it had recognized the ring as imager-compatible. Ty waited as the terminal pulled a data package out of the ring and dumped it into its own localized memory. The panel flashed again, letting him know it was working at opening up a line of communication.

Whoever was behind the avatar hadn't lied when boasting about the level of encryption involved. Ty had uploaded the same data packages into the lab's own stacks, but hadn't been able to crack them, despite several days of effort. But that didn't matter nearly so much as finding out what was really going on.

He fidgeted there in the coffin-like space for several minutes, while he waited for the terminal to establish a link. He briefly opened up his spacesuit's comms to check in on Martinez and Perez, but they were busy talking sports, so he turned it off again and waited.

The terminal chimed eventually, and a confirmation request appeared. Ty tapped the screen, and a moment later the same avatar he had encountered in Unity appeared before him.

'Mr Whitecloud,' acknowledged the voice behind the avatar.

'There was another Consortium agent on the *Mjollnir*, and now he's dead,' Ty yelled, without any preamble. 'What the hell is going on? Just how many of you people are on this ship? And . . . how the hell do I even know *you're* really a Consortium agent? In fact, what proof did I ever get?'

The avatar gazed back, silent and calm and so clearly artificial, while whoever was behind it tried to put together a response.

'We're aware of your encounter with Leo Olivarri,' the synthesized voice finally responded. 'Olivarri was in reality an agent for the Freehold Senate – *not* for the Consortium.'

Ty stared at the screen, befuddled. How could they have found out about Olivarri's death already? How—?

'No.' Ty shook his head several times, slowly at first,

then more violently. 'No, that's bullshit. I talked to him! He told me he was a Consortium agent, and I asked him why he'd approached me, when *you* had already contacted me. He didn't know what the hell I was talking about. So I *know* he was telling me the truth. He had no idea who you were – and now he's dead!'

There was another long pause, and Ty imagined whatever shadowy figure lurked behind the avatar trying to come up with a plausible response.

'It's possible,' the avatar said eventually, 'that whoever killed him might target you next.'

'None of what you're saying makes any sense!' Ty shouted at the tiny screen. 'If he was really working for the Freehold, then who killed him? Yet *another* Consortium agent?'

He pounded the hard plastic of the screen with one fist, feeling pain like hot needles being rammed into his knuckles. He was breathing hard, hyperventilating, fast using up the airlock's limited supply of air. He sobbed with frustration, and felt hot salt tears trickle down his cheeks.

'Listen to me,' he spat, both hands now gripping the sides of the screen, as if framing the face of the avatar. 'Show yourself. Do you hear me? *Show yourself.* And tell me who the hell killed Olivarri . . . and if it had anything to do with your talking to me!'

'Nathan?'

It was Martinez, his voice sounding tinny from within

Ty's discarded suit helmet. He grabbed up the helmet and opened a channel.

'Where are you?' asked Martinez. 'We can see your spiders, but we can't see you. You need to stay in sight at all times, Nathan.'

'I'm fine. Sorry,' Ty replied, a little too hurriedly. He swallowed and forced himself to sound calm, or they would suspect something was wrong. 'I'm . . . I thought some of the stern drive-spines might have got more damaged than we thought. So I figured it might be better to check them out, just in case. I'll be right back.'

'Well, okay,' said Martinez, doubt evident in his voice. 'We're heading up to one of the middle hull sections. Mr Corso's currently picking up some fail signatures from up that way, and we're off to take a look. We'll see you there in . . . make it five hundred seconds from now. Got that?'

'Got that,' Ty replied and cut the connection.

The avatar was gone, and the screen had turned black. If he wanted answers, Ty was going to have to find them somewhere else. He re-secured his helmet, cursing and muttering as he twisted around in the confined space, then paused just as he was about to pull his glove back on.

He left the same glove spinning slowly in the air, as he pulled the other one off as well. Then he tried to slide the data-ring off his finger.

The moment he worked it up to his knuckle, a deep, primal terror washed over him like a black tide. Worse, the ring actually became *tighter*, rather than looser, as it was designed to do when removed.

Ty gritted his teeth and once again tried to work the ring past his knuckle. It could only get so tight, after all.

Something like an electric current surged up his spine before exploding inside his skull. He writhed in pain, his head feeling like it was on fire, twisting around in the zero gee like a trapped animal.

When this pain finally subsided, the knowledge of how thoroughly he had been duped became unavoidable. He had suspected as much when he first encountered the avatar, but had been so desperate to escape from the residency and from Marcus Weil that he had ignored his own instincts.

Worse, he now had a pretty good idea what had been done to him.

It was still difficult for Ty to think back to his days developing military technologies for the Uchidans; conscripted or not, he had allowed himself to be sufficiently drawn into his work that it became easy to ignore the potential human cost of their research, while helping his fellow scientists develop a variety of possible means by which neural implants could be attacked or compromised. One in particular had involved the use of the body's own bio-electric field as a conduit for signals that could overcome or suppress the flow of information in implants – except that, in order to work, whatever affected the bio-electric field had to remain in constant contact with the target's own body. This, in turn, had led to the development of hardware-based neural-feedback mechanisms that could manipulate the neuro-chemical balance of the target's brain, eliciting powerful negative emotions or even generating escalating levels of pain and distress that could prove ultimately deadly.

Something like a cheap data-ring could do the job. And whoever was behind the avatar had somehow figured out how to use Ty's own research against him.

TWENTY-SEVEN

Eleven days out from Redstone, Dakota made her way to one of the airlock bays. She was surprised to find Nancy Schiller there, along with Ted Lamoureaux.

Lamoureaux nodded guardedly to her. Nancy, on the other hand, was doing her level best to ignore both of them.

'I thought Dan was scheduled for this crew,' Dakota said cautiously. Since Schiller herself was in charge of scheduling the repair shifts, she had so far arranged them so that she had never once had to work on the same crew as Dakota.

Nancy didn't look up while she ran her spacesuit's auto-diagnostics. 'Yeah, he was, but something else came up.'

'You know, me and Ted could probably handle this just fine with only the two of us,' said Dakota.

Nancy finally raised her head and flashed her a look of contempt. 'I don't think so,' she barked. 'Just get suited up, all right?'

Dakota pushed her way over to one of the racks and grabbed a suit.

What happened to Dan? Dakota sent.

<There's been a big increase in Emissary transmissions since our last jump,> Lamoureaux replied. <It's a lot of tach-net traffic for such a low-density region, and Martinez wanted him up on the bridge while they try and figure out the reason why.>

There's an increase in Emissary tach-net traffic because we just jumped straight past the Long War and deep into the gap between spiral arms, remember? So that means they have to boost their signals all the way from the Perseus Arm, and we're just picking up stray long-range transmissions. It doesn't actually mean there's more Emissaries out there any closer at hand.

Their last jump had taken place fourteen hours before, with the drive-spines running at about 70 per cent efficiency. The frigate was now nearly three and a half thousand light-years from home, and the Consortium had been reduced to a barely discernible smudge of stars lying somewhere in the direction of the Core.

<Oh, right. I didn't think of that.>

See why you need me? Dakota sent, now making for the locker next to his. He was making a typical hash of getting into his own suit here in zero gee.

Lamoureaux laughed at her expression, and Schiller snapped her head around to stare at them both.

'I know you're talking,' she said. 'Don't think I don't know it.'

Dakota turned to face her. 'Is that a problem, Nancy?'

For a few seconds, the other woman looked like she

might make something more of it, then she uttered a sound of disgust. 'Just get ready,' she muttered. 'I want this over and done with.'

Nancy turned away and Dakota stared silently at her back for a few seconds. Then she began to strip off, throwing her discarded clothing into the open locker.

Lamoureaux meanwhile kept his gaze politely averted and concentrated on checking his own spacesuit's integrity, once he had finally managed to pull himself inside it. When Dakota was completely naked, she padded towards the airlock entrance on bare feet.

Nancy's face turned a stormy red. 'I don't know what you think you're . . .'

Her jaw dropped open as the black tide of Dakota's filmsuit spilled out of its hidden orifices, rapidly coating her skin overall in a thick layer that could protect her from the vacuum and radiation beyond the hull. Dakota swallowed as the same tide of black flowed down her throat and into her lungs, stilling them as their function was temporarily abrogated to tiny power units inside her spine.

She waited as the black slick faded to partial transparency over her eyes, then opened them and squinted over at Nancy. 'Come on, surely someone told you about this already?' she asked with a smile.

Nancy stared back at her in horrified fascination. 'Yeah, but . . . look, you need to get into your suit.'

'She doesn't,' intervened Lamoureaux. 'That thing's

all the spacesuit she needs, at least for the amount of time we'll be out on the hull.'

Schiller switched her gaze between them. 'How . . . ?' she stammered.

'A present from an old friend,' said Dakota, gesturing towards the airlock. 'It's time we got started, don't you think?'

Dakota and Ted had now reached the point where they swapped control of the frigate's primary systems almost automatically: one keeping a watchful eye over the *Mjollnir*, while the other slept. As they pushed out of the airlock and on to the hull, Lamoureaux assumed primary control.

There was plenty to do, and Nancy worked away on her own, keeping any communications with them down to the bare essentials. Over the next few hours, Dakota and Lamoureaux monitored the removal of almost a dozen dead or degraded drive-spines, which was a record for a single shift. The fabricators were having such a hard time keeping up with demand that the idea of having them construct copies of themselves in order to increase the overall output had been mooted. But that idea had to be shelved once it became clear that certain essential resources for the construction processes were simply not available.

*

<Do you ever miss it?>

Glancing towards Lamoureaux's suited figure, Dakota instantly knew he was talking about the Magi ships and that powerful sense of connection all Magi-enabled human navigators felt with them.

A dozen spider-mechs floated close by, holding a failed drive-spine firmly in their grip. She had momentarily been staring towards the stern, and beyond it to the great band of stars where home lay.

Depends what you mean, she replied, making her way towards a cargo airlock just in time to see it disgorge yet more spiders, carrying a replacement drive-spine out of the ship's interior.

<That feeling of just *being* with them – there are times I can almost put it out of my mind, but it's hard, Dakota. It's really hard.>

I know. She could sense the intense regret overwhelming him, because that bond was something he would never experience again. *But why do I get the feeling you've got something else on your mind, Ted?*

<What happens when we go home, Dakota? What will you do then?>

She watched as the spiders under her immediate control incrementally lowered the new drive-spine towards its magnetic couplings.

I don't know, Ted. If you want me to be really honest, I have a hard time even thinking beyond where we're headed. And, even if we pull this off, I don't think there's a place for me back home any more. Maybe not for any of the navigators.

<You're saying we're obsolete already? Holy shit.>

Dakota merely smiled under the viscous oil-slick of her filmsuit.

The frigate's next jump would take them to their penultimate destination, and to the location of the extra shielding Trader wanted them to pick up. Corso had already brokered an agreement with the Shoal-member to use his yacht for the trip down to the cache. With its considerably more advanced propulsion systems and inertial dampeners, Trader's ship would be a lot faster and safer than any other craft stowed in the *Mjollnir*'s hold.

Dakota had declined to take part in those negotiations, but she was the one who would have to make the pick-up trip with Trader – and that meant coming face-to-face with him, whether she liked it or not.

At the end of the shift, Dakota made her way back to the airlock and surveyed the hull, noting the gaps where drive-spines had been removed but not yet replaced. Nancy had made a point of cycling back through the airlock before either of them.

Tell me what I have to do to get her off my back, Dakota asked him, as they made their own way back inside the frigate.

Lamoureaux activated the airlock access panel and a

light blinked green. <Maybe she's not so bad as you think,> he sent back.

You can't possibly be serious.

He glanced towards her while they waited for the hatch to slide open. <Most women's lives in the Freehold are pretty circumscribed, Dakota. Their career choices come down to mother, teacher and whore. She must have had a hell of a fight to get to be head of security on a ship like the *Mjollnir*. Then she lost that job when Martinez fell out of favour. No wonder she's pissed off – wouldn't you be?>

Dakota tried to think of a reply, but could not manage one.

TWENTY-EIGHT

Less than an hour later, Dakota reached the bridge just in time for Olivarri's funeral service.

The rest of the crew was already there – even Driscoll, who had been hiding in the labs ever since leaving Redstone. The overhead display was filled by an external image of the *Mjollnir*, as seen through the lens of a surveillance-drone trailing the frigate at a distance of a couple of kilometres. Floating a few metres away from the drone, and in full view of its sensors, was a single spider-mech holding a jar delicately in its multiple arms.

Martinez was in full dress uniform, as were Nancy Schiller and Dan Perez. Corso wore a formal suit, his shirt a swirl of various shades of grey. Dakota, by contrast, felt distinctly underdressed in her usual casual uniform of T-shirt and work trousers, but dealing with formal occasions like this was very far from being one of her strong points.

She watched Corso mount the dais, resting one hand on the arm of the vacant interface chair as he waited until the conversation died down. Dakota tried to listen to his brief eulogy, and then that of Willis, but waves of fatigue kept washing over her, and her attention kept slipping. All she could see when she briefly closed her eyes were the grey and black plates of the *Mjollnir*'s armoured hull.

Her mind drifted further, speculating on what the next generation of human-built superluminal ships might be like, assuming they ever survived the onslaught of the Emissaries. She decided their best option would still be to find some way to power up the Ascension core-ship, or one of the other coreships abandoned in the vicinity of the Long War . . .

Dakota snapped awake and realized the service was finishing. She looked around warily, wondering if anyone else had noticed her practically sleepwalking through the whole event.

She glanced back up at the image overhead. The spider-mech had now opened the jar, spilling grey ashes out into the vacuum, where they hung in a slowly expanding cloud. She imagined Olivarri's essence spreading ever outwards until it filled the void between the spiral arms.

'Dakota.' A hand touched her shoulder.

She turned to see it was Corso.

'We're going to be reaching our goal in a little under twelve hours' time. I really think it's time you got some sleep, don't you?'

Dakota awoke, entangled in her hammock, to the sound of a pre-jump alert. There had been several since she had stumbled back into her cabin, but she had managed to sleep through most of them.

Keeping her eyes closed, she linked into the data-space. Lamoureaux was already there, of course.

<Looks like you're just in time for the show,> he sent.

She switched over to the flow of data coming in from the ship's external arrays. The Orion Arm had already vanished behind dense dust clouds, while the band of the Perseus Arm, in the other direction, was becoming brighter and more detailed. A star barely an AU away bathed the frigate in a pale golden light.

Then the stars shifted, suddenly, jarringly, and that same star was now much closer. It formed a bright round disc, while a dark shape closer to hand partly occluded it – the dwarf planet Trader had directed them to.

Post-jump analyses started pouring in, and she skimmed over them, picking out the main details and discarding the rest. The star had thirteen planets, and a brown dwarf binary partner less than two light-years away.

Dakota untwisted herself from her hammock, despite the protest of her tired and aching muscles. She kicked herself over to an exercise frame designed for zero gee, and did some gentle stretches before hitting the shower, though half her attention was still focused on the updates still flooding in. Initial analyses showed all the planets to be either frozen balls of gas or sterile rocks, most with only a few thin vestiges of atmosphere. If there was anything more evolved than lichen to be found in this whole system, she would be greatly surprised.

Half an hour later she made her way to the nearest transport station, and was surprised to find Nancy Schiller waiting there with a pulse-rifle slung menacingly over one shoulder. Dakota just stared at her with a bleak expression.

'I'm coming with you,' Schiller announced. She reached out and slapped the access panel on the nearest car, and its door slid open. 'But don't think I like having to babysit you.'

Dakota didn't move towards the car. 'Nancy, why are you here? It's meant to be just me and Trader going down to the planet surface. Whose idea was this?'

'Martinez.'

The two women regarded each other with the keen attention of soldiers on opposite sides in a war caught in the same foxhole.

Ted, are you getting this?

<Sorry. Not my idea,> he sent back.

Dakota shook her head with a sigh and stepped past Nancy and into the car. Schiller followed a moment later, her mouth set in a thin line, and pulled herself into the couch facing her. The car began to accelerate down the transit tube, heading for the stern.

'I know you don't like me,' Dakota said carefully, 'but

if we're going down there together, you're going to have to at least try and be civil. We're all on the same side.'

'What about whoever killed Olivarri?' Nancy replied. 'Whose side are they on?'

Dakota shook her head, as if to say *I give up*, and stared fixedly at the ceiling for the remainder of their short journey, feeling disproportionately grateful when the car slid into the station close so in the main hold. As they reached the airlock bay, they found a dozen spider-mechs waiting, floating patiently just to one side.

'What do we need those for?' asked Nancy.

'For grunt work,' Dakota replied, noting with approval that the spiders had been modified for low-gravity work, as she had requested. 'We're going to be doing a lot of lifting and carrying, according to Trader, so we're going to need them. You want more details, ask him when you meet him.'

'Huh.' Nancy headed to the nearest rack and pulled down a pressure suit.

Trader's yacht was, for the first time, linked to the frigate via a pressurized tube. As before, Dakota herself did not bother with a pressure suit. Once Nancy was ready, Dakota hit the cycle button on the airlock door, and then waited until the safety light turned green and the door hissed open. The spiders followed them in, unfurling their arms to push themselves away from the sides of the tube and into the yacht's interior.

Trader had already drained his vessel's liquid atmosphere, in anticipation of their arrival, but the damp air still had a briny scent to it that made Dakota think of sunken wrecks and weed-strewn shorelines. The chamber they currently found themselves in was barely capacious enough to hold the two of them, all twelve of the spider-mechs, and a tiny, glowing, insect-sized device that hovered before them for a few moments before darting away around a corner.

Dakota glanced at Nancy, then nodded towards the departing beacon. 'Let's go,' she said.

'You first,' Nancy muttered uneasily.

They followed the beacon to an egg-shaped chamber about eight metres in length. The wall surfaces were shiny with moisture, and tiny beads of liquid still spun through the air around them. They found Trader waiting there inside a field-induced bubble of water.

Nancy stared at the alien with a shocked expression, making Dakota remember the first time she herself had set eyes on a Shoal-member, when she had probably looked just as flustered.

Several holographic projections of varying size floated close to the walls, rippling whenever Dakota and Nancy or the spiders passed through them. Most consisted of indecipherable Shoal iconography rendered in three dimensions, but one showed a real time image of the interior of the hold.

Unlike human-designed ships, there was nothing there that could be called furniture, nor were there any convenient handholds to grip on to. Similarly there was nothing that might be designated a ceiling or a floor; indeed, there were very few right angles, and most of the bulkheads simply curved into each other.

Dakota ordered the spiders to go into sleep mode, whereupon they powered down, folding themselves into multifaceted polygons that took up far less room.

Dakota moved closer to Trader. 'Did you get my briefing?'

'Received with delight,' the alien replied, manoeuvring within his ball of water until he directly faced Nancy.

His manipulators, suspended beneath the wide curvature of his lower body, twisted with what Dakota chose to interpret as distaste. 'I see we have company.'

Nancy glanced questioningly at Dakota. 'Briefing? What briefing?'

'I gave Trader a summary of what he's been missing while he's been stuck away here in the hold,' Dakota explained. 'Murder, sabotage, intrigue. The usual.'

'Life aboard the frigate is filled with much excitement, yes?' said Trader.

'Call me crazy,' Dakota replied, staring fixedly at the alien, 'but I had an idea you just might be able to throw some light on it all.'

'Most distasteful discorporation upon us all grants few hopes for the future.' Trader's artificially generated voice took on a harsher quality inside the metal-walled chamber. 'One assumes you are already hard upon the scent-path of those responsible?'

'What?' Nancy stared back and forth between them, her expression incredulous. 'What the hell did he say?'

'He said he hopes we catch whoever did it really soon,' Dakota replied, without taking her eyes off the alien.

Trader moved closer to them both. Though Nancy didn't move from where she still floated close to a wall, Dakota looked over in time to see a muscle in one of her cheeks begin to twitch spasmodically.

'We swim towards the world below,' explained Trader, 'where we will find the defensive systems we need. I have probes already performing reconnaissance, so perhaps we should take a look at what they've found.'

Dakota glanced towards the live video feed and realized with a start that they were already moving. The hold's open doors were receding into the distance, the yacht's inertialess systems dampening the effects of its acceleration.

Another projection now appeared in the air in front of Trader, taking the form of a flat black rectangle. A yawning, glass-walled abyss appeared inside this rectangle, falling away into darkness. It looked like images Dakota had seen of the Tierra cache. As the viewpoint rushed headlong into the mouth of the cache and into sudden darkness, she felt a strong urge to look away.

Some kind of filter kicked in, so that the cache's walls became visible. There were oval openings ranged on all sides, blurring together initially as the viewpoint descended at speed. But then the viewpoint suddenly slowed and veered aside into one of the doorways, moving rapidly along a smooth-walled tunnel until it arrived in a long, narrow chamber filled with the blackened ruins of some kind of machinery.

The projection then faded to black. Dakota glanced to one side and saw the *Mjollnir* receding into the distance with increasing speed.

'And it's the same throughout the cache?' asked Dakota.

'As far as can be determined,' Trader replied. 'Contact with some of my probes was lost after a certain depth, but that may be down to the sometimes unusual gravitational conditions to be found inside caches. The Meridian defence systems, however, are located near the mouth of the cache.'

'I still want to see inside the cache at the first opportunity,' insisted Dakota.

'But of course,' Trader replied, his manipulators wriggling like hungry worms.

The idea that Trader might actually provide better company than another human being would never before have occurred to Dakota, and so she found herself tremendously irritated when Trader left her alone with Nancy in the egg-shaped chamber. All she could do was crouch in the inertialess zero gee, and try to ignore Nancy's embittered gaze. But before very long the sheer tension, enhanced by boredom, drove her to at least make an attempt at conversation.

When that failed, Dakota finally lost her temper.

'Just what is your fucking problem?' she seethed. 'I used to own a *cargo ship* that was easier to talk to.'

Nancy's eyes darted away from hers. 'There's things you don't know about me. That make it hard for me to talk to you.'

'What? What things?'

Nancy swivelled her gaze back around, her shoulders rising and falling as she took a deep breath. 'I lost family in Port Gabriel,' she replied.

Dakota felt her face go red. 'I'm sorry, I—'

Nancy burst out laughing. 'No, no . . . I mean that's just the kind of bullshit you want to hear, right? I didn't lose anyone. I just . . .' the other woman shrugged and shook her head. 'I just really fucking hate machine-heads. You and the Uchidans, you're all the fucking same to me, you know that? Even that hole in the ground we're headed for isn't deep enough for you all.'

Dakota stared at her, speechless.

'Look,' Nancy went on, 'if Commander Martinez wants you on board with us, that's up to him, not me, but I don't have to pretend I like you, or that I trust you, or that I'm not sure you had something to do with Olivarri's murder. Are we clear on that?'

'As daylight,' Dakota replied through gritted teeth.

*

After that, Dakota kept her mouth shut and her eyes fixed on the projections all around. Nancy crouched in a similar pose, her helmet resting nearby. They had a spectacular view of their approach to the cache-world: the curving limb of the planet rose towards them at a terrific speed and, as they drew nearer, Dakota studied with interest the great rifts and valleys and ancient impact craters that spoke of a violent past. The mouth of the cache became visible as a perfectly round circle of black punched through the tiny world's outer crust.

Dakota felt the tug of something familiar from the surface below.

'There's more drones here,' she muttered out loud.

Nancy shot a glance at her. 'What?'

'More Meridian drones. Trader! Where the hell are you, Trader! There's—'

<I am here.> Trader replied to her directly through her implants. <Are you certain?>

Very certain. I'm picking them up right now.

<An unexpected surprise, then. Do you have a location?>

Close to the mouth of the cache, about where the field-defences are. They've buried themselves deep in the ground.

'Who are you talking to?' Schiller demanded.

'I'm talking,' Dakota replied testily, 'to Trader.'

'Did you know your mouth moves when you talk in your head like that?'

'It does?'

Schiller nodded slowly. 'Makes you look like an idiot.'

TWENTY-NINE

They made landfall not long afterwards, the yacht settling on to a cushion of shaped fields just a few kilometres from the mouth of the cache. Dakota pulled off the standard-issue jumpsuit she had been wearing, and folded it into a wad before dropping down from the yacht's open hatch, relying once more simply on her filmsuit for protection.

Her black-slicked toes kicked up a cloud of dust as she hit the ground, before she took a few bounding steps in the low gravity. She glanced behind her in time to see Nancy hit the ground only to be immediately swallowed in another billowing dust cloud that coated her pressure-suit in grey.

Dakota took a look around her. Outcrops of granite rose from a sea of dust that extended to the north, only coming to an end at the ridge-wall of a crater about ten kilometres away. To the west, and in the direction of the cache itself, the ground rose and fell in gentle inclines, like waves sculpted in stone. The overhead sun was bright enough to blot out the stars.

Trader emerged last, followed by the spider-mechs.

One by one, the spiders skittered around the edge of the hatch, in an eerily lifelike way, before jumping down and flexing their elongated legs as they scanned the horizon. They looked very different in a gravity environment: they now used most of their limbs to walk on, with just one set raised above them, so that they now looked more like six-legged mechanical crabs than spiders.

Trader led the way, his brine-filled bubble hugging the curve of a nearby slope up to its peak. Dakota trudged through the dust after him and on up the side of the hill.

<I was unaware we would have company,> he sent to Dakota as she came abreast of him.

Dakota glanced back at Nancy, who had just reached the foot of the hill. Her pressure-suit clearly made the going harder for her.

Officially, she's here to give us a hand. Unofficially, I'm top of their list of suspects for Olivarri's murder. She waited a beat. *After yourself, of course.*

The alien swivelled within his field bubble to study Schiller more closely as she struggled uphill, the spiders racing past her towards the peak. <So she is here to watch over us.>

Did you kill Olivarri, Trader?

The Shoal-members manipulators writhed beneath the wide curve of his belly. <How could I possibly carry out such a crime, seeing I have not even been allowed to board the frigate itself? Perhaps your inquiries should

first turn to those who accuse you? I am sure Olivarri was not the only one with secrets.>

Dakota frowned. *What secrets?*

<Ah.> The manipulators writhed again, and Dakota couldn't help but wonder if he was laughing at her. <Perhaps you were not aware Olivarri was secretly employed by the Consortium's intelligence division?>

Dakota actually took a step back. *What? Where did you get this from?*

<That, I'm afraid, must remain with me. I have my sources.>

If you're lying to me—

<Spare me your empty threats, Dakota.>

Trader moved off again, his bubble following the contours of the incline as he descended the other side of the hill. Dakota stayed where she was, staring off across the hilltops and brooding.

Who else, she wondered, was something other than what they appeared to be? She knew almost nothing about most of the *Mjollnir*'s contingent, particularly Perez, Driscoll and Nancy Schiller herself – all strangers to her until she boarded the frigate. They had each been vetted personally by Corso, but if Trader turned out to be telling the truth, what did that mean about the rest of them?

Who else might not be who they seemed?

Nancy finally came abreast of her, closely trailed by the spiders; her faceplate had polarized until it was nearly opaque beneath the bright glare of the sun overhead.

Dakota followed in Trader's path, soon leaving Nancy and the spiders behind once more. From the top of the next hill she could make out a low dome squatting on the wide flat plain surrounding the mouth of the cache, several hundred metres away. The dome's grey colouring made it almost invisible against the surrounding landscape, and there were the ruins of other buildings all across the plain.

Looking closer to hand, she saw Trader forging ahead of her, and jogged down into the next valley to catch up with the alien halfway up the next rise.

That dome. Is that where we're heading?

<Most assuredly.> Trader turned in his bubble to look back towards Nancy, still making her way down the slope of the hill behind. <Our companion appears to be getting left behind. Perhaps it would be amusing for us to hide and see how she reacts?>

Dakota ignored this remark as she watched Nancy laboriously make her way towards them.

That's not the way to do it, Dakota sent to her. *Run on your toes, like you're skipping.*

<I'm doing just fine.>

Then you won't mind if we leave you behind.

Nancy swore, then pushed up and off the ground with both feet. She came sailing back down in a low arc and landed on her hands and knees. Dakota watched as she picked herself up and tried again. This time it looked like she tripped over in slow motion, but managed to catch herself on the way back down.

I'm surprised you're having such a hard time. You were pretty nimble during the hull repairs.

<Yeah, well, that's different,> Nancy replied.

How?

<It just is, okay? I'm almost there.>

Dakota followed Trader downhill, herself bounding in long, low, skipping strides. Despite her mood and the shock of Trader's revelation, not to mention Nancy's seemingly boundless hostility, a part of her was actually beginning to have fun. She made good time, looking behind her once or twice to check on Schiller, who was trailing huge dust clouds behind her.

She could see the dome more clearly from the next hilltop, beyond which lay only level plain stretching towards the cache's abyssal pit. She saw now that, mixed in with the ruined buildings, there were what appeared to be the remains of a huge spacecraft broken into several sections and half buried in the dust.

As Dakota jogged down to the edge of the plain, she realized the dome was a lot bigger than it appeared at a distance. It had to be at least a hundred metres across, but no more than twenty in height, and it had presumably been designed to withstand whatever forces had destroyed the buildings surrounding it. Trader was well ahead of her by now and, as she started to make her way across the level ground, she saw him pass inside an entrance in one side of the dome, the sparkle of his field-bubble faintly illuminating the interior of the passageway beyond.

She soon reached it herself and stepped into its interior, noting how the relatively tiny inner space emphasized just how thick the walls were.

Dense drifts of dust gradually began to appear out of the gloom, as the filters over her eyes adjusted for the lack of light. She saw waist-high racks stretching from wall to wall in orderly ranks, with wide aisles running between. Identical flat, smooth plates were mounted in haphazard order within the racks, though, at a glance, less than a third of the racks contained them.

Is this what we're here for?

Trader guided his bubble down a side aisle, his huge eyes swivelling from left to right. <These are modular shaped-field generators designed for use in battle situations. One must assume the colony here was wiped out before they could be used.>

Dakota turned in time to see the spiders were now threading their way in through the entrance, sending brilliant beams of light cutting through the darkness. Nancy followed them in soon afterwards.

<I want to ask something,> Nancy sent. <What did for all those ruins out there? I saw what looked like the remains of some kind of ship.>

The Meridians slaughtered each other over possession of the cache, Dakota replied. *But it all happened a long, long time ago.*

Nancy merely watched at first as Dakota started pulling the disc-shaped field devices out of their slots, dropping them to the ground for the spiders to collect.

Then she started to help, pulling the discs loose and placing them where the spiders could get to them easily. Trader meanwhile simply hovered in his bubble; in truth there wasn't much he could do but watch them.

<Here's something else I've been wondering,> said Nancy after they'd been working away for a few minutes. <You said you detected some more of those . . . drones here, right? Like the ones you turned on those corvettes back home?>

What about them?

<How many of them are there?>

A couple of dozen, Dakota sent back. *Why?*

<I saw the playbacks of what those other things you found did to those corvettes. Don't you think its kind of weird the Meridians would leave weapons that powerful lying around here? Doesn't it make more sense if they left them here for a reason?>

Why are you so suddenly keen on giving me your opinion?

Nancy stopped working and stared over at Dakota. <I'm just saying there was obviously some kind of a fight here, right?>

A long time ago, Nancy.

<Yes but, even so, *why* were they just left here? Are they guarding something? Just waiting for something? What?>

Dakota directed an angry glance towards her. *They were at war. Shit happens.*

<I'm just not crazy about the idea of just walking in

here without carrying out a thorough reconnoitre,> the other woman replied, <and, besides, we're obviously dealing with seriously fucking advanced technology. I'd just like to be sure we're not going to get caught out by something nasty while we're digging through some dead alien's discarded trash.>

Dakota picked up one of the field-generators and studied it for several moments, thinking.

Trader, when I met you on that other world, were the drones you gave me . . . guarding anything?

<I have no idea, Dakota. Perhaps they were once but, if so, whatever that might have been is long gone.>

You said you didn't hear back from some of the probes you sent down into the cache. Any idea why?

As Trader floated in his bubble, his manipulators remained immobile for at least half a minute. <Perhaps I should investigate further,> he replied.

The discs were a lot heavier than they looked, and Dakota's implants had picked up faint queries coming from them, which were interpretable thanks to the Meridian command structures Trader had given her. Once she had built up an idea of their internal structure, she transmitted this data back to Lamoureaux on the *Mjollnir*.

Ted, take a look at this. What do you make of it?

His reply came barely a moment later. <Like I'm an expert in shaped-field tech? The real question is how hard or easy it's going to be to integrate something like this into our existing defences. Is it even possible?>

According to Trader, it is. And the interface seems to be straightforward enough, so it shouldn't be a huge problem setting up an interface with the Mjollnir's *defence stacks.*

<Okay, I'll talk to Ray about them. Leo would have been your man, but now he's gone the next-best expert is probably Nancy, I'm afraid. Have you asked her yet?>

Hang on, I'm going to try activating one myself first.

Dakota lugged the device over to a clear spot between two rows of racks, and triggered it by depressing a button on one side. The shaped field that surrounded her a moment later sparked and crackled with light.

The effect was so startling that Dakota almost dropped the device; the field was far brighter – and therefore more powerful – than anything she had so far encountered. It had started out as a sphere about four metres across, centred on herself, but then it began to shrink, slowly at first but with increasing speed. She quickly deactivated it before it could shrink any further and crush her to death.

<Be careful,> Trader warned her, from where he hovered near the dome's entrance. <These are much more powerful than the field-generators you're used to.>

<What happened?> Lamoureaux asked.

Two aisles over, Dakota could just make out an expression of shock on Nancy's face through her face-plate.

I think it's safe to say they work just fine, she sent back.

THIRTY

They had to abandon a number of the field-generators after they proved to be broken on closer inspection, their outer shells cracked and brittle. But at least fifty appeared to be undamaged.

After a couple of hours' work, the last of these were secured on top of some of the spiders, and sent back over the hills to Trader's yacht. Dakota took one last look around the interior of the dome, wondering what it must have been like in those last hours before the colony was obliterated, and if the creatures who had built it had realized what was coming. Then she stepped back outside to join Trader and Nancy, who were waiting for her amongst the ruins.

Dakota watched as the machinery-laden spiders followed one another up the slope of the nearest hill. *Maybe it's time to activate those drones I detected, see if they wake up.*

Trader's manipulators wriggled underneath his belly. <As you wish.>

The Meridian drones had either burned or dug their way deep beneath the surface long ago. As the three of them now started moving towards the foot of the nearest hill, Dakota sent out a command-level activation signal that she hoped would override whatever instructions the drones had been left with.

Less than a minute passed before she was rewarded with a faint tremor that rippled the dust beneath her feet. Dakota stopped and turned in time to see rock and gravel fountaining upwards from all around the cache-mouth, as drone after drone punched its way back out of its hiding place. They rose quickly, spinning and glittering in the harsh sunlight, with debris sliding off of their mirrored carapaces as they accelerated away from the surface.

<Shit!> Nancy exclaimed, her voice full of terror. <What the fuck is *that*?>

Dakota realized she had forgotten to warn Nancy what she was intending to do.

Sorry, I should have warned you. Those are the drones I detected on our way here. I've ordered them to head for the frigate, but they had to dig their way out of the ground first.

<How fucking stupid can you be?> Nancy raged. <I thought we were under attack!>

Hey, I said I was sorry.

<From now on, you even think about doing something, you clear it with me first. Do you hear me?>

Yes, Nancy, I hear you.

Dakota did her best to ignore the flash of resentment she felt at Nancy's tone, as she headed for the nearest slope. The spiders had already scaled the summit and were well on their way back to Trader's yacht.

Trader himself kept abreast of her as she ascended the hill, Nancy not so far behind them this time. Dakota glanced back and saw that debris was still slowly raining down on the ancient ruins. The drones were by now out of sight.

Dakota turned away and pinged the drones, finding they were functioning at peak capacity, and all accelerating hard towards the frigate. She fired a warning to Lamoureaux to make sure the others understood they were not being attacked.

<All right, for what it's worth, that was some pretty spectacular shit,> Nancy sent, her tone almost bordering on respect.

Just doing my job, Dakota sent. *Once we've got these field-generators back on board, I want to take the ship down inside the cache. We should take a good look at it while we've got the chance. Do you have any objections to that?*

<None. That was the plan anyway, wasn't it? And, by the way . . . those explosions around the cache. That was the drones?>

Yes, why?

<So what's causing that glow coming from *inside* the cache?>

Dakota stopped to look back at Nancy, who was standing just a little further downhill, with one foot up on a boulder. Beyond her, the interior of the cache had indeed become brighter, emitting light that flickered as if derived from a hundred different sources, each one moving constantly in relation to the rest. It was as if a horde of giant fireflies was flying up the mouth of the cache from somewhere deep inside.

Dakota loped up to the crest of the hill with long, striding bounds to look back down at the cache from a slightly higher vantage point. When she looked again, the light had grown brighter, becoming noticeably more so even as she watched. Another tremor rolled through the ground beneath her feet. She glanced over at Trader, who had also turned to look back, and she felt an unpleasant churning sensation inside her chest.

Trader, what the hell is that light?

<I have no idea. Query the drones, see if they have an explanation.>

Dakota felt a chill. *Those probes you said you'd lost, is it possible they ran into something down there?*

<It is not outside the bounds of conjecture. I sent another probe down, but lost contact with it a short while ago.>

The sense that something very bad was about to happen overwhelmed Dakota, and she turned to look the other way, to where she could just see the uppermost spines of Trader's yacht poking up above the crest of a hill about a kilometre distant. She also spotted the train of spiders, still making their way back, in an undulating file, across the intervening hills and valleys.

She queried the recovered Meridian drones, hoping

that they might be able to tell her what was going on. It took a few attempts to navigate her way to some kind of answer, and her eyes opened wide in horror when she got it.

We have to get out of here, she sent to the others. *We have to get out right now.*

She started running down the other side of the hill, desperate to get away from the cache, her legs moving with what felt like dreamlike slowness. She ordered the drones to reverse their trajectory and to return to the vicinity of the cache, but they had already lost precious seconds.

<Dakota?> asked Trader. <Please explain.>

There are hundreds of unmanned Emissary scouts inside the cache, Trader, and we just woke them up.

Trader started heading back towards his yacht without further hesitation. <Then we must bring the drones back here to defend us.>

I already called them back, but I don't know if they can get here in time.

Dakota stumbled once, picked herself up and kept going. She could hear from Nancy's panicky breathing that she had finally taken the hint and started running as well.

On reaching the crest of the final hill before they arrived at the yacht, Dakota paused to glance behind her. She saw Nancy approaching the foot of the same hill, but Trader had already overtaken them both. She turned back towards the yacht in time to see him slip through the open hatch, and for one terrible moment she wondered if he meant to abandon them.

By now the spiders had neatly stacked the field-generators beneath the open hatch, in which two of them stood waiting as their brethren began passing the generators up to them with their instantly extendible arms.

As she reached the yacht, she swiftly climbed up on top of one of the spiders and pulled herself through the hatch. The two spiders already inside scuttled back into the yacht's interior to get out of her way. Once inside, she accidentally crashed into a pile of field-generators, and just managed to stop them toppling back out of the hatch. At that moment, she spotted Nancy making her way down the final slope, kicking up a huge cloud of dust that must surely have been visible for kilometres around.

A torrent of dark shapes shot upwards from the location of the cache, moving with such colossal velocity that Dakota barely had time to register their passage. Part of her attention was now focused on the approach of the Meridian drones, as she caught an equally brief glimpse of them vectoring in towards the Emissary scouts.

Around the yacht, the ground began to quiver yet again, sending up thick, choking clouds of dust that soon obscured the summits of the nearby hills.

Nancy stumbled and flailed about, and Dakota heard her yelling over the shared comms.

<Did you see that? What's happening now?>

It's the Emissary scouts, Dakota replied. *Get back here as fast as you can.*

Nancy picked herself up hurriedly, staggering past a shoulder-high boulder. She was almost at the yacht.

<I fucking told you something wasn't right!> she yelled over the comms.

You were right. We should have checked things out more thoroughly.

<Next time, try listening to me. There's a reason they made me head of fucking security.>

Incandescent light suddenly blazed from the direction of the cache, as a beam of focused energy struck the crest of a distant hill, which erupted in a terrifying display of violence. At that same moment, something dark and oblong flew close above them, followed by a wave of intense heat that briefly overwhelmed Dakota's filters.

Nancy?

<I need some help here.>

Dakota dropped from the hatch to the ground, and darted over to where the other woman had collapsed. Gravel pattered down all around them, falling slowly in the low gravity. The dust was so thick it made it nearly impossible to see more than a couple of metres in any direction. Dakota finally stumbled across her where she was crouching on her hands and knees, her breathing sounding ragged over the comms link.

Dakota hooked one arm around the woman's shoulder and pulled her upright, hearing her moan in pain. Together they managed to stumble back to the yacht, where Nancy almost collapsed again once Dakota let go of her.

C'mon Nancy, need to get you inside.

She hoisted Nancy on top of one of the spiders, then climbed on behind to get a secure hold of her under both arms.

Grab hold of the lip of the hatch, and then I can help heave you up.

<I don't feel so good.>

Just get inside so I can take a look at you.

With a groan, Nancy reached out with both hands and grabbed the rim of the hatch. She started to pull herself up, as Dakota pushed her by grabbing her hips. Fortunately, the low gravity made things a lot easier, but Dakota still had to command one of the spiders already inside the hatch to grab hold of Nancy and help her up.

Dakota pulled herself in next, feeling the subtle transition from low to zero gee as she entered the ship.

We're all on board. Let's get out of here, Trader.

The Shoal-member didn't reply, but the hatch spiralled shut behind them, sealing out the dust. Dakota pulled the other woman's helmet off and found Nancy had passed out. Her skin was looking horribly red and blistered.

Finally Dakota answered a priority signal from the *Mjollnir*, that had been hovering at the back of her attention for the past minute or so.

<Dakota!> Lamoureaux yelled when she opened the

link. <We saw what looked like some kind of fight going on from out here. What the hell's happening?>

There were Emissary scouts hiding in the cache, and they just got loose. We're back on board Trader's ship with the field-generators, but Nancy's been hurt.

She opened up a visual link to let Lamoureaux see what she herself was seeing. She could sense his horror when he saw just how bad a state Schiller was in.

A lot of this is radiation damage, Dakota sent. *If you haven't already, you need to get* Mjollnir *prepped for an emergency jump. I don't know just how well the Meridian drones are going to hold up against a couple of hundred Emissary scouts, but if those scouts reach the frigate, we're in serious shit.*

<Okay. Just get back here as fast as you can. I'm picking you up on the external arrays, and it looks like you're just clearing orbit.>

Dakota glanced around the crowded chamber, where everything seemed perfectly still and silent. There wasn't the slightest clue to suggest the ship had so much as moved. Spotting her wadded-up jumpsuit, she started to pull it on, while letting the filmsuit drain itself back inside her body.

Then, for the first time, the ship rocked gently around her, sending fresh beads of moisture caroming through the air.

Trader?

<An unfortunate encounter with some Emissary

scouts following us. Might I ask that you set some of the Meridian drones to defend us?>

Dakota closed her eyes and locked into the drones, immediately finding herself submerged in a chaotic whirl of data. The drones had reverted to their original programming, and were now fighting to push the Emissary scouts back down inside the cache.

She felt one of the Meridian drones die; they were a superior technology, but the Emissary scouts had the advantage of sheer numbers.

Dakota concentrated on protecting the yacht, keeping her eyes tightly closed and letting her limbs float out around her, her fingers jerking spasmodically as she directed her side of the battle raging outside. Trader's yacht looked tiny and fragile compared with the bristling black mass of the pursuing scouts. Yet more of the Emissary scouts were pouring out from the mouth of the cache, their skins flickering with multiple bright energies as they repelled tightly focused bursts of energy directed towards them. The hulls of the machines on both sides of the battle crackled as their outer layers were burned off, while the complex nanomolecular circuitry within attempted to repair the constant damage.

<We're just about prepped for a short-range jump,> Lamoureaux sent to her. <Have you checked the monitors on Nancy's suit?>

Dakota swore silently to herself for not having thought of that already. She opened her eyes and quickly activated the data screen printed on the sleeve of the other woman's spacesuit.

It says she's absorbed more than fifty grey of radiation, Dakota sent in reply. She was far from sure whether even the wonders of modern medical technology could combat such a huge dose of ionizing radiation.

Nancy coughed, and Dakota studied the other woman's face. Her lips moved soundlessly, and her eyes had rolled halfway up into her head.

<Okay, that's really not good,> Lamoureaux remarked.

Understatement of the fucking century.

<Look, all we can do now is stick her in a medbox and hope for the best.>

I should have listened to her, Dakota sent. *She had a better idea of the situation, and I didn't pay attention. I should have checked things out more thoroughly, instead of going barging into a situation I didn't understand.*

<Don't beat yourself up too much, Dakota. She wasn't exactly going out of her way to win your trust and respect.>

The yacht shook again. *Trader, how much damage are we taking?*

<A considerable amount, I regret to say. I believe there might originally have been only a few scouts inside the cache, who would have used any available resources to build copies of themselves.>

How do you know?

<The tactic is familiar. A few enter a defended territory, multiply rapidly, then attack from within.>

And knowing this helps us how?

<The ones with antimatter cores are identifiable by the magnetic fields they use for containment. Those are suicide devices. The ones without antimatter cores control the rest.>

So if we can destroy the ones doing the controlling, we can stop the rest.

<Precisely.>

Dakota slowed her time frame until the seconds stretched out. She ran an analysis of the course of the battle so far, and noticed how just a dozen scouts kept themselves close to the cache, while all the rest pushed the attack aggressively. She watched as one of them dived towards a Meridian drone, detonating at the point of closest proximity, overwhelming the drone's wrapping of protective fields and annihilating the machinery within in an enormous blast of heat and radiation.

It was time, she decided, to stop running and go on the offensive.

As she drove the drones straight at the cache, several were annihilated instantly, but instead of breaking away again, as they had been programmed to do, she kept the rest driving relentlessly towards the cache and the cluster of controlling scouts sheltering there.

<Dakota, It's Ted. We've come up with an idea.>

I hope it's good.

<There's a couple of scouts heading towards us. We

might be able to take them out with the pulse-cannons, once they get within range, but we can't risk letting them gather intel on the frigate and then maybe sending advance warning to the Emissaries that we're in the vicinity.>

You're assuming they haven't done that already?

<Yeah, well, we still need to cut any potential losses. So here's what we're going to do, we'll jump now, and rendezvous with you at the following co-ords. Pass them on to Trader, and we'll meet you there later.>

We could wind up separated from each other by a long way, Ted. Maybe even by a couple of light-years.

<Not if we make it just a small jump, like you did back at Redstone. That reduces the chances of wide separation. There's a binary system about twelve light-years from here that might be a good recognizable target.>

A moment later an image of the binary system materialized in Dakota's mind.

<It's got about six satellites, so we'll aim for the fifth one out. Neither of us is going to hit the exact spot, but with luck we'll be in close enough range of each other to make a relatively fast rendezvous.>

What about Nancy? She needs emergency treatment, Ted – as in right now.

<The consensus is we're taking too big a risk if we let those scouts get any closer. We're going to initiate that jump immediately.>

Consensus? You mean Corso and Martinez, don't you?

Lamoureaux didn't reply, but she could sense his

tension and concern as if it were her own. Dakota pulled back into the real world, and she looked down again at Nancy. Her skin had reddened even more, and her lips trembled faintly.

Perhaps it was better she wasn't aware of what was happening.

Dakota described the new plan to Trader. By now more than half the drones recovered from around the mouth of the cache had been destroyed.

<Are any of the remaining drones recoverable?>

I don't think so, she replied. *I could pull them back towards us, but all that'll do is draw the scouts straight to us.*

<Then we must abandon them.>

We have what we came for anyway. How long before we can jump?

<Immediately.>

The frigate was already gone: it had slipped into superluminal space only seconds after she had spoken to Lamoureaux.

She switched her attention back to the cache. The scouts had rallied, throwing the last of their antimatter-equipped clones at the remaining Meridian drones with devastating effect.

Dakota opened her eyes and again checked on Nancy, thinking that, if she was lucky, she might live long enough to appreciate the irony of trying to save the life of a woman who'd like nothing better than to see her dead.

Time to go, Trader.

<Initiating.>

The stars spun around the yacht and then, for one brief instant, vanished.

'That's it,' said Lamoureaux, leaning forward in the interface chair as he reached back both hands to massage his neck muscles. 'Twelve light-years, and just half an AU off-target.'

Corso nodded, looking up at the simulation of the system they had landed in as it floated beneath the ceiling. Each of the simulation's planets became gradually more detailed as additional data arrived from the hull's sensor arrays.

Martinez stepped away from the console he had been manning and slumped next to Perez on one of the couches. 'I guess all we can do now is wait and see if they make it, too.'

The next several minutes slid by at a glacial pace. Corso glanced around the bridge, at displays of intercepted tach-net feeds originating from the Perseus Arm: most of it indecipherable gibberish.

Thirteen minutes after they had jumped, an alert sounded.

'They made it,' Lamoureaux exclaimed, his gaze fixed on some faraway point. 'I'm picking them up now.'

Martinez clapped his hands a couple of times, and Corso found himself grinning as the tension suddenly lifted away.

'They're a couple of light-minutes away,' Lamoureaux added. 'That means a couple of hours before we can rendezvous.'

'Is the med-bay prepped for Nancy?' asked Martinez.

Corso didn't miss Lamoureaux's hesitation when he answered. 'I've unlocked the seals and reactivated the medboxes.'

Martinez merely nodded, as if satisfied with this answer, yet Corso knew they were all maintaining a fiction: there was likely very little they could do for Nancy Schiller. Even if by some miracle she was still alive by the time Trader's yacht docked with the frigate, it would almost certainly be far too late to save her.

Lamoureaux stepped down from the interface chair and approached Corso. 'Have you had any more thoughts about what we found back by the reactors?' he asked him quietly.

Corso glanced towards Perez and Martinez, but they had stepped over to a console on the far side of the bridge, and were deep in a discussion over astrogational data.

'I think we're going to have to let Dakota see it,' he replied. 'If we're right about Whitecloud, she should be the first to know.'

'You realize that means telling her who he really is?'

'Yes . . . yes, I suppose I do,' Corso replied. 'Not that I'm looking forward to it.'

'Rather you than me,' Lamoureaux said softly. 'Rather you than me, any day of any year.'

THIRTY-ONE

Whitecloud sat staring at a screen and nursing a bulb of coffee as Corso entered the lab a short time later.

'Found anything new?' Corso asked him, shooting a glance at the Mos Hadroch still wedged inside the enormous machine and surrounded by probes.

Whitecloud went on staring at the screen like he wasn't even aware of the man standing next to him.

'Ty?' Corso asked again, this time in a substantially lower voice.

Whitecloud finally turned to face him. *Nobody home*, thought Corso, chilled by the empty expression on the other man's face.

Whitecloud seemed to come back to life a moment later, and jerked backwards, clearly surprised to find Corso standing in front of him. The bulb of coffee went spinning out of his hand, but Corso reached out and caught it, then handed it back. His lingering doubts about Whitecloud being under some form of control had now vanished completely.

'I was wondering if you had anything new to report,' Corso started again, keeping his voice level even while his heart hammered inside his chest. It was important not to let Whitecloud suspect anything was amiss. 'You were supposed to file an update this morning, but I didn't receive anything from you.'

In truth, Whitecloud's reports rarely made for good reading. Rather than containing actual information or providing any insights, they tended more to be a list of ᴛᴇsᴛs, ᴏʀ ᴠᴀʀɪᴀᴛɪᴏɴs ᴏf ᴛᴇsᴛs, ᴛʜᴀᴛ ʜᴀᴅ ʙᴇᴇɴ ʀᴜɴ ᴏɴ ᴛʜᴇ ᴀʀᴛᴇfact, all producing the same dismal results. The only time the artefact had shown any sign of being anything other than a dumb inanimate object had been that first time Corso had laid eyes on it.

Whitecloud blinked and pulled himself out of his chair, grabbing a rung in the low ceiling for support. 'New?' He scratched his head, staring around him as if he had been asleep for a long time. 'Yes. Yes there is, actually. Take a look at this.'

Whitecloud pushed past Corso and headed for a tabletop imager. He activated it first by passing his hand over its plate, then quickly sped through a series of holographic menus until he found what he was looking for.

A few moments later Corso found himself looking at the image of a translucent upright cylinder hovering above the plate, with thousands of hair-thin passageways extending outwards from it horizontally.

'That's a cache, isn't it?' remarked Corso.

'It is,' Whitecloud agreed. 'The one at Tierra, to be precise. I only got a chance to take a look at this for the first time the other night. The main reason I didn't get round to filing your report was because I wanted to check more of the correspondences before discussing it with you. But since you're here . . .'

Whitecloud reached up towards the floating cylinder and nudged it to one side with an expert flick of his fingers, then he quickly navigated through another menu. A second cylinder appeared, similar to the first except that, rather than having a single primary shaft, this one had two shafts that merged in the middle, forming a cross.

Corso started. 'That's . . .'

'The interior of the asteroid where we found the Mos Hadroch,' Whitecloud finished for him.

'But they look identical!' Corso exclaimed, coming forward and putting both hands on the rim of the imager's flat plate. 'Well, no, not identical, but . . .'

'But strikingly similar, wouldn't you say?'

'Yes.' Corso nodded. 'And you only just picked up on this?'

'You'll recall I was working outside on the hull during the briefing about the cache we just visited. A summary was forwarded to me, but I didn't get round to studying it until now. Still, I don't know how I missed it before,' he admitted, a touch of wonder in his voice. 'When I saw this for the first time yesterday, I was thunderstruck. The relationship was immediately obvious. Anyone with enough knowledge of the Atn could have made the connection, but there are so few of us left, really, and with the chaos of the last few years . . .'

Corso studied the two images and felt a chill that had nothing to do with the ambient temperature of the lab. 'Just to be clear, you're saying there's obviously some kind of relationship between the Atn and the machine-swarm that created the caches?'

'You sound surprised, but think about it for a moment. They're both widely distributed, self-reproducing machine species. It's certainly not beyond the bounds of possibility that they share some common point of origin. Perhaps what we're seeing here is a case of some kind of genuine machine evolution.' Whitecloud paused to think for a moment. 'Or more likely one was created from the other.'

'And the swarm was hunting down and destroying Atn clades.' Corso, too, thought for a moment. 'Can knowing this help us in any way?'

'I don't know,' Whitecloud admitted. 'Just about the first thing I did, once I realized this, was to try and crack the Mos Hadroch with the Atn's own machine-protocols. I got nowhere, though that's not to say there aren't other commonalities between the species that might give us the key we need to understanding how the artefact actually works.'

'We're running out of time, Ty. A few more days and we'll be reaching our destination.'

Whitecloud nodded. 'Did we get what we needed at our last stop?'

'Yes . . . but there were some problems. Dakota and the others are on their way back right now.'

441

'What problems?'

Corso briefly summarized the events on the cache-world, including Nancy's radiation poisoning.

Whitecloud paled at this final piece of news. 'Nancy . . . is dying?'

Corso frowned at his reaction. Whitecloud was clearly severely shaken, more than might be expected given that he hardly knew the woman. 'No, not dead, but it's really not looking good. She's going straight into a medbox as soon as she's back here but, to be honest, the delay before we can rendezvous is just going to further reduce any chance she might still have had to pretty much zero.'

Whitecloud's face became a mask. 'I see,' he said briskly, looking away from Corso. 'That's a matter of some concern, of course.'

Corso nodded, and wondered again just what it was Whitecloud wasn't telling him. 'We need to find a way to activate the Mos Hadroch that doesn't involve Trader,' Corso reminded him. 'Dakota's been down here a couple of times, hasn't she?'

'Yes,' said Whitecloud, 'but we never got a repeat of the phenomenon that occurred the first time she saw it.' He nodded towards the artefact in its cradle. 'It's been inert ever since.'

'Do what you can, Ty. It could mean the difference between success and failure. I'll see if I can get Dakota to come back down. Maybe this connection between the swarm and the Atn is what we need to finally get somewhere.'

Ty nodded, but his whole mood had changed dramatically once he'd heard the news about Nancy. *Just what have you been hiding from me?* Corso wondered as he left.

As soon as Trader's yacht had docked, Dan Perez and Ray Willis helped Dakota get Nancy out of her suit. Corso arrived in time to watch the two men lower her into a portable medbox towed away by a spider-mech, before following it back out of the bay.

'Her suit's support systems are keeping her alive, but only just,' remarked Dakota once she and Corso were alone. She wrapped her arms around herself and shivered. 'I know she's not going to make it, but why do I feel so bad? The woman hated my guts. She wouldn't *want* me to feel sorry for her.'

'Maybe you're still a little more human than you seem to think,' Corso suggested.

Dakota just shook her head, her eyes filled with regret. 'I can't help but blame myself. I let myself get careless.' There was anger in her tone. 'I was in too much of a hurry to get down inside the cache.'

Corso sighed and gripped her by the shoulders, forcing her to look at him directly. 'There's no way you could have known beforehand what was going to happen, and Nancy knew the risks before she came along on this trip. We all did. You understand that, right?'

Dakota looked away from him again. 'Maybe.'

'Maybe, yes,' he said. 'Now listen, there's something we need to talk about. Something urgent.'

She glanced back at him. 'What?'

'The closer we get to where we're going, the more nervous I get when it comes to letting Trader anywhere near the Mos Hadroch. But I just got back from seeing Nathan Driscoll over in the labs – and it looks like he's finally on to something.'

'A way to activate it?'

Corso hesitated. It had already occurred to him that there was no reason to assume Whitecloud was the only one to have been compromised.

'No, not yet,' he replied, entirely aware of how evasive he was sounding. 'Something else.'

Her eyes narrowed as she studied his face. 'Oh, for . . . You still don't trust me, do you? Listen, I already checked myself out *before* Olivarri was murdered. I went down to the med-bay and ran a full set of diagnostics on my implants almost as soon as we were under way, because I wanted to be sure. Lamoureaux did the same, and he's never even met Trader. Believe me,' she continued, 'we're both clean, and neither of us is being controlled – not by Trader or anyone else.'

'Why the hell didn't you tell me this before now?'

'Because, after Olivarri was murdered, I knew it wouldn't make the slightest damn bit of difference what I said. You read the report on the med-bay; whoever did the vandalizing, they didn't just smash the physical scanners, they did a good job of wiping the core memory as well. So how could either of us prove that we'd scanned ourselves?'

'All right, I'm sorry for doubting you. Anyway, Nathan now thinks it's possible there's a close relationship between the swarm and the Atn. He thinks one might have split off from the other a very long time ago and, given what he just showed me, I'm inclined to believe it.'

Dakota's eyes widened. 'Shit, that's . . .' She tailed off into silence.

'Pretty incredible, yeah,' Corso finished for her, then he nodded towards the exit. 'Maybe we should get going.'

Dakota followed him to the nearest transport station. 'I've run into Atn a couple of times on coreships,' she said, as they boarded a car. 'They're harmless, so it's hard to believe they could somehow be related to something as malign as the swarm.'

'It means there's at least the outside chance that Atn protocols might work on the artefact, but the fact is we're almost out of time. We're almost certainly going to need Trader to activate the thing, whether we like it or not.'

'It's strange to hear you saying that, Lucas.'

'Yeah, well, I'm still not too keen on the way you sprung him on us.'

'But I'm not the only one who's been hiding things. How long have you known Leo Olivarri was working undercover for the Legislate?'

Corso stared at her. 'Where did you hear this?'

'Trader told me,' she replied. 'And, no, don't ask me where he heard it. He wouldn't tell.'

'I haven't known about Olivarri that long,' Corso replied. 'There were suspicions, but we had to send a covert signal back home to get any kind of confirmation. It still doesn't tell us why he was murdered.'

'If he was spying on us, maybe he knew something we didn't. I could have worked on finding out more, if you'd only told me. Or do you still not trust me?'

Corso leaned forward and buried his face in his hands for a moment, before looking back up at her. The transport station lay silent and empty through the curved glass behind him. 'All right,' he said, 'I know who killed Olivarri. Or at least I have a pretty damn good idea. I think it was Driscoll.'

'What makes you think it was him?'

'Whoever sabotaged the ship's stacks didn't do a thorough enough job. It turns out there are memory overflow buffers that can hold partial back-ups in case of a major failure. We managed to retrieve some of the missing hours from the surveillance feeds, and it turns out Driscoll was the last person to see Olivarri alive. We even have partial video of them arguing not long before Olivarri was killed.'

'What were they arguing about?'

He shrugged. 'No idea. We haven't managed to recover the sound yet.'

'That's not necessarily incriminating in itself, is it? I mean, people do argue.'

'There's more. Before we left Redstone, Nathan completely disappeared for several hours. We have no idea what happened to him during that time.'

'Surely you asked him?'

'Yes, but his answer never rang true.'

Dakota leaned back and studied Corso for a moment.

'You're still holding something back, I can tell.'

Corso smiled weakly. 'All right, when the med-bay was vandalized, it made it almost too easy to pin the blame on you or Ted.'

'I think it was deliberate misdirection: a way to take the focus off someone else by making the obvious suspects look like the only suspects.'

'That occurred to me too, but now I think it was vandalized for exactly the reason we originally thought it was – so someone couldn't be scanned for compromised neural implants. But not you or Ted.'

Dakota smiled and shook her head. 'That's ridiculous. If there was another machine-head on board, I'd have known straight away.'

Corso smiled softly. 'Dakota, our friend Driscoll is a Uchidanist.'

'A Uchidanist? Why are you only telling me now?'

'Because I need your help,' Corso replied miserably. 'I'm sure he's under Trader's control.'

'How?'

'Remember, Uchidanists have—'

'Implants,' she finished for him. 'Oh, Jesus and Buddha. But that still doesn't necessarily prove he's responsible, does it?'

'No,' he agreed. 'For that, you need evidence.' He reached up to the car's list of programmable destinations. 'Let's get going. There's something I want you to see.'

She looked at him suspiciously. 'What?'

'The evidence,' he said simply. 'But before we get there, there's something else I'm going to have to tell you about Driscoll. And you're not going to like it.'

The frigate's reactor complexes were surrounded by a maze of access tubes narrow and cramped enough to induce any number of claustrophobic nightmares in the minds of anyone traversing them. Corso led the way, once they disembarked, relying on the detailed maps placed at each junction to help him navigate his way to one of the reactor bays.

Dakota followed close behind, a knot of apprehension twisting in her stomach, her mind still numb with shock from what she'd just learned. Before long they reached the main control area for the frigate's fusion-reaction systems. A screen mounted on one bulkhead showed a real time simulation of the fantastically violent processes taking place just a few metres away.

'I still can't believe you kept this from me for so long,' she mumbled, watching as Corso stepped over to a service hatch set into the bulkhead. He entered a code into a panel beside the hatch, and after a few moments it swung open.

'We've been over this before,' he replied testily. 'If I can find a way to work with Whitecloud without throttling him, so can you.'

Dakota didn't reply at first. In truth, what Corso had told her on the way still hadn't quite sunk in.

Whitecloud was, whether directly or indirectly, one of the men ultimately responsible for everything that had gone wrong in her life. The Port Gabriel incident had led to the banning of machine-head technology, and that had led to Dakota working for Bourdain – and that had led, one way and another, to Nova Arctis, and finally to the *Mjollnir*.

'I want him dead,' she announced, her voice wavering.

Corso was halfway inside the hatch as he glanced back at her. 'But we need him alive,' he said, with a warning in his tone.

'You should have told me,' she protested in sudden fury.

'And if I had, would you have been happy about him coming along?'

'No, I wouldn't,' she spat back at him. 'He's a mass murderer, don't you understand? You weren't there, Lucas. You have no conception of what it was like losing your mind like that.'

'And yet we have Trader sitting in his yacht there in

the hold, and we all know what *he's* capable of. I seem to recall he did exactly the same thing to you. So how do you square that with your conscience?'

Dakota's face paled and she fell silent, her eyes round and luminous in the light cast by the reactor simulation.

Corso shook his head in irritation, embarrassed at his own sudden sense of discomfort. A silence stretched between them, but when he ducked to continue through the hatch, she followed after only a moment's hesitation.

The area beneath the reactor control room was barely big enough to enable them to crouch together inside it, and the only light came from a single red panel in one corner. Corso pulled out a small flashlight and shone it on to what looked to Dakota at first like a jumble of machinery. He gripped the flashlight in his teeth and used both hands to pull himself closer to it.

As Dakota followed, she saw that a plastic chair had been pushed into one corner, and was covered with matt foil that she recognized as a kind of force-feedback material. A bird's-nest tangle of wiring and circuitry surrounded it, while yet more circuitry and wiring was wrapped around the arms of the chair.

'What is it?' asked Dakota, puzzled.

'See that superconductor cable running through the back? That's so it can tap directly into the reactor power feed without showing up on the logs.'

Suddenly Dakota saw the order in the chaos, and

realized she was looking at a home-brew version of the interface chair up on the bridge.

She moved abreast of Corso and brushed the fingertips of one hand along the wiring. 'So why build it at all?' she asked.

'To trigger the shutdown,' Corso explained, 'and to hide the identity of Olivarri's killer. Some of its components were manufactured from the Jab's dhidiband fabricator. That would nail Whitecloud pretty conclusively.'

'I don't see how,' Dakota muttered. 'Can Uchidan implants even work with an interface chair?'

'Apparently his can. I did a little research into his escape from custody. His implants are a custom job – far from surprising, when you think about it. All the members of his R&D unit were regularly tinkering with their own neural hardware to see what results they got.'

'There has to be a reason you're telling me all this now rather than previously.'

'Because it was going to emerge sooner or later, and I'd rather you heard it from me. We're all going to have to make compromises if we're to have a hope in hell of getting out of this mess alive.'

'What compromises?'

'I need you to keep working with Whitecloud.'

She stared at him, totally appalled. 'You've got to be fucking joking.'

'If he's close to some kind of a real breakthrough, you're going to have to. If it makes you feel any better, I've talked with him about what happened at Port

Gabriel. He doesn't deny his responsibility for what happened, and I'm not saying he's any less guilty, but I'm beginning to think he's genuinely contrite.'

A sick, acid feeling was building in the pit of her stomach. 'Oh, that's okay then,' she snapped. 'No problem. Let bygones be bygones, right?'

Corso bristled. 'That's not what I meant.'

She stared off past his shoulder for a moment, thinking. 'Look, putting all of that aside just for the moment, one thing occurs to me. If he's under Trader's control, why did he tell you he'd made a breakthrough? Wouldn't that be against Trader's own interests?'

'Trader didn't control your actions every second of every day, did he?'

'Well, no,' she conceded.

'I think it's the same with Whitecloud. That means he's his own man at least some of the time.' He nodded towards the jury-rigged chair. 'All this tells us is that Trader's planning something and, whatever it turns out to be, we're probably not going to like it.'

THIRTY-TWO

Another jump, at only 50 per cent capacity, carried the *Mjollnir* several hundred light-years further across the gulf separating the spiral arms. The Perseus Arm grew to fill more of the sky, while patterns of dust and light began to reveal themselves to the *Mjollnir*'s crew over the next several days, as they worked to keep the frigate's jump capacity above a certain critical level.

Ty's dreams became stranger and more frequent whenever he slept, sometimes almost taking on the nature of visions. At one point he dreamt that a powerful storm roared out of the Mos Hadroch, where it sat in its cradle, commanding him in a voice expressed in the form of thunder and gales.

Now she was back on board, the prognosis for Nancy was far from good; the radiation had caused deep and irreversible cellular damage. He found he dreamt of her also, suited and tumbling out of his reach, until she was lost in the depths of interstellar space. He had visited her in the med-bay a couple of times, and gazed at her through the transparent lid of her medbox, wishing his need for her could somehow bring her closer to life.

He studied his personal logs of the tests he had run on the artefact, and in them found inexplicable gaps. He was by nature a meticulous record-keeper, going so far as to date and time-stamp even his personal observations and thoughts on the tests he ran. But the more he dug, the more he discovered periods where the logs and his own memory now clearly disagreed. He found no records of certain procedures on days when he would have sworn that they had been carried out, but the more he tried to recall the specific details of what had taken place, the more his memory failed him.

Ty experienced a cold tightness in his chest when he discovered that these inexplicable blank spots displayed their greatest frequency around the time of Olivarri's murder.

He sat for a long time, his right hand splayed on the surface of a greyed-out console, the data-ring on his index finger gleaming dully in the low light of the laboratory. Then he activated the console and, from the lab's dedicated fabricator, ordered up a dozen micro-surveillance cameras with broad-spectrum capability. The request would be logged, and he might have difficulty explaining it if it was ever questioned, but that was another risk he was willing to take.

The cameras were manufactured within the hour, whereupon he spent the afternoon positioning the tiny devices in dark and secluded corners of the lab where he was sure they couldn't be spotted at a casual glance.

*

A short time later, Ty found himself back out on the hull as part of another repair shift. He watched Corso drill a hole into the hull itself with a custom-made mechanism he had ordered up from the fabs. The frigate was bathed in the ruby light of dozens of young stars shrouded in nebulae that marked the nearest edge of the Perseus Arm. It was a tremendous spectacle but, after nearly twelve straight hours on TWA, nobody was in a mood for star-gazing.

Once the plate-like Meridian field-generator had been plugged into the hull, Corso stepped back, allowing Lamoureaux room. Ted squatted beside it, laying the flat of one gloved hand on its slightly convex surface. A moment later, a flickering dome of light flared into life around them, which had to be at least fifty metres across.

'All right, I guess that's the last one for today,' Lamoureaux announced over the shared comms, fatigue reducing his voice to a dull monotone. The field shut off once more as he stood upright again.

'How much longer before we get the last one into place?' asked Corso.

'If we can keep to our schedule, it'll be another two days before the last of them is fitted to the hull,' Lamoureaux replied. 'With the spider-mechs doing a lot of the prep-work, we can speed things up, but we're still going to have to spend some time calibrating them.'

'And how long is that going to take?'

'Another day, maybe.' Lamoureaux turned and gestured at the newly installed field-generator. 'They're powerful, mind you. Whole orders of magnitude stronger than anything the Shoal let us get our hands on.'

Corso nodded. 'Ted, I need to check some diagnostics with you. So Nathan, if you don't mind—' Corso tapped the side of his helmet, then pointed at Lamoureaux, signalling they were going to talk over a private channel.

'By all means,' said Ty, unable to keep the irritation out of his voice. 'Don't let me stop you.'

Ty simmered in silence while the other two men got to talking about whatever it was they didn't want him to hear. Paranoia made him sure that he was the subject of their conversation, and he wondered if they had finally picked up on his long-range tach-net communication with the avatar.

The two men's comms icons changed back to public mode a few minutes later.

'I'm going to take a look at the rest of the field-generators we planted,' Lamoureaux announced. 'Might be able to speed up the calibration if I double-check them.'

Ty frowned behind his visor. 'You could do that just as well from the bridge.'

'Well, since I'm out here, I might as well grab the opportunity,' Lamoureaux replied, trying so hard to sound casual that it aroused Ty's suspicions further.

Lamoureaux moved away from them, carried along

the hull by the thin silver wires of his spacesuit's lanyard, and followed by a small retinue of spider-mechs.

'Ty,' Corso tapped the side of his helmet, 'switch to a private channel, please.'

With some reluctance, Ty switched to a one-on-one channel with Corso.

'I wanted to talk to you about Nancy, Ty. Word gets around.'

Ty opened his mouth and closed it. He almost blurted out a denial, then relented. 'It started long before we even got to Redstone. I—'

'Forget it,' said Corso. 'That doesn't matter. When I told you to stay away from the rest of the crew, I didn't know you were already involved with her.'

'Is she . . . ?'

'She didn't make it, Ty. I'm sorry.'

Ty nodded inside his helmet, his throat suddenly tight. 'I see. There was never really any hope of recovery, was there?'

'No,' Corso admitted. 'But you have to make the attempt, anyway.'

Ty listened to the sound of his own breathing, close and loud within his helmet. Corso moved as if to turn away.

'Then there'll have to be a funeral service?' Ty asked.

Corso stopped and looked back at him. 'No, not yet, anyway.'

'Why not?' Ty demanded, scandalized.

'This isn't the time to be burying any more of our

dead. Not when we're this close to our goal. The last thing the others need is to be reminded just how dangerous this job is. There's a real chance none of us is going to come back alive.'

'You have to hold a service,' Ty rasped. 'There was one for Olivarri.'

'That was different,' Corso snapped. 'He was murdered. Nancy's death is a direct result of our mission. We'll mark her passing properly, but not until this is over.'

'And is that what the others think, too?'

'I'm not here to debate the issue with you. I'm just telling you how it is.'

'Good of you to let me know,' Ty replied sarcastically.

'She had no idea who you really were, did she?'

'It wasn't the kind of thing that came up in conversation,' he replied, unable to keep the acid out of his voice.

'Ty, didn't it ever occur to you what you were actually doing by deceiving her like that? Did you really think I instructed you to stay away from the crew just to punish you? I've been deceiving people who would give their life for me, and for this mission, by *not* telling them who you really are. I wanted you to stay away because I didn't want to make that lie any bigger than it already is.'

'I thought of telling her,' Ty confessed, 'but I couldn't face the idea of her hatred.'

Corso chuckled. 'Keep saying things like that, and I

might end up mistaking you for a human being one of these days.'

Once he was back inside, Ty slept for a solid ten hours before waking with aching muscles and skin that had become infuriatingly itchy from pressure sores. He dragged himself into the lab's minimal toilet facilities, turned on a tap and watched a ball of water form at the end of the nozzle. Once it was about the size of his fist, he pulled it free and pushed his face into it, gasping at its icy coldness against his skin. He felt like he hadn't slept at all.

It was time to take a look at what the cameras he'd positioned around the lab had recorded. But first he was going to fix himself a drink.

Ty could count on the fingers of one hand the number of times he had ever touched alcohol, but some compulsion born of fatigue and grief, as well as the fear of what he might find when he reviewed the video feeds, made it easier to break what had until now been a habit of lifelong abstinence. Before long he was heading for an echoing, empty mess hall not too far away, where he breakfasted on freeze-dried crackers and reconstituted yoghurt. Once he had finished eating, he wandered through the kitchen area until he found the liquor cabinet he had spotted previously and randomly picked out a few squeeze-bottles of wine of indeterminate vintage and quality.

He broke the plastic seal on one of them, loaded the rest into a shoulder bag, then took a few sips from the open squeeze-bottle, careful to keep his thumb over the seal to prevent it spilling out in the zero gee. He grimaced at the taste, but kept drinking until a comfortably mellow feeling had begun to permeate into his tired limbs and his brain.

Back in the lab, Ty loaded the video feed and ran it from the beginning, watching himself go round the lab to check the cameras were properly networked before he sat down at the console and began typing some notes.

He fast-forwarded the feed an hour, and saw himself still thoughtfully typing or else pulling up data from the stacks.

And there was still another thirty hours of video to go through.

He sighed and fast-forwarded again, watching himself stand up and propel himself over to the far side of the lab, where a dedicated stack system maintained a real time back-up of all the experimental data gathered so far.

Ty frowned: this was something he definitely didn't recall doing. The only reason ever to use the back-up stack at all was because something had gone wrong with the primary system: and there had been no such issues that he could recall.

He switched views so that the feed from another camera allowed him to look over his own shoulder at the screen positioned above the back-up unit.

He leaned forward as the view zoomed in, and beads

of sweat prickled his forehead when he saw nothing on that screen but seemingly unintelligible garbage. It no longer felt like he was actually watching himself; this was someone else looking out at the world through his own eyes – a monster hiding inside his own head.

He left the video feed running and headed over to the back-up stack to run a quick search. But he couldn't find any clue there as to just what he'd been staring at so intently: the data had either been wiped or hidden. Nonetheless, he spent the better part of the next hour running increasingly aggressive queries that got him nowhere.

Eventually he gave up, turning back to the console where he had left the video running, and froze.

His own face – somehow inhuman in its lack of any discernible human emotion – filled the screen. The eyes were wide and blank, as if staring off at some infinitely distant horizon. It seemed the monster had found the camera he had hidden in a recess to one side of the stack system, and crouched down to take a close look at it.

Ty moved over quickly to forward the video feed another hour. Nothing changed: the monster was still crouching next to the stack-unit, staring directly into the lens. Its slack-muscled features betrayed all the warmth and compassion of a reanimated corpse. He – no, *it* – must have been standing there during all that time, just staring into the lens.

Ty knew he was being sent a message here. No

wonder he felt like he hadn't been getting any sleep; because he hadn't.

He slammed the console with his open palm so hard that it stung. The video feed blanked, but he could still see his own traitorous face reflected back at him in the smooth black glass.

He snatched his gaze away, suddenly sober again, and now filled with a terrible, skin-crawling chill. He hunted about for the hidden cameras and soon discovered most, but not all, were missing. He repositioned the undamaged ones in places where he hoped they might be harder to find, then he took a seat, opened another squeeze-bottle and began drinking with grim determination.

At first, the others didn't notice his condition when Ty arrived in the airlock bay for his next shift on the hull.

That was fine by him, since he felt wrung out after spending the night vomiting into a vacuum hose, and tiny gold-plated hammers still pounded with an unwavering rhythm against the inside of his skull. Conversation was certainly not something he was looking forward to, but it looked like he would once again be working with Corso and Lamoureaux, who usually spent most of the time just talking between themselves.

The two men were standing almost head-to-head, already deep in discussion. Ty paused by the entrance, where they couldn't yet see him, and listened quietly.

'So you think we can still recover more data?' Corso was asking.

'The *Mjollnir* has a lot of inbuilt redundancy,' Lamoureaux replied, keeping his voice low – but sounds tended to carry easily inside the frigate. 'There's a chance we can recover the rest of the lost data from the surveillance systems.'

'You mean the overflow buffers?'

'No,' Lamoureaux shook his head, 'we've got everything we can from them. But some of the core stack arrays can act as *virtual* buffers in an emergency. So it's possible there's still . . .'

Lamoureaux glanced to one side, spotted Ty and fell immediately silent. Corso turned and scowled when he saw him.

But Ty didn't care, and he headed for one of the suit racks, his mind suddenly racing with possibilities.

Over the next several hours, he had plenty of opportunity to mull over the brief snatch of conversation he had overheard.

Memory overflow buffers. He guessed they were talking about the data lost during the catastrophic systems failure around the time of Olivarri's murder. Clearly there was a way of recovering at least some of that data. And what else might be hidden in those buffers?

Later, on his way back to the labs, Ty once again stopped off at the mess hall, an idea forming in his head.

One bulkhead was dominated by a display of ceremonial weapons: a dozen long knives of the type used in challenge fights were arranged in a circle, their blades all pointing inwards.

It took a little effort, but he managed to prise one loose, then concealed it inside his jacket and returned to the labs. He found several messages waiting for him, including a new shift-schedule put together by Willis, who had taken over that particular duty following Nancy's death.

He activated the back-up stack system, and dug deep into its operational guts. He felt a flush of triumph when he traced the files he had seen on the video feed to a virtual buffer located in a linked stack in an entirely separate part of the ship. What those files might actually *be* was a question he couldn't yet answer, but a lot of time and effort had been taken to hide them somewhere neither he nor anyone else might think to look.

He thought again of the monster staring at him from out of his own eyes, and felt a second flush of triumph: *I'm on to you now.*

Ty now used a set of software tools to study the contents of the files, and found them to be lightly encrypted command structures of a type he had never seen before, carefully modified to run on the imager array in which the Mos Hadroch still sat.

He regarded the unmoving artefact for a moment, and felt an uneasy chill. Surely it couldn't be this easy.

He spent a few minutes loading the command structures into the imager array, set the probes to start recording, and activated them.

What happened next was far more than he could possibly have anticipated. A bass moaning sound filled the air, modulating every few seconds. The sound seemed to penetrate deep inside his body and mind, in a way that was far from pleasant.

At the same time, the artefact appeared to come apart – no, *unfold* – in some way that his human eyes couldn't make sense of. He stared, utterly transfixed, as it appeared to grow larger over the next few minutes, its shape now constantly morphing and shifting. Jewel-like shards appeared all around it, hanging in the air, and glistening and twisting like a kaleidoscope projected in three dimensions.

A message alert flashed, but he ignored it.

The only way he could explain what he was seeing was by assuming the Mos Hadroch existed in more than three spatial dimensions. What appeared to be disparate shards might instead be components of this device that normally existed only in the other, higher dimensions, but were now briefly flickering into view.

The throbbing became more intense, driving itself deeper into his mind and making it hard to think clearly. He found himself involuntarily re-experiencing key events in his own life in flashes of almost hallucinatory detail, as if the Mos Hadroch were pulling them out of his subconscious and attempting, in its alien way, to understand who and what he was.

A machine for passing judgement: that's what he had told Lamoureaux and Willis, back in Ascension. It was trying to find out if he was worthy of it.

He relived his days in the hidden R&D complex; the celebrations when the Legislate-backed strike against the Uchidan Territories floundered; the sense of betrayal when his Uchidan masters had decided to hand him over to the Legislate.

Despite his terror at what was happening to him, Ty laughed. The irony was inescapable: for all his abortive attempts at understanding the artefact, it was doing a much better job of understanding *him.*

Finally, mercifully, the Mos Hadroch reverted to something closer to its normal appearance. Meanwhile the monstrous noise that had accompanied its transformation decreased to a quieter pitch.

Ty remembered the ceremonial knife. Splaying his right hand flat on the console, he held the blade in his left so that it hovered over the finger wearing the data-ring.

If he could just do it quickly enough, the ring might not have the opportunity to send a signal through his nervous system. All he had to do was strike down, a single slash, and it would all be over . . .

His hand trembled as a cold wash of fear passed through him. He sobbed and let go of the knife, unable to go through with this act of self-mutilation; not when he knew the action might kill him.

He moved his shaking fingers across the surface of the console and set it to record, then began to speak. He did his best to summarize what he'd discovered, and what he thought they were dealing with. He tripped over his own words but pushed on regardless, knowing he was babbling but afraid that his mind might be stolen away from him before he had a chance to finish. He knew the monster inside his head could come back at any time.

Ty took the command structure he'd discovered and attached both his message and the video footage of the artefact's sudden transformation to it, then distributed multiple copies throughout the ship's networks. He left the console to continue recording in the meantime.

Even if the monster managed to track down some of the copies of the command structure, it couldn't find or delete them all. All Ty needed to do now was . . .

A glint of light suddenly manifested in the corner of his vision, like a ray of sunlight reflecting off glass.

The monster had woken up.

Ty scrabbled for the knife and splayed his fingers across the console once more, just as he heard the heavy door behind him begin to open. He took a firm grip on the knife and prepared to strike down at his finger.

Something stopped him, and he cried out. It felt like the air around him had solidified, freezing him in place.

The monster crawled back inside his skull, just as he heard someone call his name.

THIRTY-THREE

The comms terminal in Dakota's quarters began to beep insistently. She accessed the data-space and found a high-priority alert waiting for her from Corso. A moment's mental navigation pinpointed him on Deck C, close by the labs.

Lucas. What's up?

<Dakota. Where are you?>

There was an edge of panic to his voice.

I'm in my quarters, she replied.

<I need you to meet me at Deck C, near Transport 55, straight away. There's something you need to see.>

Why don't you just tell me what it is?

<Just get down here, Dakota. Right now.>

He cut the connection. Dakota checked the time and realized, with a silent groan, that she had been asleep for less than two hours.

On getting there, she found Lamoureaux waiting by the entrance to a storage room, halfway between the transport station and the labs.

He nodded towards the open door, his expression grim. 'Take a look.'

She stepped inside, but her nose had already told her everything she needed to know. The bulkheads were stained red with blood, and the air smelled of copper and rust.

She saw Corso and Martinez kneeling on either side of Ray Willis, who had been pushed into the space between two tall metal equipment bins. It was clear from the deep gashes in his throat and chest that he was very dead.

Corso glanced up at her as she entered. 'Did you see anyone else on the way here?'

'No, I came straight away.'

Corso and Martinez exchanged a look. 'Four of us here—'

'And Dan on the bridge,' Martinez finished for him. 'We should get back there as soon as we can.'

Just five of us left, Dakota thought numbly. Ray, Nancy, Leo – all dead.

'What about – what about Driscoll?' she asked. She had almost said, *what about Whitecloud?*

'Now there's a question I'd like to answer,' said Martinez, straightening up. He grabbed hold of one side of a storage module to keep himself standing the right way up. 'He's gone.'

'Not only that, it looks like he took the Mos Hadroch with him,' Corso added. 'And . . . Dakota, Eduard knows about Whitecloud. Or he does now, at any rate.'

'Please tell me you only found that out recently,' said Martinez. His tone was calm, but something in the way he looked at her made it abundantly clear he was suppressing a great deal of anger.

'I swear, I only just found out myself.' She glanced at Corso. 'You know, maybe you should have told *all* of us a long time before now.'

'Maybe I should,' Corso agreed, but she knew he was dissembling.

She couldn't stop staring down at Willis's face; he wore an expression of mild surprise that seemed utterly at odds with the violence that had been done to him. The gashes in his body were horrible, and yet she couldn't look away.

'I guess it's pretty conclusive now that Whitecloud killed Olivarri,' she said.

'I'm still not making any assumptions until we find him,' replied Martinez.

'What about Willis here? Who found him?'

'We were getting unexplained major power surges from the labs,' Corso explained. 'Driscoll . . . White-cloud,' he corrected himself, 'didn't answer our calls, so Ray came down here to check things out. That was the last we heard from him.'

Dakota dipped back into the data-space and checked on Trader's yacht.

'Trader's where he should be,' she announced. 'His yacht hasn't budged, and he hasn't tried to link up to any of the airlocks.'

Lamoureaux leaned in through the doorway and caught her eye. 'You think Whitecloud might be on his way to the hold?'

'How the hell does Trader come into this?' Martinez demanded.

'How much did Lucas tell you about Whitecloud?' Dakota asked him.

'Enough to make him a very unhappy man, Miss Merrick.'

'Well . . . he has a customized Uchidan implant, and it's possible Trader's using it to exert some kind of control over him. It's also possible he doesn't even know what's happening to him.'

'That might be the case,' Martinez growled, 'but if I happen to accidentally blow the bastard's head off, I won't cry about it.' He nodded towards the corridor outside. 'There's an arms locker near here. We get armed and we go looking for him.'

'No. No firearms,' said Corso firmly. 'We can't take a chance that the artefact might get damaged.'

Martinez pulled himself upright, took hold of a metal shelf bolted to the bulkhead behind him, and used it for leverage as he planted one booted foot on Corso's shoulder and pushed hard. Corso was sent skidding across the floor until he hit the bulkhead opposite.

'I should kill you now,' the Commander rasped. 'You've lied to me too many times, Lucas, and it's getting people killed. This is still my command, my ship, my crew. Therefore we carry arms.'

He glanced around them all with an expression of disgust. 'Nothing would make me happier than to shove the whole fucking lot of you out the nearest airlock and watch you wriggle, but right now you're going to get yourselves armed and start looking for Whitecloud. I don't care how big the fucking ship is, this time I want him *found*.'

By the time Dakota made it back to the bridge some hours later, Lamoureaux had just completed the latest in a series of jumps that had shifted the frigate deep inside the Perseus Arm. They were now only twelve hundred light-years from the target system.

She lowered herself on to a couch near Martinez and Perez, and saw they were all present for once – excepting Trader and Whitecloud, of course. Lamoureaux sat in the interface chair and looked so tired that she wondered if he might pass out. Corso perched on the edge of the dais, by Ted's feet, facing towards the rest of them. They all looked just as exhausted as she felt.

Corso nodded to her. 'Think you can stay awake a few minutes more?'

'Sure,' Dakota muttered hoarsely. A numbness, like thick black cotton pressing against the inside of her skull, kept threatening to swallow her thoughts. She had enjoyed maybe a couple of hours' sleep at most out of the last seventy-two. Her implants could modulate her hormone and adrenalin levels to give her the occasional boost, but there was only so much abuse her body could endure.

Lamoureaux climbed down from the interface chair and sat beside her. Corso now stood up and faced them all.

'First,' he said, 'there's still no sign of Whitecloud. It's the same problem as before: this ship's just too big. We've set the labs to manufacturing a couple of dozen stripped-down spider-mechs to take over the search, but they won't be much more than a camera mounted on a navigational platform. They'll search the ship systematically, and at speed, starting at the bow and finishing at the stern.'

'Who's going to be running them?' asked Dan Perez.

'No one,' Martinez replied. 'We can't afford the spare hands, not with only five of us to do all the work. The spiders will maintain their own network, cross-check everything they see, and flag anything even slightly out of the ordinary.'

'But that's still going to take too much time,' Lamoureaux protested.

'I agree,' Corso nodded. 'What we really need to be doing is using our heads to try and figure out another way to track Whitecloud and the artefact down. While he was rooting around in the lab computers, Dan found something you really need to see. Over to you, Ted?'

Lamoureaux nodded, and a moment later an image of the Mos Hadroch appeared overhead, still suspended inside the imager array in the lab.

Dakota leaned forward. There seemed to be something wrong with the artefact, as if the air around it had become distorted.

'The video you're about to see was made before the Mos Hadroch was removed from the lab, obviously,' Corso explained. 'Dan came across several crushed fab-manufactured cameras, while the rest of us were out searching the ship. He's found a few more since, still intact and apparently deliberately hidden in secluded parts of the lab where you wouldn't find them unless you looked pretty hard. Dan also found some video files that Whitecloud had apparently deliberately distributed through the ship's stacks. Run the first one, Ted.' The image jerked into life.

As Dakota watched, the Mos Hadroch appeared to explode in extreme slow motion, glittering shards diverging outwards from its central mass and twisting slightly as they did so. The central core – the artefact itself – was meanwhile changing shape, seeming to twist apart and then fold in on itself every few seconds, in a way that challenged her senses. It literally hurt her eyes to watch.

There were hints of what might be shadows, as if the artefact were trapped at the centre of a tangle of struts and mechanisms, most of which were invisible, or very close to invisible. An eerie and overwhelmingly alien throbbing accompanied these contortions.

She finally tore her gaze away and pressed her fingers

to her eyes. When she looked back up, Lamoureaux had stopped the video.

'We also found this,' said Lamoureaux. 'Lucas?'

'Run it, Ted.'

A new video began. This time Whitecloud stared into the lens of the lab's main console, a wild look about his eyes.

'My name – my *real* name – is Ty Whitecloud,' he announced. 'I suspect I may be dead by the time you see this. The files accompanying this message include a command structure I believe can be used to control the artefact. I . . .'

The image jerked momentarily as Lamoureaux jumped it forward.

'. . . artefact is composed of some form of non-baryonic material imbued with a highly self-organizing principle, possibly hylozoic in nature, in essence a classical model of a Wheeler-Korsh engine. This is the only way I can begin to comprehend the nature of the communication between myself and the Mos Hadroch.'

'*Communication?*' exclaimed Perez.

Dakota sat up, her fatigue suddenly forgotten.

'What you must understand is that the Mos Hadroch is more than just a simple weapon. It will not function for just anyone who happens to come into possession of it. If the communication I shared with it is anything to judge by, it is entirely capable of making its own decisions. It knows everything about us – about the Shoal, their war with the Emissaries, our purpose in being here.'

'He's babbling,' said Perez. 'None of this makes any sense.'

'Shut up,' said Corso.

'Someone – some*thing* – has been exerting control over me against my will, and the only reason for doing so is because they want the artefact. But what you must understand . . .' Whitecloud paused to clear his throat, clearly at his wits' end '. . . what you must understand is that whether the artefact fulfils its purpose or not will depend on the artefact's own judgement of anyone who tries to activate it.'

Whitecloud slumped at the console and brushed one shaking hand through his unkempt hair. 'You must understand that it will destroy us, if it finds sufficient reason.'

For a moment he looked like he was thinking of adding something, but then appeared to change his mind, stepping back from the console.

'He's crazy,' said Perez.

'I agree,' said Martinez. 'He's clearly lost his mind.'

'I'm not so sure,' said Dakota.

Lamoureaux pointed upwards. 'There's more.'

Dakota looked back to see that Whitecloud had splayed one of his hands across the surface of the console, while the other gripped a knife with its blade aimed at one of his fingers.

Jesus and Buddha, she thought, horrified but unable

to look away. Whitecloud kept shaking badly, muttering under his breath and clearly in great distress.

He stood like that for several seconds, then his behaviour changed abruptly. His face grew expressionless, in a way that sent cold prickles of horror up Dakota's spine. He stared towards the lab entrance, which was out of sight of the console's recording lens, then himself stepped out of view, the knife still clutched in one hand.

'Talk about timing,' Perez muttered. 'This must be when Ray turned up.'

'Yeah, I think you're right,' agreed Corso. 'Whitecloud killed him before he could see what was happening to the artefact.'

'No, *Trader* killed him,' said Dakota, turning to eye him pointedly. 'The fact that it was Whitecloud's hands actually holding the knife doesn't mean anything. You saw the way he was struggling with himself.'

'I'll move it forward by a few minutes,' said Lamoureaux, and Whitecloud reappeared overhead once again. He was now covered in blood that was not his own, and he was panting hard, his chest rising and falling. Ray Willis would not have been an easy man to kill, even if caught by surprise.

Dakota watched Whitecloud pull the Mos Hadroch out of its cradle and stuff it into a bag. There was something monstrous about his eyes, as if they had been drained of any humanity.

'Does this mean he had the command structure for

the Mos Hadroch the whole time?' asked Perez, in a subdued tone.

'There's a bit earlier on where he describes finding it hidden deep inside the stacks. How it got there, he doesn't know.'

Something clicked into place inside Dakota's head. '*I* know,' she said, thinking furiously.

Corso stared at her. '*How* do you know?'

'By putting two and two together. I don't have a shred of doubt anymore that he's under Trader's control. But here's the thing. We didn't let Trader come on board because we didn't want him getting anywhere near the Mos Hadroch, right? At least, not in person.'

'So he used Whitecloud to get to it?' said Lamoureaux, his eyes widening.

'And used him as well to run his own experiments on the artefact,' Dakota continued. 'He transferred copies of the command structure into the lab, where he could test it out and see if it worked. But, somehow, Whitecloud stumbled across the command structure and figured out what was going on.'

'But why take the Mos Hadroch now? Why not before?'

'I don't know,' Dakota admitted. 'But once Trader discovered Whitecloud had distributed copies of the command structure throughout the ship, he'd have realized we wouldn't need him any more.'

Martinez stood up, his expression grim. 'Which

means right now Whitecloud is on his way to Trader's yacht – if he isn't there already.'

He stepped over to a console and a moment later a wire-frame of the frigate appeared above them. 'We'll resume the search, but this time we'll focus exclusively on the aft airlocks, and on every access route leading to the main hold and Trader.'

'But he could be there already,' said Perez. 'He probably went straight there after killing Ray.'

'Not necessarily,' said Corso. 'As soon as we found Ray, I programmed the surveillance feeds to send me an alert the moment Whitecloud showed up on a camera.'

'Except that the cameras don't cover the whole ship,' Martinez pointed out. 'Just the main passageways and bays.'

'But including every access point leading directly to the hold,' said Corso, nodding in agreement. 'Except we haven't caught him on camera yet, which means he – meaning Trader – is staying away from the parts of the ship under surveillance.'

'Then he must still be hiding somewhere on board the ship,' said Dakota.

'Listen,' said Perez, 'there's something else you have to keep in mind before we go running off looking for him. Right now we're down to less than fifty per cent jump capacity. There are also hull defects that need serious attention. We'd be at a huge disadvantage if we tried to jump into the target system right now.'

'Dan's right,' Dakota said to Martinez, 'and I

understand you want to let the spider-mechs hunt for Whitecloud on their own and free the rest of us up for essential work, but we've still got a much better chance of catching him if you let me or Ted run the spiders. No amount of repair work is going to make a damn bit of difference if we don't have the Mos Hadroch when we reach that cache.'

Martinez closed his eyes for a moment, then took a deep breath before opening them again. 'All right, fine. I guess we don't have any choice.' He fixed Dakota with a look. 'As long as you understand we're running out of time.'

Dakota nodded gravely. 'I understand. But maybe once we've got enough spider-mechs out and looking for Whitecloud, we can flush him out sooner rather than later.'

THIRTY-FOUR

<Got him,> Lamoureaux sent to Dakota, just a couple of hours later. <We just picked him up making for an ancillary airlock on Deck D. That's the *good* news.>

Dakota herself was standing in the entrance of a deserted engineering bay close by the main hold, watching as three spider-mechs boosted themselves through its echoing empty space on puffs of gas, their lights swinging from side to side, reflecting off bulkheads and machinery, making the shadows around them seem that much deeper by contrast.

You're saying there's bad news too?

<We're picking up traces of Emissary tach-net communications that are definitely in our neighbourhood. Small, scattered but numerous.>

Shit. *Scouts?*

<Can't confirm yet, but that's my guess. Don't know if they've spotted us yet, but we're going to make the next jump before they do. I'm forwarding the video-capture of Whitecloud to you now.>

She saw Whitecloud making his way rapidly down a corridor, a heavy satchel slung over one shoulder. A sign pointing towards an airlock facility was visible behind him as he passed the hidden security lens.

Where the hell's he going? she sent back. *That's nowhere near the main hold.*

<Ask him when you see him. You're closer to that airlock than any of the rest of us. Do you think you can handle him?>

She turned her back on the engineering bay and grabbed a rung, using it to boost herself through the air, kicking off walls until she began to pick up greater speed. *I've come up against things a lot worse than Whitecloud. How long before our next jump?*

<Twenty-five minutes.>

Got it.

<Do what you can, Dakota. And good luck.>

She made her way towards the bow, moving away from the hold until she reached the same passageway in which Whitecloud had been sighted. She barrelled her way towards the airlock complex at record speed, but it still took her a good ten minutes.

When she got there, she noticed a suit was missing from the racks. Whitecloud was already in one of the airlocks, but still cycling through.

She kicked off from a wall and landed square on the airlock door. She peered in through the glass panel and saw the back of Whitecloud's head. He was wearing a helmet, his bag slung over the shoulder of his suit.

She slammed her hand against the glass repeatedly until Whitecloud finally turned to look at her. Something in his face made him look eerily different. How long, she wondered, could Trader maintain his hold on him?

There was no way to override the cycle once it had started, so all she could do was wait until he had exited on to the hull, and the external hatch had swung closed again.

As soon as the safety light blinked on, and the airlock disengaged its safety locks, Dakota yanked the door open and climbed inside, initiating another cycle. By the time the outer hatch slid open once more, her filmsuit had spread out fully beneath her clothes.

She pulled herself out on to the hull but couldn't see Whitecloud. For one freezing moment she thought she had lost him, but then spotted him making his way rapidly through the forest of drive-spines, heading for the stern, his bag bouncing around as he moved.

Ty? Trader? Can you hear me? I'm right behind you.

Whitecloud stopped just long enough to glance back at her. He turned away again, and began to move more quickly.

She pushed herself along parallel to the hull. It was a risky manoeuvre to move this fast without the benefit of a lanyard to keep her attached to the hull itself. One misjudgement could send her spinning away into the darkness of space.

Trader, I know you're behind this.

To her surprise, he answered her.

<Greetings, Dakota. I hope you are well.>

The words sounded wrong, issuing from White-cloud's throat. She found herself unexpectedly recalling the ghost stories of her youth, those tales of spirits and possessions. Hearing Trader speak through a human being was more than a little disquieting.

I know everything, Trader, You killed Olivarri and Willis and now you're using Whitecloud to bring the Mos Hadroch to you. But you can't get to the cache without fire-power to back you up, so why are you doing this?

<You betrayed me, Dakota. Is that reason enough?>

What?

<You lied when you told me Moss was dead. I have received reports that he is very much alive. What did he give you, I wonder, to persuade you not to put an end to him?>

Whitecloud disappeared momentarily behind the wide blade of a heat-exchange nacelle. Dakota kept pulling herself along one of the main plasma conduits, slowly gaining on him. But another fifty metres and the conduits would terminate; after that, she would be passing over the exterior of the main hold.

Fine, I admit it. I didn't kill him. Stop now, Trader, or I'll take over your yacht.

<You don't have the means.>

You asked me what Moss gave me. He gave me the command structure for your ship. Stop now, or I'll never let you get inside it.

<Make any such attempt, and Whitecloud will throw

the artefact away from the ship. Your chances of recovering it will then be very low indeed, given that a large number of Emissary scouts are now approaching.>

She came to a halt at the nacelle, and worked her way carefully around it. Once she was on the other side, she saw Whitecloud making his way toward an airlock leading directly into a series of access tunnels that surrounded the main hold.

She saw him falter for a moment, standing there unmoving with one hand resting on the external hatch's manual release. She wondered if Trader's control over him was finally slipping.

She pushed towards him with renewed energy.

Ted, Whitecloud's entering the hold through a service lock.

<Roger that. It looks like some of those Emissary scouts just jumped into our very near vicinity to check us out. You need to get back inside, Dakota. *Now.*>

I hear you.

She kept pushing herself towards Whitecloud. He seemed to have recovered now, quickly releasing the manual switch. She saw red light illuminating the front of his suit as the airlock hatch slowly slid to one side.

Trader! This is crazy. The Emissaries will blow you out of the sky if you try to go to the cache on your own.

<How is it, Dakota, that the approaching scouts knew to track us here to these coordinates, out of all the vastness of the Perseus Arm?>

Before Dakota could answer, Whitecloud disappeared through the open hatch.

The hull sailed past, only millimetres beneath her. Light had already begun to sparkle along the top of the nearest drive-spines, and she realized the *Mjollnir* was only seconds from jumping. If she didn't get back inside the ship soon, she risked being vaporized by the energy flow.

Something sailed past the frigate, moving so fast it was gone by the time she discerned its passage. She reached out for a rung next to the hatch . . .

The field-generators came to life, even as the first pulse-beams lanced towards the *Mjollnir*.

The world went white for several seconds, but she still had hold of the rung. The light faded quickly, and she activated the lock system, watching the door slide into its recess.

More dark shapes shot past, so quickly they barely registered. She pulled herself inside.

Trader? I don't know how they could have found us. Why don't you tell me?

The hatch slid back into place above her, lightning playing across the hull outside.

<You, of all people, know the inconceivable chances against simply stumbling across this frigate in all the depths of interstellar space. The only reasonable conclusion, therefore, is that they have the means to track us.>

The airlock finished its cycle, and Dakota passed on into a network of cramped service tunnels. She briefly dipped into the data-space until she had an idea which way to go.

Following the passageway to a heavy door, she passed through it and into a large control module overlooking the interior of the hold, designed for use by traffic controllers overseeing the movement of ships and cargo. As she entered it, she saw that the module was several metres across, with a wide window at the far end which revealed the looming shape of Trader's yacht, now free from its cradle and floating just beyond the glass. It was close enough, in fact, that its drive-spines risked shattering it.

Ty crouched beneath the window, next to a console, still gripping the bag containing the Mos Hadroch tight against his chest. He'd already taken his helmet off.

'You shouldn't have followed me,' Ty rasped in what sounded more like his own voice.

As she stepped closer, he pulled a knife out of the bag, its blade still stained with Willis's blood.

'You can't hurt me with that,' she said. 'Believe me.'

She started to move closer to him – and the yacht moved towards the window with startling suddenness. A drive-spine pierced the glass, sending dozens of fragments spinning through the air. Dakota grabbed hold of a metal shelf bolted to the wall, before the venting atmosphere could suck her out of the module and into the hold.

But the explosive decompression ripped her hands away from the shelf, and she collided with the bulkhead nearest the window. She then managed to grab hold of the console for just long enough to let the force of decompression finally relent after a few moments.

The next time she looked, Whitecloud was gone. The strap of his bag, however, had become caught on a piece of twisted metal to one side of the window-frame.

Dakota pushed herself towards it, hands outstretched.

She was not aware of any kind of explosion, or of being hit by any form of missile. Only later did she recall having a momentary glimpse of a ball of white light expanding through the shattered window towards her. She was initially only aware of now being on the opposite side of the room. The metal shelves were twisted out of shape where her body had rammed into them with sickening force.

The filmsuit had protected her, but the impact had nearly drained it of power. She might have as little as a few minutes left before it would begin to fail.

Trader swam in through the ruined window, moving towards the bag until the sphere of water enveloping him had surrounded it. The tentacles dangling from his underbelly untangled the strap from the obstruction and drew it close to his body.

She watched, helplessly, knowing that if she provoked Trader into attacking her a second time, the power drain would likely overwhelm her filmsuit.

Trader swivelled to look at her directly. <To continue our conversation, you are, of course, aware that there are sophisticated means by which cultures much more

advanced than your own can track individuals across enormous distances.>

I don't know what you mean.

<Of course you do. It's how Hugh Moss chased me all across the galaxy. Don't you realize he doesn't want us to succeed? The Emissaries are *winning*. The Shoal is retreating, world after world destroyed. You can't imagine how many lives have been lost already. Nothing would please that monster more than to see us all die, so it was hardly surprising that he might place a similar form of tracking technology on your own person. Something so small and undetectable you would never find it. Then, my dear Dakota, he gave the means of tracking you to our enemies, the Emissaries.>

Dakota remembered how Moss had touched her shoulder back on Derinkuyu, and the way his touch had stung.

You're lying. There's no way you could possibly know all this.

<I am not so alone in my endeavours as you seem to imagine. I still have those whom I can trust to supply me with certain intelligence, otherwise Moss would have found and destroyed me long ago. But the final proof that the Emissaries have a means of tracking you lies in the ease with which they found us here, out of all the vastness of this spiral arm. I cannot believe those scouts hidden in the cache were anything other than a trap carefully laid in anticipation of your arrival. The only course of action then left to me is to take the Mos Hadroch far

away from yourself and the frigate, in order to preserve it.>

This is bullshit. You were always planning to steal it.

<Once our mission here was finished I intended to return it to the Hegemony for safe-keeping, that much is true. Perhaps, if you survive this day, you will eventually come to understand that the Mos Hadroch is far too precious to be allowed to remain in the hands of a fledgling and barbaric race such as your own. The Emissaries' attention will be on the frigate or, more precisely, on *you*, while a much smaller ship like my own may be able to slip past their defences.>

A hatch began to slide open in the side of Trader's ship, and he moved towards it.

Wait . . .

<Goodbye, Dakota. I did not come to this decision lightly.>

The hull of Trader's yacht closed behind him as he slipped back inside. Flickering lightning began to form around the tips of its drive-spines.

Dakota activated the command structure Moss had given her, feeling it unfold like an impossibly complex origami flower in the depths of her mind. She tried to lock on to the yacht's primary control systems, but it was already too late; the craft was fully committed to a jump. Trying to reverse the flow of energy spilling out through the drive-spines at this point would likely destroy the yacht, the frigate's hold, and herself along with it.

She scrambled for the door and felt real panic well up

inside her when she found it had sealed itself following the decompression. She launched herself back into the data-space and found the door's override codes, but Lamoureaux was in the chair, meaning she couldn't activate them without his explicit permission.

Ted, I need you to override the safety locks at my current location. Now!

‹I've got your location, but just blowing the door will be dangerous. Won't—?›

Just do it, Ted! Do it now or I'm dead!

‹Okay. You might want to move back from the door if you're anywhere near it.›

She pulled herself into a corner, under a metal desk that projected out from one wall, and held on to its legs. The light from Trader's yacht was beginning to build in intensity, becoming almost blinding.

The exit door slammed open a second later, and Dakota clung on for her life as the atmosphere rushed past her and out the shattered window. Once it was over, she threw herself back into the access tunnel, bouncing from wall to wall in a frenzy, heading back towards the airlock.

The light followed her, still increasing in intensity. Whenever her hands or feet touched a bulkhead, she could feel a heavy vibration building up inside it.

She was back out on the hull less than a minute later. The stars had changed once again, the Emissary scouts now several hundred light-years aft.

‹Dakota!› Lamoureaux screamed to her through

their link. <What the hell is happening back there? Are we still under attack?>

She could hear priority alerts blaring on the bridge. *It's Trader. He's going to jump his ship from inside the hold. I don't know what it's going to do to the frigate, but you'd better warn the others and tell them to get ready.*

She kept pulling herself back along the hull towards the bow, hand over hand, until she reached the same heat-exchange nacelle she had passed before. She pulled herself around the other side of it and pressed herself close, the vibration now growing into a powerful tremor that in turn became a series of hammer-blows that very nearly sent her spinning off into the encompassing darkness.

Light spilled out into the void from somewhere on the other side of the nacelle. She peeked over the top in time to see the hull around the main hold tear open like putty, hull-plates silently spinning away as an inferno of light and energy burst outwards. The dazzling light pulsed as it reached a crescendo, casting off a great burning shell of plasma that expanded outwards from the frigate, before quickly dulling to a deep orange.

Trader's yacht was gone. Dakota stared in shock at the devastation left behind it.

<Dakota! Dakota, are you still there? We've lost contact with everything beyond Deck E. Please respond.>

Yes, I'm here. Trader's gone – along with most of the main hold.

THIRTY-FIVE

Half an hour later, Dakota was back on the bridge. She looked at the grim, worried faces around her, thinking how few of them were left now.

Five against an empire was not good odds.

Dan Perez was giving everyone booster shots, Dakota last of all. 'For the nerves,' he said, with an attempt at a smile, as he pressed the spray against her shoulder.

A numb, icy feeling spread through her where the spray touched her skin.

Corso sat next to a console, Martinez standing beside him with folded arms.

'All right,' began Corso, leaning forward slightly, with his elbows resting on his knees. 'Whitecloud's dead, Trader's left our ship half-crippled, and he's taken the Mos Hadroch with him. According to Dakota, we lost a third of the Meridian drones when he blew the hold apart.' He shrugged and made a face. 'But it could be worse, right?'

Dakota affected a weak smile.

'I'm not kidding,' Corso continued. 'At least we're still alive. We came very close to suffering a breach of one of our plasma conduits, and if that had happened, we wouldn't be here now. Not only that, most of our critical systems are unaffected, despite losing most of the hold. Our jump drive is still functioning. A good part of the ancillary fusion propulsion system is screwed, admittedly, but enough of the reactors are still working that we might be able to compensate for what we've lost. Manoeuvring inside our target system isn't going to be nearly as easy as we want it to be, but it won't be impossible.'

Martinez sighed and shook his head. 'Lucas, our reason for coming out here is gone. When the hold went up, it almost certainly took all our landing craft with it. The most sensible thing we can do now is turn back.'

'We're getting a response from the on-board systems for at least two of the landers,' Lamoureaux pointed out. 'I've already sent a couple of spider-mechs in to take a look, and I reckon they're salvageable, but I can't know for sure until we check them out.'

'Of course we go on,' interrupted Dakota. 'We chase Trader all the way there. Why give up now?'

'You don't make the decisions here!' Martinez exploded, stabbing a finger at her. 'You told us yourself, he's gone to do the one thing we came here to do. That means our job is over. So we go home.'

'Look, I don't know if we *can* go home,' said Dakota wearily.

They all stared at her, waiting until she continued.

'When I was chasing him – chasing Whitecloud, I

mean – Trader told me the Emissaries had some way of tracking us.'

'How do you know that's true?' Corso demanded.

'I didn't believe him at first, but the fact is those scouts we ran into back there knew just where to find us, out of a truly enormous volume of space. The chances of that being a coincidence are beyond astronomical. Trader said so himself.'

'That would make sense out of what happened back at the cache,' confirmed Perez, from beside her. 'It felt like an ambush.'

'Exactly.' Dakota nodded vigorously. 'They clearly *knew* we were coming.'

'If that's the case,' Lamoureaux said slowly, 'they could be on their way here right now.'

'Just hold on for one minute,' said Martinez, moving closer to Dakota. 'You haven't told us *how* they could track us.'

She chose her words carefully as she answered. Some things, she had decided, were better left unsaid for the moment.

'He told me there was something planted on the frigate that would lead them right to us.'

'So what does that have to do with Trader taking the artefact?' asked Perez.

'He planned on grabbing it for himself once we'd done what we came out here to do,' she explained. 'But he panicked when he realized the Emissaries knew how to find us. The way he sees it, we might as well have a bull's-eye painted on the hull.'

Martinez glared at her. 'Even if any of this is true, it doesn't fundamentally alter my original point. There's no reason for us not to turn back.'

'Because, even if we did turn back, there's a good chance the Emissaries would still come after us,' she snapped. 'And remember what Whitecloud said: the Mos Hadroch might decide not to let Trader activate it. If that's true, then it's imperative we carry on and be ready to finish the job, if we have to.'

Martinez laughed. 'You really believed that fairy tale?'

'The Mos Hadroch isn't just a weapon any more than the Magi ships are just ships,' Dakota persisted. 'And Whitecloud might have been an evil son of a bitch, but even you could see he was telling the truth when he recorded that message. Right there at the end, he did one good thing in his life by trying to warn us.'

'How the hell do you expect us to "finish the job"?' Martinez demanded. 'The artefact is gone!'

'We have the command structure,' she reminded him. 'We could activate the artefact ourselves, if Trader fails. And even if he doesn't, we have enough drones left to let us try and stop him escaping with the artefact.'

'Perhaps you're forgetting who's in charge of this expedition,' Martinez spat, his face turning red.

Dakota regarded him with a weary expression. 'You're out of your depth, Commander. You don't have any idea about the forces we're dealing with, or the kind of power they have.'

Martinez started to move towards her with bunched fists, but Corso leaped up and grabbed him by the shoulders.

'I want you to shut the fuck up for now,' Corso barked at Dakota, then turned his attention to the Commander.

'Eduard . . . listen to me. I know exactly what's going through your head right now. It's much the same thing that's running through mine. I don't want anything more right now than to go home. But I also don't want to have come this far just to turn around. Especially not if something could still go wrong.'

'I agree,' said Lamoureaux, nodding vigorously and gazing around at them all. 'We can't just turn around now – not this late in the day.'

'I'm sorry, sir,' added Perez, 'but, with the greatest respect, I'm with the others on this one.'

'We still have most of the drones,' Dakota pointed out, sweeping back the dark fringe of hair from her face. 'And the new field-generators, too. We can do this.'

Martinez stared at her like she was insane. 'Are you even listening to yourself? You already said the Emissaries know that we're on our way!'

'No, they only know where we are *right now*. And I don't see any reason to believe they have any idea exactly where we're headed, or that the Mos Hadroch even exists, let alone what it's capable of.'

A sudden alert sounded, an insistent beeping that cut off abruptly when Corso reached out and touched the console nearest him.

'Scouts,' he announced a moment later. 'Lots of them, and about one light-minute away. No details on their acceleration or specific vector, but definitely too close for comfort.'

Martinez tightened his hands again into fists before opening them wide, peering down at them as if seeing them for the first time.

'I guess that clinches it, then,' he said, dropping his arms helplessly to his sides. 'We go on.'

The frigate jumped again less than twenty minutes later, running at approximately 40 per cent jump capacity – just enough to carry them several hundred light-years across the Perseus Arm and into the close vicinity of their target system.

Dakota took the interface chair for the jump procedure, fatigue washing over her like a dark tide.

She closed her eyes and let herself sink deep into the ship's data-space. As long as she could keep up concentration, she could stay awake.

The power of suns flowed out of the fusion reactors and then through the drive-spines, tearing a hole in the fabric of the universe. The stars twisted, then changed.

A flood of new data immediately began to stream in via the sensor arrays: spectral analyses, mass estimates, number of visible planets, evidence of technology. They were still at least half a light-day out from the main-sequence star at the system's centre, but they would get up close to the target world through the next couple of jumps.

Dakota was distantly aware of Lamoureaux guiding a small contingent of spider-mechs out on to the hull, intending to make a quick assessment of the hull degradation.

Dakota activated the command structure that Moss had given her, and tried using it to locate Trader's ship. Before very long she got an automated response from the vicinity of a low-albedo object somewhere deep in the heart of the star system. She compared the object with the data she had received from Trader, and they matched. That meant they had reached the target cache.

She checked in on Lamoureaux once more, and found he was analysing video feeds scraped from the spider-mechs that had been sent into the hold. Pieces and fragments of hull-plate clung to those sections of the underlying skeleton that had survived the blast.

I can see the landers, she sent to Lamoureaux.

<Yeah, they must have been at the farthest point in the hold from where Trader's yacht was when it jumped.>

Feeling a hand on her shoulder, she opened her eyes to see Corso bending over her.

'Do we know where we go from here?' he asked.

She nodded, her throat dry. 'The target cache is on a small planet in the inner system, not much over a thousand klicks across and tidally locked to its star. The cache is on the dark side, however.'

'And how long before we get there?'

She let her head fall back against the head-rest, almost afraid to close her eyes in case she passed out from exhaustion.

'At least another hour before the drive is up to making another jump.' She raised a hand, stopping him before he could speak again. 'I know what you're going to say. The scouts will reach us before that, but it's just not possible to do it any sooner.'

'Then you're going to have to find a way to keep us safe from those scouts in the meantime.'

'Sure.' She nodded wearily. 'Of course.'

He studied her. 'How are you holding up?'

Dakota laughed weakly. 'Just barely.'

He started moving away, but she reached out to stop him. 'Wait. I need to show you something.'

She put on display the video feeds from the spiders.

'You can see how badly trashed the hold is, but Ted was right: those landers look like they survived pretty much intact.'

Corso nodded and stepped back down from the dais. 'Dan, come with me,' he said to Perez, then stopped, before he left the bridge, to look back at her. 'See what else you or Ted can discover before we arrive there,' he said.

'I'll send a spider out on to the hull to retrieve a couple of field-generators,' she said. 'If we're going to attempt a landing, we're going to need all the protection we can get.'

Corso nodded and left, with Perez following.

Dakota linked into the remaining Meridian drones and prepped them for combat. At the same time, she noticed it was early evening, shipboard-time. She settled back in the chair and wished she had asked Perez for another shot.

Whatever happened after this, she already knew it was going to be the longest night of her life.

Trader swam through the dense, pressurized waters that filled his craft. Schools of tiny fish swam around him, and he snatched some up with his tentacles, devouring them as he studied the multi-coloured projections all around him. The first jump had brought him within a few light-hours of the target system; subsequent jumps brought him closer to the inner system.

Defensive networks pinged his yacht constantly as it accelerated inwards, but he had obtained automatic response codes, leached from captured Emissary vessels, which fooled the networks into thinking he was one of their own. They would see through it eventually – particularly once he got within range of the cache – but it would meanwhile get him close enough.

He entered the chamber in which he had placed the Mos Hadroch. It hung there in the air, suspended in a series of interlocking shaped fields. Its mass was much greater than might be expected, but of course much of that extra mass was hidden in non-local spatial dimensions.

His ship spoke to him: *All propulsion systems are currently optimal. The local Emissary population is primarily located aboard habitats orbiting the fourth world. Local comms traffic implies they are engaging in one of their periodic purges.*

Trader's fins shivered at the mention of the purges. The Emissaries were bad enough when it came to dealing with other species; they were hardly less harsh on themselves. Every now and then, they would set about destroying their weaker members in orgies of slaughter.

The ship provided him with images of the system's innermost world. He saw enormous machines scattered and apparently abandoned all across its scarred and airless surface. Great holes had been drilled deep into the planet's crust, so that Trader could see manufactories extending deep into the core. Godkillers guarded it, patrolling the volume of space surrounding the star, their hulls black and crystalline, and forbidding in their sheer strangeness.

Even a cursory analysis made it clear that almost everything in this system was old. His yacht was still pulling in data from local data networks which did nothing but assure him of what he already knew, that this system was a backwater, and therefore only lightly guarded by the Emissaries' usual standards.

*

<We're coming under fire out here. Can you get them off our tail?>

Working on it, Dakota sent.

She had folded the interface chair's long petals up around her, enveloping her in silence and darkness. She could see the suited figures of Corso and Perez through the eyes of a single spider-mech hovering in the twisted wreckage of the hold. One of them was using a welding torch to cut away wreckage blocking in a lander.

She switched her viewpoint back to the battle taking place all around the *Mjollnir*. So far, the Meridian drones in conjunction with the field-generators were doing a good job of protecting the frigate but, for all their extraordinary power, they were being pushed to their limit by the onslaught of scouts. Worse, a godkiller had now appeared a couple of light-seconds away, vectoring towards them on an intercept course.

Dakota didn't want to think about what would happen if it got within range before they had a chance to jump.

<Dakota.> Corso's voice sounded terse and strained. <I think something got in here with us.>

She switched her view back to one of the spider-mechs and searched through the shadows until she saw it: the scout that was part hidden in the twisted shadows of wreckage. As she watched, its carapace began to slide apart, revealing a variety of deadly-looking machinery. The hold was now a weak spot, since most of the field-generators meant to protect it had been destroyed during Trader's jump.

The scout began to cut and burn its way through an exposed bulkhead leading to the frigate's interior.

I've got it.

A Meridian drone peeled off from the rest, darting back inside the wreckage and reducing the scout to white-hot slag within moments.

How's it going with that lander?

<Nearly done,> Perez replied. <She'll be good to go just as soon as we've finished mounting the field-generators on her hull.>

One hundred and eighty seconds to the next jump. Get back inside the instant you're done.

<We'll be done by then.>

Dakota drew the drones back inside the frigate while Corso and Perez retreated through a still-functioning airlock that led into the rest of the ship. Less than three minutes later, the *Mjollnir* fell once more between the folds of the universe.

The frigate dropped back into space less than twenty thousand kilometres from the surface of the cache-world. The system's star now filled the sky, huge and terrifying, while the hull's sensor arrays showed the world itself as a circle of black imposed against this seething light.

New data came in: vast, apparently abandoned craft

circled the star in long, eccentric orbits, along with a halo of less easily identifiable junk. The surface of the target world itself, outside of the cache, was pocked with what might have been machinery or habitats of some kind. There were two . . . no, three godkillers in orbit around the target world.

As she watched, they started to move out of orbit. *Because of me*, she thought, with no small amount of horror.

A few moments later, Emissary scouts began to materialize all around the frigate.

She picked up Trader's yacht, already dropping down towards the planet's surface. He was being chased by several scouts himself, and automated defences positioned on the surface of the planet were firing on him.

Trader became aware of the *Mjollnir*'s arrival at about the same time his ship warned him that its primary defences were approaching catastrophic failure. The scouts that had been chasing him decelerated almost at once, reversing their thrust and heading back towards the frigate.

Within his yacht, the waters remained dark and cool. Trader studied the data coming in from his hull arrays, but no matter how often he looked he still couldn't quite believe what it was telling him.

*

\<Dakota. I see that you are still alive.>

Trader?

\<I did not expect you to make it this far.>

What can I say?. I'm tenacious when I'm really fucked off. When we're done, I'm going to take that damn arte-fact and ram it up your—

\<Dakota, according to my instruments, the Emissaries have just dropped a nova mine into their own star. The neutrino flux is quite unmistakable.>

You can't be serious.

He waited while she checked the readings from her own ship's sensors. When she came back, he could feel her panic surging across the connection between them in bright hot waves.

But why? They can't possibly know about the artefact. Can they?

\<Perhaps Hugh Moss knew about the Mos Hadroch. If so, he may have passed the information on to the Emissaries.>

I told Moss you had a way to stop the war. I thought he might . . .

\<Listen to reason?>

Go to hell.

\<A most infelicitous disclosure, Dakota. Certainly enough for him to infer the existence of something approaching the nature of the artefact.>

But why blow the whole damn system up?

\<It is in the Emissaries' nature to lay waste all around them. If the sun detonates before I can implement the

Mos Hadroch, the cache will be destroyed, and with it any chance of stopping them. They are, after all, not lacking for other caches in other parts of their empire. Do not attempt to take over my yacht again, Dakota. Not if you value our purpose in being here.>

Trader! Wait—

But once again, he was gone.

THIRTY-SIX

As some of the field-generators were finally over-whelmed, scouts began to whip in towards the frigate's hull, their blades and cutting implements slicing through the thick armoured plates. The Meridian drones were meanwhile dying, overwhelmed by the sheer numbers of the scouts.

Dakota watched it all with a growing sense of frustration and panic. The scouts were attacking the *Mjollnir* because of herself, specifically because of whatever it was Moss had put inside her.

It was time for something drastic.

A minute or two later she sensed Lamoureaux entering the bridge. Indecision froze her for a moment, then she forced herself to stand, the chair's petals folding back around the base of the dais in response.

Martinez was still on the bridge, crouching over a console, talking to Perez over a comms link. He was paying no attention to either Ted or Dakota.

She stepped down and seized Lamoureaux by the arm, as he approached her, pulling him instead towards the exit. Her voice was just above a whisper as she spoke.

'I need your help, Ted. Things just went from bad to worse.'

'What do you mean?'

'Take a look,' she said, transferring the neutrino flux data to him via a link.

His eyes became momentarily unfocused, and his jaw flopped open. 'How long have we got?' he exclaimed, once he had recovered.

'Quiet!' she hissed, nodding towards Martinez, but the Commander was still talking to Perez, still oblivious to the pair of them. 'We've got maybe twelve hours maximum before this whole system goes up.'

Ted looked befuddled, glancing quickly at Martinez and then back again. 'And you want to keep this a *secret*?'

'No, just . . . wait for twenty minutes before telling them.'

He eyed her with increasing suspicion. 'Dakota, what the hell are you up to?'

'Here.' She linked with him again and transferred over the command structure for the Meridian drones. 'You can handle them just as well as I can.'

Over Lamoureaux's shoulder, she saw Martinez glance up and study them for a few seconds, then look away again.

She nodded silently towards the passageway outside the bridge. He picked up the hint and followed her.

'Take the chair and run the drones for me,' she told him once they were outside.

'Why can't you do it yourself?'

The ship's data-space informed her that Corso and Perez were on their way back from the hold. One of the landers was hooked up to an airlock and ready for launch.

'Do you remember what I said earlier, that there was something on board this ship that was leading the Emissaries straight towards us?'

He nodded.

'That something is me, Ted. I don't know what it is or how he did it, but a man called Hugh Moss planted something on me. Not even my Magi ship realized it was there. While you're running the drones, I'm going to get on board that lander and use it to draw the scouts away from the frigate. That way you'll have a better way of staying alive, while I can go after Trader. Nobody else needs to be down there at the cache but me, anyway.'

'Dakota, no.'

'For God's sake, Ted! I need to do this. I need to put an end to it all.' She could feel tears prickling the corners of her eyes.

'We should wait for the others to get here. Besides . . .' He shook his head. 'No, this is beyond just crazy. Even if you're determined to go down there on your own, nobody's going to be mad enough to let you.'

Her expression became icy calm. 'Don't get in my way, Ted, or I'll shut down the drones. The frigate would be left totally defenceless.'

He swallowed. 'I'd reactivate them.'

'But it might take you too long. There are already

things out there trying to burrow their way through the hull.'

'I don't think you'd—'

'Try me, Ted.'

She watched him studying her, trying to make up his mind whether she was serious.

'You're out of your mind,' he said eventually. 'That's what they've all been saying, and I th.. finded you. But they were right, Dakota. You're out of your fucking mind.'

'Don't let anyone come after me. Do you understand me?'

He stared back at her in silence, filled with impotent fury, as she turned and ran down the passageway.

Trader's yacht had utilized a maximum-evasion pattern as it descended towards the surface of the cache-world, but it had still suffered enormous damage from the ground-based defences. Once his ship had dropped into the cache's main shaft and begun its descent deep below the planet's surface, however, the shooting stopped.

Thousands of passageways had been cut into the rock all the way down the shaft. Before very long, Trader guided his yacht to a landing in one specific passageway where he knew he would find the cache's drive-forge. Once he had exited his ship, he took a moment to approach the lip of the passageway, in order to gaze down into the abyssal depths below.

Rows of lights descended the shaft's smooth walls, all the way down to where they appeared to converge tens of kilometres below his vantage point. On the far side of the shaft he saw a city-sized factory complex imbued with that same ineluctable air of decay and abandonment.

The walls around him had a half-melted look, with more ruined machinery lying abandoned. It didn't require a great deal of conjecture to realize it had been a very long time since any new drive-cores had been manufactured here.

The Emissaries, despite the advance warning, had clearly not expected the cache itself to be targeted. That they had then chosen to destroy the entire system made it clear they had finally recognized their error, even if much too late.

Trader swivelled in his field-bubble, then guided it deeper into the gently curving passageway, dodging past the blackened hulks of dead technology.

'I don't give a damn what she said!' Corso screamed. 'We have to go after her!'

'You want to go after her, fine,' said Lamoureaux, 'but I'm not willing to call her bluff. She looked crazy enough to do it.'

'It's too late anyway,' said Martinez, from across the bridge. 'She's already boarded the lander and taken it out. She must have sneaked right past you and Dan while you were on your way here.'

'We got a distress call,' explained Perez. 'That's why we came back here as fast as we could.'

'Ship-wide or direct to your helmets?' asked Lamoureaux.

'Direct,' Perez replied. 'Not . . .' He fell silent mid-

Lamoureaux nodded. 'She faked that alert.'

Perez rubbed his face with both hands and dropped into a nearby seat. 'I knew we should have stayed with the lander.'

'Here's the thing I don't understand,' Corso growled, moving closer to Lamoureaux. 'You could have warned us – and you didn't even try to stop her. Why?'

Lamoureaux's nostrils flared angrily. 'I already told you. She threatened to shut the drones down, and leave us defenceless. What did you expect me to do?'

Corso shook his head vehemently. 'I refuse to believe she'd make a threat like that, let alone follow through on it.'

'She *did* make a threat like that,' Lamoureaux yelled. 'Maybe, Lucas, you don't know her nearly as goddamn well as you think you do.'

Corso punched him in the nose.

Lamoureaux staggered back, then stumbled, collapsing to the deck. Corso loomed over him, his expression furious.

Strong hands pulled Corso away. A moment later he

was pushed into a chair and found himself face to face with Martinez, the Commander's hand planted firmly against his chest.

'I was on the bridge when all of this happened,' said Martinez. 'Now, I didn't hear what Dakota and Ted were saying to each other, but the responsibility is still with me. So if you want to take a swing at anyone, try me.'

Lamoureaux wiped blood away from his nose and glared at Corso. 'Want to know what else she told me, Lucas? *She's* the reason the Emissaries knew where to find us.'

Corso stared at him. 'What?'

Lamoureaux laughed, and then coughed. 'That's exactly what she told me. The Emissaries are tracking *her*, not the frigate. That's all I can tell you.'

'He's telling the truth.' Martinez nodded towards the overhead display, which still tracked the ongoing engagement. 'The scouts are breaking away and going after the lander.'

Corso stared up at it, too, with a stricken expression. 'She'll never make it.'

Lamoureaux staggered upright and pulled himself back into the interface chair.

Martinez let go of Corso and stepped over to Lamoureaux, handing him a handkerchief. Ted took it from him with mumbled thanks.

'Dan, keep an eye on Mr Corso here. If he tries taking a swing at anyone else, find somewhere to lock him up. Meanwhile, Mr Lamoureaux, I want you to do some calculations. Work out how long you think we have left before the star blows, and how much power we'll need to jump out of the vicinity in time, before it does.'

'She's abandoned us,' Corso muttered, half to himself.

'Don't be so sure,' said Martinez. 'I'd say she's given us some breathing room. Ted, put her current trajectory and location on the overhead.'

An image of the cache-world and its star appeared overhead, complete with outsized representations of both the *Mjollnir* and the lander, the latter already fast approaching the planet's surface.

Lamoureaux's reply was muffled by the handkerchief pressed to his face. 'If she can stay alive long enough, she should reach the cache itself in about fifteen minutes.'

The lander received a direct hit that sent it spinning so hard that Dakota was almost ripped out of her seat restraints. A sudden roar blanketed out the whine and screech of the bulkheads as the atmosphere vented, while her filmsuit enveloped her instantly.

Prior to this, dozens of direct hits and near-misses had finally overwhelmed one of the two field-generators attached to the lander. Apart from her filmsuit, the only thing between her and certain death was a couple of Meridian drones she had peeled away from the main pack. She had been worried Lamoureaux might not allow her control over them, but in the end he hadn't tried to stop her.

On the screen, she could see the cache growing bigger as she dropped towards it. According to the signal she was still picking up from Trader's yacht, he was more than thirty kilometres directly down the throat of the shaft.

Something about the thought of descending into that bottomless hole made her skin prickle with terror.

Down, down, down she went, the cache expanding towards Dakota like a wide and hungry mouth.

More pulse-beam fire blasted out from defensive structures scattered around the mouth of the cache. The lander spun under another direct hit, and alert messages flared across her screens.

She caught one brief glimpse of vast fields of slag and rubble around the mouth of the shaft, before the lander began to drop down into limitless darkness. Faraway lights, mounted on the sides of the shaft, illuminated what looked like abandoned cities or factories clinging to the walls.

She left the two drones on guard near the surface. They wouldn't be able to hold off a full-frontal assault for long, but at least she would have some warning if the Emissaries were about to follow her in.

The lander dropped down farther, while the mouth of the cache seemed to grow smaller and smaller, increasingly far overhead.

Trader, I'm not going to let you get away with the arte-fact. Do you hear me?

Silence.

Either something had happened to him, or he wasn't interested in talking.

Trader? Are you there?

It had all been going so well until he had tried to activate the Mos Hadroch.

Trader had placed it in the mouth of the drive-forge, and then accessed the command structure he had retrieved from the Greater Magellanic Cloud so very, very long ago, activating it through a meshlike apparatus woven around two of his secondary manipulators.

The effect had been spectacular.

During his initial experiments, using Whitecloud as his proxy, it had become rapidly clear the artefact was much further beyond his understanding than he had anticipated. Aspects of its operation pointed to a power-ful, almost godlike intelligence buried somewhere within its depths.

At first, the device had appeared to unravel, its outer shell peeling open to reveal internal components that defied comprehension. Its shape had mutated rapidly, expanding well beyond the drive-forge, and Trader had felt the presence of that overwhelming intelligence, for the first time, as it ransacked his yacht's onboard systems and even, to his shock, his own mind.

He had turned to flee, recognizing that events were already spinning far out of his control. But it was far too late: the artefact had already expanded to surround him, its malevolent intent suddenly and startlingly clear.

THIRTY-SEVEN

The lander kept following the signal from Trader's ship, until it dropped down on to a shelf extending out from a darkened side passage no different from the thousands of others she had seen during her long descent. The onboard systems told Dakota there was a protective field placed over the mouth of the passageway that retained a breathable atmosphere.

She exited her craft quickly, a torch in hand, and soon spotted Trader's yacht resting nearby in the gloom, on a bed of shaped fields. Most of its drive-spines were either broken or melted or both. She flicked the torch on, then bounded forward in long, loping strides due to the minimal gravity, manoeuvring her way past cluttered wreckage and abandoned machinery.

After a couple of minutes, Dakota reached a side chamber. When she shone the torch inside it, it was to see a machine she recognized as a drive-forge. As she moved closer, she observed that the Mos Hadroch had been mounted inside it.

A moment later she nearly stumbled over Trader himself.

The tiny field-generators that normally held a protective sphere of briny water around him now lay scattered across the floor of the chamber. His enormous bulk somehow looked much smaller, lying unprotected on the dusty ground. His skin looked grey and cracked, as his manipulators twisted and slithered helplessly across the grey stone underneath him.

<Dakota.>

Jesus and Buddha. You're alive?

<For now.>

Trader's movements were growing ever weaker as she watched. She knelt beside him and touched the fingers of one hand to his side. His flesh felt rough, abrasive.

<It knew everything about me. Secrets buried so long I had forgotten them. But it will not function.>

Let me try, Trader?

The great bulk of his body shuddered one last time, and became still.

She remained kneeling by him for a few more seconds, wondering why she didn't feel anything, not even vindication or triumph. Instead she only felt hollow, as if all this had been an anticlimax.

Finally she stood up and stepped past Trader's inert form and towards the drive-forge.

She had been able to hear the artefact from the moment she entered the chamber: a high-pitched ululation like a thousand amplifiers feeding back all at once, throbbing constantly from low to high. But she had a sense of an underlying order that hinted at something else, something vast and cool and powerful.

She stumbled to a halt just short of the forge, and watched as the artefact flowered open the way she had seen it do on Whitecloud's video recordings. The sound filled her head until she couldn't form a single coherent thought, hammering its way into her brain almost like something physical.

And, just when she thought the worst was over, she felt that same intelligence she had sensed earlier suddenly focus all its attention on her.

She stood again on a snow-blasted highway on Redstone, surrounded by the bodies of the dead. Found herself in a bar called The Wayward Dragon with Lin Liao, waiting for his sister to arrive. Looked across the rooftops of Erkinning along with half a dozen other students with whom she had lived and loved and warred, and none of whom she would ever see again after that night.

She was dragged back farther and farther, reliving memories that she thought she had lost for ever half a galaxy away, suddenly as real in that moment as if she were experiencing them for the first time.

The last image that came to her was that single glimpse of a street in winter, and the memory of her mother's hand laid on her head.

But this time, when she looked up, she saw her mother's face clearly.

Dakota came to, some indeterminate time later, to find herself sprawled on the chamber floor.

She pulled herself to her feet and stumbled closer to the drive-forge. The Mos Hadroch had unravelled yet more, like some multidimensional kaleidoscope expanding to surround her, penetrating deep inside her body until she had no idea where she ended and the artefact began.

And in that instant, she discovered the terrible price she was going to have to pay.

'That's another drone gone,' Lamoureaux cried hoarsely. 'And more scouts on the way!'

Corso looked up at the overhead display and saw that only one of the three godkillers guarding the cache remained and, by the looks of it, was charging up for an imminent jump. But now a constellation of pixels showed an enormous number of scouts were heading for the frigate. More than they could possibly fight off.

Lucas.

'Dakota?' Corso spoke out loud, unconsciously reaching up to touch the comms bead in his ear. He ignored the looks he received from the others.

Are you ready to jump out of the system?

'No, not yet. We won't be for some time. There's severe damage to the drive-spines, we've lost functionality in more than threequarters of them. It's not looking good.'

You can still get away in time if you stick to short incremental jumps. As long as you can stay just ahead of the shockwave, you can gradually build up enough power for a long-range jump – particularly if you can get into the shadow of one of the outer gas giants. What's happening back there?

'The Emissaries' bigger ships are starting to jump out of the system, but I don't see how they can get more than a fraction of them away from here before it's too late. What's happening with the artefact? Did it work?'

I think so, yes.

'What do you mean you *think* so?'

It's going to be a little while yet before it takes effect.

'Then you need to get back here. Their main ships may be leaving, but we've got a force of their scouts currently on the way. Is the lander still operative?'

Lucas . . . I'm not coming back.

Corso stared across the bridge with a stunned expression. 'What?'

I'm not coming back. I can't.

'Bullshit, you just told me you activated the damn thing. We won, right? So now we can go home.'

No, Lucas. I have to stay here with the Mos Hadroch. I won't ever be going home. The artefact can't function unless it's merged with a living mind. In the meantime you need to get the Mjollnir *as far away from here as possible.*

Corso felt a sudden tightness in his throat. 'I won't allow this. There's always a way.'

Goodbye, Lucas. I'm glad we had a chance to know each other.

*

She cut the connection before he could say anything more. Dakota felt numb, as if the reality of what was happening to her hadn't sunk in yet.

The artefact pulsed with light, all around her, inside her, even entwined with her. She had since lost all sense of her own body. She seemed to see the floor and walls of the chamber from a dozen different points of view simultaneously. Her mind was being unravelled like a piece of cloth slowly teased apart into disparate threads.

She slipped in and out of consciousness, as the hours passed like minutes. The artefact occasionally fed her glimpses of the *Mjollnir*, which had already started taking incremental jumps away from the cache, making the most of its remaining drive-spines. Hordes of scouts followed her, diving towards the frigate in a strategy all too reminiscent of the swarm's tactics. She could see that the frigate was taking heavy damage.

She sensed the artefact was beginning to approach some kind of peak of activity. The chamber began to shake, while a shell of burning energy surrounded the drive-forge.

Lamoureaux gazed down at Martinez with haggard eyes. 'We can initiate one more jump, on your call,' he said. 'After that, nothing. I'm sorry.'

They had lived through hours of endless terror since their last communication with Dakota. The scouts had chased them throughout the night, tearing and hacking at the hull wherever the field-generators failed. The frigate had already executed more than half a dozen short-range jumps, but every time the scouts caught up eventually, materializing all around and diving inwards towards them with the mindless efficiency of machines. The star system might be doomed, but the Emissaries clearly weren't going to let them escape.

Martinez was sweating profusely, still being careful with his injured arm. A scout had reached as far as the bridge before being taken out by Perez and Martinez, both armed with pulse-rifles. The air still smelled of burnt wires and plastic.

'Do it anyway,' said Martinez. 'I don't want to have to stay—'

'Wait. Wait a second,' interrupted Lamoureaux.

The machine-head gripped the arms of the interface chair, staring at some point far beyond the bridge as if he couldn't quite believe what he was seeing.

'What?' said Corso, speaking for the first time since the scout had tried to cut its way in. Ever since they had successfully repelled it, he had remained collapsed in a seat, too weary and shell-shocked to say or do anything.

'Look,' Lamoureaux stuttered, pointing to the overhead display. 'Just look.'

They all stared up and saw the Emissary scouts were self-destructing.

'Perhaps it's just local,' Martinez mumbled.

'No,' insisted Lamoureaux vehemently. 'The last god-killer – it's burning.'

'It's Dakota,' Corso yelled, standing up at last. 'It has to be!'

Lamoureaux didn't say anything to that. He just stared past them all, like a blind man seeing visions, with sweat breaking out on his forehead.

'Ted,' asked Perez, 'what is it?'

Lamoureaux seemed at last to remember they were there. 'We've got bigger worries now,' he said gravely. 'I just picked up a second neutrino flux. The sun just went nova.'

The nova mine had been in close orbit around the star for over fifteen hundred years. Before receiving its activation signal, it had drifted insensate and silent, outwardly little different from any other piece of random junk caught in a similar orbit, betraying its purposefulness only on those occasions when it activated dormant guidance systems in order to guide it away from any imminent collision.

There had been others before it, spread out over the millennia, each one a potential sword of Damocles aimed at the heart of the star. Similar nova mines could be found in close solar orbits within every Emissary-occupied system, serving as ultimate safeguards against defeat or rebellion.

The activation signal had triggered ancient protocols and, within an hour, light had begun to build up around each of its drive-spines, reaching a crescendo in the moment before it briefly vanished from the visible universe.

It rematerialized less than a hundred kilometres from the star's core. In the few brief nanoseconds before it was vaporized, a chain reaction deep within its drive caused a bubble of false vacuum to form, expanding outwards at the speed of light before collapsing within seconds.

Billion-kilometre tongues of fire rose up from the star's surface like fiery wreaths, and over the next few hours it began to shrink in size. Its heart had been cut out, and its remaining lifetime was now numbered in hours.

When the star finally exploded, the shockwave reached the cache-world within minutes, sending rivers of molten fire pouring down the narrow valleys between the tiny planet's mountains.

Tidally locked until now, it began to spin for the first time in a billion years, the light of a million dawns creeping slowly towards the mouth of the cache itself.

But it was already too late. The Mos Hadroch, the 'Judgement of Worlds', had sent out a signal that propagated itself across the galaxy instantaneously.

The last thing Dakota saw was a brilliant light, almost liquid in its intensity, surging in through the entrance to the chamber housing the drive-forge.

'Explain this to me again,' Commander of Shoals demanded, swimming across the command-chamber of a coreship located some tens of thousands of light-years away.

'I can't explain it,' the aide stammered, instinctively darting closer to one wall as Commander of Shoals bore down upon him. 'But something's happening to the Emissary fleet. It's . . . it's self-destructing. There are no other words. Look.'

The aide's stubby little tentacles, reflected Commander of Shoals, had never been used in combat, had never been used to slash an enemy's belly open, or to tear away that same enemy's fins. These were the soft appendages of a civilian, with no place on board this world-sized warship.

They were deep within the ruins of a star system whose population had numbered in the billions until it had been destroyed, more than a year before, by the Emissaries. This was the first time the General had returned here since that awful day. He and the forces he commanded had done their utmost to prevent that particular tragedy, but the Emissary ships had continued to fill the skies, intent on carrying out surgical strikes against the defensive installations on all the system's worlds – while one single enemy drone had found its way past their coreships and dived into the living heart of the system's star.

The Shoal's forces had rescued pitifully few in those last frantic hours before the star detonated. Even if there had been enough coreships to carry away every last one of the system's inhabitants, the basic logistics of such a mission would have rendered their efforts almost point-less. It would have taken the better part of a year to transport all of them safely away from the various planetary bodies.

Instead, they had a scant few hours to save what and whom they could.

And therein lay the terrible tragedy of the nova war: those left behind had no choice but to wait for the end as the departing coreships jumped to safety. It was a scenario that had been repeated in so many other systems that he could not even bring himself to contemplate their number.

They had now returned to retrieve certain items of value from the wreck of a coreship partially destroyed by that nova, but had themselves been ambushed by a cloud of Emissary scouts hidden within the tangled smoke of the newborn nebula. A godkiller had unexpectedly appeared, drawn there by the scouts, jumping to a point less than a light-minute distant and then quickly vector-ing inwards to deliver the final death-blow.

Commander of Shoals stared at the data coming in from his ship's external sensor arrays. What it told him was utterly preposterous. And yet, despite this, more data was pouring in from other sources, all appearing to support the most unlikely conclusion: that the scouts had somehow, inexplicably, self-destructed.

There had also been an enormous explosion on board the godkiller. Adrift and aflame, it now spun out of con-trol through the nebula.

Fresh data-glyphs kept appearing in the murky water filling the chamber, carrying high-priority reports from far-flung sectors of the galaxy – indeed, from the very farthest corners of the beleaguered Hegemony. Huge swathes of the Emissary fleets were reported to be spontaneously self-destructing.

Commander of Shoals found himself looking at images of other godkillers, their shattered hulls tumbling through the skies of a thousand worlds.

It was as if something had affected them all instantaneously.

It was only in that same moment that he recalled his final meeting with Trader in Faecal Matter of Animals.

Commander of Shoals whipped around in a half-circle, his enormous bulk smacking into that of the timorous aide, sending the underling tumbling and squawking with fright.

Commander of Shoals's manipulators twisted with giddy joy and he spun wildly around the chamber, while his support staff fled, unnerved by this most uncharacteristic behaviour.

Trader had done it. *The vicious old fool had actually pulled it off.*

He had ended the war.

THIRTY-EIGHT

Five Years Later

Corso glanced to the west and saw the Lantern Constellation rising into view as the sun set. He checked his pressure suit's filters, took one last glance at the ruins that had been his principal occupation for the last few years, and was on his way back to the truck parked nearby, when suddenly Dan called in over the short-range.

'Got some news, Lucas. Commander Nabakov says the landing party should be here a little after noon tomorrow. When will you get back here?'

'I'm finished,' Corso replied. 'I should reach there just after they land. Thanks for the heads-up, Dan.'

Four and a half years before, the *Mjollnir* had limped away from the expanding nova, reaching a star system less than a hundred light-years away only after a difficult and hazardous six-month journey, their long-range sensors having picked up a potentially habitable world there. Its atmosphere had proved deadly, but it carried life in the form of hardy flora and small brown-pelted animals, even the largest of which had soon proved to represent no threat, as well as the scattered remnants of a long-abandoned Emissary settlement.

They had named the world Pit Stop, and started the work of repairing the *Mjollnir*'s drive system, but it soon became clear this was going to take longer – much, *much* longer – than any of them might have suspected.

Only lichenlike growths studded the sandy, gritty soil. The sun was far away and dim, even during summer, and at night the ground frosted over. It was nobody's idea of paradise, therefore, but – as Corso soon realized – it wasn't really so different from Redstone. He'd found himself getting used to the idea that he might have to spend the rest of his life here.

Once the exploration ship *California* had come within range of the *Mjollnir*'s transceivers, a few weeks before, Corso had known he should feel elated. But, instead, he had felt only an obscure sadness he couldn't begin to explain.

He got back in the truck, pulled the door shut, and waited for it to cycle out the toxic atmosphere and replace it with something he could breathe, before pulling off his helmet with a gasp of relief. The dashboard came to life, automatically downloading the new data he had imaged from the site of the ruins, and filing it along with the rest. He had recorded thousands of samples of Emissary glyphs and art, all gathered from a hundred different locations, and in the past year or two he had finally begun to make some kind of headway. For somewhere in Pit Stop's myriad ruins, he felt sure, lay the key to understanding the Emissaries.

Corso opened his mouth to tell his truck to get moving, then he paused, turning to glance out of the window once more at what he and the others had come to call the Lantern Constellation.

It was hard not to think of Dakota every time he saw it. Four stars, forming a rough rectangle, with a fifth and brighter star in the middle; and, slightly to the right and much fainter, the star system whose destruction they had barely evaded. It still shone as serenely as ever, and would continue to do so for nearly another century, when the light from the nova would finally reach Pit Stop.

In that moment the memory of Dakota was so clear and sharp that he could almost imagine her stepping out from amongst the ruins, as if everything that had happened all those years ago had been merely some kind of dream. He didn't like to think this way, even though he always did, because of the regret that inevitably followed.

They had all found ways to keep themselves busy, as the years on Pit Stop stretched out. The *Mjollnir*'s entertainment systems had been stocked with centuries' worth of music and books and 'viros, but mostly they had each filled up their time with work and with personal pursuits.

Corso had returned to his academic roots in alien

machine-linguistics, while Martinez spent most of his time up in orbit aboard the crippled frigate, directing an army of spider-mechs, sometimes with Lamoureaux's help. Perez occasionally joined Corso on field trips that could last for weeks, while they sought out derelict computer-systems and buried data storage-sites. At other times, Perez joined Martinez back on the frigate, and they would work together on patching the hull. Lamoureaux had meanwhile taken charge of setting up their tiny encampment, as well as refurbishing and repairing the frigate's long-range tach-net transceiver so that they could finally send out a distress call.

And now, at last, rescue had come, but Corso couldn't help wondering just what there was for them to go home to. Certainly, he wouldn't be returning to Redstone, and neither would Martinez or Perez. They had stolen one of the Freehold's major military assets, and people there had long memories.

The truck rolled on through the night, while Corso slept in its rear cabin. He woke late the next morning, less than fifty kilometres from home, and ordered his truck to a halt so that he could have breakfast, mostly consisting of supplies brought down from the frigate in orbit every couple of months by the one remaining lander.

While he was eating, he saw a light like a flare burning its way down through the atmosphere, and realized it was a lander dropping down from the *California*.

*

'Senator Corso.' The woman who had just taken a seat next to him looked impossibly healthy as she reached across to shake his hand. Pretty, too, with short dark hair and large round eyes. The skin of her hand felt silky smooth, so much so that he only just resisted the impulse to stroke it, like some love-starved prisoner on his first day out of jail.

'I've not been a senator for a very long time now, Miss . . .'

'Zukovsky. Meredith Zukovsky. I'm the liaison officer for the *California*.' The lander was clearly visible outside one of the pre-fab's windows, a massive, squat boulder of a ship resting on a dozen legs.

Corso could catch a strong whiff of himself after so many long nights sleeping in his truck's tiny cabin, so either Meredith had no sense of smell or she was doing a valiant job of pretending he didn't stink.

Apart from himself and his fellow exiles, there were a dozen members of the *California*'s crew now gathered around a long table in the tiny settlement's largest enclosed space: a mess hall where the four of them would meet for meals whenever they were all down on the surface at the same time. But now the room could barely hold all sixteen of them – four times more people than it had seen in the last half-decade.

The table was covered with dishes of a variety that Corso had almost forgotten existed. The *California*'s commander, a bluff, broad-shouldered man by the name of Casimir Anders, was meanwhile talking with Martinez and Lamoureaux.

'It's nice to meet you, Meredith. You'll have to excuse my manners and my body odour. I don't get to talk to people for long periods sometimes, and the bathroom facilities here still leave something to be desired.'

'But the main thing now is that you're able to go back to the Consortium.'

'That depends . . .'

She raised her eyebrows, tilting her head back slightly as if to get a better look at him. 'I'm not unaware of your circumstances, Mr Corso,' she said. 'The political situation on Redstone still hasn't stabilized, and you don't need to tell me it wouldn't be safe for you to go home. Not for most of you, either.'

He bit his lip and looked at her thoughtfully, then decided there wasn't any reason not to be honest. 'I'll admit that, in my more candid moments, I've wondered if there'd be any point in going back even if rescue did come. In a sense, this . . .' he waved a hand around the prefab, 'all this is my home now. And, besides, I've made real progress trying to decipher the records I've dug up. It's . . . hard to think I could end up just walking away from it all. But I'll have to, I realize that. I'm not some insane hermit. I don't want to stay here for ever on my own.' He could hear the sadness in his own tone.

Zukovsky nodded and smiled broadly, as if pleased with this answer. 'That's exactly why I came over to talk to you. How *would* you feel about staying here?'

He eyed her askance, as if she was kidding him.

'I should maybe be more candid,' she continued. 'We didn't just come out here to look for you, though that was part of it – in fact we also wanted to know exactly what happened to the Emissaries. It seemed prudent to try and assess whether they might still represent some kind of threat.'

'And do they?'

'What happened up there,' she said, shifting her gaze towards the ceiling as if she could look straight through it at the Lantern Constellation, 'wiped out most of their space-going fleets and crippled their empire, but it didn't put them entirely out of action. They have other surviving caches, so they could regroup and come back at us – and we need to be ready for that.'

'So what does that have to do with me being here?'

'We've taken a look at the research you've done here, and it's obvious you already have a better handle on the Emissaries than most of the specialists back home. That counts for a lot when it comes to making the kind of assessment I'm talking about.'

'You want me to keep working here?' he said. 'Seriously?'

'You wouldn't be alone,' she replied quickly. 'We came here intending to leave a permanent outpost behind. There'll be other ships visiting after the *California*'s returned, as we want to use this place as a stepping-off point for deeper exploration into the Perseus Arm. We've already talked to Ted Lamoureaux, who's willing to stay and help us set up the outpost, but I got the feeling he wanted to hear what you had to say first. We'll still be here for at least another six months, and in that time we'll build up what you've already established here, and then some of us are staying behind to get things up and running.' She smiled. 'I know it's a lot to ask of you, but nothing you say meanwhile would be binding. And if you ever changed your mind before we headed back, there'd still be a berth waiting for you.'

Corso cleared his throat and looked her in the eye, almost supernaturally aware of the proximity of her hand to his. There were glinting depths in her pupils, in which he saw himself reflected.

'What about you, Meredith?' he asked. 'Will you yourself be staying?'

She looked back at him with an amused expression. 'As a matter of fact, I will be, yes.'

Do it, he could imagine Dakota urging him. *What else do you have to go back for? Your life is here now.*

'I'll stay,' he decided.

EPILOGUE

Dakota drew in a sharp breath, filling her nostrils with the sickly-sweet scent of flowers in early spring, before opening her eyes and squinting into bright sunlight.

Fields of blossoms stretched out all around her, while the bright cerulean blue of the sky curved overhead like a ceiling. The sun was high, almost at its zenith. Tall, tree-like growths, at odds with the terrestrial flowers, formed a small copse nearby like great black squid frozen in the act of leaping out of the soil, their leaves wide and oval and glossy.

She stood up, uncertainly at first, and looked around. The breath caught in her throat as she sighted the cloud-breaching towers of a Magi memory-complex on the horizon, the soaring towers and great fluted domes of a deserted city surrounding its base like steel and concrete waves breaking on the shores of an island mountain.

She trailed her fingertips across the tops of the flowers around her, and tried to piece together her final memories. She had been in the vicinity of the red giant, with the swarm briefly at bay . . . the star had turned nova, and then . . .

And then she had found herself back here, in this place.

She gazed over towards those distant spires for a long time, remembering the conversation she'd once had in just such a building, with a Magi entity calling itself the Head Librarian. That had been during the heat of the battle for Ocean's Deep. One moment she'd been on board a ship with missiles closing in on it, the next she'd been here, in this otherworldly realm generated from the virtual memories of the Magi ships, and weeks of subjective time had passed.

She sat on the ground, her mind numb, and watched as the sky slowly darkened until the Milky Way came into view, the great cloud of the Sagittarius cluster spreading before her in all its glory.

And then, finally, she began to walk.

When she finally reached the city, more than a week later, she found that the building under the onion dome hadn't changed since her last visit. A chair and a chaise-longue stood next to an orrery composed of oiled brass and copper. This time, however, an old man she had never seen before was sitting in the chair, watching her with amused eyes that looked out from amidst a mass of crinkles.

'Dakota,' he said, rising to greet her as she crossed the carpeted floor. She stared at his long white hair, neatly held out of the way with a small silver clasp. His face was a patchwork of lines, but the set of his mouth and the way he looked at her suggested he knew her from somewhere.

His voice was warm and firm. 'It's been . . .' He paused to shake his head and sigh in a good-humoured way. 'It's been a long time since I last saw you.'

'I . . . I don't recognize you. I'm sorry.'

'My name is Lamoureaux. You don't remember me, but I remember you.'

She couldn't think of anything to say, so she perched carefully on the edge of the chaise-longue. 'I don't understand how I could be here,' she said. 'I only remember I was at the red giant with the swarm, and then—'

'And then the star turned nova,' he finished for her.

Dakota nodded faintly. 'How do I know you?'

'We met after your first resurrection a very, very long time ago.'

'Resurr . . . how long ago?'

'Over three thousand years, Dakota.'

She stared back at him, too stunned to think of anything to say, or how to react at first. Lamoureaux, however, waited with apparently endless patience.

'I still don't . . . How can I even be sitting here?'

'That,' he said, 'will take time to explain. But I can tell you this much: the ship that took you to the swarm gathered and preserved your thoughts and memories, and transmitted them outwards in the last few seconds before the shockwave from the nova reached you.

Another Magi ship much closer to home used these thoughts and memories to recreate you. But your mind was preserved in other Magi ships also, and they kept you in stasis for a long, long time. We didn't manage to retrieve a proper copy of you until close to the end of the Thousand Year War.'

She stared at him slack-jawed, then dropped her head towards her knees with a groan. 'I'm sorry, but it's so hard to take all this in.'

He smiled sympathetically. 'There's a lot more to explain, and we're going to give it to you gradually. But here's what you mainly need to know: the Mos Hadroch was discovered, and used to stop the war between the Shoal and the Emissaries. That was followed by the Great Diaspora, as the human race scattered across the galaxy.'

'So you brought me back,' she said, raising her head slowly up again. 'Why?'

'Because we need you. The Accord of Worlds is a successor of sorts to the Consortium, but it's facing its greatest threat since the Emissaries. A Shoal fleet is currently heading for the Greater Magellanic Cloud, intent on building an empire.'

'The Accord of what?' Dakota asked weakly.

'I played a small part in its creation, towards the end of my sixth iteration.' He pointed up: 'If you will.'

Dakota glanced up to see an image of the Greater Magellanic Cloud materialize overhead, filling the space directly beneath the onion dome.

'A few decades ago,' Lamoureaux continued, 'a small fleet, led by Shoal-members intent on recreating the Hegemony, left our galaxy on a secret mission for the Cloud. There's now reason to believe there's more than one Mos Hadroch. If they do find more, they'll have the means to cripple the Accord. So we have to stop them.'

'And what does this have to do with *me*?'

Lamoureaux smiled. 'If there was ever a time we needed you, Dakota, it's now.'

She felt like weeping. 'I can't tell you how out of my depth I feel, just being told all this. I mean, Jesus and Buddha . . .' She laughed. 'I don't know what else to say.'

'The Accord is something special. It's much more than the Hegemony ever hoped to be. And its name is no accident – would you like me to show you why?'

Dakota nodded warily.

A moment later she found herself bathed in the sound of a hundred trillion voices, all talking at once. But, rather than cacophony, it was more like a single, infinitely complex piece of music constantly mutating and shifting. She saw through a million eyes, heard a million voices. She felt the touch of an untold number of lovers, smelled the air of a thousand worlds. She felt alien limbs sprouting from her body; tasted the armoured chitin of her brood with her long tongue; swam through sentient corals, sniffing out delicious plankton with a nose resembling a flower.

'There's a lot more I have to explain,' he said,

reaching out his hand as he stood up. His movements were fluid, not at all those of an old man. 'And a lot for you to see. But, if we're going to get started, I don't see any reason why we should delay.'

She licked her lips and glanced around the onion dome, then reached out tentatively and took his hand.

FINAL DAYS

By Gary Gibson

The new novel in an explosive new space opera
series, from the author of the Shoal Trilogy.

It's 2235 and through the advent of wormhole technology more than a dozen interstellar colonies have been linked to Earth.

But this new mode of transportation comes at a price, and there are risks. Saul Dumont knows this better than anyone. He's still trying to cope with the loss of the wormhole link to the Galileo system, which has stranded him on Earth far from his wife and child for the past several years.

Only weeks away from the link with Galileo finally being re-established, Saul stumbles across a conspiracy to suppress the discovery of a second alien network of wormholes which lead billions of years into the future. A covert expedition is sent to what is named Site 17 to investigate, but when an accident occurs and a member of the expedition, Mitchell Stone, disappears, they realize that they are dealing with something far beyond their understanding.

When a second expedition travels via the wormholes

to Earth in the near future of 2245, they discover a devastated, lifeless solar system – all except for one man, Mitchell Stone, recovered from an experimental cryogenics facility in the ruins of a lunar city.

Stone may be the only surviving witness to the coming destruction of the Earth. But *why* is he the only survivor – and once he's brought back to the present, is there any way he and Saul can prevent the destruction that's coming?

The first chapter of *Final Days*
follows here . . .

ONE

Gate Delta, Site 17, $1{\times}10^{14}$ AD
(Home Date: 5 January 2235)

They were making good time along the East Rampart, on their way back to Vault One, when all four life-support indicators for Stone's team suddenly faded to black. Jeff Cairns came to a halt, his pressure suit informing him, in a soft contralto voice, of a sudden spike in his adrenalin and heart rate.

You don't fucking say, Jeff thought sourly. He glanced automatically over the ramparts, his eye following the bright parallel lines of the path markers towards the truncated pyramid of Vault Four in the distance. He waited to see if the indicators would flicker back into life, his mouth suddenly dry and sticky.

Three other life-support indicators – representing Eliza Schlegel, Lou Winston and Farad Maalouf – still glowed on the curved interior of his visor. All three, along with Jeff himself, had been assigned to the first and second vaults for the duration of this particular expedition. Other icons – representing suit pressure, air supply and bio-functions – floated near the bottom edge of the visor, registering clearly against the black and starless sky.

Eliza and Lou, who had been walking a couple of metres ahead of Jeff, both came to a stop at the same time, their helmets also turning towards the fourth vault. Jeff listened, over the shared comms, as Eliza tried to raise Mitchell and the others, the strain becoming evident in the sharply clipped tone of her words.

The comms hissed as they all waited in vain for a response.

The East Rampart was one of four hundred-metre-high walls that connected the vaults together, forming a square when seen from above. For safety, the edges of the rampart were illuminated to either side by rows of softly glowing markers placed at regular intervals. It was a long way down if you somehow managed to wander too close to the edge.

Jeff turned to see Farad standing just behind him, his frightened eyes staring back at him through a smeared visor. The fingers of Farad's gloves were wrapped tightly around the handlebar of a steel containment unit, mounted on four comically bulbous wheels, and his lips were moving silently in what Jeff suspected was a prayer.

'Maybe we should go look,' said Lou, sounding like he was thinking aloud.

'No.' Eliza's voice was sharp, decisive. 'The artefacts are our priority. We have to make our scheduled rendezvous with Hanover's team at the Tau Ceti gate.'

Jeff turned to look back towards her. 'We can't just abandon them,' he heard himself say.

'Nobody's abandoning anyone,' said Eliza. 'If something *has* happened, I don't want to risk any more lives until we know exactly what we're dealing with. Besides, it might just be a temporary communications breakdown.'

'*Might* be,' said Jeff.

Eliza turned and shot a quick, furious look at him. *I'm tired of your insubordination*, she'd warned him more than once.

'Maybe Eliza's right,' said Lou, his tone conciliatory. 'We have to be careful.'

'So just what is it you're saying we should do if we don't hear from them?' Jeff demanded. 'Just *abandon* them?'

'You're not in charge here,' said Eliza, 'and we have our orders from Hanover.'

'I know we're expendable,' said Jeff. 'I'm under no illusions on that count.'

'Nobody's saying anyone is exp—'

'We can get to Vault Four with time to spare if we start out now,' Jeff snapped, his fear flowering into sudden anger; all that adrenalin couldn't go to waste. '*Fuck* the artefacts.'

'Really?' said Eliza. 'Would you like to share that sentiment with Hanover when we get back?'

'That could be *us* stuck in there,' Jeff insisted. 'If they're trapped and still alive, a rescue team won't get here from Tau Ceti for several hours, probably longer. They'd run out of air long before that.'

Eliza's expression suggested she was contemplating murder. *Typical military mindset*, he thought, almost able to see the wheels spinning in her head. It wouldn't be too hard to engineer an accident for him, not with a long, hard drop on either side of them. Unfortunately for her, everything they saw, heard or did was recorded by their suit's A/V systems.

'Dan,' Farad spoke into the sudden silence, 'his life-support indicator. It's back online.'

Jeff glanced down and saw that Dan Rush's icon had indeed flickered back into life, and it was followed a moment later by Lucy Rosenblatt's. Mitchell Stone's icon remained dark, however, as did Vogel's. The suit interfaces felt clumsy and old-fashioned, and again Jeff found himself wishing that a tangle of security precautions didn't prevent them from using UP-linked contact lenses.

'Dan, Lucy, can you hear me?' Eliza shouted into her comms. 'We lost track of you. Can—?'

She was interrupted by a brief burst of static, followed by a voice.

'Hey! Hey, is that you?' Jeff recognized Dan's voice. He sounded panicked, very nearly hysterical. 'Mitch and Erich are gone. It's just Lucy and me. We—'

'Slow down,' urged Eliza, as the rest of them listened in silence. 'Who else is there?'

'Just Lucy. Mitch and Erich, they . . . they just . . .'

Dan paused, and for a moment they listened to the sound of his amplified breathing, sounding loud and urgent and close within the confines of their helmets.

'What happened to them?' asked Eliza.

'We were up on Level 214. It's filled with these deep pits, dozens of them. They were down taking a look inside one, while Lucy and me stayed up above. Then it started to fill up with some kind of liquid.'

'And they didn't get out again in time?'

For a moment, it sounded like Dan was trying to suppress a sob. 'Not exactly . . . no. I'll send a video squirt over, maybe it's best if you just see what happened for yourselves. And . . . get here soon, okay? The toka-maks packed up all of a sudden, and it's pitch black in here.'

Jeff found himself watching Eliza as they listened. She had turned away, to look back towards Vault Four, but from where he stood he could still see her face through her visor, and her lips were pressed together in a thin and bloodless line. She clearly didn't want to have to go into Vault Four, but none of them did, not really, not when there was a chance that whatever had happened to the others might happen to them too. But Jeff knew that didn't matter. He knew, deep in his gut, that they had to make the attempt, regardless.

'We'll be there soon,' Eliza finally replied, glancing towards Farad's cart filled with its precious treasures. 'There's no way you can find your way back out to us?'

'No. It's too dark to avoid the chance of getting lost,

and this part of the vault hasn't been secured yet. We can see some way with our suit lights, but not far enough to be sure exactly where we are. Don't want to wind up like Rodriguez, right?'

No, thought Jeff with a shiver, nobody wanted to end up like Rodriguez.

Dan's voice faded for a moment, and then came back. Jeff glanced down and saw the man's life-support icon flicker in that same moment.

'Lucy,' continued Eliza, 'how about you? Can you hear me?'

'Yeah.' Lucy's voice sounded tense with pain. 'I'm good.'

'You don't sound it.'

'Hurt my leg,' she replied. 'Had a bad fall.'

'Hang on and we'll be there soon enough. But send that video squirt over so we can get some idea what we're dealing with first.'

They watched the A/V from Dan's suit in silence, projected on to the curved surface of each of their visors.

Standard operating procedure specified that, even once a chamber had been declared safe by the reconnaissance probes, and pressurized prior to a thorough eyeball examination by the artefact recovery teams, pressure suits must be kept on until a team leader was certain there was no danger of contamination or some other, less predictable risk. Mitchell Stone's team had been tasked with just such an assessment.

The A/V showed two suited figures, as seen from Dan's point of view, kneeling at the bottom of a pit that looked about five metres deep, with a series of wide steps cut into the sides. The two men's helmets almost touched as one pointed at hundreds of indentations ꜰꜰꜰꜰꜰꜰ ꜰꜰꜰꜰ ꜰꜰꜰ ꜰꜰꜰꜰꜰ ꜰꜰꜰꜰꜰ, ꜰꜰꜰ ꜰꜰꜰꜰꜰꜰꜰꜰ ꜰꜰ ꜰꜰꜰꜰꜰꜰꜰꜰ, looping patterns. One turned to glance towards Dan, and Jeff saw Mitchell Stone's face behind the visor.

The video blurred as Dan looked up suddenly at the shallow, copper-coloured dome of the chamber's ceiling high overhead. Jeff noticed a fourth suited figure waiting up above, and Lucy's face was visible through the visor: small and imp-like, loose wisps of her blonde hair pressing against the clear polycarbonate.

As Dan clambered up the wide steps, Jeff saw that half a dozen carbon arc lights had been mounted on tripods close to the chamber entrance. They cast incandescent light across dozens of pits, each one only narrowly separated from the next.

Dan then turned to look back down at the suited figures of Mitchell Stone and Erich Vogel, still crouching at the bottom of the pit. Without any warning, a viscous, oil-like substance began to gush out of the indentations, flooding the pit with astonishing speed. Jeff heard Lucy yell a strangled warning, and Stone and Vogel both jerked upright as if they'd been scalded. The liquid was already covering the top of their boots.

It was Rodriguez, all over again.

From the subsequent sudden blurring of the video, it was obvious that Dan had descended into the pit once more, in order to try and reach the two men. Stone and Vogel were already making their way towards the steps but, even as Jeff watched, he saw their movements become slower, as if the oil were congealing around them. By now it was up to their knees.

The oil appeared to defy gravity, racing up the sides of their suits and soon swallowing them both up in a black tide. Stone was the first to collapse, followed by Vogel a moment later. Jeff watched in mounting horror as their suits began to disintegrate, the metal and plastic dissolving and falling away from their bodies with astonishing speed. Jeff had one last glimpse of Stone's eyes rolling up into the back of his head, before they were both swallowed up by the still-rising tide.

The oil had behaved purposefully, like something alive, which made Jeff think of childhood monsters, of yawning black shadows filled with imaginary horrors. Tears pricked his eyes but he couldn't bring himself to stop watching.

The video jerked once more as Dan hurried back up and out of the pit, with understandable haste. Jeff saw Lucy step back, her face aghast, then, with a terrified cry, stumble backwards over the lip of an adjacent pit.

Dan said 'Oh shit' very softly, and Jeff watched with numb despair as he hurled himself down the steps of the neighbouring pit.

It was clear from the way one of Lucy's legs was bent under her, as she lay on the floor of the second pit, that she was badly hurt. Dan grabbed her up in a fireman's lift and rapidly made his way back to safety. And, even though Jeff could see nothing but the chamber ceiling through Dan's A/V, he felt an appalling certainty the second pit was already filling with the same deadly black oil

And then, just as Dan reached the top, the lights went out.

They followed the rampart to where it merged into a tunnel leading deep inside Vault One. They moved on past branching corridors and ramps to either side, each leading up or down to other levels and chambers. The beams projected from their suits flashed reflections off hastily epoxied signs printed with luminescent inks, which were mounted near junctions that had not yet been fully explored. All carried explicit warnings never to leave the already lit paths.

Catching sight of these warnings, Jeff found himself thinking once more about Rodriguez.

David Rodriguez had been an engineer recruited to the ASI's retrieval-and-research branch several years before to help run the remote reconnaissance probes, but instead had quickly become the stuff of legend for all the wrong reasons. He was the one recruits got told about during their training and orientation, as an example of how *not* to conduct oneself when exploring the Founder Network.

He had been part of a standard reconnaissance into a then unexplored level of Vault Two, and had ignored the warnings about sticking to the approved paths. Instead, he had wandered into a side chamber, trying to find a probe that had failed to report back.

He had found the probe and, some hours later, his team-mates found him.

Time, it turned out, worked differently in the side chambers of that particular level. It became slower, the farther inside them you got. Rodriguez had discovered this when he stepped up next to the probe, probably thinking it had simply broken down.

He was still there, to this day: right foot raised and looking towards the far wall, his face turned away from the chamber entrance as he headed forward, still clearly oblivious to his fate. That alone was what really sent the shivers down people's spines; the fact that no one could see his face got their imaginations working overtime.

Rodriguez's team-mates, when they finally found him, had been a lot more cautious. One had thrown a spanner just to one side of Rodriguez's frozen figure, from the safety of the chamber entrance. It still hung there now, motionless, caught in the course of its long trajectory through the air, on its way to eventually land-ing in some future century. The reconnaissance probe – a wheeled platform mounted with cameras and a range of sensitive instrumentation – stood equally immobile nearby.

David Rodriguez, as new recruits to the most secretive department of the UW's retrieval and assessment bureau were told, had been a fucking idiot. The vaults were filled with unpredictable dangers, which was why they had to stick to the paths already pioneered by the probes. You wandered away from them at your own risk.

The current popular theory was that these slow-time chambers were stasis devices designed for long-term storage. Time-lapse cameras had been set up at the entrance, to try to estimate how long it would take Rodriguez to set his right foot down, turn around and walk back out of the chamber. The best estimates suggested anything up to a thousand years.

Sometimes Jeff woke from nightmares of Rodriguez still standing there, his face turned away, as the years turned into centuries. Sometimes he *was* Rodriguez, waking to find himself lost in the darkness of some future age, all alone on the wrong side of a wormhole gate that bored its way through time and space very nearly to the end of everything – a hundred trillion years into a future where most stars had turned to ashes, and the skies were filled with the corpses of galaxies.

They re-emerged from Vault One and followed the North Rampart until they reached Vault Four, half an hour after receiving Dan's distress call.

Beyond the vaults lay nothing but the blasted, airless landscape of a world that had been dead for immeasurable eons. The planet on which the vaults stood orbited a black dwarf: the shrunken, frozen remnant of a once bright and burning star whose furious death had long since stripped away any vestiges of atmosphere.

Dan, who was an expert in such things, had once told Jeff the vaults themselves were tens of billions of years old, meaning they had stood for longer than the entire lifespan of the universe as it had been measured back in their own time. They were constructed, too, from a material that resisted all attempts at analysis. Despite a near-eternity of bombardment by micrometeorites and other debris drawn into the planet's gravity well, the exterior of the vaults appeared as smooth and pristine as if their construction had just been finished.

Jeff glanced up at the towering slope of Vault Four, at the moment before they passed into its interior. He could hear Eliza talking to Dan and Lucy over the general comms circuit, trying to keep them calm, assuring them that help was almost at hand. He found himself wondering what they'd have to say once they discovered Eliza had been all for abandoning them.

Farad came abreast of him and tapped the side of his helmet: a request for a private link. At least Eliza had let him leave his cart of goodies back at Vault One, rather than wheel them all this distance.

'I have come to believe,' Farad told him, his eyes wide

and fervent, 'that God must have abandoned the universe long before this time-period.'

Jeff regarded him in silence, but with a sinking feeling.

'Do you know what occurred to me when we heard about Stone and Vogel?' Farad continued, an edge of desperation in his voice. 'I could not help but wonder what, in the absence of God, happens to their souls.'

This wasn't a conversation Jeff wanted to be having right now. His feet ached, and the interior of his suit stank from the long hours he'd spent inside it. Stress knotted his muscles into thick ropes of fatigue.

'Their souls?'

'This far beyond our own time, the universe is dark; no new stars are being created. Most of the galactic clusters have retreated so far from each other that they are no longer visible to one another, and most of the galaxies themselves have been swallowed up by the black holes at their centre—'

'I know all this, Farad. They covered it in the orientations.'

'Yes but, if God is no longer here, what happens if you *die* here?' he demanded, his voice full of anguish. 'Where do you go? There is only one conclusion.'

'Farad—'

'Hell is, by its very nature, the absence of God, is it not?' the other man persisted.

Jeff stopped and put one hand on Farad's shoulder,

finally bringing him to a halt. Farad stared back at him, his nostrils flaring.

'Listen, you need to calm down a little, okay?' Jeff told him. 'You're letting your imagination run away with you.'

Jeff glanced to one side. Eliza and Lou had moved ahead, apparently unaware that the pair had stopped. Up ahead lay a wide atrium, containing electric carts they could use for zipping about the 'designated safe' parts of the vaults.

Farad was a large, bluff man with a thick dark moustache, and he sometimes compared his attempts at picking apart the self-adjusting routines controlling the Vaults to a pygmy poking at electronic circuitry with a spear. He was intelligent and sharp, an excellent poker player – as some back at the Tau Ceti station had discovered to their cost – and also in possession of a keen sense of humour. But something about the black, unforgiving void that hung over the vaults, like a funeral shroud, could get to even the best of people.

It seemed to Jeff that the more intelligent people were, the harder it was for them to deal with witnessing a darkened universe far advanced in its long, slow senescence. Self-declared atheists began sporting prayer beads, while the moderately religious either discovered a new fervour for their faith or, more frequently, abandoned it altogether.

Farad refocused on him after a moment, and Jeff

could see that his face was slick and damp behind the visor.

'I'm sorry,' said Farad after a moment. 'Sometimes . . .'

'I know,' Jeff replied, with as much sympathy as he could muster. 'But we'll be home in a few days. Remember, we've got a plan.'

'Yes.' Farad nodded, his upper lip moist. 'A plan. Of course.'

'You just need to hold it together for a little while longer. Okay?'

'Yes,' Farad said again, and Jeff could sense he was a little calmer. 'You're right. I'm sorry.'

Jeff gave him his best winning smile. 'You already said that.' He nodded, indicating somewhere further up the corridor. 'I think we'd better catch up.'

Eliza had glanced back once, but chose to say nothing as the two of them caught up.

They pulled a spare tokamak fusion unit from a prefab warehouse established in Vault Four's primary atrium and loaded it on to the rear of an electric cart, before letting it zip them up a steep incline that switched back and forth the higher they rose. When they reached Level 214, they found the passageways and chambers shrouded in darkness, so had to rely on their suit lights while they swapped the new fusion unit for the failed one. There was no telling why it had shut down, but inexplicable power-outs were far from unusual.

The lights strung along the ceiling flickered back into life, revealing closely cramped walls on either side. An airlock seal had been placed across the passageway, and they stepped through it one by one, emerging into the pressurized area beyond.

Jeff wanted nothing more than to crack open his helmet and breathe air that didn't taste like his own armpits, but Eliza would have none of it. He understood the reasons for her justifiable caution, but still felt resentful.

When they entered the chamber that Stone's team had been studying, they found Dan had now managed to drag Lucy on to a narrow strip of ground located between four adjacent pits. The pit that had swallowed up Stone and Vogel was now full to the brim with black oil, its calm stillness looking to Jeff like a black mirror laid flat on the ground. It seemed strange that none of the reconnaissance probes first sent into this chamber had triggered a similar reaction.

The furthest walls of the chamber faded into darkness beyond the pools of light cast by the carbon arc lights. There were hundreds more of the pits, Jeff could see, stretching far out of sight. He watched from the chamber entrance as Eliza guided a limping Lucy back to safety, Dan following close behind. They had to shuffle along sideways, one at a time, wherever the edges of the pits came closest together.

He found himself wondering what purpose these pits might have served for the vault's architects. A garbage-disposal system, perhaps, the black oil being some universal solvent for breaking down unwanted items? Or perhaps they represented something more inexplicable, a puzzle that could never be solved – like so many of the artefacts that had already been recovered and brought back to their own time . . .

Something suddenly moved just beyond the illuminated part of the chamber, snapping him out of his reverie. Jeff stared hard into the shadows, then stepped forward. Lou and Farad were too busy arguing to have noticed anything, as they discussed how to recover a sample of the black oil, should it prove equally adept at dissolving any type of container they might attempt to collect some in.

'Did you see that?' asked Jeff urgently, turning back to look at the two men.

'See what?' asked Eliza over the comms, audibly puffing with exertion.

Jeff stared into the shadows once more. 'I'm not sure. Maybe it's . . .'

Maybe it's nothing, he thought. The vaults lent themselves effortlessly to the imagination, after all.

But he saw it again; a slight movement almost on the edge of his perception. Lou must have seen it, too, for he stepped up next to Jeff, unclipping a torch from his belt and shining its powerful beam across the chamber.

The torch revealed Mitchell Stone, naked and shivering, kneeling between two empty pits and blinking up into the light.

It's not possible, thought Jeff, in the shocked silence that followed. But a moment's reflection suggested otherwise. After all, the lights had failed almost immediately, so Stone might have managed to crawl out of the oil-filled pit, unseen by either Lucy or Dan, and then got lost. But why hadn't he called out for help?

'Jesus!' he heard Eliza exclaim, followed by a muttered prayer from Farad.

Stone raised one hand towards them, and then slumped forward soundlessly.

Without thinking, Jeff stepped forward and began to navigate his way towards him.